LOVENOTES

Lovenotes

Justine Valenti

Heywood Books

© by Justine Valenti 1981

First published in Great Britain by
Sphere Books Ltd in 1982

ISBN 1 85481 018 9

This edition published in 1989 by
Heywood Books Limited
55 Clissold Crescent
London N16 9AR

Printed in Great Britain by
Cox & Wyman Ltd, Reading

PART I

WINTER: 1978

1

As soon as Anne Lurie saw Nicola standing in the doorway she made her way across the crowded room. 'Nicola, I'm so glad to see you. You look fabulous.' Anne's quick eye took in her friend's Yves St Laurent black silk dress, belted at the waist, and beautifully set off by a necklace of faceted Victorian amber at her slender neck.

'So do you, Anne. I like you in red velvet. Very lush.' Nicola hugged her warmly.

'Maybe a little too lush, like Little Lord Fauntleroy. But I do need the colour with my dark hair. In black you look like Mata Hara whereas I'm taken for a widow from Bleecker Street.'

Anne patted the bun at the back of her head. 'Janet once told me that I couldn't wait to reach forty-five. What are you laughing at? We haven't that many years to go, even if *you* don't look it. Where's Edward?'

'I'm afraid he couldn't make it after all,' Nicola apologised. 'Out of the blue, Bianchi had to cancel a show in his downtown gallery and decided at the last minute to substitute Edward's new protégé, an exciting painter. Tonight of all nights was the opening.'

'It's all right, I understand,' Anne murmured, making every effort not to be hurt that Nicola's husband was passing up her son's debut as a composer.

'Edward asked me to be sure to convey his best wishes for Paul's success tonight,' Nicola added, not entirely truthfully.

'In that case,' Anne smiled, 'I'll just have to forgive him. Besides, two-thirds of the Harrington family is here. I've already said hello to your beautiful Julie. Let me take you over to Paul. It must be a year or two since you've seen him.'

'Longer than that. You know, Anne, I think the last time was when he graduated from Curtis, and you had a party –'

3

'Impossible. I know he's not been down from Yale often, but surely –'

'No, I assure you.'

Nicola, peering across the room, packed with people, saw a dark young man in smiling conversation with a group surrounding him.

'Don't tell me that's Paul,' she murmured, startled. 'God, he's attractive.'

'You sound surprised.'

'What I mean is that he's so grown up, so manly –'

'Here, Nicola, let me introduce you to Max Furst. Max, this is my closest friend, Nicola Di Candia Harrington . . .'

Anne was suddenly wrenched away and swallowed up, leaving Nicola jammed next to the well known elderly impresario. Max Furst held her hand in a crushing grip and looked her up and down as if about to kidnap her for a role in one of his operas.

'I believe we met a couple of years ago –' Nicola began, but her partner, talking at the same time in the loud tones of the hard-of-hearing, barrelled ahead relentlessly. 'Nicola Di Candia, how great to meet you in the flesh –'

'Do you know, I've followed your work in all the museums and galleries for years.'

Nicola had the sinking feeling she always got when she was cornered by an admirer who insisted on discussing her sculpture at great length. She never knew what to say, after thank you.

'Take your collage on the wall, the one over there with the cello and violin. I'd love to buy it from Anne if she would part with it.'

'Well, you see, I did it especially for her twenty-first birthday,' Nicola murmured, drinking her champagne too quickly.

'In that case I'm sure I couldn't get it for a million bucks. But I really would like to have something of yours to fit in my living-room. What if I came to your studio some time . . .'

It was all very *déjà vu*. Nicola was sure she and Max Furst had gone through the same conversation when they had met before.

'I'll trade you a sculpture for an aria in your latest production,' she offered, smiling.

'What is this? You think I'm pulling your leg? Listen, I mean it, kiddo. I hope you're not one of those artists who hates to part with anything.'

'Not at all, Mr Furst. I'm flattered by your interest. But in fact my dealer, Marshall Faber, handles all sales –'

'Max, stop monopolising my favourite gal.' A slight, bald man slipped an arm around Nicola's waist.

'Al, how wonderful to see you.' Nicola turned to her host as Max Furst melted into the crowd.

Al Lurie smiled broadly. 'I didn't really spoil a sale for you, did I? That old windbag hasn't got a kopeck to spend on art. He's been reduced to throwing his own money behind his productions.'

'Don't be silly. I badly needed rescuing, and you're my first choice for a knight in shining armour.'

Al grinned. 'You always make me feel brand new. How're you doing, babe? You look tremendous. The old you – or should I say the young you, untouched by time. Some set-up here, eh? A *schlemiel* like me doesn't belong in this crowd. Not unless I was dolled up in a white jacket and serving out the wine and crackers. But even the servants aren't servants, they're music students. It's the musical social register in here tonight.'

Al's jokes, as usual, hit very closely upon the truth.

'So which one is Julie? Not that gorgeous blonde babe over there in the beige top and skinny pants? She could go right to Hollywood.'

She probably could, Nicola thought, sighing. Julie was talking to Paul. But her daughter could look so stiff in conversation with an attractive young man. What a pity Julie had not inherited her father's charm instead of her mother's shyness.

'Hey, our kids make a dynamite couple, don't they?'

'Yes, yes, they do,' Nicola agreed hastily, wanting it to be true.

'She seems a quiet type, Julie, like you, with people you don't know well,' Al noted shrewdly. 'Well, that's okay. Only one of a couple ought to shine. Two prima donnas trying to walk first through the door are gonna bump shoulders.'

Nicola laughed. 'Do you think your son is a prima donna?'

Al shrugged. 'He's got lots of talent, even more than he

5

knows. I predict that the whole music world is gonna be at his feet in a couple of years. Paul's the real thing, not like his old man.'

'Oh, Al –'

'It's true, it's true. What am I? A junk dealer, like my pop, only my junk is more expensive. Instruments, sheet music, records, tapes, all the latest electronic this and that.'

'But you play wonderful jazz and you always have.'

He shrugged. 'Strictly weekends. I'm a Sunday saxophonist. In fact, I had to cancel a gig tonight. Feast or famine, that's my fate. If I bend down and smell a flower you can bet a bee will bite me on the *schnoz*. The only luck I ever had was to marry Annie, and even then it ran out after sixteen years. But she's still my Annie. Just look at her. Did you ever see such a ritzy babe? I think she's lived her whole life for tonight,' Al finished, a little sadly.

Nicola impulsively kissed Al's cheek. 'I've always thought that you were the best person that ever happened to her.'

He made a self-deprecating gesture. 'Sure, sure.'

Observing Al's hurt expression, although he tried to cover it with a funny face, Nicola felt a tinge of anger. Much as she loved Anne, she had always disapproved of the capricious way her friend behaved to Al. The two were not divorced, and even though Anne had thrown Al out she always expected him to come running when she wanted him.

'Anyway, I'm certainly a proud papa. Wait until you hear Paul's music.'

'Nicola, haven't you said hello to Paul yet? Al, see to the champagne, please.' Anne scooped her up and tried to propel them both across the room.

'Wait a minute, Anne. Paul's talking to Julie, and I don't want to interrupt.'

'If not you, someone else will. Come on.'

When Julie saw her mother advancing arm-in-arm with Anne she stopped speaking and took a long swallow of her champagne.

'Paul, look who's here,' said Anne.

Paul turned to look at Nicola with an expression of surprise. Then a flicker of interest showed in his fine dark eyes.

'It's nice to see you,' he muttered after a moment's pause,

6

shaking Nicola's hand, his face serious.

'I'm Nicola Harrington,' she said, hating guessing games. Her smile felt as forced as when she was posing for a photograph, and she cursed her awkwardness. 'It's been years, Paul. You may not remember me.'

'But he must,' Anne broke in. 'Really, Paul, Nicola's my oldest friend, and Julie's mother.'

'Of course she is,' Paul said, exasperated. 'Stop treating me like an idiot son, Anne.'

Nicola recalled that Paul had been allowed to call his parents by their first names. Anne had thought it cute, but Nicola wasn't so sure.

'Julie, don't go away,' Nicola called out to her retreating daughter, who ignored her.

'Nicola was like an aunt to you,' Anne persisted.

'Not quite like an aunt,' Paul contradicted. A slow, tantalising smile illuminated his features. 'I remember you very well, Nicola Di Candia. I still have the sculptures you made for me when I was a kid.'

Anne, sighing with relief that her son would be able to converse intelligibly after all, moved off to set things in motion. She saw to it that chairs and stands were set up for the musicians – a cellist, trumpet player, vibraphonist, and two percussionists – and began to lead her music critic friends and a couple of famous performers to the choicest seats.

'You called it *Paul Learns the Recorder*, remember?' Paul was saying to Nicola. 'It's a wooden torso standing on what passes for its head, with the recorder upside down, too.'

'Oh, God, yes.' Nicola smiled shyly. 'That must have been one of the last pieces I did in wood.'

'I know. The sculpture you did for my tenth birthday was made out of brass. A terrific thing, very abstract and witty. Hey, let me show you.'

Paul suddenly grabbed Nicola's hand and pulled her towards the door.

'Now? But we can't. All those people are waiting for the concert to start.'

'It won't start without me. But we'll only be gone a minute. I'm saving my etchings for next time.'

Nicola laughed nervously. This was hardly the moment to be bothering about her old sculptures, but she didn't feel up

7

to making a fuss with this determined young man.

Julie, watching Paul lead her mother out of the living room, drained her glass of champagne and reached for another.

2

At the end of the long hallway in the huge apartment Paul flung open a door and made an exaggerated bow. 'Enter.'

Feeling foolish, Nicola obeyed. Then she grimaced at the sight of her long-forgotten *Boy On A Bicycle*, sitting on Paul's night-table.

'I loved the boy's arms up in the air, to show "no hands". That's the way I rode a bike in those days, Nicola. Youthful bravado. I thought it was brilliant of you to have guessed. Here, come and sit on the bed for a moment. Don't worry, your virtue is safe with me,' he assured her, smiling wickedly and tossing his heavy black hair back from his forehead.

Nicola perched awkwardly on the edge of the bed, astonished by Paul. He had more self-assurance at twenty-two than she would ever acquire.

Studying her two early pieces critically, Nicola was dismayed by their crudeness and didn't want to dwell on them. Her eyes darted around the room, noting the musical awards, the chess set, the sheet music flung carelessly on the carpet, the tennis racket stuck on a nail in the wall.

While she surveyed Paul's room, Paul surveyed her.

Looking up at him suddenly, Nicola caught an expression of such intensity on his face that she felt her skin grow hot with embarrassment.

She jumped to her feet. 'Thanks for showing my old pieces to me. I view them as curiosities, something out of the past. But now we really must get back. Your mother will be frantic.'

Paul laughed. 'My mother thrives on being frantic. Keeps the adrenalin flowing.'

8

'I'm so looking forward to your concert,' Nicola told him as they made their way back to the living room. She was hoping, actually, that the music wouldn't be too atonal. Ultramodern composers like Cage and Stockhausen left her cold.

'I'm not an élitist,' Paul said, as if he had penetrated her thoughts. 'I write music that anyone can understand. At least that's my intention. I don't see why so-called "serious" music must reflect only what is ugly and discordant in life. Anyway, I hope you won't have to put your hands over your ears,' he finished with a smile.

'Even if I wanted to I wouldn't dare, with Anne watching me. Good luck, Paul,' Nicola murmured, liking him enormously.

As soon as Anne caught sight of her son, she waved to him wildly, and Nicola went to sit on one of the chairs set up for the audience.

'Julie, over here,' Nicola called.

Obediently Julie took a seat at Nicola's side. 'Isn't it exciting, darling,' Nicola said, squeezing her daughter's arm. 'Paul has certainly grown up well, don't you think?'

'Yeah,' Julie agreed sullenly.

'It's too bad he's away from home so much, studying and composing. Anne hardly ever sees him, and we never do. Maybe while he's in New York we can all get together.'

'No thanks. You don't have to fix me up,' Julie said.

Nicola frowned. 'I didn't mean it that way at all, Julie. Of course you don't need to be fixed up. I only thought you might find Paul interesting and amusing. I certainly do, and –'

'Oh, God!' Julie jumped up and moved several seats away.

Al slipped into Julie's place and patted Nicola's hand. 'I went through the same thing with both my sons. Trying to prove they're all grown up, didn't want any advice from their old man any more. Julie's how old, seventeen? Yeah, it figures. She's not sure where she's at. I was watching her, trying to swill champagne like an old pro.'

Nicola smiled wanly. 'Everything I do or say lately is wrong.'

'Well, it can't be easy for her, living up to a mother who's so young, beautiful, and talented. Julie's a beauty herself but she acts as if she doesn't know it.'

9

'But Al, how could she not know it? People turn to look at her on the street.'

'It will all straighten out in time. Now Timmy writes to me regularly from Toronto, and Paul sounds me out about his music, even though his mother considers me a middle-brow. Don't go away, babe. I'll be right back. Annie wants me.'

Nicola took heart from Al's optimism, but she found it difficult to control the intermittent stabs of guilt she felt towards Julie. Nicola's work had kept her at the studio a great deal when her daughter was small. Then, when her sculpture began to be known and commissioned, there had been the trips abroad. Every moment she could spare Nicola had spent with Julie, but perhaps it had not been enough. If Nicola had managed to make more time for her, would Julie have become a better painter? Or would she have felt pressured and turned off?

Watching Anne fuss over last-minute details, Nicola remembered the first time she had been in this forty-foot living room so many years ago, when Anne's mother, Henrietta Kadin, ruled with a professional pianist's iron fist. Henrietta was determined that her cellist daughter would follow a similar path to the concert halls of the world.

Brooklyn-born Nicola – tiny, shy, gauche – had followed Anne around the High School of Music and Art for months like a disciple, learning from her how to chew with her mouth closed, to look up words she didn't know the meanings of in the dictionary, and not to start a sentence with 'lookit'. She had been thrilled that Anne actually liked her and thought her sculptures were terrific.

And finally she had been invited to her friend's elaborate apartment on West End Avenue, so different from her own crumbling brownstone in Bay Ridge.

While Anne sat at the cello playing chords, Henrietta Kadin entered and took a seat on the sofa next to Nicola.

'Let me hear the first movement of the Dvorak *Cello Concerto*,' she said in a soft but icy voice.

While Anne played, Nicola went through the ordeal with her note by note.

'Stop. I've heard enough! Is that what you call a cadenza?

10

I'd call it a travesty. Pablo Cassals you're not, Anne, but you could do a lot better than that.'

'But Mother –'

'Don't "Mother" me, play the finale.'

Nicola cowered in her seat, tears of pity standing in her eyes for her friend. In spite of her riches and fine home and expensive clothes, Anne was stuck with a terrible mother who never even gave her a smile.

Forehead damp with perspiration, Anne sat poised at the cello, frozen for a moment. Then a look of tense determination hardened her features, and from the minute she drew her bow across the strings, she threw herself whole-heartedly into her playing. Even Nicola could hear the difference. Anne was completely caught up in the music this time, not just playing to please her mother.

It sounded so wonderful to Nicola that she clapped enthusiastically. 'That was brilliant!'

She caught her breath, frightened, as Mrs Kadin turned to look at her. 'Yes, I agree, it was brilliant – a little too brilliant. Your playing, Anne, goes from one extreme to another. You want to be a steady, reliable performer, now that you're too old to be called a child prodigy ...'

In others words, heads I win, tails you lose, thought Nicola.

She had never watched Anne practise again under the eye of her relentless mother, hating to see her friend so humiliated.

Although Anne had never admitted it, Nicola felt that Henrietta Kadin was the reason that the gifted girl had 'accidentally' got pregnant the week of her seventeenth birthday, made a hasty marriage to Al Lurie, and put an end to her professional career.

Al was handing out printed programmes. There were to be three original works by Paul Kadin-Lurie: *Serenade for Flute and Ensemble*, *Duet for Flute and Cello*, and *Celebration*. Nicola thought it was a lovely compliment to Anne that Paul had elected to use her name as part of his own. Then she overheard someone whisper, 'Look at that, cashing in on his grandmother's fame.' Nicola didn't think that was the reason, and was annoyed by the spiteful cynicism of the remark.

11

Paul had every reason to be grateful to his mother. As a patron of the New York Philharmonic, the Metropolitan Opera, and other music organisations, Anne was in a position to cultivate everyone in the music world. She had spared no effort to gather together a number of important people for this private recital of her son's compositions.

The room grew quiet. Anne slipped into the seat next to Nicola and hugged her. The two women smiled at each other like conspirators.

'Anne, I'm so excited,' Nicola whispered, 'though not half as much as you must be. But try to relax. Paul will be fine. You're more nervous than he is.'

'I know,' Anne acknowledged. She clasped her hands in her lap and forced herself to sit absolutely still.

Certainly Anne was more nervous. That was the point; she was nervous for both of them. Paul was supposed to be calm. She had seen to it that her son had absolute confidence in his talent, in his ability to give a brilliant performance, and to let his imagination as a composer take him where it would. Whatever torments Henrietta Kadin put Anne through, she had avoided with Paul. From an early age Paul had found musical instruments in the house, and he picked the recorder by himself at four, going on later to learn the flute. Paul had been given lessons, but never terrorised into practising. He hadn't been threatened, blackmailed, ridiculed, or made to feel that Anne's ego had any part in his musical life. She had had her own cello lessons – although she had never quite reached concert standard – but she remained a competent amateur and played in a string quartet.

Music in the Lurie household had been fun. Al, she had to admit, was a kind, indulgent father. Anne had tolerated Paul's enthusiasm for jazz and rock, although it had been an effort.

Paul, she felt happily, had been a joy from the moment of his birth, in spite of everything.

Anne watched with deep pride as her son took his flute from its case, wishing that her younger son, Timothy, had been able to make it to New York for his brother's debut, although he wasn't musical himself.

Al sat down on the other side of Anne, taking her hand and winking at her. 'What a cold hand you have, Annie,' he whispered. 'Take it easy, like our boy is doing. You know,

12

sweetie, I have to hand it to you for not making the kid into a child prodigy the way your mother wanted. Even I was tempted. But you were right not to let it happen. Yetta was a good musician but a lousy mother. Still, she's proud of her grandson and would have given her right hand to come up here if she could get out of that nursing home. Anyway, Paul's grown up being normal and happy, to go with the talent.'

'He certainly has, Al. I just know he's good enough to earn his living composing. But if that takes time, at least he'll have a master's from Yale so he can teach.'

'You know, babe,' Al said thoughtfully, 'Paul may not be the academic type. He's hinted that he's never even had a break from the schooling.'

'Don't be silly,' Anne interrupted, feeling Al was projecting his own lack of studiousness onto her son. 'Of course he'll get his master's.'

Anne, glancing around her, found her eye arrested by the fragile beauty of Julie Harrington, and she had a momentary flutter of apprehension, remembering that Paul and Julie had been talking together earlier that evening.

'Al, I hope Paul's not interested in Julie Harrington. She's a beautiful girl, but there's something wrong there. I know Nicola's not happy with their lack of communication. Nicola may have been lucky in everything else, but I think we've got the more satisfactory child.'

'I wouldn't be so sure of that, Annie. You're looking at it from the outside.'

'I'm not. Nobody knows Nicola better than I do – and that goes for that elegant husband of hers. Nicola feels guilty about Julie. Her paintings are so pale and fragile, like Japanese watercolours. They're pleasant enough, but what a contrast to her mother's powerful, authoritative work. The fact is that Paul has benefited because I stayed home developing his talent while Nicola developed her own. You can't have it both ways. Anyway, Julie's not the kind of girl I'd pick for Paul.'

'I don't think, sweetie, that he's gonna let you pick for him.'

'No, I guess not. But at least I've prepared Paul for today's woman – dynamic, strong, independent –'

'You don't say.' Al looked at his wife in amusement. 'All he's got to do is remember that before he gets the hots for some babe.'

Anne abruptly drew her hand away from Al's. 'I hate it when you're vulgar,' she hissed.

Anne stubbornly told herself that Paul would take his time before he got involved with a woman. This was not the moment for a romance but for singleminded dedication to his music.

Her son couldn't possibly be sidetracked by little Julie, who hadn't much going for her except a pretty face.

3

From the very first note, Nicola's attention was caught and held. How pleasing the sounds were – light, melodic, with wondrous harmonies and changing rhythms. The instruments were unusual – wood blocks, cow bells, Chinese cymbals, and several kinds of drums. Paul's flute wove a magical tapestry up and down and around that was simply delightful. Although there were intimations of jazz, the patterns were classically intricate, subtle, and impossible to anticipate.

Paul played compellingly, drawing a fine tone from his instrument, as his body bent and swayed with the rhythms. During some passages, when his dark hair fell forward on his thin face, with its interesting irregular features, Paul reminded Nicola strongly of the way Anne looked when she played the cello. Nicola simply couldn't take her eyes off him.

At the end of the first number, amid the enthusiastic applause, Nicola, glancing at Anne's beatific expression, saw that Paul was living up to her expectations.

The duet followed, and Nicola thought that the cello and flute, playing with, and against, each other, created some of the loveliest harmonies she had ever heard. Undoubtedly the piece had been written as an acknowledgement to his mother.

The final and longest piece, *Celebration*, reminded Nicola of a bird soaring over a street festival. Vivid colours and shapes flickered momentarily into Nicola's consciousness and vanished in a blur. The shapes, sometimes curving, sometimes linear, were always colourful and joyous. The bird, dipping and soaring with the notes of the flute, was at the same time a part of the kaleidoscope and removed from it. When the music ended, the bird folded its wings and vanished.

Nicola felt happy. Waves of well-being washed over her, followed by a slow tremor down her spine. She didn't know whether it was the music, Paul's playing, or just Paul himself who created such stirrings of delight in her. She clapped wildly at the end, swept completely up in the magic of the music. 'Oh, Anne, he's absolutely magnificent,' Nicola cried.

'He is, isn't he,' Anne agreed, with tears in her eyes.

Paul accepted the audience's response with smiling dignity. Nicola had never seen such poise in a young man, and so utterly without smugness.

Anne and Al jumped up to go to Paul, and the crowd around the Luries was so thick that Nicola decided to hold back.

'Julie,' she said, momentarily forgetting her daughter's earlier hostility, 'wasn't it wonderful? I haven't enjoyed music so much in years.'

The look Julie gave her mother caused Nicola to stop in mid-sentence. Without a word, Julie walked away, and again Nicola felt a stab of guilt. Was Julie jealous because Nicola didn't go into such raptures over her flower paintings? She tried to encourage her daughter, even though she found it hard to enthuse genuinely over the uninspired pastel bouquets that Julie produced.

Sighing, Nicola moved towards the buffet table, laden with food, lavishly displayed. She bumped into Janet and Tom Markham, who had been fellow students at Music and Art.

After a few words about their respective children and Janet's and Tom's shared workshop, in which she did ceramics and weaving and he, graphics, they talked enthusiastically about Paul's music.

'Oh, Anne,' Janet said as she approached, 'Paul's so original, so talented, I don't think anything is more satisfying to parents than seeing their children do well. It makes all the early mess worthwhile.'

15

Nicola remembered the Markham's rambling, disorganised house on Long Island. They had never had much money, but Nicola had always found their home a place of great joy and love.

'You two hardly ever come to us,' Janet was saying to her friends without resentment. 'I know we're far away but I hope you'll make it out for our twenty-first anniversary party this summer.'

'Of course we will,' Nicola promised, already composing excuses for Edward's certain absence.

'Jan is doing some really exciting new things with pottery,' Tom said proudly, 'a total departure from her earlier designs.'

Janet and Tom exchanged a look of such love, such mutual admiration and respect, that it quite stunned Nicola. At the same time, it made her feel suddenly empty. How many years had it been since she and Edward had looked at each other like that?

Julie waited until her mother had walked away with Anne before approaching Janet Markham.

'Hi,' she said shyly.

'Hello, Julie. Don't you look lovely.' Janet hugged her warmly. 'I haven't seen you in ages. Was the last time at your sweet sixteen party?'

'No, not mine, Emily's,' Julie said glumly. 'I didn't have a sweet sixteen party.'

Janet caught the expression of tight defensiveness in Julie's eyes and was about to say something when the girl quickly added, 'I didn't want one. But I had a wonderful time at your house. How is Emily? How's she doing at Pratt?'

'Just fine. Really enjoying it. Why don't you come out and visit us? Emily was asking about you only the other day.'

While Janet spoke in a warm rush of words, Julie's face gradually lost its guarded tenseness, and she granted her mother's old friend one of her infrequent smiles.

Then Tom joined them, putting an avuncular arm around Julie's shoulders. 'You get prettier by the hour, Julie. Looking more like your mother every time I see you.'

A shadow passed over the girl's face. As soon as she could,

she excused herself and went in search of a glass of champagne.

Absent-mindedly Nicola put some food on a plate. She didn't see Julie anywhere but felt they should leave shortly.

Paul came up to Nicola and lightly touched her elbow. 'Was it so bad, that it makes you avoid me and vent your frustration on the food?' Although he smiled as he spoke, Nicola had the distinct impression that he cared very much what she thought.

She hastily swallowed the artichoke heart she was chewing. 'I thought your music was exquisite, and no doubt everyone has been telling you the same. It certainly is music that anyone can understand, even me.'

'Good. Tell me what it meant to you personally.'

'I – I can't really describe it, in words –'

'Sure you can. Try. Please, Auntie Nicola,' Paul implored, grinning.

'Well, I – I like the jazz motifs to start with ...' Nicola was suddenly aware that Julie was hovering nearby, listening. Maybe Nicola could force herself to be articulate for once, and set her daughter a good example.

'Your music has an earthy quality, and yet it soars. I loved the strong rhythms and melodic lines. I especially liked *Celebration*. It made me think of a bird flying over a street festival.'

Paul listened intently, smiling with such pleasure that Nicola was encouraged to complete the vision she had had. Then she lowered her voice. 'I must excuse myself for a moment. Oh, here's Julie. Please wait for me, dear, I'll be right back.'

As Nicola swiftly moved away she hoped that Julie would not be angry at her clumsy efforts to draw her into conversation with Paul. Nor was it only altruism, she admitted to herself guiltily. The fact was that Paul had a very disturbing effect on her, and she thought he might better use his charms on a girl of his own age.

Nicola made her way into the kitchen, where she had some more champagne. Anne and Al came in, laughing gaily, their arms linked, looking almost like a courting couple.

Al, catching Nicola's eye, winked at her, 'Annie's so full of *gemütlichkeit* tonight she's even throwing a little my way.'

Anne giggled like a schoolgirl and gave her estranged husband a kiss on the cheek. 'You've been very sweet tonight, Al,' she said. 'In fact, you've been wonderful. Everyone's been wonderful.'

Nicola realised that Anne was slightly drunk.

'Isn't she adorable?' Al laughed. 'Now I see what went wrong with our marriage. I didn't drench her in champagne.'

'Oh, God, Al, I forgot to talk to Mrs Bruge about Carnegie for Paul.'

Anne tottered out of the kitchen, Al closely upon her heels.

Nicola thought being drenched in champagne was a lovely idea, and had another glass.

'Nicola,' Paul said behind her, making her jump. 'Stop trying so hard with Julie. She'll be okay, if you just let her find her own way.'

For the first time since she was a girl, Nicola blushed deeply.

Paul put his hand on her arm. 'I was talking to you, and you deliberately walked away and left me with your daughter. Why?'

'Because – because I thought you young people might have something to say to each other.'

'Was I boring you?' he asked in a low voice.

'No, of course not. I enjoyed talking to you, and you know it. I wanted Julie to do the same. What's wrong with that?'

'When you put it that way, nothing. Julie's a sweet kid, but I hadn't finished my conversation with you.'

Nicola looked at him, and quickly looked away. 'You make her sound like such a child. She's not that much younger than you.'

'Wrong. She's many, many years younger.'

As he said the words, Nicola saw the truth in them. Paul was mature far beyond his years, whereas Julie ...

'Men find her beautiful,' Nicola said, her heart aching for her daughter.

'She is beautiful – but not as beautiful as you.'

'Oh!' Nicola was astonished. It was a lovely compliment, spoiled only by being at the expense of her daughter. Nicola tried to make a joke of it. 'Now that's what I call chivalry.'

'I didn't say it to be chivalrous. I mean it.'

Nicola felt a fluttering in the pit of her stomach. To prove to herself there was nothing to be afraid of she defiantly lifted her face to his. What she saw when their eyes locked did not reassure her. His eyes were burning with the same intensity that had unnerved her earlier that evening. Nicola suddenly remembered that he had sometimes looked at her like that when he was a child. It had not been a child's look, it totally lacked innocence. It lacked innocence now.

'I – I've got to leave, Paul. It's terribly late.'

He bent his head and quickly brushed her lips with his. 'Good night, Nicola. Thank you for coming.'

'Good night, Paul. It was a pleasure to hear your music,' she murmured, returning his intense look in spite of herself. She turned and went in search of Julie.

Nicola felt wildly elated, as she hadn't been in years. She blamed it entirely on the champagne.

4

Paul lay in bed, one arm behind his head, smoking, something he did only when he was tense.

He inhaled deeply, the events of the evening tumbling through his head like colours in a kaleidoscope. His debut had been a success – even a triumph, if he dared admit it. Although musicians and composers tended to stick together, to encourage each other, there was a total honesty among them, and nobody ever paid an insincere compliment. What elated Paul was the knowledge that he really must be good if he had managed to strike a balance between pleasing his peers, the critics, and the public. If only there weren't this other thing nagging at him.

Paul had seen with horrifying clarity this evening that he had been in love with Nicola Di Candia since he was a child.

He had always looked forward to the visits of his mother's friend with great excitement – a slim, warm, laughing woman, with shiny blonde hair, clever, hot eyes, a wonderfully expressive mouth, a tawny complexion ...

'Nicola's here,' Anne called out to seven-year-old Paul as he sat on the floor playing with his array of trucks and trains.

'How's my Paul?' Nicola asked, sweeping him up and embracing him.

He liked to be hugged by her more than by anyone else. He liked the smell of her hair, the velvety feel of her skin. But today she was also holding a squirming little Julie.

'Oh, God, Anne, I simply must sit down. Julie's going through her terrible two's and I can't rest for a minute. I've been thinking of tying her to one of my metal works just to have a little peace for a few hours.'

'Paul,' his mother said, 'show Julie your toys. Oh, I know, play her a tune on the recorder. I bet she'll like that.'

Paul didn't much care what Julie liked or didn't like, but when Nicola smiled at him and said, 'Oh, please do, I'd love to hear you play,' he jumped up and ran to get his recorder. Then he stood holding it awkwardly in front of Nicola. She was busily talking to Anne and didn't immediately notice him, so he moved away, sulking.

Julie, gurgling in the silly way that babies did – which reminded Paul of his little brother – toddled over to him and tried to take the recorder.

He snatched it back, and his mother saw him. 'Paul, don't be so mean. She's only a baby.'

When Nicola looked at him, he felt bad and handed his instrument to Julie. Immediately the baby flung it on the floor and it rolled under the couch.

'Never mind, Paul, I'll get it,' Nicola said, rising from her chair.

'Paul, help her please. Go on, dear. It's easier for you to crawl under things than old people like us,' Anne said.

'Nicola isn't old,' Paul protested sulkily, his eyes on her jean-clad rear end, as she squirmed under the couch. 'Not as old as you.'

'We're exactly the same age,' his mother corrected him sharply.

Paul didn't believe her, but he did hurl himself under the couch next to Nicola. 'I've got it,' he called triumphantly, retrieving the recorder, which had rolled to the far end next to the wall.

As he and Nicola tried to scramble up again, they became entangled, and both started to laugh. Paul's hand accidentally touched her breast.

While Nicola and Anne talked to each other, Paul tried to behave well so that Nicola would approve of him. He played patiently with Julie, even though she drooled onto his toys and everything she touched felt sticky afterwards.

But Nicola wasn't paying any attention to him. She, like his mother and all grownups, noticed you more when you did something wrong or made a lot of noise.

'I've been agonising over whether it would be worthwhile to go back to Juilliard, Nika. It's so difficult, with the two boys and the house to keep.'

'Oh, Anne, I think you should. You're so talented. You play beautifully and it's still not too late. Even if you don't become a soloist or member of a quartet, you could join an orchestra based in New York.'

'Not feasible.' Anne shook her head. 'A musician has to be prepared to travel, and I simply can't leave the boys.'

'Nicola could take care of me,' Paul broke in.

'No, she couldn't. She has her hands full with Julie.'

'Well, I could play with Julie.'

'Paul, please let us talk for a while. Be a good boy, dear,' his mother begged.

He moved away from the two women and picked up his recorder. What if he were to make up a song, something Nicola had never heard before? Would she notice him then?

Paul began idly to experiment, hitting on an interesting combination of notes after a few moments. He repeated the phrase, looking all the while at Nicola. I'm playing for you, he said with his eyes. I love you, Nicola, and when I grow up I'm going to marry you.

As he created his own sounds and rhythms, he suddenly had a wonderful feeling of power. He watched his fingers,

21

moving so quickly, doing as he wished.

'Paul, that was beautiful,' Nicola called to him. 'What's the name of the song you just played?'

He looked at her intently. 'It has no name,' he mumbled.

'But what is it, Paul? An exercise your teacher gave you?' Anne asked. 'I never heard you play it before. It's really charming. Why are you looking so funny? Have you done something you shouldn't? Come here, darling. Tell me.'

Dragging his feet, Paul approached his mother. He wished she were not so persistent in wanting to know everything about him.

'I made it up,' he finally mumbled.

'You made it up?' his mother shrieked. 'But darling, that's marvellous. Can you play it again? I must write down the notes. Oh, Paul, I'm so proud of you.' Anne jumped up and rummaged for paper and pen. 'What made you compose it? What were you thinking of?'

'I don't know,' Paul replied, looking at Nicola.

Fleeting memories came to Paul of when he was twelve, rapidly losing his innocence, helped along by a humorous discourse on the facts of life from his father, and occasional fumblings with a female music student on rainy days when their teacher was delayed.

Paul had been embarrassed for Nicola to see him with a slightly spotty complexion, or to be present when his voice went from high to low in a matter of moments, and he kept out of her way, though on the few occasions when he saw her he continued to find her enchanting. Of course, he had long ago put aside his childish wish to marry her. However, Nicola had always remained special for him, even though in the busy next few years he rarely saw her, nor thought much about her. His life was too full of studying and music and, from the age of sixteen, girls. 'Nice' girls from his classes to take out on a date. Or 'friendly' girls from town, who would willingly go driving with Paul and his friend, the evening ending with their car parked and the two boys trying to go all the way and having various degrees of success.

Paul had ardently treasured the sculptures Nicola had made for him. In his boy's way he realised that it was okay to love her work, but not okay to have fantasies about an older married woman.

Whenever he had come upon one of Nicola's works at the Museum of Modern Art or the Whitney, Paul was struck by the beauty and power of them, his memories of her always a pleasure to cherish.

Lying in bed, Paul lit one cigarette after another, fearful of where his thoughts about Nicola might be leading him. It had been so long since he had thought of her romantically. After all, she would be, how old? Thirty-nine, like Anne. Was it possible? Anne had fine lines around the eyes and the beginnings of a sagging chin. His mother was large-boned and matronly, not fat, not unattractive, but definitely middle-aged.

Nicola had hardly changed at all. That was why it had been such a shock to see her this evening, and why he had been momentarily speechless. He had felt as if he was stepping back in time.

Surely that sophisticated blonde in the simple black dress that clung subtly to her slender figure, flat-tummied and round breasted, was no older than twenty-eight. Her glossy hair fell in soft waves. Her long-lashed, slightly oblique blue-grey eyes were as clear as he remembered, and still what he thought of as 'hot'. Her mouth was richly tantalising and even more expressive than in his memory. An adorable mouth, and one he had had a wild impulse to kiss. And when she smiled at him his heart had flipped over, making him realise that Nicola Di Candia was his golden girl still.

As if that weren't unnerving enough, she had understood his music. She had talked to him, in her thrilling low voice, as a friend and an equal. Struck by her sensitivity and vulnerability, he had wanted to put her at her ease. He hadn't succeeded, with not-very-funny jokes. Paul sometimes disguised deeply disturbing feelings by speaking of them in an off-hand way, hoping that would take the curse away. Telling Nicola he'd save his etchings for next time, or that her virtue was safe with him, was meant as a kind of exorcism.

The fact was that he wanted her as he had never wanted anyone else.

Paul lit a fresh cigarette from the stub of his old one, even though his throat felt raw. He definitely had to give up smoking when he finished this pack.

Was Nicola the reason he had never truly been in love? Was

23

it because of her that his occasional infatuations didn't endure beyond a couple of months? Had she imprinted upon him, in his infancy, a particular ideal of femininity that no other woman could ever match?

Be careful, Paul, he told himself. Don't get carried away. Inspiration is one thing, the carnal pursuit of a married woman, something else. So spoke the rational Paul.

The passionate Paul continued to imagine what it would be like to kiss those lips – really kiss them – to touch those golden strands of silken hair, to caress that exquisite body and feel her heart beating next to his.

Paul extinguished his cigarette, crumpled the package and threw it away, and opened the window to clear the smoky room.

He wondered about Edward Harrington III, whom he hadn't seen since childhood, vaguely picturing a big, fair man, very personable and self-assured and charming.

How much did Nicola love Edward? What was their relationship like after at least seventeen years?

Paul was certain Nicola knew he had found her attractive. Although she hadn't encouraged him, she hadn't entirely discouraged him either. Wasn't her clumsy attempt to interest him in her daughter proof of her uncertainty about her feelings?

The peculiar thing was that Paul did not feel younger than Nicola, but in a way older. There was a touchingly childish quality about her – and not only the traditional naïveté of the artist. It was as if a part of her had been stifled in her youth and had therefore never matured.

Paul sensed that Nicola was capable of a more passionate kind of loving than she had ever experienced. And what did he dare to do about it?

SPRING, 1979

5

Nicola, shivering with cold, climbed into the truck and smiled a greeting at Mickey Wright, who was going to help her assemble her playground at the Buckleigh School, Kent.

'Typical English weather,' Mickey remarked in his rapid London accent. 'I hope your thingee's designed to hold up. Wood rots, metal rusts –'

'Yes, I know,' she answered gently. She'd been in London many times, and had also studied architecture, but she hesitated to say too much to this budding sculptor. She had already pegged him as a macho working-class young man, edgy and defensive.

They drove in silence for a while. Nicola had been feeling very unsettled since the evening of Paul's debut, two months previously. Although she had succeeded in blurring the experience, when she least expected it an image of Paul's face, his smile, his burning glance would suddenly flash into her consciousness, leaving her weak, excited, and faintly guilty. Paul had left for New Haven two days after the concert, to Anne's distress and Nicola's relief.

She had welcomed this trip to England, hoping a change of scene might soothe her restlessness.

When they arrived at Buckleigh School it had stopped drizzling, and a pale sun threatened to break through the clouds. But the air was still damp, and it made Nicola's nose feel as if it had been dipped in ice water.

She and Mickey fixed the base of the playground in concrete, in the grassy quadrangle used by the younger boys in the lower school. While they waited for the concrete to dry,

Alfred Steadman, the headmaster, insisted upon giving them tea in his study. They were hardly attired for the occasion, in their jeans, but the tweed-clad Steadman, a proper English gentleman, seemed not to notice. No doubt they fit his preconceptions about artists.

If Nicola felt slightly uncomfortable in the presence of this corpulent and over-jolly fellow, looking like her idea of Holmes' Doctor Watson, Mickey was visibly squirming. Nicola could see, in spite of the supposed ending of class distinctions, that when it came down to it, they still remained strong among the English.

'No sugar, my dear?' Steadman asked. 'Well, do have a bun then. Surely you have no need to be slimming.' He smiled in a friendly manner, and Nicola smiled back.

'It's such a pleasure to meet Edward's wife at long last. How is my old chum? Did Edward ever tell you of the splendid times we had in '43 and '44? Of course Lieutenant Harrington was only a lad then, but very lively and full of fun. His family was well acquainted with the Lockes of Philadelphia, related to the Locke-Winsteads of Buckinghamshire, who are cousins of mine, and we took Edward under our wing when he was stationed at Earl's Colm, near Colchester . . .'

Nicola observed the look of contempt that passed over Mickey's face. 'Uh, Edward is very well, thank you, Mr Steadman, and asks to be remembered,' Nicola lied, hoping the warmth now suffusing her cheeks was not readily observable by the two men.

The fact was that Edward had neglected to tell her he knew Alfred Steadman at all. Until this moment Nicola had not suspected that the commission given to her by Buckleigh School might be the result of that connection.

Mortified though she was, she kept her cool and sipped her tea, entering into the polite teatime conversation of the English upper middle class as best she could, given no help from the monosyllabic Mickey. All the while she wondered how Edward could have done such a thing without even consulting her.

After tea she and Mickey worked extremely hard to assemble the playground. Watching Nicola use a wrench on the bolts, her welding torch on the steel, he shook his head in wonder. 'Three cheers for women's lib. If we get a flat tyre you can jack up the wheel.'

'Okay, why not,' she agreed amiably.

Mickey stepped back and looked at the playground. It was made of wood and Cor-Ten steel in twisting shapes, low slung and sturdy. Around it snaked a horizontal distortion mirror made of synthetic glass. Nicola had sprayed the wood with acrylic paint in bold colours to preserve it and give interesting reflections.

Mickey, looking at it critically, did not comment on the design. 'I'd better try it for strength,' he muttered, flinging himself onto the curving bars. 'I guess it'll hold the lads okay,' he said grudgingly.

Nicola laughed. 'I can see that you don't think much of it. How would you design a playground, Mickey?'

'Well,' he drawled, as they got into the truck and started back to London, 'I have some ideas but there's no bloody use talking about them. I haven't got tuppence to mount anything. My dad could lend me the money, but he won't. He doesn't understand what the hell I'm playing at and wants me to get a real job and be a real bloke,' Mickey said bitterly. 'Not the sort of problem you would know anything about.'

'I might.' Nicola recalled the day she came home and found a letter from the California School of Art waiting for her.

'What's it say?' Theresa asked, a glittering fear in her eyes as if she already knew.

'Oh, Mama, I've won a scholarship!'

Theresa Di Candia, brown-haired, young, and fretful, had always been overanxious about her only daughter, whom she simply could not understand. 'What scholarship? All the way in California? Are you crazy? Papa would never let you go.'

'But he has to. It's only San Francisco,' Nicola specified, as if somehow that part of California was closer to New York.

'*Dio mio*, what are you talking about? An unmarried girl doesn't go so many miles from home by herself, scholarship or no scholarship. I tell you to forget it. Papa wouldn't let you go. And even if he would, I wouldn't.'

'But Mama, if you only knew what it means to me! To be a sculptor! It's the only thing I want in the world.'

'Oh, is that so? Sculpture you want, eh? Not a husband? Not babies? What's the matter with you anyway? Have you gone crazy? Dom! Dom, come in the house!' Theresa shouted through the window into the backyard. 'Dom, I can't do anything with your daughter.'

Dominic Di Candia, wiping his greasy hands on an old towel, sat down in the parlour, prepared to hear both sides and decide fairly, as he believed he did with all family decisions.

Nicola stood tensely in front of her father and explained, 'I didn't tell you I applied because I knew that you could never afford to send me unless I won a scholarship, but I have!'

Dominic was a good listener, an unusually calm man in his Neapolitan milieu. Theresa often found his reasonableness maddening, and had always suspected that the family of her blond, blue-eyed husband had originated in the North.

'But why sculpture, Nika?' Dominic asked. 'I always thought commercial art was the thing for you. It pays good, you could live at home, life could go on.'

'I don't want commercial art,' Nicola cried. 'Papa, I don't want to work only with my hands but with my *whole body*. I haven't brought home any of my latest pieces yet, but I've been working with metal. You know, welding things, the way I help you weld the auto fenders out in the back.'

Her father and mother gave Nicola a blank look. She began restlessly to pace their small parlour, decorated in what she privately dubbed Early Woolworth – all floral chintz, wax fruit, and badly framed still-life prints, as well as a hideous rendering of The Nativity. How could she explain to them what sculpting meant to her?

'You know, Nika, it doesn't sound to me like a good job for a girl who will soon be thinking of starting her own family . . .' Dominic's voice was soft, low, persuading, and Nicola felt a hard lump forming in the bottom of her throat that would soon cause her to erupt in tears.

'Look at you,' Theresa shouted at her daughter. Fear, which made Dominic even more calm, rendered his wife shrill. 'You just want to be different. Skin and bones, like we didn't feed you, and dressed in those dirty dungarees all the time, like we didn't give you money to buy some decent clothes.'

Nicola's control snapped. 'Do you know why, Mama? Because I skimp on lunches at school and use every penny to buy art materials, that's why! Because I know if I asked you for money for things like that you'd never let me have it!'

All at once Nicola poured out all the little secrets she'd been keeping from her parents for more than a year. How she had scoured junkyards and car graveyards, gathering railroad spikes, old gas and water pipes, links of chain, rusty nails, bent auto fans, old bicycle parts. How she had been consumed with inspiration. How she had had such an enormous output that her impressed teacher had been the one to encourage her to apply for a scholarship.

While she spoke, walking up and down and waving her hands, Nicola became another person to her parents, a stranger. 'Other sculptors have used metal, only not the way I will. You should see the works of Julio Gonzales, for instance. Gonzales taught Picasso himself.'

Theresa's anger turned to fear for her daughter, investing such emotion in hunks of metal instead of in a man. 'At your age I was already engaged six months to your papa. I don't know what will happen to you,' she moaned, rocking her face in her hands.

Dominic listened carefully, observing his daughter, who looked so much like him but had her mother's volatile temperament.

'Please, Papa. You wanted Vincent to be another Michelangelo, remember? You used to buy him clay and help him make things.'

'How do you remember that?' Theresa asked in wonder. 'You were so little.'

'I remember because I loved my big brother and wanted to be just like him. I wanted to model in clay too. And – and when he was run over, and you and Papa cried and cried, I thought I could take his place, and make you as proud of me as you would have been of him. Remember, Papa, when I convinced you to show me how to weld the way Vincent did so I could help you in the shop? I have helped, haven't I?'

'Of course, Nika, but this sculpture business is different. You're talking about spending four years of your life three thousand miles from us, with total strangers.'

'That's what I say,' Theresa broke in tearfully. 'It's just crazy ...'

Nicola grew desperate to make them understand. 'Look, there's something mysterious in me that I've felt since I was a kid. I feel it everywhere in my body. I don't know, working with clay, wood, stone and metal –it just thrills me. I become reborn. My ears sing and my head rings with all sorts of shapes and forms. I think of them before I go to sleep, and dream of them, and wake up with them.'

'Nika *mia*, you've got the gift!' Dominic suddenly declared, his face lighting up with comprehension. 'I always thought I had it but I didn't know what to do with it. And I needed to make a buck. Vincent, may he rest in peace, had it, that special spark, that sacred gift given only by God. Theresa, we can't fight it, our daughter's got the gift!'

When Nicola heard her father say that, she knew, in a rush of joy, that he would let her go to California.

'Yeah, I can see you had it tough,' Mickey said sarcastically. 'So you went to art school and then you just happened to marry Edward Harrington III, who just happened to be a rich art collector. Don't you think that had a teensy weensy bit to do with your success?'

Nicola bit her lip and didn't reply. He had opened up old wounds and revealed old doubts. She wasn't sure she had an answer for herself.

As they drove across Westminster Bridge, Mickey said in an off-hand way, 'I don't suppose you'd care to come to a disco this evening.'

'Well, I am rather tired.'

He shot her a look of class hatred.

'– and much too old. People would think you were taking out your mum.'

'Bloody hell! If it's no, just say so, without the excuses.'

'Well, yes, I mean, if you grant me dispensation as an old married woman and don't expect me to dance every dance.' She smiled tentatively at him.

'Right, then.' His angry frown changed into a sheepish smile.

Nicola felt trapped but she couldn't bear to bruise his delicate ego. These young artists were very touchy and very self-deceiving. Mickey was another Jimmy Porter, another Angry Young Man who, much as he might argue to the contrary, was turned on by her success and wealth. Aspiring artists of twenty didn't ask out women of nearly forty if they happened to be only housewives.

She didn't like discos, and because she really was tired, didn't look forward to the evening. To her surprise Mickey took her, not to some basement dive, but to Regine's, a new, trendy rooftop place catering to the jet set. Bianca Jagger and Princess Caroline were among the celebrities that night.

'Just look at the view! Some posh place, huh? Costs two hundred quid to join, but it's worth it,' Mickey assured her, making her wonder just how serious he was about his work.

From the way he looked at her, and gyrated his slim-hipped body, she knew he was hoping to turn her on but was too afraid to make a real pass in case it might be rejected.

Nicola was careful not to insult Mickey by offering to pay for the expensive drinks or anything else. And he did treat her civilly, even keeping to his promise to deliver her at the Dorchester before midnight.

'You come on tougher than you really are,' he muttered, giving her a peck on the cheek and an aggrieved final look before opening the door of his truck.

Nicola went to her room, stifling a yawn, and feeling great relief that the evening was over and she no longer had to tread on eggshells. Young men were to be taken in small doses and preferably from a distance.

6

Nicola wandered through the sculpture exhibits at the Tate Gallery. Looking at the work of other artists was always a mixed experience for her. She felt in turn critical, elated, and often envious – especially when someone else's vision caused a slow tremor down her back.

She was admiring a large, low sculpture in red-painted steel by Anthony Caro when she caught sight of one of her own pieces. Called *Forward Rhythms*, it was composed of wing shapes of various sizes in welded steel and cast bronze and looked from afar like a mobile pinned to the ground which would at any moment take off. Nicola approached it with some trepidation and looked at it for a long while.

'What does Di Candia think of Di Candia?'

Nicola jumped and turned to see Paul Kadin-Luri, looking unbearably attractive in a navy blue blazer and crimson turtleneck sweater, and smiling at her tensely.

She felt flustered and as foolishly vain as if he'd caught her making faces at herself in the mirror. Before she could explain that she'd come upon her own work quite by chance - the Tate owned several of her pieces and rotated their displays - Paul laughed and headed her off.

'I'm sure you're not admiring it. More likely you're a little put off. You'd do it differently if you could. You wish you could somehow get it out of here and shove it away where nobody could see it.'

'God, that's right, that's it exactly. How on earth do you know? And what are you doing in London?'

'It's the same way I feel about an early composition.'

He never did answer the second question, and Nicola didn't dare to ask again. Instead, to cover her nervousness and the ridiculous fluttering she felt in her stomach, she led him from one piece to another, giving him a kind of guided tour.

'Here's Louise Nevelson's *Black Wall*. She really inspired me when I was just beginning. Because her father owned a lumberyard, and mine an auto body shop, I was terrifically impressed. I wanted to do in metal what she did so ingeniously in wood, using table legs and old knobs. She fused them into such perfect compositions, so powerful, like her private monuments to heaven.'

Paul suddenly touched her arm, giving her an electric shock. 'Could we possibly have some lunch, Nicola?'

'Oh, I'm sorry. I've been blathering on, boring you to death.'

'Quite the reverse. It's just that my stomach feels the way Henry Moore's stomachs look - a great gaping hole.'

While they ate in the museum restaurant, Nicola's

apprehension returned. 'I take it you've been to London before?'

'Yes, I spent a summer here a couple of years ago. Going to concerts, playing a little myself, and visiting the Tate and searching out Di Candias. Are you busy this evening, Nicola?'

The question was so unexpected that she blurted out, 'No, not really,' before she could think.

'Good. There's a concert at South Bank. James Galway playing Mozart. As for this afternoon, as long as there's what the English call "sunny interval", I'd like to drive down to Buckleigh to see your playground. Come on, say yes.'

He smiled at her so charmingly that her objections withered on her lips. Paul insisted on paying for the lunch. 'I invited you. You can pay next time. Don't start fussing like my mother –'

'Why not?' Nicola challenged. 'I'm your mother's contemporary, don't forget.'

'All the more reason to hang onto your money – for your retirement,' he teased, grinning at her.

Paul drove well, as he appeared to do everything. There was an air of competence about him that made Nicola feel peculiar.

As the older person, she felt she ought to have been the dominant one, but Paul did not permit it.

When they arrived at Buckleigh, the playground was not in use. Nicola, staring at it from a distance, saw a dozen things that didn't please her.

Paul, however, rushed to it and plunged himself onto the bars, standing on his hands and hoisting his legs upward like a gymnast, while making faces in the distortion mirror. 'I love it. It's whimsical, fascinating. Deceptively complex. I would have enjoyed climbing around on a thing like that when I was a kid.'

Nicola couldn't help comparing Paul with Mickey, although she knew she wasn't being quite fair. Paul was an accomplished musician and composer, whereas Mickey, although about the same age, had hardly begun. Also Mickey had seen Nicola as a competitor.

At recess the small boys came rushing out of the school and swarmed all over the bars and rungs.

'You see, Nicola? They love it.'

Nicola smiled with relief to note that despite its faults the playground was functional.

'Have a little more confidence in yourself,' Paul said as they drove away. 'You seem embarrassed, as if you don't deserve to be successful. Can't you see that your playgrounds in America are so famous that even the English are impressed?'

Loyalty to Edward kept Nicola from telling Paul the real reason she had been granted this commission. She had tried to phone Edward last night but he wasn't at home. This morning she hadn't been able to reach him either.

Paul's mention of her success had plucked a very fragile chord in her self-esteem, and she pushed all thoughts on the matter deep down, as she had done for years.

She was more immediately worried about the evening ahead of her. While she dressed, Nicola tried to get her emotional bearings. She was slightly afraid to go to the concert with Paul, but at the same time she was excited by the prospect. Seeing him so unexpectedly had sent her imagination soaring.

She toyed with calling his hotel and cancelling at the last minute, but it would make her seem so stuffy. Worst of all, it might give him an inkling that she thought she had something to fear, which had to be ridiculous. Like spinsters always worrying that they were going to be raped.

Nicola chose a suit of camel-coloured chenille with a slim slit skirt and classic belted wrap jacket. Very tailored and no-nonsense.

When Nicola went downstairs to meet Paul, his elation, which was already considerable, increased, although he tried to conceal it. Nicola was dressed in what she probably considered a matronly fashion. Would she have done so if she weren't attracted to him? In fact, the severity of the outfit only emphasised her graceful sensuality.

Nicola quite enjoyed the first part of the concert, the music heightened by Paul's knowledgeable comments during the intermission.

'I think you play at least as well as Galway, Paul.'

'Well, I'm no Jean-Pierre Rampal and I never will be. In truth, I'd rather compose than play someone else's music.

Some day I hope to write something for Rampal. Have you ever seen him play?'

'Of course. I'm practically a Rampal groupie,' Nicola said, drawing a laugh from Paul. 'I've heard him in London and Athens as well as New York. He reminds me of Pan, piping music written by the gods.'

'That's a lovely image, from a lovely woman.' He looked deeply into her eyes.

Nicola moved away from him quickly, saying, 'We'd better get back to our seats.'

During the second half of the concert she didn't really hear a note of the music. She was too aware of Paul sitting beside her, of his leg almost touching her, of his beautiful hand resting on the arm of the seat. Most of all, she was aware of her frightening attraction to him.

When it was over, Paul suggested walking back over Waterloo Bridge. 'It's such a fantastic night. I can pick the car up in the morning.'

Nicola was trembling with such breathless longing for him that she had to force herself to respond with mere words when she admired the architecture of Somerset House, and the striped effect of the moon, half-concealed by clouds.

Each time Paul looked at her, Nicola had the eerie feeling that he was going to kiss her. It was nonsense, it must be, just her overactive imagination. For the first time Nicola understood why men of a certain age pursued young girls. Youth had great appeal. The difference was that women were content with just the company – or so she told herself.

She tried to keep the conversation to Paul's music, listening intently as he talked of a work in progress, a tone poem for seven instruments. When he had finished she began to tell him about an idea she had for a sun monument, inspired by Stonehenge.

'I'll look forward to seeing it,' Paul murmured, stopping and turning to face her. Nicola hadn't realised that they had actually walked all the way up Park Lane and were standing in front of the Dorchester.

'I want to do my monument in aluminium, with sheets of glass over it –'

He took her arm. 'I want to kiss you good night,' he murmured, drawing her closer.

Nicola's heart suddenly pounded a warning, and she twisted her face so that his lips connected with her cheek.

'Good night!' she almost shouted. 'Thank you for the concert.' She was in such a hurry to escape that she tripped on the pavement. 'Say hello to your mother, if you get back to New York before I do.'

In a terrible panic, Nicola ran into the lobby. She was losing her grip, and it terrified her.

A while later, lying in bed tormented, she was able to think more calmly. 'This is Anne's *son*, twenty-two years old. Okay, he acts older and he's an interesting companion. His mother brought him up to be interesting.'

Nicola continued to talk to herself, trying to remove the turbulent feelings within her. 'Okay, he wanted to kiss you. Remember, he kissed you at his debut. A peck on the lips, that's all. Nothing to panic about. You're just being ridiculous.'

Nicola calmed herself sufficiently to get to sleep, but she awoke later in the night from an erotic dream.

Watch out, she warned herself grimly, watch out.

Nicola was awakened by the telephone. 'Hello.'

'Good morning, Nicola. Sorry if I woke you. I'm down in the dining room. I've ordered breakfast.'

'I – I can't Paul –'

'What, can't eat breakfast? Of course you can. See you in ten minutes.' Paul hung up.

Nicola ran into the shower. This was preposterous. She would have to put a stop to it immediately. When she entered the dining room, she intercepted the waiter and made certain the meal would be put on her bill. Then she approached the table, spotting Paul before he saw her.

'God, he's gorgeous,' she thought, immediately furious with herself. She was acting like a depraved old maid instead of a happily married woman. Edward certainly didn't neglect her in bed. Then what the hell was she doing, even thinking of Paul like that?

He glanced up and got to his feet politely, but the expression in his eyes was not polite. It was seductive. He was divesting her of her tan velvet jacket, her dark green silk shirt, and her black velvet trousers.

Paul smiled, and the intensity vanished. 'You're grumpy in the morning, don't like to talk, and feel very shadowy because reality is not yet with you.'

Nicola relaxed and smiled back at him. 'That's right. And you're awake the moment you open your eyes. Probably whistle a complete flute concerto in the shower.'

'Guilty. Since I'm the morning personality, you must let me make the morning plans. First I suggest a walk on Hampstead Heath.'

'I couldn't possibly. I have some shopping to do.'

'Excellent. You'll do it in Hampstead. Antique jewellery. Ethnic clothes. Scottish tweeds and tartans. Rare books and prints. Loose tea or freshly ground coffee. Second hand junk. Mats and baskets made in Hong Kong. 'Ere, luv, you name it, we 'ave it.'

Somehow Nicola couldn't bring herself to refuse.

They visited some of the most charming shops she had ever seen, and she bought extravagant gifts for Edward and Julie, as well as for Anne, trying to make up for the prickles of guilt that kept dampening her elation from time to time.

'I shouldn't feel guilty,' she kept telling herself. 'Nothing is happening except that I'm having a marvellous time with my best friend's son – as if I were his aunt or something.'

They walked on the Heath, got caught in the rain, and ran for refuge to The Spaniard's Inn pub. Just inside, Paul took out a handkerchief. 'Hold still a moment, love,' he murmured, gently wiping the raindrops off her face.

Nicola shivered with something besides the dampness, and she couldn't look at him for a moment, simply frozen in time and space. He mopped his own face, and they went in.

While he got drinks at the bar, she sat down, her head spinning with thoughts that were ecstatic one moment and riddled with anxiety the next.

'A cold day for the time of the year,' said a rather staid-looking Englishman with mutton-chop whiskers.

'Yes,' she replied hesitantly.

'Spring's likely to be late, so the forecasters say.'

Paul appeared holding two mugs of Guinness in one hand, a plate of Cornish pasties in the other.

He glared at the Englishman and slammed down the food

37

and ale. 'What ees thees?' he said, assuming a frightening truculence. 'Do you dare to talk to my vooman? Een my country thees ees not permitted.'

The Englishman looked at Paul in alarm. 'Sorry, old man, I didn't mean any harm. Just passing the time of day.'

'Such behaviour een the Spaniard's Een.'

Mumbling apologies, the man jumped up and fled the place, while Nicola nearly collapsed with laughter.

'How was I?' Paul asked, pleased. 'Think I could make it on the stage, if all else fails?'

'I'm sure of it. You certainly could pass for Spanish. That poor man was terrified you'd pull out a stiletto and run him through.'

'Would have served him bloody right, too,' Paul said in a proprietary manner that thrilled and frightened her.

Later, Paul looked for a genuine country teashop, against Nicola's protests that she had to get back.

'Nonsense, my dear,' he said, in an exaggerated upper class accent. 'It's half three and I must have my tea or I'll go into a decline.'

They finally found a lovely place for tea in a pretty country cottage with a flowered border around the lawn.

Nicola poured the tea while Paul buttered the scones and tried to apply strawberry jam to them, in the process making his hands all sticky. He compounded the mess by slathering thick Devon cream on top. By then he had reduced the scones to crumbs under his fingers.

Nicola laughed more freely and helplessly than she had in years.

When he took her back to the hotel, she suddenly had a flat, letdown feeling. She realised uneasily that she didn't want him to go.

'Thank you for a lovely day.'

'– and night. As a matter of fact I have tickets for Tom Stoppard's *Night and Day*.'

'No! I – I mean, I can't possibly –' She had said the same words to no effect earlier. 'I can't, really I can't, Paul.'

'You will,' he contradicted quietly, 'because I hate to go to the theatre by myself, and if you don't come with me you'll be depriving both of us. I'll tell my mother on you.' He smiled mischievously.

Nicola felt the blood pouring into her face. How did he dare laugh about it? And yet, if he was joking, didn't it prove that all this was simply a lark for him, and that she was reading too much into it?

Right. She was supposed to be a mature woman. She would act her age. She would behave the way Anne would have done had the situation been reversed, with Nicola's son taking her to an innocent play in the West End.

As she dressed, Nicola imagined the future conversation between mother and son. 'I ran into your old friend, Nicola Harrington, and she looked a little lonely so I invited her to the theatre ...'

Nicola put on the only dress she had brought with her, a pale blue silk crêpe de Chine. It was a kind of shirtwaister, with the sleeves rolled to the elbow, and a plunging lapel neckline. Clasping a strand of small freshwater pearls around her neck, she dabbed some perfume on her ears, neck, and wrists.

'Paul is harmless,' she told herself, 'He's just teasing you, the way he did when he was a kid, trying to make you feel young and desirable. Don't make a whole meal out of one abortive kiss.' And yet, her pulse raced wildly.

They had dinner in Covent Garden in a dimly lit restaurant boasting fine continental food and discreetly hovering waiters.

It was seldom that Nicola found herself at dinner vis-à-vis a man other than Edward, and she felt suddenly as awkward as a schoolgirl out on a date – even to the extent that she drank too much wine and got quickly high on it. That helped her to keep up her end of the conversation, which was sharp, light, and heady. Yet, every so often, she was assailed by pinpricks of guilt that scorched her like sparks from an otherwise beautiful bonfire.

With time, and more wine, Nicola began to feel reckless. So enthralled was she to be dining with Paul that she forgot that she was not really as attractive and contemporary as she felt.

'Do you remember me much, when I was a kid?' Paul suddenly asked.

Nicola tumbled to earth. 'Yes,' she said, sighing painfully.

'Yes, of course. You were an interesting boy, and so musically talented.'

'I don't mean that. I mean did you know what I was feeling when you used to visit?'

'No. How could I?'

Paul tilted his head back, resting it on top of the banquette. 'I thought you might have noticed that I have always been madly in love with you, ever since I can remember.'

Stunned, she didn't say anything. After a long silence he said, 'You look shocked. Are you?'

'I – I don't know what I am,' she whispered. 'Little boys often admire their mother's friends. It's not something to be taken seriously.'

'I took it the only way I could.' Paul reached for her hand, which trembled icily in his. 'Nicola Di Candia, I loved you then as boy loves girl and I love you now as man loves woman. Since the night of my concert, I've thought of nothing else. Except my tone poem, which means thinking of you because you inspire me, as you did long ago.' He told her how he had happened to write his first song.

'Stop, please. I can't listen to any more, it frightens me too much.'

He increased his pressure on her hand, looking at her with adoration mingled with anguish. 'I know. It frightens me too. I've been going through hell trying to decide what to do because I don't want you to be hurt.'

'Oh, Paul,' she murmured, in a voice so low that he had to lean forward to hear her. 'This isn't real, it can't be. It's just a carryover of a childish infatuation. Now that you've told me, it will go away forever, if you let it.'

Paul shook his head slowly, his gaze arresting her. She forgot how to breathe.

'Nicola, I want you. Every which way. Friend. Lover. Mate. It's very real to me.'

Nicola was attacked by such a clash of emotions that her brain reeled. She felt joy and hope on a level she hadn't experienced in ages. The next moment a searing fear gripped her, the way it would a person with chest pains who has just had a doctor's confirmation that it's a heart attack.

'You may not be aware of it, Nicola my love,' Paul

murmured softly, 'but you've been sending me answering signals. The way you look at me, your body language, every gesture tells me you're available for loving by someone – even if it's not me.'

Not him! Nicola rested her burning face in her cold hand for several minutes.

'All right,' she capitulated finally. 'All right. I find you devastating. If I were twenty years younger, and had no husband and daughter, I'd probably follow you to the ends of the earth. But. *But* I have both a husband and daughter, *and* a friend who happens to be your mother – which I'm old enough to be. To do anything about my feelings would be unthinkable.'

His look of joy at her confession faded. 'Unthinkable?' Paul questioned, leaning forward tensely. 'People fall in love every day of the week. Your age – which you don't begin to look – is irrelevant to me. Your daughter is old enough to look after herself. And my mother is too fond of me to meddle in my emotional life. The only valid point you've raised concerns your husband. I have little doubt that you care for him. I'm sure you could never live a lie. The question is how much you care for him, and if you could give him up. Nicola, don't misunderstand me.'

Paul impatiently pushed his heavy dark hair off his face. His eyes burned with passion.

'I don't honestly think that if I spent even one night with you I would ever be able to share you with anyone else. I don't want a backstreet affair. I want you totally.'

'Oh, God!' Nicola lowered her face and put her hand to her eyes. 'You followed me to London.'

'Of course. I was at home briefly and overheard Anne's end of a conversation with you. She was good enough to mention your hotel.'

'Paul, it's impossible. We just can't do it. Anyway, what you call love is more likely youthful libido.'

'Stop it!' he hissed. 'Don't trivialise my feelings just because you aren't courageous enough to come to terms with your own. Do you think I'm going to force you to be with me?' He lifted his hand to summon the waiter.

Nicola watched him in amazement. His tone was so calm,

41

even cold. Was this some strange sort of macho game on his part? If he really wanted her would he drop the ball into her lap and leave it there?

But when she glanced at him as he helped her into her coat – tensing against the touch of his hands on her shoulders – she saw the pain in his eyes, and she felt ashamed. Paul was not playing any game. His early love for her had matured to this, and with every moment she felt herself weakening.

Nicola knew she should have taken a taxi directly to the hotel. Why then, did she go to the theatre as planned? How was she able to sit in her seat, so close to him, and concentrate on the play? Had Paul known that one of the subplots of *Night and Day* concerned the deep infatuation of the wife of an older man for a much younger journalist?

Nicola realised with a sense of shame that Paul was right about her. She was available for an affair, even though she deplored her restlessness and could offer no excuse. She didn't even have Paul's rationale, for 'love' as he meant it didn't enter into it. She loved Edward. But she was overpowered with desire for Paul. She wanted that tender, manly mouth on hers, and those hands to caress her.

While she tormented herself with the knowledge that she wanted him to follow her to her room, fling her on the bed, and give her an excuse to surrender, Paul appeared to be concentrating on the play. When it ended, he said, 'I know someone in the cast. I was at Curtis with Tony Saunders. Let's go backstage.'

Nicola went willingly, because she didn't want to be alone with Paul, but reluctantly because she wanted to be alone with him more than anything in the world.

Tony Saunders had only a minor part. He was a rawboned fellow who looked at Nicola with disconcerting interest, as if she were exuding sexual receptiveness like a cat in heat. Was it as obvious as all that?

Tony invited them to have a drink, taking for granted that Nicola was Paul's girlfriend. 'We used to double-date at Curtis in the old days,' Tony told her, 'and I spent more time learning about female anatomy than concentrating on my singing. Fortunately I decided I wanted acting after all and was lucky enough to get into RADA. But oh, the times we had, eh, Paul? I bet you haven't confessed half of what you've done. How long have you two known each other?'

'Since he was born,' Nicola replied.

Tony hooted with laughter, as if she had said something terribly witty – or at least symbolic – and Paul gave her an I-told-you-so look. He followed it with the intense stare that had begun to liquefy her flesh.

During the taxi ride back to the Dorchester Nicola was too upset to speak. She had mixed feelings when Paul got out and paid the driver instead of taking the taxi back to his hotel.

She had to do this quickly. 'Goodbye, Paul,' she said in a shaky voice. Goodbye for the rest of my life.

'One kiss?'

'One kiss,' she echoed primly, determined to show him she meant what she had said, and to prove it to herself.

Steeling herself for a young man's impatient onslaught, she was unprepared for the gentleness of his embrace, the sweetness of the kiss. She felt her very bones dissolving, and when he stepped away, having exacted no more than he had asked, she felt wildly, irrationally like pulling him up to her room, ripping off his clothes, and losing herself in a night of bacchanalia.

Nicola caught the morning plane back to New York.

7

'Nicola, my sweet, how good to have you home.' Edward kissed her and then held her very tightly. When he released her he threw her a preview of his 'let's make love' look.

'It's good to be home,' Nicola said truthfully.

'Come and have a drink with me and tell me how your trip went.'

Sitting on the oversized sofa in the oversized living-room of their Beekman Place duplex, Nicola watched her husband mix martinis. She saw him as if through Paul's eyes. Tall and slim, Edward, at fifty-four, was still remarkably fit, his grey-streaked hair still thick, his face still handsome. He took excellent care of himself, playing tennis or squash daily at his club, and swimming several lengths of the pool.

Even when dressed casually, Edward gave the immediate impression of wealth and breeding. He threw Nicola a disarming smile as he handed her a drink.

'Edward, why didn't you tell me that you were an old friend of Alfred Steadman's?'

He brow wrinkled. 'Who?'

'Steadman, headmaster of Buckleigh School. My playground, remember?'

'Oh, Alf! Why certainly we're friends. Alf and I were the greatest buddies in the old days. Didn't I ever regale you with our times together when I was stationed in England?'

'If you did I can't remember it. I hadn't any idea that my commission was the result of your friendship with him, and it was so embarrassing.'

'Good grief, I hope you don't think I acted as an intermediary in any of this. Look, Alf and his family happened to be very kind to me in '44. I haven't seen him in years, although we've kept up on news through mutual friends. I guess he knows you're my wife, so it was obvious to think of you when planning a new playground for the school. Is there anything wrong with that?'

'Well, no,' Nicola said without conviction. What was wrong was the depressing jolt she felt whenever a commission came her way for any reason other than a disinterested appreciation of her talent.

Edward patted the arm of his chair and smiled enticingly at her. 'Come here and give me a cuddle, precious. I've been missing you.'

Nicola perched next to him and kissed his forehead, while he stroked her hair, his arm around her.

'Do you notice any changes?'

Nicola surveyed the walls. 'You *have* been busy. Three acquisitions. That one's interesting. Somebody new?'

'No. Frank Skoda's been around but his work never clicked. Too surrealistic. Recently, though, his painting has taken on a demonic quality that's coming into vogue. I got it from Ritter's Gallery.'

'Was it very expensive?' In truth Nicola didn't like it much but she hesitated to dampen her husband's enthusiasm.

'Not yet. I've only borrowed it to see how well it wears. The other two paintings are the work of a new artist, Tess Abrams. A name to watch. Her work is an interesting marriage of Minimalism and Pop.'

Edward bent Nicola into his lap, kissing her insistently, his hand snaking over her body.

Nicola responded with enthusiasm, trying not to feel guilty about Paul. Nothing had happened. It was idiotic to punish herself for her desire.

'Having fun?'

'Oh! Hi, Julie,' Nicola clumsily tried to pull down her skirt twisted above her knees.

'Learn to knock before you enter a room, princess,' Edward said, annoyed.

Julie stood still for a moment, her fine blonde hair curling softly to her shoulders. With her wide-spaced blue eyes, perfectly formed nose, and sensually etched lips, she could have posed for Botticelli.

But when Julie looked at her mother with glittering eyes, the innocence vanished. 'I won't be in for dinner tonight.'

'I'm disappointed. I thought we three could catch up on all the news,' Nicola murmured. 'Are you going anywhere special?'

'Yeah. Out.'

Nicola rose and went towards her daughter, but Julie passed well out of arm's reach. Hurt, Nicola didn't persist in trying to embrace her.

'What have you been doing all week? Anything new at school? Have you done any new paintings?'

'The same as usual. No. No.' Julie replied in a flat tone. She walked to the bar and poured some gin into a glass, adding tonic and a twist of lemon. 'See you.' Julie departed with her drink.

Edward looked after her. 'Very breezy, lately, isn't she?'

'Edward, since when is she in the habit of mixing herself cocktails?'

45

Edward sighed and drained his glass. 'God only knows. It's the first time she's done so in front of me. You know, the more beautiful she gets the more difficult she is to communicate with.'

'I know.' Nicola frowned. 'But it's mostly me she's down on. Do you suppose it has to do with some boy?'

'It better not,' he replied, a tightness showing around his mouth. 'She's too young for anything serious. More to the point is what she's going to do after graduation. Much as I hate to admit it, art school would be a waste of time – unless it's commercial art. It saddens me that my own daughter hasn't any talent, but there it is. She's like me, and there's no use kidding ourselves. I only hope Julie sees it in time.'

'I'm so upset about her. She says she wants art school, but I wonder if it's only a gesture she feels she has to make to us, although we encourage her to be honest.'

'Young girls have always mystified me,' Edward said, his tone slightly tinged with nuance.

Nicola immediately caught it. 'Did I, when I was a young girl?'

He smiled fondly in remembrance. 'Yes, at first. But in the most intriguing sort of way. I kept trying to find out what made you tick, and by the time I had, you'd lodged in my heart like a little time bomb.'

'Which never exploded, of course.'

'Which explodes intermittently with the force of a ten-ton charge, you beauty.'

'I was never a beauty, and that probably saved me. Maybe our Julie is just a little too beautiful for her own good.' Nicola expelled a sharp sigh.

'She could put it to work for her. She's gorgeous enough, and skinny enough, to be a professional model.'

'Oh, not that, of all things.'

'Why not? It's terrific money. She'd be good at it, and it might bolster her self-esteem. That exquisite face would soon be on the cover of *Vogue*.'

'What do you mean about her self-esteem? Surely she doesn't need her picture plastered on a magazine to know that she has a striking face. And modelling is such mindless work.'

'Don't you believe it. A successful model has to be damned intelligent. You can take my word for it that no dummy ever reaches the top in any profession.'

Nicola had always taken Edward's word for everything – except maybe in art.

'Didn't you and Julie do anything together the week I was gone?'

'Nope. She always seemed to be going out when I was coming in, and vice versa. I've been pretty swamped. Trying to get the Whitney to buy an Abrams. I have a hunch that gal is going to take off. The women's movement has made the art world more receptive to female painters, and Abrams is one of the best. What do you think?'

Nicola scrutinised the two works with as much objectivity as she could muster. 'They show skill, but there's a slickness, almost as if she were doing paintings for stage settings. I grant you she knows her colours, and her stroke is sure.'

'You're being a purist. The public craves a little panache. And collectors get tired of rough dabs and splotches. Abrams has elegance.'

'Yes, but no – passion. She doesn't paint from an inner urge to create in the only way she must. Rather it's as if she's coldbloodedly determining what's most likely to sell.'

Edward laughed, showing his fine white teeth. 'Anyone would think that it's a crime for a painter to make money. You know at first hand that talent and success are not mutually exclusive. And speaking of talent, my sweet, have you finished your sculpture for the Biennale?'

'God, no. Not even begun. I'll really have to get down to some hard work.'

'Before you cloister yourself in your studio, I humbly request *droit de seigneur*.' Edward went towards her, a purposeful look in his eye, and drew her to him. They kissed long and deeply.

Nicola was the first to break away and wave her empty glass. 'Shall we have another?'

The second martini numbed her, and the nagging ache that was spelled P-a-u-l finally receded.

She and Edward had an excellent dinner, cooked and served by their amusing imaginative Korean chef, who had mastered the cuisine of three continents, though not the English language.

Nicola, looking at Edward over the candles, began to count

47

her blessings. Edward was good company. He was kind to her and protective. From the start of their marriage he had taken care of all financial matters and surrounded her with every comfort. She had never had to cook a meal, unless she wanted to, or wash a dish, or darn a sock, or pay a bill. Her life was workable, luxurious. Most important, it left her free to sculpt.

No matter how old she grew, Edward would always be a socially acceptable fifteen years older. He would continue to treat her as his child bride, making numerous indulgences for her 'creativity' which he admired because he did not possess it, although he was a genius at recognising it in others.

Wasn't it insane, then for her even to contemplate risking this nearly perfect life just to have an absurdly reckless fling with a callow lover who was still a student being supported by his parents?

Nicola lay on her side, her back to Edward, while he curled around her from behind. She felt comforted by the strong way he held her. The dull ache in the pit of her stomach had receded. She was home, where she belonged, with the husband she loved and who loved her.

She grew pleasantly drowsy, and was on the borderline of slumber when Edward's fingers crept slowly from her waist to her breast, his thumb making a soft, circular motion around her nipple. It stiffened, and he was encouraged to fondle her other breast.

In spite of her sleepiness, Nicola roused herself. She wanted to respond to Edward tonight, needing proof that their relationship worked.

Edward, pressing against her buttocks, stiffened, and he moved his lips to her neck.

'My beautiful virgin bride,' he murmured into her ear. 'I love your body. It's as young and fresh as when you were twenty.'

Whenever he mentioned her virginity, Nicola felt uncomfortable. She had not been a virgin when she met him. Surely a man of his experience had known. And yet, if he preferred to believe it was so . . .

Edward turned her onto her back and kissed her breasts while he caressed her thighs.

Nicola reached out to stroke him.

Although he seemed hardly to move at all, he drew back from her fingers.

Nicola lay inert, remembering that too much movement on her part would turn him off. Edward liked to take the lead, to set the pace. He decided where and when he would touch her, and she him. The trouble was that passivity rarely brought her to orgasm.

Using a combination of his fingers, mouth, and tongue, Edward caused her skin to tingle warmly. He took her by the shoulders and moved her head onto his belly.

Nicola obeyed his unspoken command in order to please him, but she wished she could go down on him when she felt like it instead of only at his direction.

During the first year of their marriage she had tried several times, in a vertical moment, to discuss with him that she felt constrained during their lovemaking, but he had smiled and changed the subject.

Edward pulled away, breathing stertorously, and pushed her onto her back. As she felt him thrust into her, her breath quickened. She tightened her arms around his neck and strained towards him. She wanted desperately to come. It always pleased him so much, and relaxed her as nothing else could. But although her flesh was reacting to his pressure, she felt a hard knot of resistance from within her.

Whenever Nicola failed to have an orgasm Edward would cheerfully, afterwards, make some mention of the fact that she was sublimating her sexual energy in her art. It was probably true. Art was exciting, compelling, immortal, whereas sex was only – sex. And yet the frustration, when she did not climax, was depressing and often meant a sleepless night.

Please let me come tonight. Nicola had noticed that her resistance was strongest when they made love in her studio. Although Edward respected her need to be alone and to sleep there when she was absorbed in a work, he sometimes used his key to visit.

'Just wondering how you were getting on, and if you could spare a kiss for me,' he would say, smiling at her appealingly.

Nicola would try hard, but her true feeling was that he had violated the sanctity of her place of creation.

49

Tonight, however, they were in their marital bed. There was no reason, no reason at all to be tense.

She felt herself drawing close, closer.

'Come! Come now!' Edward hissed.

His command acted like a tourniquet to choke off her response. She strained against him but it was no use. Barely able to catch her breath, Nicola relaxed her muscles. She would not make it tonight.

Without warning she had a fleeting image of heavy, dark hair, wonderfully devouring eyes, and slender-strong musician's hands caressing her. Nicola immediately crested, shivers of ecstacy forcing a moan from her lips.

Edward, letting out a grunt of male triumph, drove relentlessly into her.

'Nicola, it's the most exquisite sweater I could ever imagine,' Anne exclaimed, rubbing the rose-coloured sleeve against her cheek. 'I've had a cashmere, but this is gossamer. It was so sweet of you to think of me, busy as you must have been with your playground. I'll put it on right now.' Anne pulled off her suit jacket and struggled into the sweater.

Nicola, taking a long swallow of her chilled white wine, was glad she had bought a big enough size, Anne had not grown any slimmer with the years, Nicola thought a little smugly.

Anne had come all the way downtown to Nicola's studio, on Eleventh and University Place, so that after lunch Nicola could immediately get back to work.

She was tense, waiting for Anne to mention something about Paul's having been in London the same time as she, so that she could casually tell of their meeting. Chances were that Paul hadn't done so.

Nicola had no intention of repeating the terrible, wonderful things Paul had told her. But she knew that when she mentioned their having been to the theatre and dinner together, even keeping it on an innocent level, it would finish the matter once and for all. Anne would know, and Paul would soon know that his mother knew. That knowledge would cool his ardour – or at least alter his tactics.

Nicola would then be able to tuck Paul, and the tantalising

love that might have been, away into the secret compartment in which she kept other, more youthful, erotica. Until now Gareth Howe had held sway in that minuscule corner of Nicola's memory.

'Shall we eat, Nika, I'm starved,' Anne declared. 'I feel like pasta, and I hope you'll humour me because with your astonishing metabolism you've never had to watch what you eat.'

Nicola smiled. 'I wouldn't quite say that, but I will humour you. In fact, I anticipated you enough to have made a reservation at the Tavola Calda.'

'Nicola, I love you,' Anne cried, rushing up to embrace her friend.

Nicola felt a momentary pang of guilt hearing Paul's mother say to her what he had so lately said.

Nicola didn't deserve to be loved by Anne. It was basically cowardice and fear that kept Nicola from picking up the phone and calling Paul in New Haven. Certainly it was not lack of concupiscence. The more she tried to forget Paul, the more obsessed she became with him.

Sensing Anne's good humour as they sat in the bright restaurant on Bleecker Street, amid the greenery and napery and gleaming crystal, Nicola felt close to tears.

Anne had always been so wonderful to her. She had often fed Nicola during her struggle to support herself on a waitress' salary when she first returned from California. And after an evening at the Luries – who in those days didn't have too much themselves – Nicola would arrive home to find that Anne had tucked a $10 bill into her purse or the pocket of her threadbare coat. When Nicola tried to repay her friends by giving them sculptures and collages, Anne had always insisted on 'buying' anything not a birthday or Christmas gift.

'I'm doing it for me, not you,' Anne had insisted. 'Al and I must pay now, so that when you're famous and your work becomes priceless we'll feel less guilty.'

She had been a constant source of encouragement to Nicola, always serenely convinced that her friend's talent was on a par with Nevelson's, and that she must never quit in a moment of depression.

'It's so hard to choose between the *fettuccine Alfredo* and the *cannelloni della Trattoria*,' Anne was saying. 'What will you have, Nicola?'

'Why don't you order the *fettuccine* and I'll have the *cannelloni*? Then we can share,' Nicola murmured, knowing that was what Anne had in mind.

Nicola privately doubted that she would be able to swallow a mouthful of food. She simply had to tell Anne about meeting Paul, and it had to be during lunch.

'Are you all right, Nika? You look so down all of a sudden. Tired? Jet lag?'

'Yes, I suppose so. I am very tired, actually.'

'Starvation,' Anne pronounced. 'You hole yourself up in that studio with nothing edible and you work away like a demon. What you need is some nourishment. Oh, look over there,' Anne whispered. 'Isn't that Janet Markham? And with a man who most certainly is not Tom.'

'It couldn't be,' Nicola said, twisting in her seat. 'No it isn't Janet. I'll grant you she's the same general build and colouring, but that's a girl of not more than twenty-five.'

'Yes, I can see now that you're right. My old eyes are going back on me,' Anne agreed, squinting, 'but the idea of Janet with someone else isn't as preposterous as you seem to think. The way the Markhams moon over each other in public makes me think things aren't quite so rosy in private.'

'They don't moon, they just genuinely appreciate each other.'

'Maybe, maybe not. Nobody really knows what goes on between two people behind closed doors.'

Anne looked sad, and Nicola knew she was thinking of her failed marriage with Al. 'I've seen couples holding hands in public, Nika, looking as if they can't wait to jump into the sack, and two weeks later they're divorced. Scratch the surface of any marriage, and you're likely to come away with dirt under your fingernails.'

Nicola's expression must have been devastated, because Anne immediately smiled at her and blew her a kiss. 'Except yours and Edward's marriage, of course. I don't suppose you've ever dreamed even a tiny dream of being unfaithful to him, have you? God, look at you, you're blushing. Relax, I'm only teasing. I can tell a one-man woman when I see one. You

52

know, the damnedest thing is that the four or five times I've had a lover, since Al and I split up, I was never able to enjoy it. I can only come with Al, isn't that ridiculous?'

'No,' Nicola managed to get out from between dry lips. 'Underneath everything I think you love him. Maybe he's never been your ideal, on paper, but the body has its reasons.'

'No, I think you're wrong. Habit is more likely. And Al has such patience. Most of the men I've been with were so worried about their own performance they had little time to choreograph mine.'

Nicola laughed nervously, feeling her voice edge into hysteria. 'Ah, here's the food. Oh, God, the smell is enough to put five pounds on me. Shall we have some more wine?'

'I'll tell her after we eat,' Nicola promised herself. By deftly giving Anne the bigger portions she managed to disguise how little she ate herself.

They ordered espresso.

'After we drink our coffee, I'll tell her without fail.' Nicola dug her nails into her palms to act as a string around her finger.

'How was your trip to London? You've hardly said a word. You know, it's been ages since I've been, and London is one of my favourite places, too.' Anne blew out cigarette smoke. She looked as happy, sleek, and well fed as an indulged tabby.

Nicola took a deep breath and poked herself painfully in the palm with her sharpest nail. 'As a matter of fact, I happened to run into –'

'Oh, damn, my cigarette's gone out. You, of course, don't have a match. Waiter!'

'– into Paul.'

'What?' Anne asked, smiling at the waiter and thanking him for the light. 'Paul? Oh, hell, I don't know how he is. I'm really irritated with him. From the time he took off for New Haven, after his debut, he's been almost like a recluse. He came down for one weekend after that, moped around the house, and then scooted back. He doesn't phone, is never there when I phone him, tells me he's doing nothing but working, is evasive about when he'll be ready for his public debut at Carnegie. I've set a date for the fall, so he must be. His tone poem is probably not going well, and that's why he doesn't want to talk to me. You know, I thought it might be girl trouble, or something. Remember, the night of his concert, he was talking a lot to Julie. You don't know if she's heard from him, do you?'

Anne forced a laugh. 'They're both way too young, of course, but at least if your daughter had a romance with my son we'd know they were in good company.'

Nicola had to force the words. 'I don't know anything of Julie's private life. She doesn't say –' Nicola stopped and swallowed painfully.

Anne, feeling she had touched a sore point, immediately changed the subject.

Nicola felt as if her skin were being prodded with an ice pick. Paul had lied to his mother. Anne had no idea that he had been in London. How could Nicola say anything and precipitate a family rift – especially when she was the reason for his mendacity?

For days after her lunch with Anne, Nicola was unable to work. She sat crosslegged on her scaffold looking at the sketches for her sun monument. The only thing that was missing was inspiration.

Only the day before she had met Paul in London, Nicola had paid another visit to Stonehenge. She had been haunted by her memory of the huge boulders that seemed to have burst through the ground, to stand like giant monoliths in the barren Salisbury Plain. One theory about their origin – and the one she was most sympathetic to – was that they had been placed there by sun worshippers in a particular arrangement to show sunrise and moonrise at different times of the year, and even solar and lunar eclipses.

Nicola had been so excited at the idea of mounting a sun monument of her own. Now, nothing remained of her vision but a lifeless architectural drawing and cold sheets of glass and aluminium.

The longer she sat and contemplated her materials, the less she had an impulse to begin. Nicola came down off the scaffold and lay on her bed, staring at the huge, slanting windows facing north.

Edward had bought her this beautiful studio as a wedding present. She had gasped at its size then, apprehensive that her work would never justify such luxurious space, on two floors, half of one broken through the ceiling to rise forty feet high. It was a studio that all sculptors dream of, and Nicola had welded her first massive sculpture almost in self-defence to propitiate the gods for her good fortune. Afterwards, her visions had conformed to the size of her work space, and even beyond. It was here she had been able to visualise her first environmental sculptures.

Nicola tried closing her eyes and making her mind a blank. 'I will not think of Paul, I will not,' she ordered fiercely. But it didn't work at all because she thought of nothing but Paul – of that last look he had given her, of the first – and what would have to be the last – kiss. She could taste the sweetness of it, feel again the gentleness of his arms, and the restraint of his youthful muscles.

Nicola put her hands over her ears and shut her eyes. No good. She decided to meditate. She didn't do so on a regular basis, but it had often helped to ease her tenseness, especially when starting a new work.

'Toes of my left foot, relax. Toes of my right foot, relax ... Ankle of my left foot ... hand of my right arm ... left arm ...'

She concentrated on her breathing, watching, as if from the outside, her stream of consciousness, without forcing her thoughts in any direction.

Then she began to say her mantra, 'clyre,' over and over. Each time the word eluded her, and her mind drifted back to Paul, she recaptured it. Clyre floated in and out of her like a ghost.

At the end of twenty minutes, Nicola took a deep breath and slowly came out of the depths of her relaxation. She opened her eyes, stood up, and stretched.

Meditating had helped. Nicola felt refreshed and ready for work. But not on her sun monument.

She went downstairs to her storeroom, cluttered with all sorts of unused materials she had been accumulating for eighteen years. Nicola could never bear to discard anything, always expecting that she would some day find a use for it. She considered it as immoral to waste material, when other artists had to scrounge, as to waste food, which showed contempt for the starving.

55

Nicola dived into the darkness looking purposefully for stone. Not any stone, but a particular piece, remembered as from a dream.

She finally found it, a large chunk of Italian alabaster in translucent white. Using her strength properly, as she had been taught by her father, Nicola dragged it out, took it up to her study and hoisted it onto a bench. She put on her goggles and went to work, not thinking at all but allowing her hands free sway, immersing herself in a three-dimensional primitive experience.

All around the alabaster she moved, bending and reaching and touching at first, making it an extension of herself. She felt the hardness of the alabaster, and its coolness, its bulk, shape, texture. Gripping her mallet and chisel, she worked with a sureness, a trancelike concentration and an authority that always amazed her in retrospect.

Although it had been years since she had carved stone, she had no hesitation as she hammered her mallet on a point and shattered away large chunks. Nicola worked quickly, like a being possessed who was afraid the vision would vanish too quickly.

The point was replaced by a toothed chisel, with which she shaped the form, and in turn made way for a flat chisel, to shave furrows.

At seven in the morning, Nicola straightened up from polishing her sculpture, a life-sized, perfectly formed, representational torso of a young male. A warming flush crept from her neck to her ears and cheeks. Slowly she made her way around the bench, examining the proudly squared shoulders, the recessed tender backbone, the shoulder blades, the slim hips, the masculine buttocks.

Nicola looked at it from the front for a long time. Then, stepping closer, she let her fingers rest lightly on the pectoral muscles, shivering at the smooth, cool texture.

Shutting her eyes, she stroked the statue slowly, starting with the hollow of the chest, moving down over the taut belly, and then below, to the softly swelling genitals. Ripples of tactile joy, helped by fantasy, made her shudder with desire.

Once she bent her head and kissed the navel, letting her tongue linger in the hollow, willing her breath to make the stony form come alive.

Nicola finally fell asleep, curled up on the bench with both arms around her creation.

SUMMER, 1979

8

'Nicola,' Edward called, stopping short when he saw his wife standing in her dressing gown at the window of their hotel room. 'The *vaporetto* leaves in five minutes.'

Nicola turned to face him. 'I wonder if you'd mind very much if I didn't go? I'm feeling very fragile. Since we arrived in Venice it's been nothing but lunches and dinners and parties until dawn. I'm so exhausted.'

'I know, precious, and I'm sorry, but I really must insist this last time. Your *Sun Monument* is the star of the Biennale. Stan Ferrin wants to interview you for *Art in America* – only briefly,' he added, seeing her face stiffen.

'Please, Edward, I'm about to collapse.'

He gave her his most charming smile. 'You won't, though. You'll be your usual gracious self, and we'll have a delicious lunch at Torcello. Afterwards, we'll come back for a siesta.' His eyes twinkled. 'I promise to let you sleep undisturbed. And by evening we'll be packed and on our way. This is the biggest, most important piece you've done in two years, and Marshall is on tenterhooks. He has several foundations interested in acquiring it, willing to pay a fabulous sum.'

Nicola faced the window once more. Fabulous sum. Was that all her work meant to him?

Mounting her sculpture at the American Pavilion of the Biennale had been one of the most exciting moments of Nicola's career. Ever since her first attendance at the Biennale, in 1964, she had dreamed of exhibiting at the oldest international art festival. For a few months thoughts of Paul had kept her from working. Then came the night she had had the extraordinary compulsion to carve a male torso in alabaster. Some strange spirit had taken possession of her, a lustful twelve-hour virus. Awakening the following afternoon, she had regained her sanity and looked with complete indifference at the torso, as if her madness had penetrated the alabaster and left her mind and body free. She had been cured of Paul, a tremendous relief.

Nicola's vision of the *Sun Monument* had burst forth, bringing renewed inspiration and energy, and she had worked like a fiend, along with two helpers, and finished it in less than two months.

Nicola felt Edward's hands on her shoulders. He bent forward and kissed her cheek. 'A good writeup in the press will be so valuable in stimulating interest in the *Sun Monument.*'

Nicola stared out at the Grand Canal, a heaviness in her chest. She was well aware that socialising at the Biennale meant a lot to Edward. Many important art deals were made informally over meals and drinks. She really had tried to enjoy herself, but so many hours of seeing and talking art had made her feel like a child that has gorged itself on candy. But today was for her, not Edward, even though she didn't want it.

'All right, I'll get dressed,' Nicola said, a little too sharply. In apology, she let her hand rest on Edward's cheek for a moment. 'I'll meet you downstairs.'

'That's my sweetheart.' He blew her a kiss on his way out.

Nicola felt sad. Edward was always so good-humoured, firmly believing that what he was doing was for her benefit. Yet, in all their years together, she had never been able to make him understand the way she felt about her art. At present she was as dewy and sentimental about her monument as a mother her newborn child. It was chilling to have to view her sculpture as if under a huge price tag.

When Nicola opened the window hot, soggy air poured into the room. July was not the best time to be in Venice, especially when the Biennale attracted thousands of additional tourists. Nicola had the illusion that their very weight was causing Venice to sink lower into the surrounding waters.

She dressed in a pale yellow Indian cotton shirt and skirt, and yellow sandals. On her head she wore a wide-brimmed straw hat, and then slipped her large dark glasses over her eyes.

At least the ride in the motorboat was cooling, even if the passengers were awash with Valpolicella. Luigi Bianchi, of the Bianchi Galleries in New York and Milan, was hosting today's luncheon, and he kept his guests' glasses filled from the moment they stepped onto his boat.

'The question, Nicola,' Marshall Faber, her dealer, was saying in her ear, 'is whether we prefer the piece to be on a little plateau on a mountain or the centrepiece of a new industrial plaza.'

Nicola sipped her wine, sighed, and kept her peace. Marshall, not the most sensitive man at the best of times, continued to chatter. Much of what he said became lost in the noise of the whirring engine and the shrieks of the dealers and collectors who, with their wives, made up much of the party. Few artists went in for this constant merriment. Nicola, as Edward's wife, found herself in company she would rather have shunned.

The Locanda Cipriani on the island of Torcello would have been a lovely restaurant, had it not been for Bianchi's two hundred guests swarming over the terrace and talking in a high-pitched babble of languages nonstop.

The assemblage was as colourful as it was noisy; the men affected expensive sports clothes and the women looked like fugitives from St Tropez.

Nicola, not really hungry, only nibbled her grilled fish and salad.

'On balance, I wasn't at all impressed with this year's follies,' Edward was saying at their end of the table. 'They're as ephemeral as a musical comedy that folds after one night. It's all very well to have set a theme 'From Nature to Art, from Art to Nature,' but a live bull impregnating a dummy cow is in execrable taste. Only slightly less reprehensible is a sculptor dressed as a shepherd, actually standing around and tending his flock. That's not art in my book.'

'I don't agree,' a rich young socialite in a purple silk harem suit argued. 'Art isn't only what you can nail into a

59

frame or imprison within four walls.'

Nicola half-succeeded in tuning out the endless familiar arguments.

'What do you think, Miss Di Candia?' asked the alert art critic, Stan Ferrin, sitting opposite her and observing her quietly. His respectful tone was contradicted by a malicious gleam in his eyes. Nicola suspected that when it came to writing up the Biennale he'd be scathing.

'It's not my kind of thing,' she said cautiously, 'though I can sympathise with some of these artists in spite of their extremism. They're tired of having their work bought and sold like real estate, and at the mercy of whim and fashion. In their despair at commercialism they deal in dirt, wrap up coastlines, create things that dealers and collectors can't get hold of.'

The critic smiled cynically. 'Is it only despair at commercialism, Miss Di Candia, or could it be an attempt to be even more commercial by shocking, in the manner of the Dadaists?'

Nicola smiled back. 'There are always people out to shock – in every profession. The critic, surely, is trained to separate art from kitsch.'

'Certainly, but we can use a little help from the artists. You, Miss Di Candia, give us something to go on. I think your piece is one of the best things here, a tour de force which still manages to be serious and original.' He spooned melon into his mouth, chewing thoughtfully and writing his column aloud.

'Soaring thirty feet into the sky, Di Candia's *Sun Monument* was conceived and angled so that the glass on aluminium reflects and bounces the sun's rays. The merest breeze can tip the astonishing construction into slow revolution under the sun. In spite of its power, Di Candia's monument exudes her characteristic feminine delicacy . . .'

Although Nicola mistrusted the critic, she couldn't help smiling with pleasure at his words. 'It may work with the sun on it,' she granted shyly, 'but on a rainy day, will it even approach the majesty of Stonehenge? That is what I was striving for –'

'We must re-examine it in the rain, then,' he said,

reaching across the table and lifting Nicola's sunglasses so that he could see her eyes.

Edward, sitting beside her, caught the motion and turned sharply, but he was smiling, and his voice remained steady. 'Don't be too long, Ferrin. My wife is rather tired.'

The critic, sensing Edward's displeasure, composed his features and asked only a few more succinct questions. He didn't care to incur the ire of one of the richest collectors in America.

During the trip back to the hotel, Nicola dozed in the *vaporetto*, her head on her husband's shoulder. She dreamed that the sky darkened and a terrible storm broke. Each crack of thunder and streak of lightning wrenched a large hunk from her *Sun Monument*. Then the rain pelted down and melted the remains of her sculpture until it was nothing but a pool of molten metal and liquid glass.

She awoke with a jolt, feeling depressed.

Back in her room, Nicola went to bed but she was too restless to sleep. Edward dozed as peacefully as a child, and she envied his ability to relax, his evenness of temperament and generally optimistic disposition. She had too many dark shadows, too many mood swings.

Impatiently Nicola got out of bed and went to the window. Although clouds had obscured the sun there was a pinkish glow, as the ancient pastel buildings were reflected in the gleaming water.

Nicola took several deep breaths, welcoming a few moments alone in the quiet of the afternoon. Venice was beautiful, achingly beautiful, with centuries of history etched into its crumbling facade, but she had seen hardly any of the city during the days of frantic party-going. As she stared at the houses, the bridges spanning the canal, a lone pigeon waddling after crumbs, she came to a decision and her depression lifted.

When Edward strirred and awoke, Nicola turned to him with a lilt in her voice that hadn't been there in a long time.

'I know you have to be back in New York by tomorrow, but I'd like to stay on for a few days.'

9

Nighttime Venice was exhilarating, with its lights and music and continuous boat traffic on the canals.

Nicola stood in a *vaporetto* with her suitcases, on her way to the Cipriani Hotel five minutes from San Marco – and hoped it would be far enough from the madding crowd.

The hotel was on the Isola della Giudecca, which sounded lovely and calm and even a little lonely. When Michelangelo was in exile from Florence, he had stayed here. But that was before the Biennale. Nicola saw, to her dismay, that the island hotel was not much less hectic than the Gritti Palace where she had stayed with Edward. The difference was that here she was simply Mrs N. Harrington, and she could spend her time as she pleased.

Feeling free and energetic for the first time since she had arrived in Venice, Nicola unpacked, showered, and changed into white trousers and a shirt. She decided to go back to Venice for the evening after all.

With no appointments to keep, she strolled contentedly under the Clock Tower of San Marco Piazza and into the Merceria, filled with shoppers. When the crowds became too much, she headed off to the Church of Santa Maria Formosa, built the year Columbus discovered America. Nearby was a sixteenth-century palace with an art gallery housing paintings and frescos by Donato, Bellini, Tiepolo, and Longhi. Having spent several days looking at nothing but modern art, Nicola was excited by the masterpieces of the Renaissance. She saw the paintings through her artist's eyes, relieved not to have to hear Edward speculating on what each work might be worth in the market.

Crossing Ponte di Cristo, she thought she recognised a man's profile. Could that possibly be Gareth Howe? It had been almost twenty years since she'd last seen him, but as she drew closer she saw it really was him. He was heavier than she remembered, and a little grey at the temples, but still attractive. He was accompanied by two women and a man.

Nicola's face grew warm. She was surprised that after all this time the sight of him could still cause her to react. She couldn't tell which woman was with Gareth, but neither was particularly striking. This pleased her, and she felt ashamed.

Gareth didn't see her as she passed him by on the street. There was no point in provoking what might be an awkward meeting.

With a thumping heart, Nicola continued walking, and thinking about Gareth. She stopped, confused, and saw that she had lost her way. Apparently she was backtracking. She turned sharply and walked directly into his path. Gareth was slightly ahead of the others, who were deep in conversation.

When he saw Nicola, he slowed, and for several moments their eyes touched.

'Gareth,' Nicola said tentatively. She stopped abruptly as he withdrew his gaze as if she were a total stranger and continued past her. The others in his party were not even aware of the encounter.

Nicola turned her head and watched him go. So he still bore her a grudge. She shook her head incredulously, trying to substitute anger for hurt, but failing. He had once been more important to her than almost anything.

'Here, let me. That's much too heavy for you.' The handsome boy with the soft southern accent wrested two sheets of iron from Nicola's hands.

Flushing, she stepped back and let him carry them for her although she could easily have done so herself.

She was awed that he should have offered. Gareth Howe, a year ahead of her at the California Institute of Art, was considered as talented a lover as a sculptor, and Nicola had often noticed the prettiest girls on his arm. She had longed to be there herself, but he had not noticed her before now.

Fixing dark, intense eyes upon her, Gareth said, 'A few people are coming around to my place later to listen to jazz. You're invited. What's your name, by the way?'

'Nicola Di Candia.'

63

'Whew.' He smiled charmingly. 'It's a mouthful for a down-home Georgia boy like me. I'll call you Candy. I bet you're just as sweet.'

In a fever of excitement Nicola went to his party, which was packed with people sprawled on the floor in jeans, shirts, and sneakers, drinking cheap wine by the gallon and grooving to Brubeck and Miles Davis.

Nicola, unused to drinking, downed glass after glass of wine, determined to be one of the gang. Gareth paid little attention to her but spent his time nuzzling one attractive girl after another, making Nicola sorry she had ever come here.

Other boys talked to her, though, and Nicola flirted, looking from the corner of her eye to see if Gareth noticed.

After somebody turned off the lights and lit a couple of candles, the kids paired off, kissing, groping, caressing.

A nice red-headed boy tried to get Nicola to do the same with him but she wriggled free and stood up. 'Got to go home,' she mumbled drunkenly.

'I'll take you,' the boy offered.

'Get lost,' Gareth said behind him. 'I'm taking her home.'

'Oh. But how can you? It's your party –'

'That's right, baby, it's my party. Host has special privileges.' Smiling in a way that made her heart beat faster, Gareth took her arm and led her from the room.

At the door of her dorm he kissed her. It was thrilling, but Nicola felt whoozy and drew back, scared she was going to fall on the floor.

'I hardly know you,' she whispered.

'We'll have to do something about that.'

They did. Within two weeks she was mad about him and they became lovers.

Nicola had never imagined such sweetness, such passion, such joy. She adored Gareth. In her eyes he could do no wrong. He was in turn passionate, tender, funny, grumpy, and spoiled. Nicola, having learned from her mother to defer to a man, was happy to do everything Gareth wanted as he wanted. She loved his good manners, his smile, his drawl, his popularity, although she lived in constant fear that one of the more sophisticated girls would take him away.

When she spoke of it to Gareth, he laughed and gave her a

64

mock punch. 'Hey, Candy, nickel candy, you've got me hooked and that's a fact.'

For her nineteenth birthday he put his high school graduation ring on a gold chain and slipped it around her neck, making her supremely happy.

Only one thing nagged at her: she wasn't as enthusiastic about his sculpture as she longed to be. Although at first glance it was impressive, a longer look showed faint pretentiousness and lack of subtlety.

Nicola was always as tactful as she could be, but no amount of love could cause her to compromise her artistic integrity.

'I like the way you fused the wood and metal here, but don't you think this section takes away from the simplicity of the main sweeping line?'

'No, I don't, sweetie pie. You're too stingy. You have to let yourself go, which is what I do. Your work is kind of coy, as if you were afraid to give it everything you've got.'

That Gareth didn't take her seriously as a sculptor depressed her, but she was learning modesty in San Francisco, where there were so many very talented students. Obviously she was not yet good enough and would have to become better.

During Nicola's third year, and his last, they shared a place together at Newport Beach. Nicola had never known such happiness. In equal amounts she was consumed with love for Gareth and inspiration for her work. She projected the pure bliss they would have when they got married, and worked side by side by day, making love by night.

In May, students began gathering work to submit to a sculpture annual held in a gallery in Los Angeles. Nicola sighed every time she looked at Gareth's mobile. It reminded her of Calder, only it was complicated in a way the master would never have allowed. Ostentatious was the word that came to her mind, no matter how she fought her feelings. She was sure she was wrong, she must be. His teacher seemed to think it was fine to submit it.

Nicola had done something at school, but she was dissatisfied with it. She wondered if she oughtn't to submit instead a small work, a maquette of a playground she had devised and worked on at home. She called it *Aquazoo*, and it was made of steel skeletons of fish and animals sprayed with acrylics in bright colours. Each animal was constructed so that kids would be able to climb, swing, slide, and do acrobatics.

Gareth looked at it with an expressionless face. Nervously, she explained it to him, finding, as she was always to do, that words were useless. The viewer either understood the piece or the sculptor had failed.

'Yeah, I see what you mean, honey. It's very decorative, very cute.'

Cute. Nicola was shattered. She was unwilling to believe that her excitement and sense of achievement could be so ill-founded. But she trusted Gareth so completely. Could he possibly be wrong? He had a good eye for talent in others, even if he sometimes went overboard himself.

She probably would have left *Aquazoo* where it was if her teacher, Jack Maxwell, hadn't happened to stop by to pick up a welding torch she had borrowed.

When Nicola came back with the torch she found her teacher standing in front of *Aquazoo*. A taciturn and very critical man, he never minced words. 'Pack this up and send it to L.A. I like it.'

Adrenalin shot into Nicola.

When Gareth came home he found her manic with joy. 'Jack said to submit it. Jack said it was good. Jack said –'

The phone rang. She ran to pick it up, and heard her mother weeping through the static of a bad connection.

'Papa is sick. We don't know how bad.'

'Mama, I'm coming home.'

The next two weeks were terrible for Nicola. She had thrown some things into a valise, asked Gareth to ship out her sculpture along with his, and rushed to the airport. During the flight she huddled in her seat and cried for her father, wondering why her joy at having had her work praised by her teacher should now be so cruelly punished.

When she saw her father lying in bed in the hospital and looking so ill, the pain was unbearable.

His heart attack, fortunately, turned out to be less severe than the doctors originally had thought.

'Nika, don't go back, please,' Theresa begged her. 'It's so

far away. If he's taken bad again, I'm all alone. You're my only family.'

'I'll stay, Mama,' Nicola said, her world in pieces.

But Dominic wouldn't hear of it. 'No, Nika, you must get your degree. I was stupid, I overdid, and now I know better. I'll hire a helper, I'll be okay.' From his hospital bed Dominic laid down the law to his wife.

Nicola repacked her suitcase, and on an impulse flew directly to Los Angeles. She felt better about her father's health and thought it would be wonderful to surprise Gareth, and also to go to the annual after all.

The gallery was a small place that could be taken in at a glance. As Nicola looked around, her stomach caved in with horror. Her *Aquazoo* was not there. It had been rejected.

Numbed, Nicola stared with glazed eyes at the exhibit, noting Gareth's work, which was not in a prominent position but off in a corner where it did not appear to best advantage.

She walked to the gallery office, steeling herself to hear the reasons for her work's rejection.

The owners, two effeminate brothers, looked up coldly as she entered. Maybe, she thought, clutching at straws, they just didn't like women, or their work.

'I would like to know why my sculpture was rejected,' Nicola began woodenly.

'Your name, Miss,' one brother interrupted. He looked through his papers. 'Nothing received here in that name.'

'But it must have been.' She described the maquette in a rush of words. 'Maybe it was sent in the name of Gareth Howe –'

The brothers shook their heads and dismissed her.

Nicola rushed from the office in a panic. She would have to go to Railway Express and see what could have happened.

As she tore out of the gallery she bumped into Gareth.

'Candy! How did you get here?'

'My father's better, and I thought I'd catch the last two days of the show. Oh, Gareth, I've missed you, but something terrible has happened. Railway Express lost *Aquazoo* –'

He held her off a little and looked uncomfortable.

'What is it, Gareth?'

Holding her arm, he led her out into the street, while she

cast frightened looks at his sober profile. He had found another love, that had to be it.

That her sculpture and Gareth might both be lost to her on the same day caused her heart to pound like a kettledrum.

'I didn't send *Aquazoo*, Candy.'

'I don't understand ...'

He stopped and faced her, taking her hands in his. 'I didn't send it. Because I thought it would hurt you too much, especially with your daddy's illness and all, to have it rejected by the gallery. They rejected six out of ten things submitted –'

Nicola looked at him uncomprehendingly for a long moment. 'I don't believe it. Are you telling me you didn't send it because you thought it wasn't good enough?' Nicola's voice was deadly calm.

'That's about it. Jack doesn't know his ass from his elbow. Not that the playground is bad. It's actually quite cute, for a kid's room.'

Nicola saw Gareth as for the first time without her love blinkers. He belittled her work because he was simply competitive and jealous. Not expecting her to turn up in L.A., he had not sent her work. Later he would have claimed it was rejected, and she would never have known the difference.

Her insight flooded through her, dissolving a year's love like acid eating into lace.

White-faced, she took his gold chain and ring off her neck with trembling fingers and held it out to him.

Gareth, pale as well, gulped and tightened his jaw. 'Don't be silly, Candy. I did it for us. You'd be making such a mistake to go on with the sculpture, instead of marrying me, and having our kids, maybe teach in kindergarten. You know I love you, darlin'.'

Nicola flung the ring at him and ran, tears of hurt and anger and self-hatred streaming down her face.

She took the next bus to San Francisco, packed up her stuff, and moved in with a girlfriend.

Gareth never tried to phone her; nor would she have spoken to him if he had. There was nothing more to be said.

A hard determination took hold of Nicola. She consciously banished all memory of their love, of their happiness together as if it had never been.

At the suggestion of Jack Maxwell, she sent slides of

Aquazoo to several elementary schools.

The Morton School in Kansas City commissioned her playground, which later won an award for good design.

She never again heard of Gareth Howe, or of his sculpture.

Nicola, walking blindly down a narrow alley in Venice, suddenly ached with the poignant memory of her first love. The passionate hours with Gareth, which she had repressed for twenty years, came back to her in a rush of pain, and a new awareness of emptiness. She had never duplicated that love, had never trusted anyone enough again – not even Edward – to give herself so completely.

But Gareth had betrayed them both when he made her choose between him and her art. For her, that had been no kind of choice at all.

10

Although it was a sultry night, Nicola felt chilled. She walked aimlessly, down street after street, passing over innumerable bridges. Accustomed to Edward's insistence upon going everywhere by *vaporetto* or water taxi, Nicola had not realised that one could walk all over Venice the way the Venetians did, and visitors who wanted to have a sense of the city.

At last she found herself back at the Piazza. The walk, instead of exhausting her, had made her more restless. She couldn't quite bring herself to return to her empty room.

A few people were standing in the Piazza holding musical instruments. Her heart jumped and her breath failed momentarily, when Nicola saw that Paul Kadin-Lurie was among them. She stopped in consternation, not wishing to walk directly in front of him but unable to turn around because of the crush of people behind her.

During the moment of her hesitation, Paul saw her.

'*Come sta*, Nicola?' he asked softly.

'*Bene*,' she replied, suddenly wildly glad to see him.

Paul's glance flickered past her, looking for Edward, and returned to rest with intense pleasure on her face when he realised she was alone.

'Can I buy you a drink?' She tried to keep her voice light but she was trembling inside with shades of feeling that mingled Paul's image with Gareth's.

'I'd love a drink. And something to chew on. I never eat before a performance,' Paul said, the magic of his smile bathing her in total, unexpected joy.

He took her elbow and steered her across the Piazza to Harry's Bar.

'Upstairs,' he directed, and Nicola was elated. The one place she had always wanted to go, Edward had somehow never taken her. Paul negotiated a table near the window, from which they could see the water, but Nicola looked only at him.

He ordered two Bellinis and an antipasto.

'Has a Bellini something to do with Giovanni Bellini, painter of the sad-eyed madonna?'

'Probably, but there's nothing sad or madonnalike about this concoction, as you'll discover.'

Paul lifted his glass and touched hers lightly, his glowing eyes filling her with excitement.

She sipped. 'Heavenly. What is it?'

'The nectar of our time, champagne, mixed with fresh peach juice.'

The champagne bounced from the emptiness of her stomach right to the top of her head, and she found no willpower to refuse the second drink.

Nicola kept studying Paul's face, tanned and smiling and more dear to her than she had dared to admit all these months. He was wearing a pale blue cotton shirt, opened halfway down his chest, where tight bunches of dark hair curled. Nicola swallowed painfully.

'Are you playing with an orchestra?' Nicola wanted him to have a valid reason for being in Venice – one that had nothing to do with her.

'Yes. A two-week engagement. I sat in at the last minute for a colleague who couldn't make it. It was my big chance to see Venice, the Biennale – and possibly you.'

Nicola's stomach fluttered. 'When I spoke to Anne last,' she ventured, trying to keep her voice steady, 'she said you were working on your tone poem. She seemed not to know that you and I – that you had been in London.'

Paul smiled. 'I don't see the need to tell her everything I do. I was working on my tone poem, and it's in very good shape. I'll be ready for my concert in the fall. That's what concerns her. I don't encourage her to snoop into my personal life. Ah, *filetto Carpaccio*, a specialty of the house. Entrecote, rare and covered with homemade mayonnaise and a dash of Worcestershire, I'm told. Quite delicious.'

It was, Nicola granted. 'Very subtle, like the light in Carpaccio's painting. I like the way Cipriani, who seems to own all the best restaurants in Venice, names things after painters.'

'He'll have to come up with a unique dessert to be called Ambrosia Di Candia, in honour of your sculpture. Your *Sun Monument* is absolutely dazzling. I've looked at it every day that I've been here. The lines are so silky and fluid, and the whole piece glitters. It's almost as if it dropped from the sun itself like a jewel.'

'I'm glad you like it,' Nicola whispered. If her monument was all that to Paul, then she had succeeded.

Paul cast her the intense look she remembered from her dreams. 'Where is Edward?'

At the hotel. He's at the hotel, she knew she should answer, but she couldn't, even though a flicker of guilt dimmed her happiness at being with Paul.

'Have you quarrelled?' Concern for her sounded in his voice.

Nicola shook her head, and her eyes suddenly welled. How much Paul reminded her of the long-ago Gareth, in his dark intensity, his sweetness of youth. Only with the addition of his exquisite sensibility, and without Gareth's faults.

'Nicola, don't be hurt. I want anything but that.' Paul covered her cool hand with his warm, confident one.

She lowered her eyes. 'It's nothing to do with Edward. Just an unfortunate revival of an old memory this evening.

Edward had to be back in New York, and I stayed.'

Paul placed a gentle, silencing finger on her lips and signalled for the bill.

'Please let me pay, Paul, at least for the drinks.'

He shot her a look that told her she was going to pay, all right. A tremor of excitement rippled through her, mingled with fear. Had she really believed she was cured of Paul? God, she hadn't even begun to want him as she wanted him at this moment.

Outside, he took her hand, and they began to walk.

They did not speak. Nicola could think of nothing she dared say. He was terribly, wonderfully sensitive to how she was feeling. He would decide for both of them, and tonight, just this once, she would follow him into the abyss.

A sleek black gondola glided up beside them, and the Venetian flashed Paul a brilliant, questioning smile.

'*Sì*,' Paul said, his voice rich with a sudden, secret excitement.

He handed Nicola into the gondola and jumped in after her. The standing gondolier poled the boat silently through the water.

Paul, instead of sitting next to Nicola, turned his chair and faced her. He reached into his case and took out the flute.

'I wrote this for you when I returned from London.'

He played a wonderful tune that captivated her and warmed her with its haunting passion. That he had written it for her moved her deeply.

Paul fixed hungry eyes on Nicola. 'It's part of my tone poem, based on Shakespeare's sonnets. This one begins, "Let me not to the marriage of true minds admit impediments. Love is not love which alters when it alteration finds ..." '

Paul's husky voice, as he looked at her, faded with emotion. 'If this be error and upon me proved, I never writ, nor no man ever loved.'

Nicola was in his arms, pressed close to his pounding heart, mingling hands and tongues and lips and breath, lost to herself and found to him.

72

11

When Nicola woke in her hotel room she was terribly thirsty.
Paul, stirring beside her, leaped out of bed without being
asked and opened a bottle of *aqua minerale*. He brought her a
glass.

'*Buon giorno,*' she said sleepily.

Paul drew her to her feet and moved back with her to a
rocking chair. He sat down in it and pulled her into his lap.

Gently he cradled her in his arms, stroking her hair.
'You're beautiful, Nicola, and I love you very much,' he
whispered. He kissed her forehead, her cheeks, and her lips.

Made weak by his tenderness, she snuggled closer, twining
her fingers into the curling hair on his chest.

He continued to stroke her hair with one hand, while his
other lightly grazed her shoulder, her arm, her waist, all the
while gently rocking in the chair.

Nicola's hands crept from his chest around to his back,
thrilling to the warm skin, the vibrant flesh, the taut muscle.
This was no alabaster. Compared to the life in the human
body, art was a shambles.

Paul leaned his head down to find her lips, then her tongue,
deep inside her mouth.

Nicola's skin stippled with pinpricks of fire. A moment
later she felt his fingers caressing her erect nipples, then her
breasts, as he grew stiff beneath her moistness.

He carried her back to the bed.

Very lightly, with a musician's sensitive fingertips, he
scouted the contours of her body, and with his lips gently,
blissfully, claimed every inch as his exclusive territory.

Nicola undulated under his touch, and his murmured
words of love. The moment she felt his tongue between her
legs she had a shimmering orgasm.

73

He loomed above her, and thrust deeply inside, but gently, slowly, tantalisingly. Her strong fingers dug into his back and shoulders, pressing him closer, increasing her rhythm. She moaned. As her eyes fluttered open and focused on his face, exquisitely contorted with passion, she came, murmuring his name over and over. Still he held back, advancing, retreating, his tongue teasing her lips, his teeth nipping her neck.

Nicola was wild, insatiable. She grasped his buttocks and pushed him nearer. Then she caught her breath, stiffened, and arched her back.

Finally he let go, giving all of himself to her, and getting all of her in return.

'Now it's a *buon giorno*,' Paul said, hours later. He was smiling, leaning on one elbow and studying her.

'It's a wonderful *giorno*.' Nicola stretched like a cat. She reached out her finger and traced a line in the damp hair of his chest.

'I need a shower,' he said.

'Me too. Together?'

'Of course.'

'In a moment.'

Nicola slowly pushed him onto his back, her artist's eye devouring his form. She touched him in wonderment. There was nothing really so extraordinary about his body, except that it was his, and he had pleased her as no man had done in years.

Lightly she sculpted his curves and crevices, lingering over every freckle, tiny scar, and the funny bumps from mosquito bites. Emotion spilling over into her eyes, Nicola bent her head and kissed his shoulder, his chest, his belly, loving the smell and the salty taste of him.

As Paul grew erect, he tightened his hands in her hair.

She looked up at him, thrilled, and beginning to throb. 'Can you, again, so soon, after all that?'

In answer, he pulled her to him and kissed her violently. 'Nicola, Nicola, I've waited so long for you!' His voice, hoarse, urgent, turned her into pulsating, liquid desire.

They fell on each other like half-starved love vultures,

clutching, biting, and moaning in a glorious frenzy of mutual fulfillment.

Nicola and Paul walked through Venice, hazy with heat and buzzing with visitors. They drank *Punt e Mes* and ate lunches of *fegato alla veneziana* and *risotto* in out-of-the-way trattorias, where the waiters were called Alessandro or Fabrizzio.

They leaned over bridges and saw their images distorted by the shimmering water. They got caught in a thunderstorm in the Piazza and ran for shelter to the welcoming portals of the Byzantine Basilica, from which they watched the torrents cleanse the square and make it as slick and shiny as glass. They visited churches and galleries, arguing the merits of Titian, Tintoretto, Veronese. They mingled with the crowds at a church festival on Giudecca commemorating the ending of a medieval plague. It was a Sunday of feasting and carnival, ending with a regatta staged by boatmen in costume, and making Nicola and Paul feel as if they had stepped into a Canaletto painting. They swam at the Lido and rubbed suntan oil into each other's back. They bought ice cream cones and laughed when they couldn't eat quickly enough to prevent the ice cream from melting onto their fingers.

Every evening Nicola went to the concert and watched Paul play the music of such native Venetians as Vivaldi, Albinoni, and Marcello. She swelled with pride at his virtuosity, remembering with quickened breath the way those wonderful hands and lips touched her and elicited a more elemental sound.

After the concert they went to eat, usually at Harry's Bar upstairs, where they rubbed knees under the table like a couple of kids, drank Bellinis, and were exquisitely happy.

Nicola was surprised by Paul a dozen times a day – especially when it came to his uncanny perception of her feelings. He knew when she wanted to be awakened with kisses, and when she needed to be left to sleep; when she welcomed teasing, and when her fragility required tenderness. All his nerve endings were alert to every nuance of her being, as if he had been created to grant her wishes and soothe her frustrations.

Images of Edward and Julie and Anne lay at the bottom of Nicola's consciousness like shadows anchored to sand which was eroding each day. But for now she revelled in the days with Paul and lived in greedy anticipation of the nights.

Nicola and Paul shared a compelling need for tactile communication, their work having honed their sense of touch far beyond the norm. They couldn't bear not to touch every moment they were together.

And while they touched hands, they touched minds, talking for hours about music and art, agreeing about wanting to create for the ordinary person, about modern art belonging outdoors instead of in museums so that it could harmonize with its surroundings and be seen and appreciated as part of everyday life.

Paul understood and shared completely Nicola's feeling about the intrinsic worth of art, and the word 'price' was never even mentioned.

When it came to making love, Nicola had more to learn from Paul than to teach him. Edward, after Gareth, had been her only lover, and for more years than she cared to admit, sex with her husband had been more frustrating than joyful.

With Paul, each episode restructured her universe. He was sensual in a way that Edward, with certain inhibitions, wouldn't even have imagined.

Paul was alive with intensity and the capacity for enjoying everything, and he could throw himself into lovemaking as Edward never could. When he looked at a painting, played the flute, listened to music, ate a meal, drank a beer or bent to stroke a kitten in the street, every part of his being was engaged, aware, open to the experience.

Nicola recovered her capacity to delight in a man, and in five days felt closer to Paul than she had to Edward in eighteen years.

12

Edward Harrington was feeling wonderful as he mingled with his friends and competitors, dealers, collectors, and critics at the stunning opening at Luigi Bianchi's downtown gallery. The excitement he sensed told him that Marc Rubetsky, an unknown, was going to be a whopping success and make him a great deal of money.

Rummaging in the grubby old warehouses of Tribeca, Edward had come upon the loft of Rubetsky, a Polish-born Jew who had managed to survive the holocaust. A glazier, Rubetsky had hoarded slivers of glass and mirrors for years. Suddenly he had burst forth as a painter. His work – collages of bits of glass, blood-red paint, barbed wire, and haunted faces – was powerful and disturbing.

Edward had taken Rubetsky's work to Bianchi, one of the most prestigious dealers in the business. Bianchi respected Edward's unerring intuition. After all, Edward had been among the first to collect Rothko, Motherwell, and Segal – not to mention Nicola Di Candia, whom he had discovered.

Always regretting that Marshall Faber had been the lucky dealer to get Di Candia, Bianchi jumped at the chance of acquiring Rubetsky.

Only Marshall Faber, his thin, pale face with its perpetual lugubrious expression, was unhappy. 'But why didn't you bring Rubetsky to me?'

Edward smiled his disarming smile, assuring Marshall that he had. 'Your phone was busy for days, and Bianchi was pressuring me.'

What Edward didn't say was that Bianchi was in a better position than Faber to make a blue-chip artist out of Rubetsky. When that happened, Edward would bring forward ten of the artist's paintings he had bought for only a hundred dollars each and make a killing.

At the opening Edward met a luscious lady named Kelly Bogan. She was extremely provocative, with long curly black hair and big, teasing dark eyes. Edward didn't know if she could paint a damn but she certainly had a good pair of tits.

'I hope I'll be as good as Nicola Di Candia someday,' Kelly said, moving her tongue suggestively over her richly red, moist lips.

Edward was quick to pick up Kelly's signal and suggested going 'somewhere quiet' – which turned out to be her loft on West twenty-sixth Street. Her work wasn't bad and he was able to pay her compliments without telling lies.

'Wow. This is terrific, Mr Harrington. I'm really flattered. You know, Nicola Di Candia has always been my ideal.'

Edward smiled and began to talk about his wife. Girls like Kelly were as eager to steal the husband of a famous woman as they were to advance their careers.

Within fifteen minutes Edward was peeling off Kelly's clothes. Her body was magnificent. The only trouble was that she immediately jumped all over him, moaning and rolling her eyes, raking his shoulder with her fingernails.

Edward suddenly had an intense longing for Nicola. He recalled their first meeting and how intrigued he'd been by her elusiveness, which had made the eventual conquest sweeter.

Lying in bed with Kelly, Edward, as limp as wet cardboard, devised a game. 'You must be a virgin. I'm a stranger, and have surprised you alone in the house.'

Nicola. Edward hadn't so much as kissed her cheek until he had told her about the show Marshall Faber was willing to give her. Nicola had been so happy, so naïvely happy. And he had been as patient as Jacob waiting for Rachel. He had waited until all of Nicola's pieces were snapped up, after the reviews came out, and Nicola Di Candia had become an exciting new name.

'I love you, Nicola, you must know that. To me you are the most exquisite girl in the world and the most talented.'

Edward had been careful to talk more about her talent than her flawless body that so enchanted him, her clever, passionate eyes that, it seemed, she reserved for her work and never cast upon any man. Those lips, those firm, perfectly rounded breasts, had made him wild with desire to possess her.

But he had proceeded slowly, from a chaste kiss to a gentle slipping of his tongue between her lips. A light caress of her beautiful breasts with his fingertips. And that was as far as he'd got until the announcement of their engagement.

Reliving their first episode of lovemaking had aroused Edward. Kelly, panting, had already opened her legs.

'No, baby, not yet. You're a virgin, remember, you need to be persuaded.'

As he sat, having breakfast in his dining room the next morning, Edward felt pretty good until his daughter walked in with the sullen look on her face she had had lately. He determined to ignore it, to cheer her up.

'Good morning princess. Lovely day today. And how's my girl feeling?'

'Terrific.' Julie's voice was flat. She crouched over the table buttering a piece of toast she had no appetite to eat, and poured out a glass of milk.

Edward flicked his eye speculatively over his daughter's sulky face. 'I got in pretty late last night, after three. We went out for a drink after the opening and wound up in someone's loft.'

Julie turned off from the rest of his words. Taking her toast and milk, she went to the small maid's room that now served as her studio. Her stomach was churning with rage. She had awakened at six-thirty and her father was not at home. What hypocrites her parents were.

Trembling, Julie drank her milk, leaving the toast untouched.

She mixed some paint and stared at the easel, on which she had started a watercolour of roses. Very lightly she began to dab at the paper, adding more water, then more white to the pink of the petals.

Her father knocked at the door and opened it. 'What's wrong, princess?'

Nicola Di Candia is the princess. I'm just the pea under the mattress, Julie thought. Without glancing at her father,

79

she continued to dab paint onto her picture.

A few months ago during one of her mother's trips abroad, she had caught a glimpse of her father with a young girl in a restaurant on First Avenue. It had made Julie sick even to look at her father with his friend, holding her hand, smiling in his simpering way at her.

She wished she could say something to him about it, but every time she tried to talk of anything real to him, or even worse, to her mother, the words just wouldn't come. She would find herself almost choking on her own saliva. Honour thy father and mother. How she detested them both!

'I asked you what the matter was. Why don't you answer?'

'Nothing's the matter,' she mumbled. 'I have nothing to say.'

Edward sighed and glanced at Julie's picture.

I know you hate it. I hate it. It's too stupid, too nothing. My work's not like her work. Her work's got balls.

'Have you decided to go to art school?'

'Yes,' she said defiantly.

'I see. Say, did you ever think of going in for textiles? Now there's a lucrative field.'

He thinks I'm only good enough for flowered wallpaper and chintz bedspreads.

Julie took a deep breath. 'I've already registered for some classes at the Art Students League. I start next week.'

Edward had a moment of depression. Julie was trying to follow in her mother's footsteps without a trace of her mother's talent.

'Oh. Okay. Fine,' he said. 'It's a good place. You'll make some interesting friends there.'

Friends! The last place I'd look for friends is in art school. Stupid artsy fartsy little shits. Just like you, just like Madame Di Candia, just like the whole gross art world. But if I could do something really good with watercolours, really simple, more real than all that pretentious crap . . .

Edward, observing his daughter's reverie, withdrew from the room, wondering if she knew he hadn't come home until seven-thirty that morning. Not that she was likely to say anything to her mother. They weren't close enough for that. Still, he would have to be more careful in future.

Edward enjoyed having his cake and eating it. It was only a fair compensation for having a part-time wife.

Julie had always felt like a wildflower growing between two oaks. Her father, rich, powerful, from a good old family, rolling in money. Everything he touched turned to gold. King Midas. And her mother, all warm smiles and oozing charm. Nicola Di Candia had shaken the spaghetti from her fingertips, and how.

Everybody loved Nicola Di Candia and Edward Harrington. Isn't he distinguished, isn't she remarkable, isn't he suave, isn't she talented, isn't he a genius at picking winners, isn't she brilliantly innovative ...

Even Paul Kadin-Lurie had treated her mother like a fucking goddess. Julie thought Paul was dynamite. But whenever she spoke to him he listened with only half his attention. Little Julie, as uninspiring as someone's kid sister.

However, when Nicola the Great uttered a few syllables, he was all burning eyes and total attention. Her mother had shown her up to be a nothing. Thinking about it caused an angry flush to appear on her cheeks. Come, Julie, don't hang back. Watch and learn, you idiot. Learn how to speak to a boy. Even if he's young enough to be my son, I can charm the pants off him.

Nicola Di Candia wasn't like Janet Markham, who acted her age, who had always been there for her daughters, helping them, encouraging them, licking their wounds. When Emily sometimes complained that her mother was into her life too much, Julie found it hard to commiserate. Janet was warm and very understanding, very human. Nicola the Great was superwoman. Nobody could live up to such perfection.

Her fingers trembling with the angers that lived just below the surface of her skin, Julie reached into a canvas bag beneath her easel and brought out a pint of vodka. She was finding it increasingly difficult to get through a day without a drink.

Unscrewing the cap, she took a slug. How she burned to pay both her parents back for putting art first, sex second, and Julie last. She *would* pay them back, somehow.

When she looked at the canvas, she saw that she had leaned too hard on her brush. The delicate rose she had been painting was now a mass of crushed petals.

'Mr Harrington,' the voice said on the phone. 'This is O'Brien again, of the Academy of Fine Arts. I phoned a while back asking Miss Di Candia to submit a work for the exhibit we're mounting.'

Hell, he'd forgotten ever to mention it to Nicola. She had been so busy upon her return from London preparing for the Biennale. 'When do you need it? That soon? Okay, I'll see to it.'

Edward dropped into Nicola's studio and explored her storeroom. God, the stuff she had lying around. Why did she do that, when collectors were always in the market for her work? Surely once she finished something she should want it to be exhibited.

Edward selected a sculpture he found very appealing – an abstract figure of a woman welded in iron who seemed about to fly off into the air. It was a charming thing, light, feminine, the sort of piece that would go over well in a small indoor space.

Having made his choice, Edward looked around his wife's studio, feeling the air of her personality. He missed Nicola terribly. Here in her studio was where he most desired her, feeling tremendous power when he could snatch some of her art-directed passion for himself.

Nicola was very dear to him, very touching in her true innocence of the compelling lusts of the flesh. He was convinced that only when he was with her did she exhibit the slightest sexual hunger. The one thing Edward had never feared in all the years of his marriage to Nicola was that she could ever want any other man.

13

Nicola and Paul were having a late lunch at Torcello, seated at a quiet table under a grape arbor.

'Nicola, my ticket home is dated tomorrow.'

Her stomach lurched. 'So soon? You said Wednesday.'

'Tomorrow is Wednesday. What date is yours?'

'I left the date open.'

'Will you come with me? Will we be together in New York?'

The colour drained from her face. 'I don't know,' she whispered. Her Venetian Interlude couldn't extend to later, could it?

Nicola stared at Paul, unwilling to believe that tomorrow at this time they would not be together.

'Don't you have to go back to New Haven, to consult with your teacher?'

'I can write music anywhere you are.'

Nicola didn't know what to say. Paul understood. He didn't press her, but his eyes were full of the love and life and passion and sensitivity she would lose if she gave him up.

She couldn't give him up yet. It was still today. Her eyes answered his. They went from the restaurant by the *vaporetto* to their hotel room.

As soon as the door was shut, Nicola reached for Paul, her fingers tearing open his shirt so fiercely that the buttons popped. They didn't even make it to the bed but sank to the carpet like two people doomed to die at dawn who feared they would never slake the hunger and thirst for each other.

Afterwards, in bed, they had an encore, and then a recapitulation. Nicola clung to Paul, not knowing if this was to be her private death in Venice or the beginning of another life. He devoured her, not knowing if he was to have future joy or gut-wrenching misery.

'Together?' he asked, after a while.

'I don't know, Paul. I honestly don't know. I don't see how we could ever make it work.'

He bounded out of bed and went to the bathroom. Moments later she heard the shower turned on full force.

It was the first shower they weren't having together.

Nicola lay in bed feeling miserable. She hadn't once told him that she loved him. She hadn't dared.

When he came out of the bathroom, she went in without looking at him.

She emerged and saw that he was flinging on his clothes, his face pained and remote. Nicola dressed as well and in silence they left the room which they had filled with their love.

It was still early. They took the boat back to San Marco. There they walked side by side, not touching. Nicola knew she had to speak, to try to make him understand, hoping that she might understand herself.

'It's been a wonderful five days. That's why we mustn't let what we've had spoil and rot in another time and another place. Which it would because too many people would be hurt.'

'Let me not to the marriage of true minds admit impediments.'

'But there *are* impediments, Paul. My age and yours, my marriage and your mother, my daughter and your father, and the rest of the world.'

'Love is not love which alters when it alteration finds. Or bends with the remover to remove.'

'Paul, even if I could do this thing, you would grow to resent me, to hate me. I would be a burden. Don't you understand that the older one gets the more one longs for youth – in someone else, at least.'

'Love alters not with brief hours and weeks, but bears it out even to the edge of doom.'

The edge of doom was where she was teetering.

With every soft word Paul uttered, Nicola loved him more.

She stopped and turned to him. His face was still, his features calm, his love unshaken. The breeze blew his hair down onto his forehead, and he tossed it back in a gesture that had become so dear to her. Aching to touch him, she clenched her hands into fists. 'We can't build happiness on the foundations of other people's misery.'

'We can't make others happy if we're miserable ourselves.'

'This has got all out of proportion,' she murmured, almost to herself.

'What were you thinking of, at the beginning? That it would be merely a quiver of the flesh between us? That we would "get it out of our system"?' His voice was gently accusing.

'I wasn't thinking at all. I was just – being.'

'Exactly. Being. You were being Nicola – not Edward's wife, Julie's mother, Anne's friend, Marshall's artist. You were, and will always be, Paul's love – which means just being Nicola.'

The exquisite truth of his words made her feel weak with pain. But there were responsibilities. 'There are responsibilities ...'

'... to adult people who would not want you to deny your feelings.'

Wrong. Edward had always forced her to deny her feelings. Julie didn't have a clue. Anne would be horrified, strangers would snicker.

Nicola turned wearily on the bridge. She stood for a moment gazing into the black water that was as unilluminating as her present state of mind.

'Paul, you're so young. I'm your first love. You'll get over me.'

'No,' he contradicted softly behind her. 'No, I won't. You spoiled me for any other woman a long time ago. And I've been hoping to spoil you for any other man.'

They prowled the streets of Venice like scavengers seeking sustenance.

'Where would we live, Paul? And how?'

'Don't be childish.' He gave her a glance of disgust. 'I'm not intending to sneak you into my room in my mother's house. We'd get a place together, not Beekman Place, of course, but it would be ours. I can support myself, if not you. I don't need to take money from my parents. Grandfather Kadin left me a trust fund, and I can give music lessons.'

Nicola had a shuddering image of the two of them living in a cramped, dark tenement overrun with cockroaches, the type of place she had been reduced to in her youth. It wasn't

Beekman Place she couldn't relinquish but her studio, the space she needed in order to work.

'Edward has dealt with all the practical matters. I don't even know how much money is mine. I haven't handled it in years. Or done the laundry. Or cleaned the house. I can hardly cook.'

'It may serve Edward's interests to keep you a child. It serves mine to keep you a woman.' Paul stopped and turned Nicola to him, taking her face tenderly in his hands. '*Te amo molto*. I'll teach you to cook, you sweet idiot. We'll do it together.'

Nicola, moving away, tried to swallow a tear and found the taste bitter. 'I can't just walk out on Edward after eighteen years. He loves me.'

'Do you love him, really?' You've given me something these last days you wouldn't have had to give if all were well between you. You're happier with me, you know you are. And freer.'

Nicola sighed. 'This is Venice, and out there is real life. Your happiness will make you irresistible to other women. To girls, sweet young things with smooth skins, girls of your generation.'

'Oh, Christ! Do you want guarantees? I face as many pitfalls as you. More. You will often be impatient with my ignorance. You may after a while compare me unfavourably with Edward, who is rich, respected, successful. I'm untried, a novice. I may never make it as a composer.'

'Of course you will. And then you'll be ashamed of me in front of your friends. "No," you'll say, "it's not my mother. It's my mother's best friend." You'll be disgusted when I turn grey.'

'I'll dye my hair, wear a full beard, walk with a cane.'

'When you get angry with me you'll call me an old bag.'

'You'll call me a dirty Jew.'

'I can't even lie about my age. It's given in every art reference book.'

'I'll lie about mine. My colleagues in the orchestra think I've found myself a beautiful babe. No one has remotely guessed we're not contemporaries.'

'Oh, come off it. I don't look twenty-two.'

'Neither do I. I was able to get a drink in a bar when I was fifteen.'

'I have a rotten, explosive temper.'

'So have I, baby, so have I.'

'You'll wake up one day and look at me and wonder how you ever could have loved me.'

He stepped behind her, pinning her arms to her sides, speaking in her ear. 'Oh no! Love is an ever-fixed mark that looks on tempests and is never shaken.' He kissed the back of her neck, and she trembled with desire and torment.

At dawn, a damp mist began to rise slowly from the canal.

Exhausted from talking and emotion, they went back to the Cipriani by water taxi. Nicola packed her bags feeling like a criminal bound for prison. Paul packed his, utterly defeated. He had offered her his life, and it was not enough.

They avoided looking at each other in the boat to the airport or in the plane to Milan, where they would catch their flight for New York.

Their luck had definitely turned. Nicola couldn't exchange her first-class ticket for economy because every seat in the plane was taken. For a wild moment she thought of a direct swap of tickets with someone in economy but decided against it. If she was going to have to get used to doing without Paul, she could begin on the plane.

She sat in first class drinking Campari and soda and trying to read a magazine, but her eyes couldn't focus on the words.

He sat in his economy seat next to the window, drinking ginger ale. His neighbours were a honeymoon couple, cooing and giggling and looking adoringly at each other until he wanted to hit them over the head in his frustration.

Nicola's neighbour struck up a conversation about the beauties of Venice, making her ache with new pain at each forced memory.

Paul took out his music pad and tried to write but all that came into his head was the theme from Schubert's *Death and the Maiden*.

Nicola could neither eat nor sleep but sat like a zombie, feeling the separation from Paul as keenly as if her limbs had been severed from her body.

Paul could not eat or sleep, and viewed with satisfaction a slight bumping of the plane in the headwind, romantically hoping they would crash into the sea.

Nicola's suitcases came off the moving platform in the first batch, and she passed through Customs before Paul had even retrieved his.

As she went through the arrivals gate and saw the people embracing returning travellers, empty, sheer panic hit her.

Paul came slowly through the gate, head down. Nicola stepped directly in front of him. When he looked up, tears glistened in his eyes.

'I love you, Paul.'

They took a taxi to her studio.

PART II

1

When Edward embraced her, Nicola turned her head to avoid being kissed on the lips. He felt the stiffness in her body and drew back, looking at her searchingly. 'What's wrong?'

For hours Nicola had been rehearsing what to say so as to cause the least amount of pain, but when it came down to it, she could only blurt out, 'I have something to tell you. And – and it's so difficult to know how to begin, and where.'

Nicola moved away from Edward and sat down, clasping her hands nervously.

Looking at her, pale and wide-eyed, Edward's first thought was that she was ill. Cancer of the breast or the uterus.

He drew closer, concern in his eyes. 'Please, I can't stand the suspense. Whatever it is, darling, we'll deal with it together.'

Nicola grimaced as if she were about to cry and put her face in her hand. 'Oh, Edward, I'm so sorry.'

'Sorry for what? Nicola, for heaven's sake, tell me!'

She couldn't look at him. 'I – I've been back for two days, living in the studio. With – Paul Kadin-Lurie.'

Edward felt as if he'd been hit. 'That's impossible. Impossible. I don't believe it!'

When he saw the way his wife sat, her face in her hand, unable to meet his eyes, he realised that however incredible it was, she was telling him the truth.

Carefully composing his features, Edward moved to the bar and poured gin into the pitcher, added ice and used an eyedropper for the vermouth.

Nicola took the drink he handed her, forcing herself to look at him. She noticed that around his finely etched lips was a white line of anger she had never seen there before.

'To sanity,' he said grimly, raising his glass. 'Now, suppose you tell me what this is all about?'

Nicola gulped her drink and sought for words. She started with her long-ago love affair with Gareth Howe, and how she had run into him again in Venice.

'What the hell has that to do with this?' Edward interrupted coldly. 'I've never questioned you about your past, have I?'

'No. But it has a bearing. Please believe, Edward, that I don't want to hurt you.' The expression in his eyes stopped her.

Taking a swallow of her drink, she compressed the story of Gareth into a few sentences and described her meeting with Paul at his debut, in London, and finally in Venice. But telling it factually, without the romance, made it come out flat and sordid.

Edward looked at her with growing disgust. 'So that was why you wanted to stay on in Venice. To meet that goddamn little creep.'

Nicola winced. 'No. I didn't even know he was there.'

'Okay, enough.' Edward made a quick decision. 'You've had a fling. Blame it on Venice, the moonlight, whatever. I appreciate being told. And I'm prepared to forgive you. Let's not speak of it again.'

Nicola felt a crushing pain in her chest. 'But, but I'm in love with Paul. We're living together.'

Edward forced a laugh. 'That's too absurd. I don't believe it!'

'Please, Edward, it's true.'

'You're going to give up what we've had together for eighteen years for – for what?'

Nicola despaired of making him understand. 'I – I don't feel we've really been friends, really been honest with each other for a long time. To start with, we're on opposite sides of the artistic fence.'

'Bullshit,' he said between tight, angry lips. 'You're not shacking up with that adolescent just because you and I have an occasional difference of opinion. What you're really saying is that he fucks you better than I do.'

Nicola pulled back, pained, and set her empty glass shakily on the table. 'It's not that simple. It has to do with basic attitudes towards everything, with understanding, with each person letting the other be himself and herself.'

Edward moved swiftly to Nicola and stood directly in front of her in a menacing attitude. 'You bitch! I haven't let you be yourself? I haven't "understood" you? For eighteen years you've lived like a queen here, coming and going as you please. You've made a success working in the very studio that I bought for you. Who discovered you, Paul? Who promoted your work, Paul? How dare you imply that I don't understand, don't let you be yourself!'

Nicola felt a pounding in her temples. She had never seen Edward in such a white heat of anger.

'I didn't say you haven't helped me. Of course you have. I'm talking about understanding my feelings. You treat me like a child.'

'You talk and behave like a child. I've loved you and cherished you for almost twenty years. And you're just going to walk out –' Edward's voice broke with emotion.

Tears sprang to Nicola's eyes. 'Oh, Edward, I'm so sorry. I don't want to hurt you, believe me I don't.'

He turned and went to make another drink, breathing deeply, trying to control his feelings. Pain kept alternating with rage. Every time he thought of his wife in bed with that awkward boy he remembered he wanted to smash her face in. How had she dared to betray him so shamelessly!

Edward handed Nicola a second drink, which she left untouched.

'I know it's a shock, coming so suddenly, Edward. I never meant it to be.'

'Never mind,' he cut in stonily, draining his glass. The alcohol numbed him sufficiently to think. This was a temporary madness. It couldn't possibly last. If he kept his cool, didn't blurt out things that could never be taken back – he had already said too much.

'You're planning to live at the studio with that – with Paul?'

'Well, yes, for the time being, until we càn make another arrangement. I don't even know how much money is mine. If you could give me an idea of what I've earned?'

'The accountant handles that, but it's not as much as you might think. You sell an occasional piece, but running this household amounts to something over three-quarters of a million dollars a year. Does that boy know he gets you without the Harrington bank account?'

Nicola wouldn't let herself be baited. She had expected the money to come into it. That wasn't as painful for her as the hurt in Edward's eyes, which now had given way to a cool, calculating look that was more his style.

'I don't expect a big settlement, Edward. I only want what I've earned.'

'Yes, of course.' Edward needed a third martini, noting with fury that Nicola had not drunk her second.

'Edward, please believe that I'm very, very fond of you.'

'That will do me a lot of good, when I'm in my empty bed.' He looked reproachfully at her, trying not to show the hatred he was feeling. 'That kid is too damn young for you. You're being utterly ridiculous.'

'You never considered that I might be too young for you,'' she said gently.

'It's hardly the same thing.' Edward leaned back on the couch, considering. 'Have you started your menopause or something?'

'Oh, God, Edward, please don't make it sound like some cheap little affair. What Paul and I have between us is ageless and timeless, a meeting of kindred souls.'

'And bodies!' he snapped. 'Stop playing me for a sucker. You're not having a platonic friendship with that kid. He's fucking you, and that's what this whole thing is all about. Okay, tell me what he does right and I do wrong.' Edward hated himself for asking that of Nicola but he simply couldn't help it. The alcohol had weakened his resolve. The idea that a green kid could please her more than he, who had had dozens of beautiful young girls screaming in ecstasy, made him wild.

Nicola felt his pain. 'Sex is only part of the whole relationship. Paul loves me for the right reasons, for what is best in me. He sees the intrinsic value of my work, whereas you immediately put a price tag on it.'

'That infant doesn't know beans about anything. He blows his little notes on his pipe and leaves the dirty work to his mother. And that goes for you, too. All your "artists" think the world goes around on your talent alone. Temperamental and mystical, a secret world, an inner sanctum. For God's sake, it's just a hunk of metal, a block of stone, a smear of paint. It's us, the collectors and dealers and appreciators, who give art its value. If it weren't for us your stuff would be mouldering in

94

attics and basements, worthless to anyone except junk dealers'.'

This was an old argument, and as Edward went on, Nicola sighed with relief and justification. She and Edward really had very little in common. That had always been the case, only she hadn't realised it quite so sharply.

'... speaking of which, I forgot to tell you that the Pennsylvania Academy of Fine Arts wanted one of your works for their upcoming show. I sent them something –'

'What? What something? Edward, you didn't just go to my storeroom!'

He laughed sardonically. 'Just look at how absurd you are. You tell me you're shacking up with a baby and that's okay, I'm supposed to take that in my stride. What's really important is that I sent a hunk of junk off in your name without consulting you! Talk about priorities.'

'It's part of the same priority, the disregard of my *feelings*,' Nicola said, frustrated at being unable to make him see her point. 'I have all sorts of things stored – maquettes, incomplete ideas, transitional pieces. What actually did you send?'

'Jesus, how in hell can I remember at a time like this. A figure, a woman, about to fly into the air –'

'Edward, that was simply a study in motion. I did it years ago. It isn't even finished.'

'Well, goddamn it, I sent it and that's that. You've got dozens of things rotting that could be bringing in big bucks. You're going to have to sell every damn piece before you've finished keeping that spoiled mama's boy in flutes and ruffled shirts.'

'If only you'd asked me first –'

'Goddamn it, I couldn't reach you! You were shacking up in London, Venice, who knows where else. Typical of you to be more particular about your sculpture than your cunt!'

'That about sums up your attitude and illustrates exactly what's wrong with our marriage,' Nicola said angrily. 'You don't give a damn about me, not really. Except that I'm like a part of your art collection. You guard your paintings not because you enjoy looking at them but because you're waiting for the prices to go higher, perhaps for the artists to drop down dead so as to make their work more valuable. You've never asked me if I've had an affair – and I never have, until now – because you didn't care, as long as it wasn't public. What really bothers you now is that people may talk.'

'What bothers me is that you could be so silly, so vain, so afraid of getting old, that the first little creep that comes along and flatters you, fucks you ...'

'Edward, please stop.' Nicola's voice was low and calm. 'I don't want to continue this argument. It has only shown me how right I am in doing what I must do. You keep talking about "fucking" me. That's exactly what it was between us. Not lovemaking. I've always felt constrained in bed with you, afraid that if I took the initiative or followed my sensual impulses you'd be turned off. I tried to tell you years ago but you didn't even acknowledge what I was saying. You even tell me when to have an orgasm, which virtually insures that I won't be able to –'

'Aha! I knew it! All this talk of understanding comes down to the basic facts of the flesh. He fucks you the way you like and I don't. I suppose he lets you get on top –' Edward stopped when he saw Julie standing at the door.

'Come on in, princess, and join the family squabble. Your mother has something to tell you.' Edward lit a cigarette, turning his back to hide his shaking fingers.

Nicola faced Julie apprehensively. 'It would be better to talk later, privately, dear.'

Julie flopped into a chair, draping her long, slender, jeans-clad legs over the arm. Her eyes glittered with malevolence. Fortified by half a pint of vodka, she was able to get the words out for once.

'I get the picture. Mommy dearest is having an affair. Who's the lucky man?'

Nicola took several short breaths. She had known it was going to be impossible. Julie wouldn't understand, not yet.

'Your father and I are separating. I've moved into my studio.' She stopped and swallowed.

Edward, putting down another drink, filled the pause with his cold, sarcastic voice. 'And tell her who the lucky "man" is, my sweet. No? Ashamed? I'll bet you are! Your mother, princess, is leaving me for Paul Lurie – Anne's creepy little kid!'

Julie turned a dull orange. Slowly untangling her legs, she rose from her chair.

'Darling, it's not just a sordid affair between us. Paul and I are in love –'

Julie, jamming her hands over her ears, groped her way towards the door.

'Julie,' Nicola called.

The girl glared at her mother, her face distorted with anguish. 'You're – you're gross!' She slammed the door behind her.

Edward was suddenly calm. Julie had reacted more strongly than he could have hoped. Nicola would not be able to carry it off. She was not going to give up her daughter for that young shit who was tied to his mother's apron strings. Nicola was a child herself. She needed Edward's support and protection. He didn't give the 'affair' longer than a month.

Without another word he opened the door and went in search of his daughter, leaving Nicola, pale and shaken, in a corner of the sofa.

Julie was lying face down on her bed.

'Your mother is simply suffering from the start of middle age. This business with Paul won't last any length of time at all. It seems they met in Venice and behaved like a couple of lunatics out of a story book. Your mother is a great lady but not at all practical or worldly. That spoiled brat, used to getting whatever he wants from his mother, simply made a fool out of a middle-aged woman. He'll realise soon enough – especially when Anne smacks his bottom for him. Your mother and I have been happily married for more than eighteen years. She'll come to her senses.'

Edward paused to light a cigarette.

'I just want you to know, princess, that whatever happens you can always count on me. Okay?'

He stood there some minutes until his cigarette burned down to a stump.

Julie never moved.

When her father had gone, Julie flung herself onto her back, her face streaked with tears. She felt as lost and helpless as when she was a child of six.

Maria, the au pair, used to escort Julie to school and pick

97

her up in the afternoon. How Julie wished that sometimes her mother would take her instead. Although other children were delivered and collected by maids, every mother of every child in her class had appeared at least once except hers.

Not until the week that Maria had appendicitis did Nicola actually take Julie by taxi to the Dalton School. She held Julie's hand all the way to the gate, just like all the other mothers, kissed her, smiled, and told her to enjoy her day.

Julie was thrilled. At last she could silence Carla and Lacey, who constantly teased her. 'That was my *mother*.'

Eagerly Julie looked forward to three o'clock. All the children would be pouring out all at once, so that virtually everyone in her class would see her mother, the prettiest of all in her wonderful sheepskin jacket, suede pants, and fur hat.

When the bell rang Julie was practically the first one out of the door. Her initial stab of disappointment that her mother wasn't already waiting gave way to a heady feeling of anticipation. Would the big Rolls pull up, or a taxi? Would her mother perhaps take her to the luncheonette on Madison Avenue where the kids went for hot chocolate? Julie had gone there with Maria once, but it wasn't the same.

The minutes crawled by. One by one the children were scooped up and led away.

Carla and Lacey, whose mothers took turns in meeting them, passed Julie standing forlornly in front of the gate. She was beginning to shiver.

'Bet she's forgotten all about you,' Carla called.

'Bet she isn't even your mother,' taunted Lacey.

The two girls giggled and ran into a waiting car, the door held for them by a smiling lady in a mink coat.

A boy somewhat older than Julie looked curiously at her. 'Mine's late too. It could be the traffic.'

'I know,' Julie said eagerly.

Julie's face grew warm when the boy's mother appeared and he whispered something to her. His mother looked at Julie. 'Would you like to wait in our car, dear?'

'No, thank you,' Julie answered politely, feeling humiliated by the expression of pity on the woman's face.

When all the children had gone, Julie really began to worry. Could her mother have forgotten? What if she didn't come at all? What would Julie do then?

A few snowflakes came down. What if it snowed harder? She had visions of waiting and waiting until it was dark and still. She would be a little white mound and nobody would know she was there. Maybe some big boys would come along and think she was a snowman. They'd wrap a long scarf around her neck or put a funny hat on her head. And if she tried to yell, snow would fill up her mouth.

She began to jump up and down. She would count to ten, and by then surely her mother would appear. But she must count slowly.

Then she counted to ten again. And again. And again.

Julie's terror grew and she trembled uncontrollably. She didn't want to cry but she couldn't keep the wetness from spilling out of her eyes.

She was the only one left, the only one nobody cared about. Her tears dried into icy streaks.

Then she saw her mother running down the street. 'Julie, darling.' Her mother hugged her. 'I'm so sorry. I was tied up with a collector. Then I couldn't get a taxi, and the bus took ages. My poor baby, you're frozen. Why didn't you wait inside?'

Julie couldn't answer. Couldn't describe the panic she had felt at having been abandoned. Her mother had come for her today. But what about next time?

Julie had never got over the burning resentment towards her mother who refused to behave as all other mothers did.

Her mother and Paul! Paul and her mother! Nicola the Great could have anyone, even a boy half her age.

Julie simply didn't know what to do, or where to turn. Her father, for all his offers of support, was just as bad, with his little sluts. Between him and her mother there wasn't much to choose.

She was experiencing the terror of abandonment as she had so long ago. She reached into her night table and took out half a pint of vodka.

2

'Paul, it's such a treat to have dinner alone with you,' Anne said, handing him the wine to pour. 'You look wonderful, so happy. What have you been up to?'

Paul carefully cut his chicken before replying. 'As a matter of fact, I was in Venice. Had a two-week job, filling in for a colleague.'

'But your work?'

'It's going very well. I'll be ready by November. Promise.' He smiled gaily at her.

'I'm very proud of you and can't wait to hear the tone poem.'

'I've played you parts of it, but of course I rewrite as I go along.' Paul continued to discuss his music. All the while the news he had to tell his mother lay as heavily on his stomach as the noodle pudding she had served him.

'Did you say Venice? My friend Nicola was there for the Biennale. Did you know her work was on display?'

'Yes. I saw it.'

'You did? Oh, tell me what it's like.'

'It's superb, so perfectly conceived and constructed that it quite took my breath away.'

Anne listened with fascination to his description. 'I didn't realise you were such a sculpture aficionado. Did you look up Nicola and Edward, by the way?'

'Mother,' Paul said solemnly, putting down his fork. 'I have something to tell you that you're probably not going to like.'

Her mother's instinct suddenly told her that Paul's glowing face came from thinking he was in love. She prayed that this infatuation would not turn out to be a nuisance. Not an Italian girl made pregnant, or something equally sticky.

'Well, tell me,' she said at length, not liking the way he was looking at her.

''You may have wondered, although you never pried, if I had any romantic attachments.'

Anne laughed nervously. 'Well, of course I would never pry. I assume that you're a normal male and have had the requisite number of experiences for someone your age.'

'I guess I have, but they've always been short-lived and shallow, as if there were something, or someone, preventing me from really caring about a woman on a deeper level.'

'My God, you're awfully serious, Paul. To tell you the truth, your romantic escapades are my least worry.'

'Good,' he said, relieved.

'You have plenty of time before you get involved. A flirtation once in a while is fine, if you don't go overboard. It sounds as if you met a girl in Venice and were swept up by the romantic setting. Nothing to be ashamed of. Tell me her name. I'll bet it's Italian.'

Unexpectedly, Paul didn't laugh. He didn't even smile. 'Nicola Di Candia.'

'What? What do you mean?'

'I'm in love with Nicola Di Candia.'

'Paul, what are you telling me?'

The growing look of horror on his mother's face made Paul defensive. 'I'm in love with Nicola. I always have been. I met her in Venice. We were together. We're together still, at her studio.' Even as he said the words he felt their brutality.

'You and my friend Nicola Harrington,' she intoned slowly, 'are living together in her studio? I don't believe it.'

'I see it's a shock, and I'm sorry to have told you so bluntly. Please don't be upset –'

'Where is Edward?' Anne asked sharply. 'Is he there with the two of you?' Anne was simply unable to imagine Nicola without Edward. Had they turned kinky and drawn Paul into something terrible?

'Nicola left him –'

'Impossible! She would never do that. She adores Edward.'

'She's left him,' Paul repeated patiently, 'Nicola and I are very much in love –'

As his words sank in, Anne felt ill. 'Love! What do you

know about love? You're an infant. You and Nicola – it's incredible. I simply can't believe that my dearest friend would do such a thing to me.'

'Not to you, but for me, for herself, for us. Mother, please listen.' Paul stood up, and on his face was a look of manly determination that chilled her to the marrow. She knew that look. It usually preceded an argument about music which she invariably won. He never called her mother unless he was about to defend a questionable position. In this case, indefensible.

'In spite of what you think, of how strange it sounds, we are in love.'

'But how could such a thing be?' Anne interrupted shrilly. 'You haven't seen her in years. Why, at your party here last winter you didn't even recognise her.'

'LISTEN!' Paul told his mother of his youthful crush on Nicola. 'I would never have composed a note if it hadn't been for her.'

'Of course you would. What you think you remember from your childhood isn't necessarily so –'

'I'll tell you what's so. We're in love and we're going to be together. Mother, if you care about me at all, please don't hassle me. Or her.'

'God, she's old enough to be your mother!'

'Edward is old enough to be her father, but nobody seems to worry about that minor point,' Paul said tensely. 'Age doesn't matter when people are soulmates.'

'Soulmates! You should be thinking of your music instead of having a delayed rebellion against me. Listen, I've been running myself ragged all around New York arranging for your première.'

'I know, and I'm grateful, I am,' he said in a softer tone. He held out his hand. 'Let's go into the living-room and have a brandy. My personal life is not going to make any difference to my music.'

'Not make a difference! If you're staying in New York, what about your master's? Starving composers are a dime a dozen. At least with an advanced degree – and I mean a doctorate – you can teach on a college level.'

'I don't want that.' Paul tossed his hair back from his

forehead in a gesture of impatience and walked out of the dining-room.

Anne followed, with a pain in her heart she hadn't felt since her adolescent fights with her own mother. Paul was just as infuriating and unreasonable.

He poured out two brandies but Anne waved hers aside. 'I would have given up the master's in any case. After a year I've had enough –'

'What will you do, while you're waiting to be discovered?'

Paul recognised the sarcasm as a family trait handed down from his grandmother Kadin. 'Although my preference is for serious music, I wouldn't sneer at movies or television or musical comedy. I'll play in an orchestra, take on private pupils. What I don't want is to remain in the rarefied atmosphere of a university music department. It stifles me.'

Anne rocked back and forth in her chair as if she were in death's agony. Paul had gone crazy. 'Musical comedy! After all I've done for you, all the sacrifices I've made –'

'Oh, God, not that. Not from you.' Paul gulped his brandy and rumpled his hair. 'I never thought I'd hear such a banal cry from you.' He strode to his mother and insistently took her hands and held them, feeling their iciness.

'You've imbued me with a love of music I'll have always. And I appreciate all the arrangements you've made for me over the years. But you can't arrange my personal life as if you were preparing me for a concert. I must compose what I choose and love whom I choose.'

Anne suddenly grew calm. It was obvious that if she wanted to put an end to Paul and Nicola, and thereby get her son back on the proper path, she would have to go about it in a different way.

'Yes, of course. I see that. I'm sorry for making such a fuss.'

'Okay, let's leave it now,' he said, grinning with relief. 'I'm on my way to New Haven to clear out my stuff. I'll call you when I return to New York and we'll talk about everything more calmly.'

Anne managed a wan smile. 'I'm calm already.'

Paul felt reassured. Nevertheless, before taking the train, he phoned Nicola. 'I'm not sure what to expect, darling. She seemed okay. In fact, she's almost more concerned about my

103

not wanting to go on with the master's for two more years than us. I'm sure she'll accept us when she gets over the shock.'

'Yes,' Nicola answered, so as not to upset him. But she knew better.

After Paul left, Anne had several brandies, wondering where she had gone wrong. She had been so careful with Paul, so modern, so stupid. Of course, he was still a child. Her dear friend Nicola was at the bottom of this so-called romance. Paul was her son, tied to her for life by blood and birth pangs. But if Nicola had really done this terrible thing to her and wouldn't quit she was going to get just what she had coming.

Julie tore open the envelope with her mother's handwriting. 'Dearest Julie. I have tried to reach you by 'phone for days. Even if you think my action terrible, talking out your feelings will help you to be less upset. I want you to know that my studio is your home, too, and you are welcome here anytime. Please, please, darling, come and see me. I love you, and nothing can change that ...'

Julie ripped the letter into tiny pieces and threw them in her wastebasket.

She turned her hi fi up louder, as if the sound of the rock music pummeling her ears would stop her thoughts. While she put on a white silk dress beaded with pearls - a relic of the twenties she had found in an antique shop - she drank from her bottle of vodka. Spike-heeled white sandals and a set of jangling bracelets completed her outfit.

At her dressing table she carefully applied makeup, using thick coats of mascara and lipstick. She used an afro comb on her fine golden hair, giving it a wet, tangled look. Finally, she doused herself with perfume. Then she stuffed her white satin purse with twenties and hundreds.

The doorman looked at her curiously but did not say anything more than good evening. He got her a cab and accepted the two dollars she handed him.

'Spring Street and West Broadway,' she told the driver.

Julie felt the welcome warmth of the alcohol as it raced through her bloodstream. She was elated at the adventure

104

ahead of her. She was a woman – young, beautiful, rich, and sexy. Wasn't she?

When the bell rang, Nicola rushed to the door hoping to find Julie.

It was Anne.

Nicola stepped aside, noting with apprehension that her friend was in battle dress – a black wool suit, in spite of the July heat (Anne had always been cold when she was upset), white silk shirt, and a white straw hat, with matching bag and gloves.

They didn't speak. Anne walked deliberately to a straight-backed chair, sat down, and crossed her legs, her face stony with anger.

For the first time in their twenty-five-year friendship the two women regarded each other with distrust. It slowly dissolved to sadness when each remembered the closeness, the affection they had always felt.

Putting herself in Anne's place, Nicola experienced a touch of pity. Anne was angry. Justifiably. Nicola's eyes grew moist.

Anne, observing Nicola's look of remorse, burst into tears. 'Nika, how could you do this to me?'

Nicola rushed to Anne's side, knelt, and put her head in her lap. 'I never meant it to be. I tried so hard to fight against it, Annie.'

As Nicola mumbled brokenly, Anne gradually stopped crying. Nicola was feeling guilty and apologetic. Surely she could be convinced to put a stop to this unthinkable liaison.

At Anne's feet, Nicola explained, 'After all those years with Edward, Paul is such a – a revelation to me. He caught me off-guard when he told me of his feelings in London.'

'You saw my son in London? And you never told me?'

'I – I did. At least, I tried. You misunderstood. And when I realised he had kept it from you – especially as I turned him down, and thought I'd overcome my attraction – I didn't want to cause trouble between you.'

'You arranged to meet my son in London?' Anne's swarthy face had gone pale under her growing anger.

'No, of course not. He followed me there.'

Anne jumped up from the chair in fury. 'I don't believe that for a moment. All these years I've never really known you.'

'Anne, Paul did pursue me. In London and in Venice. By then I couldn't deny it any more –'

'It?'

'My – my love for him,' Nicola whispered.

'Love, is that what you call it?'

Nicola's face grew warm but she forced herself to tell the truth. 'That first evening when Paul and I met in Venice I guess it was mostly passion I felt. And I'd had a great deal to drink. I thought there would be only the one night. I'd prove to Paul that what he thought was love was really – lust. Now I see I was trying to prove it to myself. But Anne, it didn't turn out to be true. Once we were together it was so beautiful. I realised that there was a lot more than just passion.'

Anne, controlling herself with the greatest effort, repeated the words, 'More than just passion. Tell me what more you find in a boy you once diapered, a kid who still has to have his nose wiped by his mother.'

Nicola realised that no matter how she explained it, Anne was not going to understand.

'I – I love Paul for every reason a woman has ever loved a man. I delight in his company. I respect his opinions. I'm in awe of his talent, of his exquisite sensibility and uncanny intuition when it comes to my feelings. With him I feel reborn, renewed, exquisitely happy, at peace with myself and the world, and I give him peace and joy too. We think and feel the same about everything that matters.'

'And the fact that he's half your age doesn't stop you! And that he's my son! And that you were supposed to be my best friend –'

'It did stop me. I've been trying to tell you. It stopped me the night of his debut, when he looked at me so provocatively that I was quite stunned. It stopped me in London when he told me he had always loved me. It even stopped me when we left Venice. I vowed to give him up, but at the last minute there was such an aching feeling of loss.'

'And what about my loss? Or are you going to say I haven't lost a son but gained a daughter?'

Nicola, pained, was silent.

'I need a drink,' Anne said harshly. 'Gin. Neat.'

Nicola poured gin over ice cubes, adding tonic to her own glass.

Anne gulped her drink and motioned for a refill. 'You have left Edward for my son?'

'Yes. I imagine you can't understand –'

'No, I can't. Is Edward impotent?'

Nicola flushed. 'No.'

'He loves you?'

'Yes, but –'

'Then your acquisition of my son is simply an extension of your avarice.' Anne stomped about the loft like the star of a melodrama. 'You have always been incredibly greedy and ambitious. When I first met you, you were a ragamuffin, out at elbows, a Bay Ridge ignoramus. I befriended you and civilised you. It was the start of your charmed life. All you had was your talent, which was as dormant as mathematical genius would be in an African bushman. With my encouragement you ended up one of the top sculptors in the world. And you're married to one of the most charming, handsome, richest men in America. You have all that, but it's not enough. You had to have my son too!'

Nicola, sitting on the bottom rung of her ladder and nervously smoothing her jeans, was living the nightmare she had tried to avoid by breaking with Paul in Venice.

'If you were a natural mother, instead of that impersonal countess you play with Julie, you'd realise the enormity of your action. I must tell you something I've always thought but never said.'

Anne folded her arms and loomed in front of Nicola like an avenging maternal figure. 'You're incorrigibly selfish. *You* have always come first. You, yourself, your art, your creativity, your sensibility, your feelings, you, you, you! You neglected Julie shamefully when she was small, and now that poor girl is hardly alive. The more famous and powerful you become, the more she fades into the walls, with her pastel flower paintings.'

To Anne's satisfaction, tears came to Nicola's eyes. All her vulnerable places were known to Anne, and now that she was fighting for her son's life she was going to prod every spot until she drew blood.

'Am I wrong?' Anne demanded.

Slowly Nicola shook her head.

'And how has Julie reacted to this caper of yours? How does she like it that her mother has taken her best friend's son for her lover?'

'She won't speak to me,' Nicola admitted. 'But she was barely speaking to me before this. Annie, you're right about my failure with my daughter, but I don't know what I can do about it now.'

'You can start by giving up my son. That might show her she's more important than your twitching cunt.'

'That's not like you –'

'Is what you have done like you?'

Nicola poured out more gin. 'I grant you that the age difference could be a problem, but at the moment we find it irrelevant –'

'Irrelevant!'

'Yes,' Nicola said, in a soft, reasonable voice. 'Anne, this isn't just animal passion between an older woman and a young stud. It's a deep, absorbing love between two creative *people*. I'm not a mother figure for Paul, nor a teacher either. He knows more than I do. I've only ever had two lovers, Gareth and Edward. With my husband, in bed, as elsewhere, there have always been problems. Whereas with Paul there is a level of mutual joy that is almost indescribable.'

'Okay, that's enough. I can't bear to hear it,' Anne shouted. 'I think it's nauseating. It turns my stomach even to think of it. You have preyed upon an innocent boy, and don't give me that shit that he chased after you without encouragement. You've always been an outrageous flirt, shaking that little ass, looking at everything in trousers as if you were ready to eat it alive. My son is no match for you –'

Anne had had too much to drink, Nicola realised. She tried to reason with her. 'If our ages were reversed, if Paul were forty and I twenty-two, would that make such a difference?'

'You imbecile, of course it would make a difference! My son would have the possibility of a normal life. He could have children. Can you give him children? Will you?'

Nicola paled. 'It's biologically possible –'

'Mongolian idiots is what women of our age give birth to.'

Nicola retreated. 'We're not planning to get married,' she

108

said, subdued. 'Probably we won't last long. Paul will stop loving me –'

'Shut up about love. Every time you say the word it makes me want to vomit. Where did I go wrong?' Anne cried, sitting down and rocking back and forth in her chair. 'How could I have done such a bad job with my son?'

'You did a wonderful job. Paul is a tribute to you for having raised the perfect mate for a creative woman. Remember, when we were girls, how we used to imagine such a man? Long before women's lib –'

'Oh, shut up, shut up. All that is shit, just rationalising.'

'It's not. The irony is that only a young man, brought up as Paul has been, has the chance of being free of male chauvinism. And you did that for Paul. I see a lot of you in him, Annie. My love for him is in many ways an extension of my love for you.'

Anne jumped up and flew at Nicola, knocking the glass from her hands. 'You predatory bitch, don't you dare tell me that! I want to hear only one thing from you – that you'll give up my son!'

Nicola backed away, biting her trembling lips. 'I – I don't see how I can. Paul would be miserable –'

'Not for long. Women have come and gone in his life, and so must you. Nicola, you must do this or I'll never forgive you. Julie will never forgive you. Edward will never forgive you. And what's more, you'll never forgive yourself.'

Nicola's face was white. She felt as if she were being torn in two. 'To give him up now would be a lie for both of us. We'd be thinking of each other constantly, building it up more in our imaginations. The relationship has a better chance of – of running its course if we follow it through.'

Anne flew at Nicola with her fists. 'You're just talking, talking, talking, like a goddamn politician. You disgusting degenerate!'

With each word Anne delivered a punch to Nicola's shoulders and breasts. Nicola was trying to ward off the blows, but the sharp pain in her breast finally snapped her temper. She pushed Anne away sharply.

'Your son? Paul is more than just your son. He's his own man, but you hardly see that,' Nicola shouted. 'You're totally hung up on Paul. You're the mother that's unnatural.

You would begrudge any woman Paul, even if age weren't a factor.'

Anne grabbed Nicola by the hair and pushed her down, banging her head against the wooden floor. 'You bitch, I'll murder you.'

The sound of the ringing phone broke the moment.

'Julie!' Exerting all her strength, Nicola squirmed away from Anne and ran to the telephone.

'No,' she said dejectedly. 'You've got the wrong number.'

When Nicola hung up she saw Anne standing at the door holding her crushed white hat.

'You'll give up my son or I'll make you wish you'd never drawn a single breath on this earth.'

3

Paul knew immediately that something had happened. The heaviness with which Nicola rose from the couch and came towards him was alarming. Although she had washed her face and applied fresh makeup, he could discern her anguish.

'Who's been here? Edward?'

Nicola shook her head and embraced him gingerly.

'Tell me what's wrong. Not my mother, I hope.'

Nicola's face confirmed his fear.

'I warned her not to hassle you. My poor darling.'

'Don't, Paul, it's all right,' Nicola murmured. 'I expected it. Nobody is going to let us be happy.'

'Wrong. Nobody is going to be able to stop us.'

'They are. They hate the idea of us. They think the worst, and say it too.'

Paul kissed her, holding her face in his hands, trying to banish the hurt. Nicola had been through an ordeal. He knew how close she and his mother had always been. He was just beginning to learn that Anne could be vicious when she felt thwarted.

'I can imagine the things she said to you, but tell me anyway. Get it all out.'

Nicola tried to make light of the matter. No purpose would be served in making Paul angry at his mother. 'Oh, what you might have expected. Middle-aged madness, preying on an innocent lad –'

'Damn it, I told her *I* was the one –'

'I believe you, darling, but she's your mother and simply can't be objective. A child is a part of oneself. When they hurt, it is so unbearable.' She was thinking, also, of Julie.

Nicola's anguish wrenched at Paul. However awkward it was for him, she was the one who would bear the brunt of their actions. Nicola had left her husband, who apparently was not going to make things easy for her. Her daughter was being difficult, and now his goddamn mother had given her a hard time.

Paul would have to make it all up to Nicola.

'I'm sorry, Paul. I'm not much fun tonight. How did it go up at Yale?'

'Okay. Fred Felix is disappointed, in a way, but I'll continue to study with him. And I've put my house up for rent. It's a tiny place but there's always a professor looking for a place to stay.'

'Good. I hope you rent it.' Nicola sighed, and Paul knew she was abstracted.

'Any word from Julie?'

'No. I don't know what I'm going to do.'

'She'll get over it. Julie has her own life to live.'

'I feel there's more to her disaffection than our relationship. There's something deeper, something frightening about Julie. And it's wrong. She's so breathtakingly beautiful, people stare at her on the street.'

'That may be, but she doesn't have your character or your talent, and she's very immature. The fact is that she'll never be another you, and she's probably intelligent enough to see that.'

'But that's terrible, Paul. That's an impossible burden. I can't bear to think that she suffers so much. Maybe she needs professional help. I've mentioned a psychotherapist to

Edward a couple of times, but he doesn't believe in that sort of thing. Not that Julie would go. She's so unreachable, now more than ever.'

'You just have to give it time, darling. I've brought some champagne and something to eat.'

Nicola tried to banish her agitation so as not to disappoint Paul. 'Any special occasion?'

'Yes.' He looked at her with burning eyes. 'I love you more today than I did yesterday, and am likely to love you more tomorrow than today.'

Nicola forced herself to return his smile, but the fight with Anne had depressed her unutterably. From the beginning, Nicola had known that disapproval of her relationship with Paul would mostly fall on her, the older woman, the vamp, the seductress. How she deplored the labels and pigeonholes people created, blinding them to individual considerations. Paul was not just any twenty-two-year-old, he was special, unique, right for her at any age.

He popped the cork and poured the champagne. 'To our happiness, and to hell with the world.'

'To our happiness,' Nicola echoed, as the first few swallows lightened her mood. 'The world isn't ready for us yet. We'll have to show them.'

'To showing the world.' He touched her glass with his, his face registering adoration.

Nicola felt weak with love for him. Momentarily her spirits rose, even though she knew the feeling to be no more substantial than the bubbles in her glass. She feared the additional burden of having to force happiness, to prove that what they had done was worthwhile. They would never be able to carry it off.

Paul unpacked two slices of quiche, Greek salad with feta and olives, and Italian bread.

He took an olive in his mouth and kissed her, moving it with his tongue into hers. 'That's known as a Greek kiss.'

Nicola chewed on the olive and returned the pit to his mouth. 'That's the Italian response!'

Laughing, he spat the pit into her shirt. 'Here's some Jewish *chutzpah*, just to liven things up!' He reached into her shirt to retrieve the pit, causing her to cry out in pain as he touched her breast.

'I'm sorry. Was I too rough?'

'No, no, it's all right.'

Gently Paul unbuttoned her shirt. 'What are these bruises all over you? Jesus, what happened here? Did my mother do this?'

'I fell off the scaffold.'

Paul took Nicola in his arms tenderly, but said nothing. He was furious with his mother. That she could have been so devious as to pretend to him that she was calm and then come here and physically attack his lover!

Nicola, grateful for Paul's silence, could already see the way their love would be eroded. Each would have to lie and pretend in order to spare the other pain. And when there wasn't honesty, misunderstanding followed, and resentment.

But not yet. Let them at least have the benefit of love right now, love they had already paid for so dearly. Nicola held Paul close, the champagne causing her skin to tingle and even edging the pain of her bruises into pleasure.

Paul's breath quickened and he bent her back on the sofa. He was always quick to note the smallest nuance in her kiss or touch or even glance. She loved the way he became instantly aroused and the honesty with which he made love to her, never playing ego games.

They undressed each other slowly, sensually. Paul dribbled champagne from the bottle onto her nipples, tonguing it off with exquisite enjoyment. He tilted the bottle, letting a thin stream of liquid trickle into her navel and just to the line of her pubic hair. Bending his head, he licked her until she was quivering with desire.

'You taste better than champagne,' he murmured, moving down between her legs.

With their lips and tongues and fingers they caressed and teased each other, waves of love and desire vibrating between them like quicksilver.

Finally they lay closely entwined, rocking in an increasing rhythm, fusing bodies and sensibilities in a shuddering climax that united them into one being.

Edward returned home after a lonely dinner and sat in his study going through his card catalogue, a pitcher of martinis beside him. His David Hockney etchings were now worth a small fortune, he noted with satisfaction. Flipping from back to front, Edward saw the name Di Candia fleetingly on a card. He pushed the catalogue aside and poured himself a drink.

How his life had changed in only a couple of days. One morning he'd been feeling wonderful, vigorous, successful, on top of the world, waiting for his wife to come home. Then she had dealt him an incredible blow.

He'd gone out to forget. Phoned a delicious morsel he had been saving for a special occasion, a sweet, pale blonde eighteen-year-old who had been haunting his office, imploring him to look at her slides.

Edward could tell by the girl's behaviour that she was resigned to sleeping with him, at the same time hoping somehow to avoid it at the last moment. Her ambition, he had noted with heightened interest, was colliding with her morals. He was sure Diana was a virgin, just the type he liked. She would be reluctant, somewhat fearful, but he would awaken her, he would show her how wonderful sex could be with someone of his discernment and experience.

The trouble was that the hurt Nicola had done him got in the way of the evening. He couldn't forget it, couldn't concentrate, and in the end, couldn't get it up at all.

The humiliation had been terrible. There they lay in bed, Diana trembling deliciously with uncertainty, and he as helpless to assault her as a eunuch.

Damn Nicola for doing this to him! In truth, the alcohol made him feel worse. What he needed was escape, diversion. It was too soon to be thinking of other women.

On the way to his bedroom, Edward knocked on Julie's door and had no answer. When he opened it and looked in, he was surprised and annoyed that she was not yet home. It was already twelve-thirty. She hadn't left word that she would be out so late. He would have to speak to her.

Edward propped himself up in bed, trying not to look at the empty space that should have been occupied by Nicola. He turned on the television and found a Clint Eastwood film just beginning.

There was a lot of action, but because Edward was unable to concentrate on the plot, the violence did not act as a catalyst for his own. Instead, he turned it inward, for the first time ever wondering if life was worth all this pain.

During the commercial he took off his glasses to wipe them. Silent tears were running down his cheeks.

Julie walked tentatively into the Spring Street Bar, momentarily dazed by the noise, crowd, and mingled aroma of beer and perfume.

Before she could decide what to do a dark stocky man intercepted her. 'What'll it be, sweetheart?'

'Nothing,' Julie mumbled sullenly. She didn't like the look of the man or the insolent way he took in her expensive dress and shoes.

'Ginger ale?' He grinned at her. 'You might be eighteen, and then again you might not. Very strict about underage drinkers in here – unless they happen to be with me.'

To the bartender the man said, 'One ginger ale, one Cutty Sark on the rocks.'

'Make the ginger a vodka martini, Stolichnaya, very dry, with a twist.'

The bartender looked from Julie back to the man.

'I buy my own drinks,' Julie said boldly, 'and I carry my birth certificate.' She took a twenty from her purse, dangled it snottily in front of the barman's nose, and slapped it on the bar.

At an amused nod from Julie's companion, the bartender began to make the drinks. The man looked at Julie curiously. 'It's okay with me, if you want to pay for your own booze. What I can offer you is a little snort.'

'I don't dig dope,' Julie answered sullenly.

'You in college?' the man said, trying another approach.

'No, I'm not in college,' she mimicked. 'If that's the best you can do –'

He suddenly grabbed her shoulder and hissed in her ear, 'Watch it, kid, don't press your luck just because you're a looker. This is my turf, and if you don't shape up you'll be out on your ass.'

Julie, already halfway through her drink, felt a warm glow in spite of the menace. He thought she was good-looking. She suddenly smiled dazzlingly at him. 'I'm an art student. How about you?'

'Rich kids,' he snorted. 'Me, I'm in the food business. Name's Vic.'

'Julie,' she murmured companionably, and slowly licked her lower lip the way she had seen a girl do in a movie.

Vic took her to a one-room efficiency in a renovated building around the corner. The room contained little besides a king-sized bed and a giant television.

'Do you really live here?' She was finding it difficult to phrase her words after three drinks, maybe four.

'You might say it's my home away from home,' he parried.

She lay down carefully on the bed and kicked off her shoes. This was it. She was really going to do it.

Julie believed she was the only girl graduate of Music and Art who was still a virgin. She had always shied away from the more aggressive boys. Sex was what they wanted, not romance. She hated to think she was only an object. However, since she had started to drink her feelings had changed. There was something wonderful in the vodka that made her body warm, made her want to get close to a man, to find out what it would be like, to test her powers of attraction.

Vic glided around the room, deftly adjusting the light to very dim, getting her another vodka from the well-stocked bar, slipping off his jacket as he went.

When he joined her on the bed an unpleasant sensation of heaviness and a rather sour odour of perspiration hit her. His lips were wet and rubbery, his tongue and hands insistent.

Julie was faintly revolted but she put her arms around his thick middle and kissed him back. When he moved his hand under her dress she jumped away involuntarily.

'Relax, Julie, just relax.'

He flipped a switch and television came on.

In a moment, Julie realised it was a pornographic movie, one of those video tape things. She watched, curious. The two girls in the film appeared cheap and dumb but the man turned her on. He had long, greasy hair, a hollow chest, and a look of haunted misery. He was even having trouble getting aroused, in spite of the way the girls slithered all over him. His pathetic quality appealed to Julie. That was the sort of fellow she had been hoping to find, not this overfed sweat factory beside her.

Vic, observing her, saw her lips part and her eyes glisten with interest.

'If you like the size of his, wait until you see mine.'

'Can I have another drink,' Julie mumbled, nausea rising.

Vic stood up and pulled off his pants. Through his black bikini shorts she could see him jutting out. He hadn't exaggerated.

Watching Vic swagger to the bar and fill up her glass, Julie had a moment of fear.

'What're you drowning anyhow, Julie? Your folks do you wrong or something?'

'Yeah. They made me an orphan.' She reached for the drink and gulped it.

Vic took it from her hands when she had drunk only half. 'Easy. Don't want you passing out on me. How's about taking off the dress.'

As she undressed, Julie tried to keep her eye on the man on the screen, but Vic's sleek head kept blocking her vision.

'Jesus, you're one gorgeous kid.'

She liked being appreciated, but when he began to caress her she shut her eyes and clenched her teeth. She felt something hard and large between her legs.

'Don't. It's too big. It will never fit!'

'Course it will, baby. It'll fit just fine.'

'Stop, please. I've never come this far before. I mean it –'

As she struggled, opening her eyes in panic, she realised he thought she was teasing him.

The more she squirmed and protested the more insistent he became. He was very strong, and succeeded in holding down her arms with one hand and jamming her legs open with the other. His tongue was halfway down her throat, preventing her from crying out.

There was a moment of searing pain, then a sensation of heaving, and a sound of groaning. When he finally lay still, Julie was covered with his sweat, and her hair was sticking to her scalp.

Easing off her, Vic noted with astonishment the tears of pain glistening on her heavily made-up eyes. Then he saw the blood on the sheet.

117

'Mary, mother of Jesus,' he swore. 'You meant it. Jesus, I never figured you for a virgin!'

'I'm not – now.'

4

When Paul arrived at Anne's apartment with a suitcase, she was sure Nicola had come to her senses and sent him home.

'I've come to pack up some things,' he snapped. 'Then I want a word with you.'

Anne followed Paul. 'Please leave your things here. You're being silly. I'm not going to rent out the room. You'll want to come back, when you find out how little integrity your girlfriend has –'

'Integrity,' Paul echoed contemptuously. 'You're one to talk. You promised me you wouldn't cause trouble, and yet you went over there and attacked her.'

'Is that what she said?' Anne asked.

'Never mind what she said. *You* said you were calm –'

'I am,' she assured him. In fact, she was feeling much better. She had remembered something about Nicola that had been filed away for years, something that would give Paul pause.

Anne watched silently as Paul pulled open drawers and stuffed clothes into his suitcase.

'I'm very angry at you for interfering in something that's none of your business.'

'Not my business? That my son and my "friend" move in together.'

'No, not really,' he said, storming down the hall. 'Your attitude is high-handed, and to attack Nicola physically – don't deny it, I saw the bruises for myself. No, she didn't tell me anything about it, but I'm not the idiot you take me for.'

No? What kind of idiot are you then? Anne bit down hard

on her tongue. A hostile exchange would do no good.

'Come and have a bite to eat before you leave.'

'I've eaten.'

Anne wanted only one thing: an end to Paul and Nicola, and she would do anything to bring it about.

'I was making coffee. You have to pass the kitchen on the way out anyway.'

Paul sat tensely in the chair gulping hot black coffee. His mother appeared pale and subdued, and he felt a tinge of sympathy for her anguish, although not the least bit guilty at having caused it. Any mother who meddled in her offspring's love life could expect no satisfaction.

'In a way, this is all my fault,' Anne began softly. 'Nicola has been my friend for years, but that doesn't mean I've always admired her. Maybe I should have told you how self-seeking she always was.'

Paul banged down his cup. 'I don't want to hear it, Anne. You'll search for any excuse to try to break us up, but it won't work. All you'll succeed in doing is alienating me.'

'When Nicola was living in her old studio, years and years ago,' Anne continued, as if Paul hadn't spoken, 'I used to drop in quite often to see how she was getting along ...'

Anne had climbed the stairs to the dilapidated, cluttered loft Nicola shared with two sculptors and one painter and pushed open the door. She couldn't see Nicola but heard voices. She caught sight of Edward standing at the window with another man, older and very distinguished.

Anne caught her breath. That was surely Gifford Silversmith, a prominent art critic. Nicola had pointed him out once.

'It's hard to choose,' Silversmith was murmuring. 'The mobile has immense charm, but the sculpture I can visualise on my wicker table, just next to the African violets –'

'Mobiles can be tricky,' Edward said, 'unless you know exactly where to put them.'

'I think you may be right. I'll take the sculpture.'

Anne was excited. Wouldn't Nicola be thrilled that Silversmith was buying one of her pieces, and even before her opening at the Marshall Faber Gallery.

She saw Edward shake Silversmith's hand. 'Then we'll look forward to seeing you at the opening.'

Silversmith looked away for a moment, obviously uncomfortable, and nodded.

Anne's quick mind suddenly took in the true meaning of the transaction. Silversmith wasn't buying the sculpture, Nicola was giving it to him so that he would review her show. And she had gotten Edward, gentleman that he was, to do the dirty work.

Anne left the loft before Edward saw her.

'I never said a word to a soul, Paul, though it did make me wonder about Nicola's character. Silversmith's review was a rave, and every piece in the show was bought up in a matter of days.'

'I don't believe a word of that story,' Paul glowered.

'Oh? You think I just invented the whole incident?'

'Jesus, I don't know what you're capable of, after you attacked her –'

'Ask her,' Anne said confidently. 'Ask your girlfriend what ever happened to that piece. I remember it to this day – an abstract nude female, in welded metal, twisted almost into the shape of a pretzel.' The way I'd like to twist her, she thought.

Paul stood up. 'I don't want to hear any more. I'm discovering a spiteful side of you I don't like. You should be glad I'm in love with a wonderful, warm woman who makes me feel joy, who inspires me to create at the very highest level I'm capable of ...'

Hearing Paul rhapsodise over that venomous snake turned Anne murderous. She wanted to slap Paul, something she had never done even when he was a child. Instead, she shouted at him, 'Was it only a coincidence that she happened to get so chummy with Edward Harrington, a wealthy art collector, when she hadn't dated at all for months after returning from San Francisco? Was it only a coincidence that the grand Silversmith came down to a brand new gallery and gave her a terrific review? Was it a coincidence that Nicola married Edward, although to hear her tell it, he didn't "understand her" and never did? From the moment she met Mr Edward Harrington III her future was assured. He made her, and now that she didn't need him anymore –'

Paul grabbed his suitcase and made for the front door. 'You don't want to hear anything about your girlfriend because you know that I'm right.'

Not having slept for most of the night, Edward dozed off towards dawn and woke up with a start to see sun streaming into the window. It was just after one o'clock.

Even after a shower and two cups of black coffee he felt like a piece of frayed rope.

'Julie, where the hell were you last night?' Edward demanded, unceremoniously bursting into her studio.

Julie fixed large, surprised, innocent eyes on her father. 'I went to a party at my friend Monica's house and slept over.'

'Fine,' he said, expelling a relieved breath. 'From now on, leave word if you're planning to be out later than midnight – and that's your absolute limit, young lady.'

A curious smile lurked in the corner of Julie's mouth. 'You seem awfully worried all of a sudden.'

'Not all of a sudden, princess. I always assumed your mother knew where you were. But now I'm responsible for you.'

Responsible. He didn't really care. He just didn't want the cops ringing the bell in the middle of the night.

Suddenly, Julie flung down her paintbrush and ran out of the room. Edward looked after her, annoyed and perplexed.

Edward got on the 'phone to his lawyer. 'I'm having some difficulties with my wife. She's living over in her studio with a – a young punk. She claims to be sculpting him. I want it kept quiet. The sooner she runs out of money – yes, yes, exactly. Just in case.'

Edward hung up the 'phone and drummed his fingers on the desk. Nicola had turned him inside out and upside down. He had always been able to concentrate on anything he did, but now she flickered into view every time he blinked, as if a photo of her were hidden just above his eyelids.

When the 'phone rang, Edward contained his impulse to

lift it. He despised the way he had been grabbing the receiver, the tremulous anticipation in his voice turning to deep chagrin when it turned out to be whoever it was and not Nicola.

Edward's secretary was taking all his calls.

'It's Anne Lurie, Mr Harrington.'

'Hello, Edward. I suppose you're feeling pretty lousy about what's happened?' Anne paused for his reaction.

'Yes, certainly it was an unwelcome surprise,' he answered carefully.

'I'm right downstairs, as a matter of fact, and I'd like to come up for just a moment. I know you're busy,' she rushed ahead, giving him no opportunity to object. 'I promise to make it very quick. Please, Edward?'

He shut his eyes and reached for a cigarette. This was the last thing he wanted. But he knew from past dealings with Anne that she was a persistent woman and that he would have to see her sooner or later. He doubted even she could make him feel worse today than he did already.

When Anne came into his office, Edward was jolted by how much she had aged. She looked forty-five at the very least. Her face was sagging, and she had gained about a dozen pounds since he'd seen her last. Which was, he realised, maybe a year or two ago.

Anne had dressed for the occasion in a navy linen suit with accents of red and white. She looked like a goddamn American flag he thought.

His smile felt frozen on his face. 'Well, Anne, you're beautifully turned out.'

'Thanks. The worse I feel the better I dress. I keep hoping a good appearance will give me a lift. Edward, I'll get right to the point,' Anne continued briskly, marvelling at how sleek and smooth and almost unconcerned he seemed, at least at first glance. A closer look indicated slightly swollen rims around the eyes, and a grim set to the jaw. He was suffering, all right, in his wasp-like way.

'I want you to know, Edward, that I'm absolutely appalled at what's happened. I can't for a moment understand it. In fact, I still can hardly believe it. I suppose you're stunned as well.'

'Yes,' he agreed, though stricken would have been the more appropriate word.

Anne took a deep breath. 'That your wife and my son have set up housekeeping together can only mean that both of them have gone crazy. I'm convinced it can't possibly last, but I feel we have to do something to put an end to it as soon as possible.'

'I see. Do you have anything particular in mind?' Every word wrenched out was torture. He deplored being expected to join forces with this woman, a woman he had never liked, had always felt exhibited all the worst traits of her class and ethnic group – cultural pretentiousness, pushiness, and bluntness bordering on vulgarity.

'Without going into explanations, without assigning any blame, Edward, I think both of us have good reason to make life as difficult as possible for those two.' She looked expectantly at him.

'Yes? In what way?'

Was the man being deliberately dense, or was he such a nice guy that he was going to accept martyrdom and let Nicola get away with it?

'I've never been taught to turn the other cheek, Edward, and I don't intend to do so now. My son has very little money. A small trust fund left him by his grandfather. I have been subsidising his education. Except for his music, he's never worked a day in his life. The best he can do is give flute lessons. Not very remunerative ...'

Edward sat listening to a mother plot the misery of her son. At the same time his gut reaction was to agree to everything so that Nicola would come back to him within days. But he felt like a bystander, watching with objective curiosity while this woman summoned up a crafty vengeance.

'I know you gave Nika the studio as a gift, but she probably doesn't have the smallest piece of paper to prove it. To be frank, Edward, however much she may be infatuated with my son, when the crunch comes she'll choose her art. If Nicola had no studio, if she suddenly had to find a place big enough to hold her materials – which has to be impossible in New York at the moment – the rosy bubbles blinding her to

123

reality would suddenly burst.'

'It's a thought,' Edward granted.

'It's the only way,' persisted Anne. 'Even a couple of months can ruin a lot of lives. My son will have fallen behind in his master's program, probably not be able to write a note, and have to postpone the première of his compositions. And it won't do him a lot of good for the news to get around the music world that he's with a woman old enough to be his mother.'

Anne stopped short, as she felt a lump in her throat interfere with speech. She couldn't bear the thought of what her friends would say, how they would speculate. Would they think she actually condoned Paul's relationship with the famous sculptor? Even encouraged it, perhaps? Anne wouldn't be able to face some of them, jealous and backbiting, who envied her as the mother of a young man with so much potential.

Edward's eyes grew hard as he, too, imagined the gossip in the art world. The smirks of competitive collectors and dealers who had always begrudged him his inherited wealth. Too old to cut the mustard, eh? Wife shacking up with a kid less than half your age! Why, it would even hurt his chances with the young girls, to whom he represented a challenge precisely because he was married to Nicola Di Candia.

'Are you going to let those two live in the studio?' Anne broke in on his musing.

'I'll think it over.'

'But you must have some sort of plan to get your wife back.'

'No, not really. I can't force her. I have always allowed her to be free,' he finished, grimacing at the irony of his words. 'I can only hope she'll want to return very soon, when the – the affair has lost its immediacy.' When that young shit you raised, lady, realises that the unattainable Di Candia is only another piece of ass.

Anne's eyes filled with tears. 'You're a wonderful man, Edward, and you don't deserve this. Success has made Nicola arrogant. She forgets what she was once, and what we both did for her.'

When Edward did not respond, Anne perceived that she was overstaying her welcome. She had made her proposal.

Edward was essentially too decent to have thought of throwing Nicola out, perhaps, but once he mulled the idea over, got used to it, he would see that this was the most practical course of action.

She rose. 'Thanks for taking the time. Just believe that I'm on your side. Anything I can do, anything we can do together, you have only to ask.'

He stood up politely. 'Certainly, my dear. I'll see you to the door.'

Anne, on an impulse, kissed his cheek before slipping out of his office.

Edward returned to his desk, reached into it, and pulled out a half pint of scotch. He didn't blame Anne, in a way. However much she had spoiled that snot, however crass she might be, she was undeniably sincere in deploring her son's relationship with his wife.

But kicking Nicola out of the studio would be only a last resort. There were other ways of undermining a relationship. Anne's appearance had had a positive effect, though not the one she foresaw. It made him think creatively, and he began to concentrate without distraction on how he was going to handle the Nicola-Paul abomination.

Paul was watching Nicola work. Absorbed, she didn't see him. The piece she was cutting was not going the way she wanted. 'Damn,' she muttered, taking up a hammer. She pounded at the stubborn metal, and then stepped back and frowned.

Nicola was totally committed to her art, Paul mused. That Anne could believe Nicola would ever bribe a critic only showed how irrational on the subject his mother was.

'Nicola,' Paul called.

'What?' she asked, abstracted.

'I love you, that's what.'

Her face softened. 'Me too.'

He held out his hand. 'Let's go out.'

'It's raining.'

'Stopped.'

'I can't get this right.'

'Leave it for a while. You can get me right.'

Nicola sighed and looked at him, so handsome, standing smiling and waiting for her.

She took his hand and jumped off the ladder.

Outside, her arm in Paul's, Nicola suddenly felt lighthearted. The rain had cooled off the humid streets, and a fresh breeze was wafting off the Hudson River.

They walked down Christopher Street, looking in shop windows. Paul picked up a stray kitten and placed it in an antique cradle. The kitten, its paws hanging over the edge, looked adorable and bewildered, as the cradle gently rocked, making them laugh.

Nicola, pulling Paul by the hand, led him into a thrift shop and began to rummage through a carton containing random objects. She came up with two stove burners dating back about forty years.

Paul smiled and shrugged to indicate he couldn't imagine what she wanted them for.

When she turned them upright, holding the seven-spoked burners by their connecting pipes, they looked like sculptured iron asterisks. 'For the mantel,' she assured him.

The long-haired proprietor pondered behind his granny glasses and quoted a price. Nicola shook her head vigorously and counterquoted, while Paul looked on, amused.

Finally they agreed on a price and the burners were put into a wrinkled shopping bag showing a big red apple with the legend 'I Love New York' across it.

On their way out Paul took a navy beret off a hook and popped it on his head. He positioned it in the French fashion, making a Charles Boyer-like face. '*Combien?*'

The proprietor grinned and held up two fingers.

Paul paid, and he and Nicola went out gaily, their arms around each other.

They found a sidewalk coffee shop.

'Oh, darling, the seats are damp.'

'*Jamais,*' he declared, whipping out a handkerchief and wiping each chair with a flourish. '*Madame?*'

She sat down.

When Paul asked the waitress for '*deux croissants, deux cappucines,*' Nicola doubled over with laughter.

'You've just ordered two monkeys.'

'*Mais, non!*' He mimed drinking, and the waitress, a bored

126

bushyhaired girl chewing gum, shook her head at such idiocy, scribbled on her pad, and went inside.

Paul unfurled a *Village Voice* and turned to the film section, pointing and gesticulating and speaking fractured French.

'Please stop,' Nicola begged finally, trying to swallow her coffee.

They took a bus uptown to Fifty-ninth Street and went to see *Young Frankenstein*. Sitting with big boxes of popcorn, they laughed all the way through the movie.

Nicola, turning to Paul and sharing a silly moment, reflected that she and Edward had never done anything remotely frivolous.

Paul, looking at Nicola, loved the way she could enter into the spirit of the moment.

In the lobby, Paul suddenly held himself rigid, and his eyes began to bulge in imitation of Peter Boyle's imitation of Boris Karloff playing Frankenstein's monster. Paul let out a menacing growl and lurched forward.

Nicola shrieked with laughter and took off, fleeing all the way to Central Park South, with Paul, his beret hanging lopsided, in stiff-legged pursuit.

5

Julie squeezed into a pale green flowered silk dress imported from China which fit her as tightly as if the silkworms had spun it around her. She looked at herself with satisfaction. In spite of her thinness, she had decent breasts, small but very well shaped. She unbuttoned the neck of the dress to the spot where her bosom began to swell.

'Julie, a package for you,' called Ella, the perky young black girl who worked days for the Harringtons.

'Thanks. Leave it, Ella, please.'

'Wow, you look fabulous. Going to a party?'

'Yes. Lunch at 21,' Julie lied blithely, flashing the girl a secret smile.

'Lucky you,' Ella said, putting a narrow white box on Julie's dressing table and exiting.

Julie eyed the box with contempt. Had that gross sweat factory actually sent her flowers?

Curiously Julie undid the pretty ribbon. Inside the box was one perfect, fragrant pink rose. She didn't see a note.

Julie liked the rose and stuck it in a bud vase with water.

Her hair and makeup finished, she picked up her bag. On her way out she noticed a card stuck in the folds of the tissue paper of the box.

'Julie, dearest, I miss you so much. I'll phone you at three this afternoon. Much love, Mother.'

Crumpling the card in her fist, Julie threw it in the wastebasket along with the rose.

When she got out of the taxi in SoHo it was just twelve-thirty. Julie sauntered down West Broadway until she came to a Chinese restaurant called Oh-Ho-So. She liked the look of the place, with its tinted windows and inviting bar in front. Pressing closer, Julie noticed a very elegantly dressed woman sitting next to a fellow in paint-spattered jeans.

Inside, Julie took a seat at the bar in such a way that she could observe the pair surreptitiously from behind her dark glasses. The woman was lushly dressed, and her long red-lacquered nails were beringed with diamonds. She seemed to have difficulty keeping from touching her companion constantly on the shoulder, wrist, sleeve.

The *maître d'hôtel* came discreetly up to the woman and murmured that her table was ready.

The woman, from a front view, looked to Julie much as she had imagined – rich, bored, married, and of a certain age. The painter had a lean and hungry look. It was clear he was going to satisfy all his appetites.

Julie gave him a provocative glance as he went by, quite startling him. From the mirror of the bar, she saw him stare at her repeatedly.

She drank vodka and tonic, noting the way young men passing by would slow down and glance in to see what the

128

possible action was. She was careful to look away from anyone who didn't interest her.

Then she saw the one she wanted, standing in the doorway and lighting what was obviously a butt. When he looked up, his eyes met hers. She smiled at him, took a long expensive cigarette from her pack, and held it up.

He hesitated for a moment and then came in.

'Thanks.' He was not very tall or attractive but he had appealing light blue eyes and a sensitive look.

'What would you like to drink?' Julie, well lubricated, laughed at his surprised expression. 'Don't look so scared. It's for real.'

'Well, I'll have what you're having. Thanks. My name is Dan.'

'Julie Harrington,' she said, blowing smoke through her nostrils. 'I paint too.'

Dan looked at her curiously and began to sip his drink. 'What is this, a joke? A bet? A dare?'

'I told you, it's for real. My father is a collector, and I think he cheats painters blind, so I'm giving a little of it back. Do you mind?'

She put her hand intimately on his arm.

'Well, no,' he said warily.

At the table, Julie ordered the lunch, making sure to leave her companion a little hungry. She had him interested in her, excited by the way she kept leaning forward so that he could see down her dress. While waiting for the check she jammed her knee against his.

'Do you live far from here?' She slid her hand up his thigh and felt his erection.

'No,' he whispered.

Julie looked round his crummy apartment with satisfaction. His abstract paintings didn't interest her, but she was feeling elated. She had loved paying for his drinks and his lunch, loved making the first moves while he held back, mistrustful at first, then horny but still a little afraid of her.

Julie took off her clothes in as provocative a manner as she could, but when he tried to approach she held him off. She insisted on pouring vodka for both of them from her pint.

129

'Sit still. I'll get your gear off.'

It was neat, the way he obeyed her. He acted as if he didn't trust his luck.

When he was naked she explored his body, the male body, for the first time. She liked his leanness, his scrawny, hairy, slightly bowed legs. His penis, she noted after careful scrutiny, was not as large as the other one she had seen but it was hard and throbbing with desire.

'What would you like to do to me?' she asked.

'Kiss you, make love to you. You're so beautiful.'

'How beautiful. Tell me.'

Dan humoured her, growing more aroused by the moment. He went down on her, to her exquisite delight. This was more like it. This man was truly appreciative.

'Get on top of me,' she demanded in a fierce whisper.

He shuddered and screwed up his face tightly as he came.

She had planned the whole thing, and it turned out just as she wanted it.

He fell asleep shortly afterwards. Julie lay on her side, looking at him curled into the fetal position, breathing evenly like a child. His thing looked shrivelled and pathetic. Then she began to caress him. Dan, only half awake, was muttering something but Julie neither heard nor cared. She rubbed herself against his thigh while fondling him, feeling wonderful when he began to grow under her caresses. Her power excited her to orgasm.

A few moments later she got up and dressed.

Dan was now awake. 'Do you have to go? I'm just getting started.'

Julie said nothing. She had had enough.

'I'll walk you down.'

'Don't bother.'

Made wary again by her cool tone, Dan lay back watching her apply lipstick. 'You're beautiful,' he whispered. 'I really like you. I hope I'll see you again.'

She smiled bitterly.

'You never did tell me what you paint.'

'Nothing that would interest you. Flowers. Watercolours.'

He looked sceptical. 'Is your father really a collector?'

'You mean you never heard of Edward Harrington?'

'Well,' Dan said apologetically, 'I know dealers rather than collectors. I mean, nobody's collecting me yet.'

'Bet you've heard of my mother. Nicola Di Candia,' Julie said, making him a mocking bow.

'Hey, you're putting me on.'

'I am not,' Julie said fiercely.

He saw it was true. Julie didn't see him looking at her speculatively, beginning to understand.

She was dipping into her handbag for a hundred dollar bill, which she laid on the bed.

He frowned, hurt. 'Look, I don't know what you think I am, but –'

'But nothing. I think you're very nice and I'm giving you a present, from all of us,' she said in a hard voice. 'We're loaded. We'll never miss it.'

Nicola let the phone ring twenty times, hung up, and dialled again. Her chest felt heavy, but no matter how many times she sighed it didn't ease her distress. Julie must have got the flower and the note.

Nicola climbed up on her scaffold and began to work. She was putting together an interesting, complex piece, but doing without the helpers she usually had to assist her. Having had no word from Edward, she didn't know how much money there was to draw upon. Nicola had no savings account, and her checking was joint. For all she knew, Edward had already cut her off. She would have to learn to live frugally again.

She wished Paul would get back. He had gone out with a suitcase right after lunch. Nicola was afraid he would have a fight with his mother, which she didn't want. It was bad enough she and Anne had quarrelled so terribly. Paul would eventually be forgiven by his mother, though she suspected that *she* never would be. It hurt that her love had to be paid for with such pain and guilt.

After twenty minutes Nicola put down her torch. She looked at her work in despair. It was as if her bad feelings about Julie were being directly translated into ugly shapes.

At four Nicola dialled Julie again, without success. Then she called Marshall Faber. 'I wanted to ask you how much we got for *Sun Monument*.' It had been sold to a conglomerate in the midwest, to be reassembled in a new outdoor plaza. Nicola realised it had been years since she had been interested in the price paid for any of her works. She could hear the surprise in Marshall's voice when he said one hundred thousand.

'Has it been paid yet?'

'Yes, about a week ago.'

'Uh, to my husband's account?'

'Well, to his accountant, as usual.'

Nicola hung up, annoyed with herself. If she had only anticipated, had only asked Marshall to send the money to her. Now she would have to go to Edward and try to pry it loose.

When Nicola entered his office, Edward was standing behind his desk. A quick glance at his expectant face wrenched at her insides. He was hoping she had come back to him.

'I hope you're feeling better, Edward,' Nicola said sadly, 'and that we can discuss certain financial matters.'

'Certainly we can discuss financial matters, but I definitely am not feeling better.'

Nicola forced herself to look directly at him, to accept responsibility for the hurt she had done him. 'I'm truly sorry.' She sighed. 'I spoke to Marshall and he told me the payment for *Sun Monument* has already come through. If I could have it, please –'

'Out of the question. You spent more than that during the last year alone.'

'Edward, that couldn't be.'

'Here are the figures. If you look at the papers the accountant prepared, you'll see for yourself. Materials, salary for your helpers, travel, hotel bills, clothes.' Edward continued to read in an unrelenting voice.

Nicola was appalled. She had never questioned whose money was paying for what. She had assumed that Edward was supporting her, that the money from her sculpture, while covering some of the expenses, was basically hers, tucked away into an investment, perhaps. Did he really expect her to emerge from a marriage of eighteen years without a penny?

132

'Edward, I'm astonished. I mean, over the years I have sold so many things –'

'And have had so many expenses.'

'But you always encouraged me to stay at the best hotels, to fly first class, to buy the most expensive clothes ...'

'Of course I did. You were my wife. Now you have become somebody else's whore.'

Edward shoved a folder across his desk to Nicola. She tried to read it but found it all a blur.

Sitting back in her chair, she took deep breaths, trying not to cry with humiliation. He was going to make life impossible for her and Paul.

'I will make you an allowance of a thousand per month. And continue to pay maintenance on the studio, which runs to more than a thousand. It costs a fortune to heat that huge barn.'

'But I won't be able to manage,' she whispered.

'You'll have to manage. Of course, if you'd prefer to live elsewhere, and I could sell the studio ...'

Nicola grew faint. Where else could she live? How could she possibly get another studio with no money? Besides, he had given it to her as a present, not that she could prove it.

'I could cut down on Julie's allowance, but she's disappointed enough at the moment.' Edward leaned forward tensely. 'I never planned for such a situation, never dreamed it could happen.' His voice suddenly broke.

'Nicola, come back to me.'

She couldn't bear to look at him, torn as she was between guilt and resentment. He was blackmailing her.

'I can't come back, Edward.'

He swallowed and with an effort set his jaw. 'I see. In that case, my offer stands. You can't reasonably expect me to go into debt to subsidise you and your – your playmate.'

Nicola wanted to get up but was afraid her legs wouldn't hold her. She was more dependent upon Edward than she had imagined. And she was sure he was lying. He was a multimillionaire, everyone knew that.

'From this day forward the proceeds of your work will not be my concern. But as I told you, the money for *Sun Monument* has already been spent. I am counting on it to pay off some of your bills. You didn't give me as much notice of your impending decampment as a typist gives her boss.'

Edward's phone rang. He picked it up and began to talk to a dealer as if Nicola were not even sitting there.

She lowered her head to hide the tears of anger and self-disgust. It was her fault that she was in such a spot. She should have been responsible for her own expenses always and not allowed Edward to take charge of her as her father had done when she was a child. As for getting a lawyer, bringing Edward to court, having her name and Paul's in the newspaper – Nicola felt like hurling herself out of the window.

She waited for him to get off the phone. 'I've been unable to reach Julie and I want to know if she's all right.'

Edward smiled grimly. 'Nice of you to remember you have a daughter.'

'Edward, please. My feeling for Julie has nothing to do –'

'It has everything to do. She's hurt and disgusted, as she has every right to be.'

Nicola didn't argue. 'Has she started taking classes at the League?'

Edward stood up and cut her short. 'I have an important painter coming in five minutes. I can't force Julie to see you, can I? She's not a child.'

'She's my child.'

Nicola recognised the impenetrable look on Edward's face and got wearily to her feet.

They parted without another word.

Nicola was relieved that Edward had not changed the locks. The bedroom looked the same. Her spring and winter clothes were still in the closet. As she glanced at her wardrobe, at her shoes and bags, Nicola realised that she had enough stuff to start her own boutique. She'd have to sell most of it. In the meantime, she wanted only the jewellery.

As she fingered the exquisite pieces, mostly antique, Edward had given her over the years, her emotions churned. It was not possible to go from one life to another without dying a little bit. It wasn't that these baubles could for a moment compete with her feelings for Paul. Only that they reminded her of so many occasions when she had worn them, of so many evenings enjoyed, words exchanged, pleasures shared.

Julie wasn't at home. Feeling like an intruder, Nicola walked slowly around her daughter's room, noting what a strangely impersonal place it was. No special books or paintings, not even her own. Only a map of the world decorated the wall over her bed.

Her eye fell on the wastebasket, and the rose lying in it. Nicola left the room quickly.

When she reached the street it was pouring with rain. The doorman wasn't around, and she stood in the doorway, waiting vainly for a taxi.

Suddenly she saw Julie walking down the street, dripping, holding her shoes.

Nicola's heart stopped for a moment, and she retreated from sight.

Julie, in a reverie, didn't see her mother lurking in the lobby. It wasn't until the elevator arrived and Nicola rushed into it after Julie that the girl seemed to snap back to reality.

Nicola didn't speak for a few moments. Julie looked pale and angry. Where had she got that dress? It looked as if it belonged on a – a callgirl.

'Julie, I know you're very angry. I don't blame you. But silence doesn't help. Please talk to me, even if what you have to say is terrible.'

Julie fixed her eyes on the wood-panelling behind her mother's head and didn't answer.

When the elevator stopped, Julie rushed out, but couldn't find her keys quickly enough.

Nicola unlocked the door, holding it open.

Julie slipped in ahead of her, slammed the door and pushed the bolt.

Nicola stood for some moments. Hot tears stung her eyes as she walked down the hall.

When Paul came home, Nicola was back on her scaffold, trying to work. She had every intention of concealing from him her interview with Edward, but her face was drawn with the anguish she was suffering over Julie.

Paul, himself drained, saw her strained face.

'A hamburger and a beer will do us good. We can celebrate my getting two music students.'

During their meal, Paul spoke with enthusiasm, smiling at her, taking her hand every so often. She began to feel better.

'Let's splurge and order another beer. I've managed to rent my house in New Haven. My trust fund gives me more than seven hundred a month, plus the teaching.'

'That's wonderful.' Nicola ached with adoration. Paul was trying so hard, but there was simply no way to come up with the thousands they would need for a down payment on an adequate studio. Unless she could finish her work and sell it very quickly.

'We'll be fine, Paul. You mustn't let teaching keep you from composing.'

'It won't.' Paul kissed Nicola's fingers, his hot breath making her catch her own. 'With you, I have unbounded energy and inspiration. There's nothing I can't do, no hurdle too great to overcome, as long as you love me.'

Nicola put her hand on his cheek, her face glowing with tenderness. For Paul, that was answer enough.

'Tomorrow, Paul, I'm going to go through my storeroom and see what masterpieces are lurking there.' Nicola was attempting humour, but she could tell from his expression that he wasn't fooled. 'Marshall is always after me to bring him smaller works, even older pieces, that he can dispose of to apartment dwellers who don't have room for my skyscrapers.'

Paul knew she was worried about money, in spite of the brave front she put up. Ripples of love went through him. This wonderful, talented, beautiful woman had given up a rich husband and a comfortable life for him. He simply had to make her so happy she would never for a moment regret it.

When they returned to the studio, he put his arms around her and bent to kiss her neck. 'A greater artist even than you was at work to make such a masterpiece of a woman. And she breathes,' he murmured, between kisses, 'and holds, and fondles –'

'And loves you very, very much.'

'And makes love very, very exquisitely.'

136

In bed they shed their clothes and their worries, losing themselves in each other.

'My darling,' Nicola murmured, 'no matter how much I give you, you always give me more.'

'No, you give me more. Inspiration –'

'Spiritual, emotional, and physical fulfillment –'

'All the joy it's possible to feel –'

'All the joy it's possible to imagine –'

'My very life. Now stop,' he smiled, putting his fingers on her lips. 'I want the last word.'

6

Nicola opened a bank account in her name, into which she put Edward's allowance and the proceeds from her old works that Marshall was selling successfully.

Her jewellery she took to a discreet antique dealer on Madison Avenue and sold every piece outright. They represented her life with Edward – a life that was now over.

Day-by-day living with Paul was wonderful for Nicola. She sculpted while Paul, at the other end of the studio, set up his music, desk, files, and flutes and recorders. It exhilarated her to catch snatches of his music, to know that his absorption allowed him to have the greatest respect for hers. Unlike Edward, Paul would never dream of interrupting her at work in order to make love. Between Paul and Nicola, there was the unspoken understanding that sex vitiated creativity and was to be savoured afterwards.

Each day they knew each other a little better and loved each other a little more. At night they lay locked in each other's arms, believing that any sacrifice was worth being together.

Their only disagreement was over Julie.

'She knows that her refusal to see you is hurtful, and that your love for me has nothing to do with her,' Paul said repeatedly.

'It's not that simple. If you had seen the look on her face, the anger, which I think is only a mask for the hurt. It embarrasses her, I suppose, to think of her mother attracting a younger man.'

'Stop it,' Paul interjected. 'The only thing you can do to irritate me is to see our love through conventional eyes.' He pinned her arms to her sides, the intense look in his eyes setting her blood racing. 'What we have together is ageless and you know it. The rules cannot be the same as for other people, who are subjected to the kinds of pressures we avoid, must avoid, to keep ourselves free to create.'

Nicola smiled and kissed him. He was so much the earnest young artist and she loved him. She mustn't make him feel that he had come between her and Julie. After all, her daughter had been hostile to her for months before Paul.

Nevertheless Nicola awoke every morning with a feeling of despondency. Finding Paul beside her, she would sigh, glad he was there. But thoughts of Julie kept haunting her.

One morning Nicola had a call from Janet Markham. 'I'm going to be in town today. Are you free for lunch?'

'I'd love it.' Nicola chose the Prince Street Bar & Restaurant, in SoHo. It was a simple establishment where one could get an inexpensive sandwich or a salad.

Janet was already examining the ceramic-tiled table top when Nicola arrived. The two women hugged warmly.

'Isn't this fun, Nika? Quite a change from grabbing a tuna sandwich in the kitchen at home. Hey, what's going on? You look absolutely glowing, and yet a little apprehensive. As if you had something to tell me but didn't quite know how.'

'You've guessed it.'

'Before you tell me, and before I forget, I just saw your daughter.'

'My daughter?' Nicola asked stupidly. 'Julie?'

'Of course Julie. Unless you've been hiding another all these years,' Janet joked. 'Julie in the flesh. She came in a few minutes before me and was just buying a pack of cigarettes. She looked awfully beautiful. So grown up, though I was a little sorry to see that she smokes. You don't.

138

Does Edward? It's been so many years I can't remember.'

'Edward smokes,' Nicola said woodenly, her brain reeling with questions. Julie in this place buying cigarettes? What was she doing down here? What about her art classes?

'Did you talk to Julie?' Nicola asked, an edge to her voice she failed to hide.

Janet looked closely at her. 'Yes, of course. We said a few words. She asked after Emily. Nicola, for heaven's sake, what is it?'

'Edward and I have separated. I've moved into the studio altogether. The fact is I haven't spoken to Julie in almost two months. She won't see me or communicate with me in any way.'

'Oh, Nicola.' Janet touched her arm in sympathy. 'I'm so sorry.'

'Janet,' Nicola said, moving her arm away abruptly, 'that's not the whole of it. I – I left Edward because there's someone else.' Nicola continued hastily, 'He's much younger, eighteen years, to be exact.'

Janet looked at her intently for a moment. 'Well, if the separation between you and Edward makes you happy.'

Nicola refilled their wine glasses.

'We'd better order or I'll be looped.' Janet asked for a mushroom and watercress salad.

Nicola ordered the same, but when it came she could only pick at it.

'Julie will feel better by and by,' Janet assured Nicola. 'It's not as if divorce is uncommon. When Kate was little, she came home from school pouting one day because she said she was the only one among her friends whose parents hadn't been divorced!'

Nicola tried to smile but didn't make it. 'You haven't asked me who my friend is.'

'No, I've been waiting for you to say. The time has come for women to be as foolish, possibly, as men have always been. If you tell me you've taken home a tattooed Hindu fakir who charms snakes out of a jug I won't admire you less or love you less than I have always done.'

Nicola shut her eyes for a moment to keep back the tears and get a grip on her voice. When she opened them Janet was looking at her expectantly.

'The truth is probably worse,' she whispered. 'I'm living with Paul Kadin-Lurie. With Anne's son,' she added, so as to hear the shocking sound of the words as they would appear to Janet.

Janet's eyes grew wide, and she put down her fork and sat back in her chair. 'Good God!'

Nicola lowered her head and poked viciously at a raw mushroom with the tines of her fork. 'I'm sorry if I've shocked you.' She forced herself to look Janet in the eye. 'I'm not going to offer any excuses. There are none. We simply fell in love. For me, it was like discovering the ideal man of my youth ... Paul delights me, Janet, he renews me. I have always envied the respect, adoration, and compatibility between you and Tom. Edward and I have never had that.'

'But you do with Paul?'

'Oh, yes. Unfortunately, I'm feeling almost as much pain as pleasure because Anne and I had a terrible parting. Edward is devastated, and Julie –'

'It can't be easy,' Janet acknowledged softly. 'I'll admit that it certainly sounds bizarre. I mean, not just any younger man but Anne's son. But as I rearrange my bourgeois morality, I begin to see how it can be. Both of you so talented.'

Nicola looked at Janet ruefully. 'That's just it. Anne created the ideal mate for me – about twenty years too late. I know it can't last, but I find it impossible to give Paul up yet. Not when we're so happy with each other, so mutually supportive, understanding, loving. At the same time, I can see that it strikes other people the wrong way.'

'All pioneers have to be strong enough to withstand disapproval. It puts an extra burden on a relationship, of course, like a black-white couple. Men have been leaving their wives for younger women for ages. Now women can't be prevented from enjoying that particular pleasure, but it will take people some time to accept it.'

'If it were only the age difference. Anne's son is what makes it so horrifying. And having to lose either Anne or Paul has cost me a great deal, Julie and Edward aside. I don't know how I'll ever tell my parents. I'm glad they're in

Florida. Oh, Janet, it's such a mess.'

'If it will ease your mind about Julie I'll suggest that Emily invite her out to spend a few days. Emily is so sensible. Too much so, sometimes.'

'Julie has always liked you.' Looking at Janet, at her warm brown eyes, her kind smile, her giving nature, Nicola had a moment of self-loathing. Anne was right about her as a mother.

'Artists have no right to marry or have children,' Nicola said dejectedly. 'It's impossible to play both roles adequately. Anne gave her own career for motherhood, and you worked your life out ideally. Your weaving and your pottery haven't detracted from mothering –'

'Stop berating yourself, Nika. I have a minor talent. Anne, well, Anne is another story. You were the one with the real talent, with the vision and the determination to make sculptural history. You had to do what you did. I'm sure some of your toughness has been transmitted to Julie somehow, only she's a little slow in putting it all together to work for her.'

Nicola allowed herself to be comforted because she needed it so badly.

'You're welcome at our house any time, you and Paul. Tom is likely to feel as I do. You know we rate love very highly.'

When Nicola returned to the studio she found Al Lurie perched on a chair listening to Paul playing his new music.

'Please don't stop,' Nicola exclaimed. 'I don't want to interrupt –'

'You're not interrupting,' Paul murmured, giving her a kiss.

Nicola felt self-conscious, and looked guiltily at Al.

He shrugged. 'Who knows what brings two people together. And not knowing, who has a right to judge?' He sighed as he spoke, and Nicola knew he was thinking of Anne.

'We're not just any two people, Al,' Nicola said quietly. 'I understand the way Anne feels. Every mother hopes for the best for her child, and feels such a failure if it doesn't happen –'

'You're the best for me, darling. If my mother cared about my feelings, instead of what the neighbours will say, she'd be happy for us.'

Al shook his head in a way that indicated a hopeless case. 'To be honest, I was sent here by Annie to try to convince you two to break it off. I wish she'd butt out.'

Al gave Nicola a hug. 'Annie, she's a killer.'

'What did she tell you, Al?' Paul asked, alert to his father's serious tone.

Al shrugged in a deprecatory gesture. 'Oh, she gave me some cock and bull story about a critic and a sculpture a long time ago. Maybe I'd better tell you, Nicola, because this kind of gossip could hurt you where you breathe.'

Nicola listened in shocked silence. She turned so pale that Paul was alarmed.

'Darling, I don't believe it for a moment, and neither does my father.'

'Of course I don't believe it.' agreed Al. 'Not that Annie would lie outright. She probably just got it wrong –'

'Gifford Silversmith,' Nicola whispered, 'paid me one thousand dollars for my sculpture *Grief*. He was the first collector, aside from Edward, to have bought my work.'

Al looked at Nicola, and she could see the hesitation there. 'Well, Annie probably just doesn't remember.'

Nicola wondered just what Anne had really seen and heard. 'Al, I feel terrible to think that you're in the middle between Anne and me –'

'That's my luck,' Al said wryly. 'Anyway, I don't intend to continue as her errand boy. I've seen and I'll report, that's all. Annie'll lay off in time.'

'Paul, did Anne tell you that story?' Nicola asked, after Al had gone.

He hesitated. 'Yes, but I knew it was hogwash. Saw no reason to upset you.'

'For God's sake, I'm forty years old! I'm tired of being treated like a child. I want to *know*. What I can't handle is going through life stupidly, blindly, trusting people maybe I shouldn't trust. Please promise me, Paul.'

'Okay. I did mean to tell you eventually.'

At eight the following morning Nicola used her keys to

open the door to Edward's apartment, and she burst into his bedroom.

'Edward, I want to know exactly what transpired between you and Gifford Silversmith. I want to know why I'm under the impression that he bought *Grief* for a thousand dollars, and Anne Lurie thinks I gave him the piece as a bribe.'

7

Bernard Lassiter sat at his cubbyhole at the *Times* correcting galleys of his latest story about the debut of a Philippino violinist of sixteen. For two years Lassiter had been reviewing peripheral performers. When Polini played or Zuckerman, or Fisher-Dieskau sang, or Mehta conducted, the Star Critic had the honour and not he.

Lassiter was inundated by 'phone calls, letters, and fliers from hopefuls and their agents, announcing debuts, clamouring for interviews and reviews. Most of the mail was addressed to the Star Critic, screened by his secretary, and fobbed off down the hierarchy, reaching Lassiter at the bottom.

Just this morning he had been handed a letter from someone called Anne Lurie, touting the talents of her son. It was the usual stuff: a genius on the recorder at four, a prodigy on the flute by seven, a scholarship to Curtis, awards, a bachelor's from Yale ... and then he played ... and then he wrote ...

Lassiter flung the letter from him contemptuously. Where would the Paul Kadın-Luries of this world be without their mothers cutting a swatch for them through the crowded and competitive music jungle? In this case, the lady wielded a machete!

At ten, Lassiter's 'phone began ringing, jangling his

nerves, making his head throb until he wanted to rip the instrument out of the wall.

'Hello, is this Bernard Lassiter? My name is Anne Lurie. I understand my letter has been passed on to you. I'm a close friend of Minna Harper's, who's on the board of the New York Chamber Sinfonia –'

'Yes, Mrs Lurie, I have your letter,' he interrupted curtly. 'I'm sorry, but it would be impossible to interview your son before his debut ...' If you put them off, sometimes they went elsewhere or forgot or dropped down dead from their exertions.

Lassiter held the phone away from his ear and read his latest review. Let her talk herself hoarse.

'Mm hm, mm hm,' he intoned, paying no attention until a name registered. 'Henrietta Kadin?'

'Of course. She's my mother. Paul not only had her example when he was a child but she took great pains to give him a feeling for composition ...'

The relationship between this young man and one of the best known woman pianists of her day was the only thing so far mentioned that had any news interest.

Lassiter thumbed rapidly through his desk calendar. 'The only possibility would be this Wednesday at noon –'

'Wonderful. Come for lunch. You know, we still live in my mother's apartment. Her piano is here, and all her music and books.'

When Anne replaced the receiver she felt good for the first time in weeks. For the lunch, she would make a simple veal scalloppini with lemon and have snowpeas, scalloped potatoes, a bottle of fine wine, a fresh fruit tart.

Things were moving along well. In addition to the interview with Lassiter, she was planning to engage a publicist to work up fliers for the première, to get items in all the newspapers, advertisements on the radio.

Anne got busy with her notebook and cheque book. She had to present her son with such a barrage of dates, appointments, duties, and rehearsals that he would have no breath left afterwards to satisfy that treacherous old bitch.

Nicola didn't know what it was like to live with a

professional musician and composer. A couple of months of neglect and she would crawl back to Edward on her hands and knees.

'Edward, I will not be put off,' Nicola declared, following him into the dining-room.

'I have no idea what you're talking about.'

'My first show, when Marshall Faber opened his gallery –'

'That's almost twenty years ago. How do you expect me to remember that far back –'

'You can remember if Silversmith bought *Grief*, or if you gave it to him, and if the thousand dollars you claim he paid came out of your own pocket! Edward, I must know the truth.'

Edward poured himself a cup of coffee. His cool assurance was maddening to Nicola.

'If I said he bought your piece, then that's what happened. And I consider it an invasion of privacy for you to come and go as you please in my house when you ostensibly have left it.'

'I'm sorry. I still have a lot of things here, my clothes and such –' Nicola stopped, feeling foolish. She was only beginning to see how devious Edward was. He had deflected her question by attacking on another front and she, as always, let him set the condition of their conversation.

'Please tell me how Silversmith happened to ask for one of my pieces. If you reconstruct the situation you'll remember –'

Edward jumped up, anger making him white around the mouth. 'I have better things to do with my time than dredge up the details of a transaction going back two decades.'

'At least you must remember that Anne came to my studio looking for me, and you were there with Silversmith –'

'I don't remember anything of the sort. That woman is irrational with anger at her brat's latest caper. She'd say anything, do anything to make trouble!'

'Edward –'

'No! No more.' He fixed cold, angry eyes on Nicola. 'I don't want to see you or hear from you unless what you have

145

to tell me is that you're ready to return. And, by the way, the offer won't be open forever.'

Edward went upstairs, furious with himself for having risen to the bait, for having shown Nicola how really hurt and angry he was. But he was getting worried. This affair was going on too long. He was fearful, also, that Anne, that stupid cow, in her maternal rage, could cause a lot of unnecessary trouble.

Nicola left the apartment, regretting her refusal all those years to take an interest in Edward's financial transactions. His conversations had always been peppered with the prices he had paid for various acquisitions. He must have a ready reference somewhere. At his office or in his study at home?

She simply had to find out, and she waited in a doorway across the street until she saw him leave the building. Then she returned and let herself in quietly, feeling like a criminal.

Nicola peeked into Julie's room. Standing in the doorway looking at her sleeping daughter, Nicola had an intense longing to awaken her with a kiss, as she had done when she was a little girl. But she didn't dare risk the certain rejection.

For more than an hour she examined every piece of paper in Edward's desk and file cabinet. Finally she located a card file of his collection, including purchase price, and another file for works since disposed of. There was even a folder of cancelled checks, but nothing going back more than five years.

On her way out she opened the closet door. The closet was filled with file cabinets. Up on top she saw the years 1955 to 1965.

The folders were yellowed but the years were visible and the cheques neatly held by rubber bands.

Nicola took out a stack marked 1960 and thumbed through them.

Her heart fluttered when she came to a cheque made out to Gifford Silversmith for five thousand dollars. In the lower left-hand corner was the word 'Grief'.

Paul didn't notice the black Rolls-Royce parked in front of the house until a man sitting in the back called out his name.

The man was wearing a natty straw hat and dark glasses,

like a mafiosa. 'Yes?' Paul said warily.

'Lurie, I'd like a word with you.'

Paul drew nearer. 'I'm sorry but I don't –'

'Edward Harrington. Please get in.'

Paul, after a moment's hesitation, did so. Edward signalled the driver to move off.

They drove in silence. Paul was uneasy. Nicola's husband had staged this dramatic near-kidnap as a sure way of forcing him into a confrontation.

Paul refused to be the first to speak. It wasn't until they were halfway to the George Washington Bridge that Edward told the driver to pull off the highway into a quiet side street.

'Please let my wife go,' Edward began, in a smooth, cool voice. 'I've no doubt you feel strongly about her at the moment, but I speak with the advantage of greater age and experience. The two of you can't possibly last. And when you tire of her, or she gets tired of living like a pauper, your career will have suffered, and our marriage, my wife's relationship with our daughter, as well as yours with your mother.'

Edward took off his dark glasses and ran his hands across his eyes. Then he looked directly at Paul and smiled weakly, as if in pain. 'I'm asking you to do the honourable thing and not steal another man's wife.'

Paul resisted the impulse to speak sharply. 'A wife is not an object to be stolen. We did not easily come to the decision to be together, but our deep feelings for each other have made our commitment inevitable.'

Edward took a deep breath, and Paul perceived that he was trying to settle the matter amicably, like a gentleman. Any moment he would assure Paul that they were both 'men of the world' and Paul's lapse of etiquette could even be forgiven.

'Lurie, if all men were forced to stick with the women they thought they loved at twenty, divorce would be unheard of, and infidelity, and unhappiness –'

'To state the obvious, not all men are the same,' Paul countered. 'My father, for example, has always been a one-woman man, in spite of my mother's insisting on a separation –'

'I, too, am a one-woman man,' Edward interrupted sadly.

147

'My wife and I have had eighteen wonderful years together. You come along, a novelty, flattering her just when she's reached an age of needing to be reassured about her attractiveness –'

'You are not a one-woman man, Harrington. You have quite a reputation as a womaniser. In spite of my love for Nicola I wasn't going to force the issue until I learned of your little diversions with art students.' It gave Paul a certain satisfaction to watch Edward shrink back into his seat.

'Did you tell my wife?'

'No, I did not,' Paul said firmly. 'That would be contemptible. It would hurt her, and it's my intention to give her happiness. How any man could be married to Nicola and crave other affairs is incomprehensible to me. Call that stupidity of youth, if you want, I have loved her since I was a boy. I've never loved anyone else, and most likely never will.'

Edward, exerting all his self-control, veered. 'One of the things you no doubt admire is my wife's talent, her achievement. I've encouraged it, provided the money, the studio, and maids, au pairs and cooks so that she would be free to create. I believe that all creative people need someone in the background to be supportive morally and financially. As your mother has been with you. My wife, Lurie, is a great lady but she's a total egotist. If she's busy welding, and you get stuck on one note, do you really think she'll come down off the scaffold and say, "There, there," to you? Like hell!'

'Your line of reasoning is futile. We've had two months to test our relationship and it works.'

Paul felt that Edward's purpose was to break them up, and nothing Paul could say would change his mind. 'Anyway, Nicola and I feel as we feel. Even if love is blind or foolish or whatever people say it is –'

'You goddamn little snot,' Edward exploded, 'talking to me as if you knew the difference!'

'That's more like it. Let's get it into the open, and stop laying that super-civilised crap on me. You hate my guts, and I'd rather you said so. You and I can't be civilised because we're natural enemies. I can't forgive you for having affairs with other women when you had the supreme honour

148

to be married to Nicola. I don't believe you love her as a woman at all but only as a talent. You've kept her a child, having to come to you for money.'

'Is that what she told you?' Edward shouted.

'No. She doesn't talk against you to me –'

'Then how do you dare give me your ridiculous theories?'

'They're not theories. Nicola couldn't be the way she is with me if you and she had a really good, understanding, free, equal relationship –'

'You little punk, you don't know what the hell you're talking about. Your mother babies you and does all the dirty work while you compose in a goddamn ivory tower. And you repay your mother by shacking up with her best friend!'

Paul glared at Edward and spoke through clenched teeth. 'Vulgarising our love to make yourself feel better doesn't take away one ounce of the joy we have together, the ecstasy –'

'Ecstasy!' Edward snorted. 'I've screwed more women than you'll ever even meet. The one thing my dear wife doesn't provide is ecstasy – which is why, at times, I've had a need for more giving women. That's right, giving. My wife takes and takes and takes.'

'Well, to me Nicola gives and gives and gives.'

'It's only your pathetic ignorance that could make you think that the crumbs she may throw you in bed – and it's early days yet – are one tenth of what a real woman can give a man. My wife, if you must know, is a lousy lay.'

Paul's hands formed into fists, but he resisted the impulse to crash them into the man's jaw. 'Not so lousy that you don't want her back.'

'Let her go,' Edward said, suddenly despondent. 'The world is full of gorgeous gals of your own age.'

'Many of whom are busy sleeping with you.'

'That's not the same thing, as you'll find out someday. Having a young girl is like biting into a fresh, crisp stalk of asparagus –'

'Jesus,' Paul hissed, opening the door.

'Hold it.' Edward put his hand on Paul's arm. 'I'd think it over carefully if I were you. Your mother is half out of her mind with anger and grief –'

'Did she speak to you about it?' Paul asked angrily.

'She came to see me, yes. She's worried and revolted, and I don't blame her. It's disgusting –'

'But you and your girls are appetising, huh?'

'It's not the same thing, as anyone will tell you.'

'Damn right it's not. Nicola and I are in love. We're not just having a dirty affair.'

'Like hell you aren't. Your affair is as dirty as they come, as all affairs are –'

'If I don't get out of here I'll damage us both for good!'

Paul wrenched open the door of the car and jumped out.

'Watch it or you'll be playing that flute down in the fires of hell.'

'Is that a threat?'

'You're living on my property –'

'That's disputable, since you gave it to Nicola as a gift. Aside from anything else, you'd throw her into the street because you "love" her only in relation to you, but you don't care if she's happy –'

'With scum like you?'

'With whomever.'

Paul walked quickly away.

For a long time Edward sat in the back of the car motionless. It was even worse than he had imagined. Paul had him over a barrel. All that bastard would have to do is tell Nicola about his affairs. Edward would deny it of course, but he would be at a definite disadvantage.

The thought that this intolerable liaison was going to go on, that there seemed no way he could put an end to it, made Edward wild. Even if he kicked them out of the studio it wouldn't help. Most likely it would draw them closer together.

Every time Edward imagined Nicola in bed with Paul he wanted to kill her. She was giving Paul what she had always withheld from him! In spite of the way he had baited Paul, Edward sensed it was true, and tears of rage and self-pity made him shake with frustration.

Gifford Silversmith answered the door. 'Miss Di Candia,' he greeted her uncertainly, stepping aside to let her enter his mews house in the Village.

'Sorry to barge in on you this way.' Nicola followed him to the small garden in the back.

If Silversmith had been rising to prominence in the fifties, he was now formidable. His opinion was considered the last word in art criticism, and in addition to writing for prestigious publications he put out his own monthly newsletter. Only people he designated could become subscribers to this esoteric service, and they included the biggest dealers and collectors. Edward, Nicola knew, was one of them.

She and Edward had sometimes socialised with Silversmith and his wife, though usually in a crowd. He had struck Nicola as effete, and she wondered if his marriage, to a wealthy patron of the arts, had been more of a convenience than a love match.

Nicola could not deny that Silversmith had, from the start, praised her sculpture as having great potential.

She declined a drink and went right to the point. 'I always thought that you bought my early work, *Grief*, for a thousand dollars. But I have just discovered that – that my husband gave you the piece –'

'My dear Miss Di Candia,' he said sharply, frowning, 'I can't possibly cast my mind back so many years. I do vaguely remember having acquired the sculpture in question. After a while I believe I disposed of it to a German collector.'

'Mr Silversmith,' Nicola said, summoning up her courage. 'In addition to the sculpture, Edward apparently gave you five thousand dollars, presumably so that you would review my show favourably.'

'*Apparently* gave me five thousand dollars?' He stood up. 'Let's go inside, for God's sake. This conversation might just as well be televised.'

Nicola noticed how frail he was, thin and stooped, and he walked with a slight shuffle. The skin across his face was tight and shiny, as if he'd had a facelift.

In the living room Silversmith looked her squarely in the eye. 'I deny absolutely the allegation you have made and will continue to deny it. In the matter of your work, I have always been fair and honest in my appraisals. End of conversation.'

151

Nicola awkwardly reached into her handbag and pulled out a photocopy of the cheque, both sides, and handed it to him.

'If you had this document,' he said at length, almost inaudibly, 'why did you put me through this third degree?'

'I'm sorry. I guess I was hoping for some valid reason. I see I've been incredibly naïve all these years.'

'Naïve is just the word. What do you intend to do with this piece of information?'

Nicola had a moment of compassion. He looked to her like an old queen about to be exposed as a fraud.

'Nothing. All I want to know is what you really thought of my work.'

His tensely clenched face muscles relaxed when he realised she was not going to blackmail him but was concerned with her ego. 'Harrington came to me with your slides, oozing extravagant praise. It was obvious that he was in love, but I knew him to be a man of sound judgment. I looked at the slides and detected some promise. But before I could say a word he offered me one of the pieces, plus an auxiliary payment, as an inducement to attend the opening. He did not request that I write a favourable review, mind you, only that I appear. The fact is that I needed money badly at that time.' Silversmith's mouth turned down in an expression of remembered misery. 'It was the most unfortunate period of my life. I was having to pay out a vast sum for a purpose that cannot possibly interest you. The point is that Harrington offered me money I desperately needed, and since I was not expected to compromise my integrity –'

'Integrity,' Nicola repeated incredulously.

'Exactly.' Walking to the door, Silversmith turned. 'I would never,' he said haughtily, 'accept a work from an artist I didn't truly like.'

8

'Anne's invited me to lunch. She's found a rehearsal hall. I'll have to start rehearsals very soon. Darling, I'm going to be very busy until the première, and probably horribly neglectful of you at times.'

Nicola kissed Paul's cheek. 'Part of what I love about you is your absorption in your work. It makes me feel less guilty for doing my own. And I so want you to have a stunning première.'

Paul kissed her eyes, cheeks, tip of her nose, and her lips, murmuring 'love' after each kiss. 'I'll set Anne straight about Silversmith –'

'No, Paul, please don't. There's no point. Anne won't think any better of me. I promised Silversmith I wouldn't spread the story. He's an old man, and probably no worse than any of the other critics.'

'All right, if that's what you want.'

'Enjoy your lunch, and please don't fight with your mother no matter how she may provoke you.'

'You provoke me,' he whispered. 'I'll see you later.'

Anne had fussed to get every detail correct. Her best luncheon china was on the table, and fresh flowers. She had hired a young couple, music students, to serve and clean up.

When Paul arrived at eleven she glanced critically at him. 'Oh, Paul, I wish you'd worn a tie. But never mind,' she amended quickly, when she saw his look of dismay. 'You might as well be comfortable.'

He looked at her suspiciously. 'Who's coming for lunch? I assumed it would be just us, to talk about rehearsals.'

'We will, of course, but I have a special surprise for you. First, before I forget, I've set up an appointment next

Friday with Bachrach. You must have some decent photos.'

Anne led Paul into the living room, talking all the while. 'I've met a wonderful cellist, a young woman named Patricia Earle. She plays the way I would if I'd continued my studies. She would be so magnificent in your ensemble.'

'What? I *have* a cellist. You've met Sondra, and heard her.'

'Yes, and frankly, she stinks. She plods through everything with so little verve and imagination that it makes me want to weep.'

'You've never said a word against her before –'

'I know. There seemed no point, since it was the best you could do. Now you could get Patricia Earle.'

'Anne, I'm sure you mean well,' Paul said steadily, 'but Sondra will remain my cellist. She's a very gifted performer.'

'Not like Patricia. Wait until you hear her – don't jump,' Anne added quickly. 'The final decision is yours, of course. All I ask is that you audition her. She's a find, teaches at Hunter, and she's only your age. A wonderful girl, with a lovely personality.'

Paul looked reproachfully at his mother. 'You mean she just happens to be invited for lunch.'

Anne's glance wavered. 'Well, yes. I thought you'd hear her afterwards. Besides, I think our principal guest might be impressed. She happens to be beautiful.'

'No way, Mother.' Paul stood up. 'This girl will not substitute for Sondra even if she plays like Jacqueline DuPre.'

Anne raised her voice. 'I've knocked myself out to hire a PR man, to interest critics, to get you a rehearsal hall with such good accoustics that a dying cat would sound like Oistrakh, and all you can do is criticise –'

'I'm not criticising.'

'You are. I've been working for weeks on your première, months, in fact, in spite of what you've done to me that has shortened my life by years, and all you can say is that Sondra must be your cellist.'

'She understands the music, interprets it beautifully.'

'She's fat and splotchy-faced and makes a terrible impression, if you must know. Appearance matters. Use

154

Sondra for recording, if you get that far, but a beauty like Patricia –'

'Jesus, I'm not running a beauty contest.'

'Of course not. And I'm not suggesting a no-talent beauty but a fabulous girl who has both.'

'I have something to say, Anne.'

She quickly gave him all her attention. Could it possibly, miraculously be that Paul was parting from Nicola?

'You've been a wonderful mother to me,' he said unexpectedly. 'I wouldn't be a composer at all if you hadn't worked so hard for me. I know it, I'm grateful to you, and always will be. But the time has come for me to take charge of my own affairs. I'm no longer a student. I want to earn my own living and take the responsibility for my own life, musical and otherwise.'

'But you don't know the first thing about it. I've acted as your agent –'

'I know. I want to be my own agent now.'

'This isn't your idea,' Anne snapped. '*She's* put you up to it. She wants to get you as far away from me as possible, hoping you'll become so dependent on her you'll never drop her even when you're sick to death of her –'

'Anne, be careful. Leave Nicola out of this. She has nothing to do with it.'

'I can't leave her out of it. Oh, she's clever, you fool, she has more guile in her little finger than you could ever imagine. She doesn't show it directly, of course. On the contrary, she probably hasn't said a word against me.'

'I told you to lay off about Nicola,' Paul said flintily. 'You've caused enough trouble already with your insinuations about her integrity which were totally unfounded. And going to Edward was disloyal to me.'

'Who told you I went to Edward?'

'He told me. He gave me some very unpleasant moments, but never mind about that. I handled him without knocking his teeth in as he deserved.'

'You knock *his* teeth in? He's the husband, the injured party. He could kill you, God forbid, and no jury would convict him.'

'I don't want to talk about that now. You think Edward is a great guy, but for your information –'

'I'm not interested!' Anne cried. 'Every suggestion I make you oppose. You want to be your own agent, you won't listen to Patricia Earle –'

'That's right. I'm not interested in her. If you're hoping she'll seduce me away from Nicola you'll be disappointed because your meddling won't get you anywhere.'

'How dare you!' Anne shrieked at him. 'You wretch, to impugn such a motive to me! It never even crossed my mind! That's a disgusting insinuation. I won't forgive you for saying such a thing to me.'

Paul grew calmer. 'Okay, I take it back. It was probably unconscious on your part.'

'Don't you trot out your pocket Freud to me! I don't recognise you, Paul. You're not my son since that bitch got her claws into you. That oversexed creature has pulled you down into the mire where she is.'

'Mother, if you call Nicola one more name I'm walking out of here.'

'*I'm* walking out! I'm the one that set this whole show on the road. Without me you'd be nothing!'

Paul recoiled, stunned. 'If you think that, I'm going to have to find how just how much of a nothing I am.'

'You've let her wrap you round her finger! There are millions, billions of girls in the world your age. You didn't have to pick a mother figure, for pity's sake. Didn't I mother you enough?'

'She's not a mother figure –'

'Of course she is. There can be no other explanation.'

Paul's rising anger peaked. 'Nicola is my lover. You can be many things to me, Mother, but not that.'

Anne rushed to him and slapped his face with all her strength. 'I've always loathed your father's vulgarity, and now I see it in you.'

Paul turned and walked to the door, but Anne rushed to intercept him. 'Before you walk out, I'm walking out! I mean it. I wash my hands of you from now on. And your career. You can get your own photographer, your own rehearsal hall, your own PR man. I am withdrawing my services, *and my money*. You undeserving little bastard!'

Anne rushed down the hall and slammed out of the front door.

Paul, trembling with a mixture of anger and anguish, remained, his face smarting, his eyes burning. He lost track of the minutes he stood there trying to fight the hurt of her brutality. Not that he was blameless. Nicola had been right to caution him against a fight with his mother that neither could win.

Finally, Paul realised that the doorbell was ringing, and nobody seemed to be answering. He went himself.

A small, slight man stood there, crisply dressed in a suit, shirt, and tie.

'Good afternoon. Bernard Lassiter.'

Paul shook his hand. He had read Lassiter's criticism. So this was his mother's surprise guest.

'Come in, Mr Lassiter. I'm afraid my mother has been called away, and I don't know how long she'll be. If you'd like to wait.'

'Okay. We can have the interview meantime, Mr Kadin-Lurie.'

'I'm sorry but I'm not feeling very well. I'll have to excuse myself.' Paul turned and raced to the bathroom, where he was violently sick to his stomach.

Bernard Lassiter, standing awkwardly at the door of the living room, felt like an idiot. He had accepted an invitation to lunch from a hysterical, obviously unstable woman who was standing him up. And not only was the son a complete nonentity, he had actually had the arrogance to refuse to be interviewed!

Lassiter's rage went to his head and started one of his migraines. Bristling at having been dismissed by that snotty mama's boy as if he were a servant applying for a job, the critic stormed out of the apartment.

He was not going to find that insult easy to forget!

Anne strode down West End Avenue oblivious to everything but the shooting pains in her chest. She wouldn't be surprised if she were having a heart attack. There was just so much a person could stand.

She had given up her career because of Paul. For twenty-two years – and nine months – she had been concerned with his life as with nothing else. Paul, Paul, Paul. He had always

157

come first, before Al and before Timothy, a quiet and obedient son who had never given her a moment's trouble.

Paul had been a problem from his conception.

When Anne missed her period she wasn't unduly concerned because she had always been irregular. She and Al had advanced from petting to lovemaking so imperceptibly that she never really thought of the danger.

True, she wasn't feeling too well. She had lost weight and couldn't face breakfast, but that pleased her, since she was always dieting. It wasn't until she noticed that her skirts weren't closing properly at the waist that she went into a panic. Anne bought a wedding ring at the five and ten and under an assumed name had a pregnancy test.

Learning it was positive, she looked pleadingly at the doctor. 'I'm only seventeen. I'm a music student. My husband isn't working ...'

'I'm sorry, but I can't help you. After your baby is born I'll fit you for a diaphragm.'

Anne left the office feeling that her life was worthless. If she jumped from her eleventh-floor apartment window she would be killed instantly. Or swallowed a whole bottle of aspirin, slit her wrists in the bathtub.

She began to be sick in the morning. The more fearful she was, the sicker she became. Nicola noticed something amiss but Anne simply couldn't tell her. Her friend was innocent and wouldn't be able to help. Anne made inquiries for a cheap, reliable abortionist but without success.

One afternoon she came home from school and found her mother waiting for her, on her face a look of loathing. 'You slut!'

'What do you mean?' Anne whispered.

'I never thought you'd go this far to spite me, you tramp. You're caught, aren't you?'

Anne began to cry. 'Please don't be angry.'

'Why should I be angry? Because you're throwing your life away? Because I've been knocking myself out so you'd get into Juilliard?'

'Who told you?'

'Nobody needed to tell me. I could see for myself. The

box of Kotex unopened for more than a month, you heaving your guts up in the morning for the last week.'

'Oh, Mother, what am I going to do?'

'You'll marry that slob and go to Paris. Study at the Paris Conservatory. Your father and I will pay. When you come back after a year, nobody will remember when the baby was born.'

'I don't want a baby,' Anne cried. 'I don't want to marry Al.'

'You should have thought of that sooner.'

'No, please –'

'Don't tell me no, you whore. You have to learn once and for all that your actions have consequences. You've probably destroyed your career by this spiteful, low thing you did. But even if you've ruined your life, you have no right to kill a life you created.'

'But lots of girls have abortions –'

'Not a Kadin. That child could turn out to be a musical genius. My mind is made up, Anne. We'll say no more about it.'

Al was foolishly happy to agree to everything.

In Paris Anne could have found an abortionist but she was married and over three months pregnant by then. Throughout her pregnancy she was constantly sick and only sporadically attended classes. How could a pregnant woman play the goddam cello anyway?

Anne hated Paris. It was cold and damp, and Al embarrassed her in front of her friends with his stupid jokes.

Paul's was a difficult delivery, a breach birth, and he was a demanding infant. After a horrible year and a half, during which they returned to New York and lived in a crummy walkup on the lower East Side, Anne had had to capitulate to her mother. She couldn't stand the smell of the halls, the roaches, the dirty diapers, the endless drudgery.

Al earned only a sketchy living playing in Broadway shows, which invariably closed on the third night. Henrietta swept in triumphantly and moved them uptown near her. She and her husband set Al up in the music business.

Anne was startled from her reminiscences when she saw that

she had walked all the way to Lincoln Centre.

It was twelve-fifteen. She called her home. 'Is my son there?' she asked the young woman she had hired. 'He's left? I see. Well, when my guests come, apologise and tell them the lunch has been cancelled. Tell them there's been a death in the family.'

Anne hung up in a cold fury, wishing she had aborted Paul when she had had the chance.

Marshall Faber phoned Nicola to tell her he had received a commission for her work in progress, from an oil company in Houston.

'How much?' Nicola asked, feeling traitorous to her art.

'One hundred and ten thousand. But it's got to be thirty feet high at least. You know Texans. To them bigger is better.'

Nicola had mixed feelings. She had always dreaded having to work to specifications, having to conform to somebody's size of living-room or building frontage. But she needed the money.

For the first time in weeks Nicola had a productive day.

When Paul came home she saw from his face that he had had a harrowing time with his mother.

Nicola greeted him with a kiss. 'Was it that bad?'

'As bad as it is good with us. I'd rather not talk about it, if you don't mind.'

Nicola hugged him. 'Could you eat a dish of spaghetti with fresh clam sauce?'

His weary face relaxed into a smile. 'I appreciate your efforts in the kitchen, but the way to my heart is not through my stomach. You have more important work to do. Say, your piece is shaping up since I saw it last.'

Nicola told him about her commission. 'Pretty soon we can go looking for our own place, Paul.'

When his tense expression returned, she knew something terrible had happened with Anne.

Nicola made a supreme effort to soothe his hurts and banish his worries, but his eyes remained clouded with unhappiness.

Seeing Nicola looking at him anxiously, Paul decided on a

version of the truth. 'I told Anne today that I wanted to take over my own arrangements from now on.'

'Was it perhaps too soon, Paul, coming so close after the shock of us? I mean, she may blame me.'

'I've got to break away,' he replied fiercely. 'She's been too much involved with me. That's why she takes our love as a blow aimed against her, the action of an ungrateful son.'

Paul said no more, and Nicola didn't ask. She had planned to return to work after dinner but she changed her mind. Paul needed her.

Nicola poured them a brandy and led Paul to the sofa. He lay down and put his head in her lap.

'You're wonderfully asymmetrical,' she murmured, as she touched his face.

'Thanks. I love you too!'

'I mean it as a compliment, silly.' She kissed both sides of his nose. 'I can sculpt an Adonis but your face has interesting planes, elusive. From every angle you look slightly different. I can see the structural development from infancy. That piece is left over from age two, I'd say.' She kissed it. 'The curve of the cheek I remember from about ten. But the manly jaw is of recent vintage, and the wicked expression in those gorgeous eyes.'

Paul, smiling, put his arm around her neck and moved her head so that he could kiss her.

'I think we're way overdressed for the occasion,' he whispered, flicking his tongue to her earlobe.

'Way over,' she agreed. She pulled his shirt out of his trousers, unbuttoning and unzipping.

Paul unhooked her bra under her T-shirt. Then he knelt beside her, kissing her belly and inching her trousers and panties to her ankles.

She stepped out of them and took his hand. She was shivering with cold, and he realised she was being careful of how much heat she used.

'I wish I had enough money to give you everything you need –'

'I have everything I need, right here, right now.' Nicola flung her arms around him. 'I love you so much, Paul,' she whispered, 'there are times I can hardly bear it.'

All his worry converted to adoration and desire for this

woman who could turn him inside out with her passion.

They made love for hours, while the candles they had lit burned to stumps.

'Hadn't we better leave something for another day?' She smiled radiantly at him.

'Of course. As soon as I say goodnight to this, and this, and this,' he murmured, kissing her armpit, her navel, and each toe of both feet.

When they finally fell asleep they were exhausted but they had succeeded in shutting out the hostile world.

'Al, this is Anne.'

'I know who it is, sweetie. I've been hearing your lovely voice for twenty-five years. How are you, babe?'

'Rotten.'

'Someday, Annie, you'll call me up just to tell me you're feelin' good.'

'Don't make it worse. I've got to see you right away. If it would be convenient,' she amended, after a pause.

'Sweetie, all you've got to do is call, and I'll come runnin'.' Al motioned a small, chunky woman with dark hair and sad dark eyes to leave the room.

'I'll just grab my tie and be at your place say a quarter to six. I'll pick up some deli on the way.'

'I couldn't eat a bite. I'm too upset.'

Al knew better. 'How about Chinese? Something from that Szechuan place on Broadway?'

'Anything, only please get here.'

'Of course I'll get there. Have I ever let you down, Annie?'

No, he never had. Although she tended to find him unbearable in public, when it was just the two of them he could be amusing. Sometimes he cheered her right out of the doldrums.

'So tell me, Annie,' Al requested, later, over a scotch and soda.

'Oh, God, I hardly know how to begin. You won't believe what Paul did to me today!'

Al listened without interruption.

'He made me so mad, Al, I actually hit him. I never did

that before in my life. And to think it had to be now, and for such a reason. I could tear Nicola's arms out by their sockets. She put him up to it, I know she did. My beautiful lunch was ruined. I had to throw it in the garbage, and with veal at nine dollars a pound. I'll have to send a note of apology to Bernard Lassiter. When I think how I knocked myself out to get him to come here.'

'It'll all blow over. Paul spent his whole life studying and practising. And letting you do for him. Now he's got his own woman and he realises he should take charge of himself. That's all it is.'

'Are you siding with him?' Furiously, Anne removed Al's arm from her shoulder. 'After everything I've told you –'

'I'm not taking sides, sweetie. I can understand how you feel, but I also can put myself in his place. Annie, if you love him you've got to let him do what he wants and be what he wants and with whoever he wants to be.'

'I can't accept him with her, I just can't. She was so sneaky about it, too, meeting him in London and never even telling me. Bringing me back a gift, as if she were still my friend.'

'Well, it's hard to argue with love, sweetie, as I know very well.'

'You don't know. You're just trying to make peace but it won't work. Paul may be a child but she's old enough to know better. Love! She's ridiculous.'

'People can love at any age,' Al said, taking Anne's hand.

'I'll never forgive Paul for what he said and did today, never.'

'You don't mean that, Annie.'

'I do mean it. He made a fool out of me. Well, we'll see how far he'll get on his own.'

'Don't you think that's a little extreme, to just drop him when he was counting on you?'

'He should have thought of that before saying such horrible things, before defying me the way he did. It's my money and I'll spend it how I please. Let his girlfriend pay for him.'

Al took Anne in his arms, stroked her hair, and kissed her cheek. 'I know it hurts, babe, but after you simmer down a little the two of you will kiss and make up.'

'I won't lift a finger. I'm the injured party. He can apologise to me. I've spoiled him rotten, given him everything he might want even before he wanted it. Well, from now on he's going to have to beg me.'

'If I beg you, do you suppose we could heat up the food now? I'm starving. I got some terrific stuff, sesame chicken, sautéed string beans, Szechuan shrimps ...'

Although Anne had unburdened herself she lacked her usual appetite.

'A little aggravation does wonders for the waistline,' Al joked. 'Hey, babe, do I see a little smile lurking? Take another swallow of the chicken and a gulp of beer and it might just break through.'

Anne began to feel better. They watched *The Magic Flute* on television, which she had hooked up to her mammoth speakers. Although opera wasn't Al's favourite kind of music, he sat through it patiently.

'Do you have to go home tonight, Al?'

'Nope. I'm staying right here with my sweetie.'

Anne, hungry for affection and reassurance, let Al make love to her. He did so gently and sweetly, caressing her for a long time to make sure of her pleasure before his own orgasm exploded.

In the morning Al called Paul from his office. 'Have you got time to have lunch with your old man? I'm buying.'

'Sure, Al. Thanks. It'll be good to see you.'

They ate at P. J. Clarke's. 'You know me, kid. Simple tastes. Give me a steak and french fries and I'm happy.'

Paul knew his father had seen his mother, and that this lunch had a purpose. He was curious to know what it was.

'Your mother is upset, as you can imagine. And I think you are too. A quarrel can be made up with a 'phone call.'

Paul worked his mouth. 'I can't do that. She said some pretty terrible things to me.'

'Sure she did. And you said some not-so-nice things to her. It was a fight. People hit a little below the belt.'

'More than just a little. My dear mother assured me that without her I was nothing.'

'You know she doesn't mean that –'

'Wrong. I think she means it exactly. She doesn't respect me because I've been lazy and spoiled and weak enough to let her run my life. I have to arrange my own première or forget about it.'

'Yeah, I see what you mean. What does Nicola say?'

'I didn't tell her much about it. I don't want her to worry. She had cautioned me against fighting with Anne.'

Paul sighed heavily.

'Listen, Paulie, I know your mother has withdrawn her support, and I'm here to fill in with the bread for the première.'

Paul looked at his father gratefully. 'Thanks but I can't accept, though I appreciate the offer. This is something I have to do myself.'

'Sure you'll do it yourself. I won't turn up at rehearsals with my sax. Listen, timing is everything. I don't want you to postpone the concert because you don't have the money. Your musicians won't be able to hang around indefinitely. Please, kid, do me a favour and say yes.'

Paul hesitated. 'If I did accept, it would be only a loan.'

'Sure. Whatever. Someday when you're rich you'll pay me back. Listen, you're my son too, and I'm proud of you. Let me give you something for a change. I mean it, Paulie.'

'You've always given me a lot. The gift of laughter, for instance.'

'So let me keep you laughing by giving – lending, *lending* – you a few bucks.'

'Okay, if you really want to do it.'

'You bet I do.'

It struck Paul, looking at his father's earnest face, how sensitive and caring he was. Without strings.

'So what's the boy genius thinking now?'

Paul smiled. 'Nicola says I've inherited the best of both my parents.'

'That's better than the worst. Take me. I got my father's bald head and my mother's *touchas* instead of the other way around.'

Paul suddenly lunged across the table and hugged him. 'I love you, Dad.'

It took a while but Paul eventually found an inexpensive rehearsal hall, in a warehouse soon to be renovated. Then he allowed himself to tell Nicola a laundered version of his break with his mother. 'She's not to be reasoned with. Took it as a personal insult that I want to be in charge of my own musical life. I told her several times that I was grateful for her help, but she just blew her top.'

Nicola was sure that Anne had blamed her for Paul's decision, but she didn't mention it. 'It will work out for the best. Artists have too great a tendency to let others handle practical matters, and it makes them too dependent.'

She was, of course, thinking of her own relationship to Edward.

'Yes, I know. My father has turned out to be absolutely great.'

Nicola smiled. 'I've always thought he was. And it will give him pleasure to do something for you, a pleasure that maybe Anne has monopolised.'

Paul agreed, but he was still feeling touchy about accepting his father's money. 'Well, we're going to start rehearsals tomorrow. I've invited the ensemble for a wine and cheese thing tonight here to celebrate, if that's all right with you.'

'It's fine. I look forward to meeting them.'

Paul caught a look of apprehension in her eyes. 'Afraid they'll disapprove?' he asked gently. 'They won't, you know.'

As soon as Paul introduced the six young people to Nicola there was an exchange of compliments. She had loved the way the ensemble had played Paul's music; they were entranced by her sculptures and walked around the studio, awed.

Nicola, alert for any intimations in their speech or behaviour that smacked of the generation gap, saw none.

Joe Yarrow, the oboist, tall and thin, with thick glasses, was Paul's closest friend in the group. Apparently he knew all about Nicola, and his attitude towards her was warm and approving.

Sally and Nat Cohen were fairly recent newlyweds. She played the piano, he drums and assorted percussions. They smiled a lot and held hands, reminding Nicola of Paul and herself.

Jayson (Nicola never did catch his last name), the violinist, and Taylor Whitley, the French-horn player, were, at first glance, prototypes of serious musicians – quiet, self-contained, and remote.

But Paul was such a relaxed host that his charm and easy banter were communicated to the others, as well as to Nicola. She knew that Paul considered Sondra Thomas a very gifted cellist. Immediately she felt an empathy for the lumpish, unattractive girl who seemed highly intelligent and sensitive.

There was some shop talk, revolving around Fred Felix, the music department at Yale, and individual concert tours. Jayson, flushed from the wine, told an amusing anecdote about a concert in Ohio, where the conductor's daughter was intent on seducing him.

'Of course you resisted,' Paul said, smiling.

'Of course I didn't,' Jayson countered, a sly expression replacing his customary earnestness. 'She was awfully attractive. I later learned she makes it a habit to sleep with all visiting musicians – and she has a special liking for violinists.'

'Ha! Sheer ignorance.' Nat tapped expertly on the table. 'If she really wants experienced hands she should try a drummer.'

His wife gave him a playful shove.

'What did the conductor's daughter look like?' Sondra asked wistfully.

'Oh, reddish hair, good figure, sort of a Jill Clayburgh type.'

'Wow. I adore Jill Clayburgh. She was great in *An Unmarried Woman*,' Sally declared. 'Anybody see that?'

Sondra had. 'It was a pretty fairy tale, but not very illuminating. She's young, beautiful, and rich. So what if her husband left her – and he was a creep, anyway.'

'True,' Sally agreed. 'You just knew she'd find someone like Alan Bates in about five minutes, even if they had to drag the film out for two hours to make it work.'

'I'd like to see an Alan Bates fall in love with a woman of forty, poor and fat and living in the South Bronx.' Sondra's tone drew a laugh from her peers.

Nicola felt very self-conscious, but nobody even glanced in her direction.

Later, when the others were talking music once again, Sondra asked Nicola, 'Do you use anything special on your hair to get it so soft and shiny? Mine is always so dull and dry.'

'Mine can be dry too. But my hairdresser put me on to a wonderful shampoo and rinse.' She jumped up to get the brochure for Sondra. The firm produced a comprehensive line of nonallergenic cosmetics. Perhaps Sondra would benefit from a skin preparation to fight acne.

The girl seemed to divine Nicola's thought. She flushed as she read, but kept the brochure.

'Where is your hairdresser, Nicola?'

'In the East Thirties. I'm due for a trim next week, in fact. If you'd like to come along, I'm sure my wonderful Anita would do your hair too.'

'I'd love to.' Sondra smiled happily.

It was a lovely smile, Nicola thought. Sondra could be far more attractive if she were given a little encouragement.

As the group was leaving, Sondra hugged Nicola. 'I'm really glad Paul's found you.'

In the weeks that followed, Paul and Nicola saw a few artist friends of hers, who also accepted their relationship, and Janet and Tom Markham called in on the studio late one afternoon.

'You're sure we're not interrupting the creative mood?' Tom asked.

'Not at all,' Nicola said, happy to see them. 'As I said on the 'phone, we were coming to a good stopping point.'

'The studio looks wonderful,' Janet said, admiring it.

'I'm glad you think so. I was beginning to wonder if we hadn't made too obvious a statement, with my artworks here, Paul's musicworks there, almost like a backdrop for *La Bohème*.'

Janet and Tom laughed.

'Not a hope, unless we get someone in to do the singing,' Paul said.

Tom looked sceptical. 'You could probably get out some notes, a musical fellow like you.'

'Nope. Strange as it seems, although I know what the notes should be I can't convince my vocal chords to reproduce them. How about a drink? We have white wine and white wine.'

'Oh, I can nip out for something else,' Nicola began nervously.

168

Tom put a hand on her arm. 'Don't you dare. White wine is great.'

'If you start fussing as if you were giving one of your formal dinner parties,' Janet added, 'I'll feel out of place in my jeans.'

Paul smiled at Nicola and kissed her cheek. 'It's not Beekman Place,' he said gently, 'but it's our place.'

'Right. Please forgive my bourgeois lapses.' Nicola kissed Paul a little defiantly, and grinned at the Markhams.

It turned out to be a wonderful evening. Drinks led to dinner out in Little Italy. Paul was relaxed with the Markhams and behaved like a contemporary rather than somebody's son.

'Nika,' Janet said afterwards as they walked arm in arm to the Markham's car, the two men a short distance up front, 'I've never seen you so radiant. You and Paul are wonderful together.'

'You – you don't find us ridiculous. I mean the age difference is so much.'

'Not a bit. It's something one forgets after five minutes. Paul is unusually mature for his age. I only wish Kate or Emily would find someone so together.'

'Anything from Julie?'

Janet's question rippled through Nicola's happiness. She shook her head morosely.

'Be patient, Nika. Julie will come to accept it in time.'

'It was a super evening,' Tom said, kissing Nicola on the cheek and hugging her for a moment. 'You look gorgeous. Happiness is good for you. Don't let it go.'

Paul and Nicola strolled home arm in arm. 'They're almost as much in love as we are,' Paul murmured.

'I used to envy them. Paul, do you know their daughters?'

'Slightly. Emily I haven't seen in years but I used to run into Kate at Yale occasionally. She's at law school there.'

Nicola had completely forgotten. 'What's Kate like? Attractive?' She deplored the tone of jealousy she heard in her voice.

Paul suddenly stopped and took Nicola's face in his hands. 'Yes, very attractive. And nice. And I like her. But I haven't the faintest interest in her as a woman. She has a legal mind, sharp, interesting, but dry. No fire. No passion. No creativity. I love you and only you and always have and always will. So stop being silly.' He kissed the tip of her nose.

Nicola laughed nervously as they resumed their walk. She was being silly, she knew. And yet, stealing a look at Paul's profile, she saw a grim expression. Was there something more to Kate Markham that he wasn't telling her?

Paul was remembering his last meeting with Kate, when she had mentioned in passing that Emily had said a friend of hers at Pratt was boasting about having had an affair with Edward Harrington.

9

Joe Yarrow came out of the University Settlement House on Eldridge Street carrying his oboe. When he got to the corner, he stopped and waited for the light.

'Excuse me,' a voice called behind him. 'You're Joe Yarrow, aren't you? I just missed you at your music class.'

Yarrow looked at the thin grey-haired man wearing a baggy suit.

'Reilly's my name. Reporter for *Soho News*,' the man said, flashing a card briefly in front of Yarrow's face. 'Wonder if I could interview you for a piece we're doing on young musicians ...'

Giving Yarrow little opportunity to object, Reilly took his arm and led him across the street. '... how you make a living, what your aspirations are ...'

'I'm playing with the Felix Ensemble, a group from Yale led by Paul Kadin-Lurie ...'

Yarrow was on his way to rehearsal, but Reilly was insistent. 'Come and have a beer. Look, it won't take more than ten minutes, and I'll drop you off in a cab.'

Reilly led Yarrow into a busy place. 'You sure you don't want a burger?'

'No, thanks. I don't want to eat until after rehearsal. A beer will be fine. Thanks.'

Reilly came back with a hamburger and two beers. He took out his notebook. 'You also play the bassoon?'

'Yes, and the English horn.' Yarrow drank his beer.

While taking notes, Reilly watched his companion through small, shrewd eyes. 'What's the matter?'

'I don't know. I feel terrible. Dizzy, sort of.'

'I'll get you some water.' Reilly jumped up and went around to Yarrow as he groaned softly and passed out with his head on the table.

Quickly Reilly moved his half-eaten hamburger next to Yarrow. Then he shouted, 'Hey, someone get an ambulance. This guy's passed out. Maybe something in your hamburgers.'

Reilly extricated himself from the crowd that had gathered and ran out of the restaurant.

He found a phone. 'Okay, man, go to work.'

'Where's Joe?' Paul asked. 'It's not like him to be late for rehearsal. We'll have to begin without him.'

A few minutes later, a slight young man with very straight brown hair slipped quietly into the rehearsal hall and stood at the back for a moment, listening.

Paul, conducting, noticed him standing there, holding an instrument case. 'Hello. Can I help you?'

'Hi. I'm a friend of Joe Yarrow's. He can't make it. A stomach upset. He asked me to fill in for him. We're buddies from the settlement house. Poor Joe had to go home and lie down.'

'Okay,' Paul said. 'Glad to have you.' He shook hands and introduced himself.

'John,' the man said briefly, taking his oboe from the case.

Paul explained what was being done, to which the oboist listened carefully.

After a while, Paul, relieved that Joe's friend was a competent musician, stopped worrying about him.

While the ensemble played, the oboist reached into his case on the floor next to him and secretly turned on a tiny tape recorder.

'Hello, Nika, it's Mama. It's so long since we talked to you. Is everything all right? Julie, and Edward?'

'Yes, Mama, fine. Didn't you get my cards? How are things with you?'

'The same. We swim, we sit in the sun, I cook and clean. And no matter how I try to stop him, Papa is always helping the neighbours fix their cars. Listen, I got the most stupid phone call from Mrs Kadin, you know, your friend Anne's mother. I swear, the woman must be senile. What a story she told me.'

Nicola felt an empty sensation in the pit of her stomach.

'That you were having an affair with her grandson, and what kind of daughter did I bring up. I never heard anything like it in my life. I told her she was watching too much television.'

'Hello, Nicola, I'm on the extension.' Dominic's voice sounded weak, as if every word cost him an effort.

'Papa, how are you feeling?'

'Every day brings me closer to God, but I'm not complaining.'

'Nika,' Theresa Di Candia broke in, 'you should tell Anne to speak to her mother. I was so upset. I don't ever want to have another conversation like that the rest of my life.'

'Mama, Papa,' Nicola had to shout into the phone to be heard, 'I'll write you a long letter soon.'

'We don't want a letter, we want you,' Dominic said. 'You haven't been down to see us in a long time. It's getting cold in New York. Why don't you and the family come down for a week or two. It'll do you good –'

'I can't, Papa, I'm so busy.'

'Nika,' her mother said, 'what's wrong? I hear something in your voice.'

'Nothing is wrong, exactly. I can't tell you on the phone –'

'It's true, what that woman told me! Dom, I'm going to faint!'

'Please listen, Mama, Papa, and don't judge until you hear the whole story –'

Her mother gave a shrill cry of anguish.

'It is not for us to judge,' her father said. 'God judges.

And he punishes. Is it true that you've committed such a sin?'

'Well, Edward and I have separated –'

'You're with that boy of Anne's?' Dominic's voice was barely audible.

Nicola couldn't reply, as her mother's sobbing filled the phone.

'Where is my granddaughter?' Dominic asked.

'At home. I – I mean, with her father –'

'Many things we have tried to understand,' Dominic went on in a strained voice. 'The way you live, the work you do. Mama and I have prayed for your soul, prayed God to forgive you for your sins. Marriage out of your faith, our granddaughter not a Catholic. But now, no more. We cannot go where Satan rules. We have no daughter.' He hung up.

'I've come to pack my trunk, Edward.'

He let Nicola in, but his face was stony. 'You know where everything is,' he muttered, walking quickly away.

Nicola felt a peculiar wrench. She had spent half her life with Edward, and even though she didn't doubt that being with Paul was what she wanted, in a strange way she didn't want to lose Edward entirely either.

Emptying her drawers and closets, Nicola found the process as painful as when she had left her parents' home so many years before. In many ways, Edward had been like her father.

It came to her with painful clarity that her parents and her husband had very little understanding of her. She had written her parents a long letter but doubted it would make them any less hurt or fearful for her soul. Times changed but not for them. To some extent, though, Nicola respected the intensity of their religious belief. It was the way she felt about art.

On her way out, Nicola stood at the door of the living room where Edward was reading the papers. 'Edward, I don't want to part on bad terms. Please believe that I'm fond of you and wish you the best.' She held out her keys.

He didn't take them but rattled his paper stiffly. 'I can't

believe that you can just walk out of here after all these years.'

Nicola's heart ached. 'Please don't make it harder –'

'Why in hell not? Why should I make it easy? Would you?'

Nicola stopped at her daughter's room, from which rock music was coming. She knocked.

'Come in.'

Julie sat at her dressing table in her tight Chinese dress applying makeup to her eyes. She saw her mother in the mirror.

'Get out.' Julie's voice was flinty. She had already drunk over half a bottle of vodka.

Nicola swallowed painfully, taking in the bed littered with clothes, high-heeled shoes flung around the floor. Her daughter looked ten years older and harder.

A chill of apprehension overcame Nicola. 'Julie, why are you dressed like that?'

'None of your business.'

'Don't let your anger and hurt push you into something you're too young to handle –'

Julie laughed harshly. 'One of us has to grow up. It damn well isn't you. Now get out of my room. You're trespassing.'

Nicola couldn't move. The pain rooted her to the ground.

Julie suddenly flung her hairbrush, narrowly missing her mother's head. 'I said to get out.'

'I – I just want to say one thing,' Nicola whispered, close to tears.

Julie looked at her mother with loathing. 'Anything you have to say to me will be obscene, like you. I hate you. Get out.'

Nicola fled to Edward. 'What's happened to her? Is she on drugs or something? She's not acting normal. And she's dressed up like a – a call girl. Edward, can't you do something?'

'What do you want me to do, lock her up? She's made a few friends at the League and is going out, that's all. She's home before twelve every night. What more do you want? For her not to enjoy herself? To remain a child forever. You just don't want to be reminded that it's her turn to have

174

some fun and that you're the goddamn fool who's not acting her age!'

Paul arrived at rehearsal with a splitting headache. He had spent all morning trying to clear up a muddle with Carnegie Hall, first on the phone, then in person.

'It's a mess.' He accepted the two aspirins Sondra handed him, and gulped them down with water. 'The guy that books the appointments wasn't there, and someone else insisted we were down for October and not November. I thought he'd given away our day.'

Joe Yarrow arrived just as Paul was coming to the point of his story.

'Sorry about yesterday, Paul. The strangest thing happened to me –'

'It's okay, we managed. Hope you're better. Anyway, when the guy actually looked up the schedule for November ...'

Joe Yarrow, relieved that Paul wasn't going to chew him out for missing a rehearsal and not even phoning, was happy to forget the whole thing.

'Paul, I didn't recognise my daughter. She looked grotesque. And her hatred ... I don't know what to do. Edward is simply blind.' Nicola was trembling with agitation.

Paul put down his flute, irritated. He had been on the point of making a very important change in the finale when Nicola had burst in on him.

'Julie is just laying a little emotional blackmail on you. Maybe she can't connect with any one guy so she's jealous of us.'

'Regardless of her reasons, she's not acting normal. She's taking drugs or drink, I know it. She's still a minor. I can't let her do anything she pleases.'

Paul patted Nicola's shoulder. 'There's nothing you can do. Julie's going to have to make her own mistakes –'

'You think it's perfectly okay to dress up like a streetwalker, to call me the most awful names –'

'No, darling, I don't think that at all.' Paul tried to put his arms arounds Nicola but she moved away angrily. 'Well, maybe I do identify with her somewhat. She's trying to grow up and be independent. Mothering can go just so far. Her father seems to think she's all right. She probably is. She was always a sensible kid. You're overreacting, my love. Maybe out of guilt, because you're living with me.'

Nicola rubbed her face, wondering if he could be right. When he put his arms around her this time she leaned against him. 'I'm sorry, Paul.'

'Our first quarrel.' He kissed her hair. 'Let's see how good you are at making up.'

Nicola let herself be soothed and persuaded. The alternative – leaving Paul and returning to Beekman Place to supervise her daughter – was the one thing she couldn't face.

Ivor Lewes flung himself into a seat in the waiting room. His stomach felt as if an electric drill were boring a hole in the lining. Fry wasn't even there, as he had promised.

The receptionist finally called him over. 'Mr Fry has been detained. You're to go directly to this address.' She extended a piece of paper. 'He'll meet you there.'

It was a hell of a sleazy business. Lewes walked into the lobby of a posh building and underwent the scrutiny of the doorman, who didn't bother to disguise his contempt for his visitor's appearance. And when Lewes asked for Fry, the doorman maintained nobody by that name lived there. If Fry himself hadn't emerged just then from the elevator, Lewes would have found himself out on the street.

Fry, looking rumpled and flustered, pulled Lewes into a doorway and stuffed some money into his fist.

A few minutes later Ivor Lewes stood on the corner feeling rotten. He'd done the deed, he'd gotten paid off, and he'd been dismissed. Okay, he had bread, lots of it. So what? He felt as bad now as before, maybe worse. He simply didn't have the guts for intrigue. Literally.

Ivor Lewes had been a scholarship student at the Eastman School in Rochester, a good musician. He was doing fine until some asshole of a teacher gave him a hype about writing music. So he switched to composition but found he couldn't hack it. He went on drugs. When he was high he felt he could outcompose the greats, but when he came down he saw he'd written nonsense. So he took more stuff to feel better, only the more he took the more he needed. Studying became so remote he dropped out in his senior year. Unable to return home, he hitched down to New York and was living rough for the summer, and then Fry found him.

Shit, he'd been happier playing the oboe on Fifth Avenue for pennies than now. Yeah, hot and sweaty and ragged, but his stomach had felt better hungry than guilty. Why had Fry had to pick him out anyway?

'Simple little thing you have to do. Just sit in for someone at a rehearsal, tape the music, and bring it to me. Presto, you've earned yourself five grand.'

Fry, the slimy bastard, hadn't told him the truth. He had to do a lot more. And now his conscience was like a brick crushing the cornflake of his self-esteem.

A sharp jab in his stomach reminded him he had to get some stuff and quick. But where? At least he had the money now. He felt the big wad. It seemed to be burning a hole in his pocket to complement the one in his gut.

'Hi, Annie, how're ya doin'?'

'Not so good, Al. The fact is I'm worried sick about Paul. That's why I'm calling you. I haven't heard a word from him, after all this time. I hope he's not in any trouble.'

'Paul's fine, sweetie.'

Anne felt a gnawing in her chest. 'What's happening? Has he done anything about the première?'

'Sure. It's on, firmed up. Everything's going smoothly.'

'With whose money has he done all this? Hers?'

'Nope. I've staked him. He considers it a loan. Well, someday when he makes it big he can pay me back. Meantime, call it a gift.'

Anne didn't know whether to be grateful to Al that Paul could go ahead after all or furious with him for having made it unnecessary for her son to come to her. But better Al helping than Nicola.

'Is Paul still with her?'

'Yep. Try to accept it, sweetie. They're good together.

Paul's happy, honest.'

'He'd put up a front even if he were miserable. I know him better than you do. Stubborn and pigheaded.'

'Gee, I guess he must take after me.'

'Never mind your jokes. Tell me how the music sounds. He was so worried about the parts for percussion.'

'I don't know, babe, I haven't heard a note. I don't go near rehearsal. Paul wants to do it all himself, and frankly I think it's better that way. Listen, all this talk on the phone gives me an earache. How about I come over –'

'No, no, that won't be necessary.' she said quickly. 'Thanks. I just wanted to know how he was.'

Anne hung up, feeling torn. Paul really was a cold-hearted opportunist. He didn't care how much he had hurt her. As long as he had the money he was going right ahead. It would serve him right if he fell on his face.

And yet she ached to think he wouldn't be brilliantly successful. She had wanted that for him ever since the day he had composed his first song and she had realised how talented he was.

Another thing churning inside her was the wish that something would happen to break him away from Nicola. Why hadn't Edward thrown them out of the studio as she had suggested? Why weren't the two artistic temperaments colliding as she had predicted?

Nicola, I despise you. All this is your fault. I would do anything to get my son out of your clutches.

Julie scanned First Avenue for a taxi. Not a hope. It was six, and people were either coming home from work or going out for the evening.

It was her mother's fault for holding her up earlier. And afterwards her father had come sniffing around her room, asking dumb questions. Like where she was going and all the rest of it. As if *he* could afford to talk. Almost every night he sneaked some girl into the guestroom, if he bothered to come home at all. Julie, whose drinking caused her to awaken at two-hour intervals, would hear female giggling.

She had been doing her number in the daytime because her father didn't hassle her as long as she was home at night.

Well, tonight might be different.

Julie felt triumphant, stimulated, and very reckless. At long last she had conquered her awe of her mother.

Maybe if Julie had acted up as a child she would have been given more attention. Being a good girl had never got her anywhere.

Julie was suddenly aware of a man standing across the street, very shabbily dressed in threadbare jeans and an old summer suit jacket over a T-shirt. His sneakers were so beat up that his toes were showing.

What attracted Julie was his haunted look, as if he hadn't eaten in days, although he didn't strike her as a beggar. She liked his face, narrow, intense, intelligent and young.

Julie crossed the street. 'If you get me a taxi I'll drop you wherever you say.'

He looked at her warily. 'If I get a taxi I'll drop you.'

Julie liked his drawl. Educated. 'Where are you from?'

'Texas, originally.'

'Don't look so scared. I don't bite. I mean, I do bite, but I don't make people bleed.' She laughed impudently when he gave her an appreciative smile.

Suddenly she saw a taxi. 'Come on. I'm going to SoHo.'

He hesitated for a moment, sizing the girl up as rich and wild. Then he got in. What did he have to lose?

'Where do you live?' she asked, looking at him curiously.

'Uh, here and there.'

At West Broadway Julie paid the driver. 'What're you into? Booze, pot, hash, coke?'

He shrugged. 'Anything but booze.'

Julie laughed. 'Too bad. That's my poison. But I'll be happy to get you some coke.' She rubbed his arm suggestively with her fingertips, giving him her most seductive look.

'I wouldn't say no to a snort.'

'You've got it.' Julie walked him to Houston Street. They went into a local bar where she ordered a vodka gimlet, Perrier for him, and then said a few words to the bartender, both her hands in his. It looked a friendly greeting, but she was actually exchanging a hundred dollar bill for a gram.

Julie had learned a lot on the street in the past few weeks. One thing being that a number of her impecunious artists would do anything for drugs, and it made her feel like lady bountiful to supply them.

Julie took her friend to the room she had rented on Bleecker Street, mainly to be able to keep control of the situation. Her landlady was a lesbian who was never at home until the wee hours.

Some of Julie's pickups lived with wives and girlfriends, and she liked those best of all. It gave her a thrill to think that no matter what they were getting at home they wanted what she could give them. And she made no secret of her name, half-hoping it would get back to her folks.

'Okay,' Julie said, once inside her room. 'Here you are.' She threw him the envelope.

'Thanks. I carry my own spoon, anyway. Want a blow?'

She shook her head. 'I don't like stuff up my nose.' She poured out a drink from her bottle of Stolichnaya. 'To good times.'

'Good times,' he echoed, grinning and waving his spoon at her. Julie liked his smile. He seemed sort of helpless, like a guy who came from a nice background but had something eating at him.

Julie lolled on the bed, knees up, her tight dress around her thighs. She opened her legs so that he could see up to her black lace bikini.

He wasn't looking at her but holding his spoon to his nose and sniffing.

'How much do you need?'

'This is plenty. I'm feeling tremendous.'

'What do you do?'

He shrugged. 'A little of this and that. Whatever's going.'

'Why did you leave Texas?'

'No questions, okay?'

'Okay.' Julie felt sympathetic to him. She didn't like to be pumped either. Besides, the answer was obvious. 'I guess you don't like your folks much.'

'You'd better believe it.'

'I don't like mine either. You ever hear of Nicola Di Candia, the sculptor?'

He put his spoon into his pocket. 'Vaguely.'

'Well, she's my mother. And my father is richer than God.'

'He seems to throw some of it your way. Mine hoards it. You're lucky.'

'Yeah, I've got it made,' Julie said bitterly. 'He gives me a thousand plus a month to keep me out of his way.'

'Heavy.' Looking at her with interest, he noticed that her legs were parted invitingly.

Julie followed his eyes, smiled, and waited.

He unbuttoned her dress while she watched his crotch, her desire keyed to the passion she could stir in a man. And this one was stirring very nicely.

When they were naked on the bed Julie found him surprisingly clumsy. 'You aren't afraid of me, are you?'

'No. I just sort of forgot how. It's been so long –'

'How long?'

'A good two, three months.'

Julie pressed against him, taking the initiative. He was very hard and they went at it with vigour, but he didn't climax.

After a while he rolled off. 'Sorry. I'm wearing you out. I sometimes have trouble coming.'

'What does it take? Do you want me to do anything special?'

'No, only make me forget my troubles.'

To Julie a man who couldn't come was virgin territory. She worked on him enthusiastically, doing everything she had learned, including tying him up to the bed with neckties.

She positioned herself on his chest and rubbed against his face, making him thrash and moan and beg to be untied. Julie teased him until his eyes were bulging and then climbed on top of him.

He came, all right. Several times that night.

Julie kept dozing off, but he couldn't sleep. Every time he felt himself going towards unconsciousness he had the most awful sick panic, which jolted him awake.

He looked at the girl as she lay sleeping. She really was a beauty and a wonderful lover, the best he had ever had.

Julie awoke and smiled at him.

He smiled too and folded his hands behind his head. 'I'm thinking of going to Paris for a while. A buddy of mine told me about a great little hotel on the rue Jacob.'

Julie looked at him in surprise. 'You have enough money?'

'Yup.'

'Can I come with you?'

'Sure, if you have your own bread.'

Julie fell asleep once more but he still couldn't. Suddenly he had an urge for a cigarette. He had given up smoking when it was a choice between tobacco or food. Maybe this cute little sexpot had some cigs.

In his previous life he would have hesitated to go through someone's handbag. It just showed the depths someone could stoop to once he broke the ice.

He rummaged through her purse, made of expensive buttery red leather, a little startled by the hundred dollar bills stuffed carelessly into it. He had taken her story about rich parents with a dose of scepticism. Wild chicks like this made up all kinds of stories. More likely she was a hooker.

He didn't find any cigarettes but he did come across her admission card to the Art Students League.

'Jesus Christ! I'm spooked. I'm fucking well spooked,' he muttered, jumping into his jeans. He tore out of the room, convinced he was being pursued by an avenging fate.

NOVEMBER, 1978

10

'How was rehearsal, darling?'

'Terrible. I'm ready to cancel the whole thing. I can't possibly be ready by next week. No sooner do I get the part for oboe worked out when the drum sounds off, or the cello section has to be completely rewritten.'

Paul flung himself on the sofa, where Nicola joined him, taking his head in her lap.

'That's it, soothe my fevered brow.' He kissed her hand and sighed. 'It wouldn't be so bad if I could just concentrate on the music, but having to send out fliers, take an ad in the paper and on the radio, get a new tuxedo ... It just takes so much damn time.'

'What's wrong with your old tuxedo?'

Too tight across the chest, too short in the arms.'

Nicola smiled. 'You're still a growing boy.'

'I'm growing wider, not taller. All that good stuff you've been feeding me.'

'It's muscle, from all the exercise –'

He gave her breast a playful squeeze.

'Conducting, I mean, and helping me to haul my sculpture up and down the scaffold.'

'How did it go today, love?'

'Okay I guess. Next week is Julie's eighteenth birthday. If only I could think of something that would show her I care.'

Paul was silent, so Nicola stopped talking about Julie. It only led to arguments.

'Did you send your mother any tickets?'

'Yes. I wrote Anne a note that I was sorry we had quarrelled and I hoped she'd come to the concert. These last two months I've really appreciated the job she did, all the irksome details she took care of. But it makes me feel good to know that I can do it myself. With Al's money, of course.'

Nicola was trying to make enough money to ease the way for him. At present, she had only about twenty-five thousand and had been quietly looking for a studio, but it seemed hopeless. She needed space, and space cost the earth. If only she could finish her present work. Somehow it was never exactly right. In addition to her anxiety about Julie, she had to do without helpers. And cleaning the loft, going to the laundromat, shopping, and cooking were time-consuming. Paul was wonderful about doing his share. The point was that she had never done her own before.

Still, Nicola wouldn't change her present situation for her old one with Edward. Emotionally, intellectually, and physically Paul gave her everything she had ever wanted.

Nicola continued to stroke Paul's forehead until he drifted into a light sleep. When he awoke after a few minutes, smiling, she bent and kissed him. 'You're exhausted, poor darling. I'll start dinner –'

'No, let's go out tonight. I know this wonderful little place –'

'Italian,' she smiled. 'With checkered tablecloths and chef-proprietor who says "*Mama mia*".'

Paul swatted her playfully. 'Japanese, in fact, where the fish is as fresh as you are.'

When they stepped into the street it was snowing heavily. Paul drew back. 'I wouldn't put a lover out on a night like this.'

'Well, I would, coward. I can already taste the *sushi*, and the *sashimi*, with slivers of ginger –'

'You're pretty full of ginger now.'

'Come on.' Nicola ran into the street, scooped up a handful of snow, and flung it at Paul.

'This, madam, means war.'

They made their way to Second Avenue behaving like a couple of children who had never seen snow before, and arrived at the restaurant red-cheeked, breathless, and glowing.

'You look beautiful, my snow maiden. I may just keep you outside my window all winter long.'

'I'll press my nose against the glass and rub my tummy and make you feel horribly guilty.'

'We'll fix your tummy right now and stoke it up against the elements,' Paul promised, 'starting with a bottle of *sake*.'

They duelled with their chopsticks as they reached for morsels on common serving dishes. Nicola, concentrating on lifting rice to her lips, caught a look of intense love in Paul's eyes.

'You are the only being in the world who can make me feel such joy.' Tears of emotion made his eyes very bright, and Nicola's heart swelled. For a moment waves of love passed back and forth between them like electrical charges.

Then Paul's eyes turned inward. He reached into his jacket for a notebook and a pen and scribbled a few musical notations. 'I've got it! That's it, a phrase that's been on the tip of my imagination all day.'

'I'm so glad you've captured it. Sometimes it helps to relax, to let the imagination float where it will.'

'Mine is floating right now over your beautiful body,' he

184

whispered, pushing his knee against hers under the table. 'I want you.'

The magic of his eyes and touch made Nicola quiver. 'Mmm, me too.'

When they got outside, Paul pressed Nicola against a building and kissed her hard and long and urgently, heedless of the snow falling thickly on their faces.

They took a taxi, during the short ride locked in a damp embrace.

'That driver thought we were mad,' Nicola giggled afterwards.

'Wonderfully mad. He shot me a look of green envy, ready to forfeit the fare for your favours.'

Nicola laughed and whacked his bottom. 'Darling idiot.'

Paul grabbed her arm and held it in an iron grip. 'For that blow you must pay with your virtue.' He lifted her in his arms and moved towards the bed.

'We're all wet,' she protested, laughing.

'I'll dry you,' he promised, his words sending a shiver up her backbone.

'Paul, Paul,' Nicola murmured, much later, 'No matter how much I pleasure you, you always pleasure me more.'

Nicola was awakened from her dreams by the insistent pealing of a bell. She groped for the telephone.

'Yes.'

'Julie's gone. I just got home, found a note, something about Paris. I wondered if she's been in touch with you –'

'No! Oh, God, Edward, I'm coming over –'

'Not now. There would be no point. It's after two and we can't do anything until tomorrow. First thing in the morning I'll get on it and call you back.'

Paul was awake, touching her arm. 'What's happened?'

'Julie has gone to Paris. Paul, I'm so scared. She's only a child.'

He sat up and drew her to him, holding her, stroking her hair. 'There's no reason to think the worst.'

'Paul, I've got to go to Beekman Place.'

'Edward didn't want you to, did he? Try to get some rest, and in the morning –'

Nicola shook him off. 'I can't, I simply can't.'

Her pained look, replacing the one of happiness only a few hours ago, hurt Paul and also made him angry. That son-of-a-bitch had called her just to upset her. There was no damn reason he couldn't have waited until morning.

Nicola began to throw on her clothes.

'Don't go, Nika, please. Chances are he – he has a woman with him.'

Nicola paused, then crumpled into a chair, looking like a lost, frightened child.

Paul got out of bed and sat with her. 'It's cold, darling. Please come back to bed.' Gently he persuaded her.

'I'm sorry to have awakened you, Paul, when you have such a hard day ahead of you.'

'If you rest, I can rest.'

Paul fell asleep with his arms wrapped around her. When she was sure she wouldn't disturb him, she carefully disentangled herself and slipped out of bed.

Julie was in terrible trouble, Nicola knew it, felt it as only a mother could. Against all her instincts, she had let Paul and Edward convince her that the girl was all right. A vivid picture flashed into Nicola's head of Julie in provocative clothes.

Nicola almost screamed with anguish and self-disgust. She had seen, she had *known*, and she had done nothing.

'One of us has to grow up,' Julie had shouted at her during their last terrible meeting.

Growing up, to Julie, probably meant sexual experience. Nicola shook with anguish to imagine what sort of trouble her daughter was in that had caused her to leave home.

'But Edward, how could you not have known what was going on?' Nicola cried, at the door of Julie's room.

'Are you blaming me?' he shot back. 'You think this is my fault? Goddamn it, if it's anyone's fault it's yours. How in hell could you expect Julie to face her friends, knowing that her mother is making such a fool of herself. I did the best I could. A father can't be a mother. She seemed okay.'

'Oh, Edward, we can't kid ourselves, not now.' Nicola accepted her guilt, but she knew that Julie had acted rashly in some way. 'How are we going to find her? Did she go with someone? How much money does she have?' Thinking of her little girl, alone in a strange European city, made Nicola panicky. She read for the tenth time the one-sentence note her daughter had left.

'We'll find her very quickly,' Edward said. His tone of almost patronising determination, sometimes so irritating to Nicola, was now comforting. 'I'll get my people on it.'

'What people?' Nicola wanted to be told that everything was going to be all right.

'Private investigators. I want to know what art courses she was taking, who her friends were, when she left the U.S., when she arrived in France –'

'She could have said Paris to throw us off. She could be anywhere!'

'Calm down. I'll get operatives not only in Paris but in every city in Europe. I'll pay whatever it costs. The best thing you could do is to come home, so that when we locate Julie I can tell her that you're here where you belong.'

'I can't. It would be false reassurance –'

'Goddamn it, if anything happens to Julie,' Edward threatened, pointing his finger. 'It's on your head!'

Nicola couldn't concentrate on her work. The third time she called Edward's office in one day she finally reached him.

'There's no news yet. Give me a chance. But I did find out Julie's been taking only one morning class at the League.'

'You mean she lied?' Nicola gripped the phone tensely.

'Well, you set her a good example.'

'I never lied to her.'

'You omitted to tell the whole truth, to her and to me,' he said bitterly. 'For that matter, Julie hasn't exactly lied. She, too, has simply kept things back. Not saying how many classes or how many hours, or what she's been doing every afternoon. I'm hanging up. Stop 'phoning me every hour. I won't speak to you. When I have news I'll let you know.'

Anne attended Paul's première with Al. For Paul's sake, Nicola was glad. But observing Anne greeting people in the crowded hall, Nicola ached with the loss of their friendship.

Janet and Tom Markham, on either side of Nicola, noticed her longing glances in Anne's direction.

'She'll accept it eventually,' Tom whispered.

No, she wouldn't. Nicola knew she had gone beyond the bounds of Anne's tolerance.

Every seat was filled. Not, perhaps, with all the leading lights Anne could have garnered but with a mostly young, enthusiastic audience. In the first row was Fred Felix, Paul's teacher at Yale and a distinguished composer himself.

When the music began, Nicola forgot all else. She had heard snatches of it but not the entire work. The melodic rhythms filled her with delight and pride, and she listened, enraptured.

At the end, the audience gave Paul a standing ovation. Nicola applauded until her palms tingled, and then hugged Janet and Tom, but declined to go backstage. Anne would be there.

As people were leaving the concert hall, Nicola caught snatches of conversation. 'He's a real composer, not just a musician playing around with notes.'

'Terrific nervous energy that works for him.'

'Full of surprises ... variety of textures ... wonderful harmonies.'

Al had arranged for a buffet supper party at a friend's apartment. Nicola stuck close to Janet and Tom, warmed by the smiles Paul cast at her, but keeping her distance. She had insisted that he allow her to remain in the background.

Al managed to slip his arm around Nicola. 'Well, babe, what do you think of our boy?'

'Absolutely magnificent, Al. But if Anne sees you talking to me –'

'She won't. She's too busy flattering Sam Wright, from the *Times*.'

Paul was persuaded to make a short speech. Nicola's heart swelled to observe his radiant poise, his controlled excitement.

But as he saluted his performers, Nicola felt a tinge of

unhappiness that things could not have been different. If they were contemporaries, she'd be at his side now, openly adoring.

'And thanks to my grandmother, Henrietta Kadin, and to my parents, whose absolute taste in music directed my own ...'

Nicola, stealing a glance at Anne, saw her chagrin at not being singled out.

'And I want to thank especially someone who has been an inspiration for me always, whose work in another field has reached a level of perfection I have always aspired to, and who has encouraged me and understood. My dear friend, Nicola Di Candia.'

The blood rushed to Nicola's head, as surprised exclamations and applause sounded all around her. After a moment's shy acknowledgment, Nicola lowered her head. When Paul saw her embarrassment he went on to focus attention on Fred Felix.

Nicola dared glance up at last. Across the room Anne was standing stiffly, shooting laser beams of hatred in her direction.

'Paul, you promised.'

They were at home preparing for bed. Nicola's head felt swollen from fatigue and champagne. 'It can't do you any good to be linked with me romantically.'

'Now stop it.' He put his hands on her shoulders. 'I *am* linked with you romantically, and proud of it.'

'The way your mother glared at me –'

'Too bad for her. She shook plenty of hands and basked in my glory, considering the fact that without Al there would have been no première.'

He pulled off his dress shirt. 'She's not as selfless as she pretended all those years.'

'Nobody is,' Nicola whispered, thinking with a sudden feeling of wretchedness of Julie.

Paul saw her face. 'Cheer up. Please don't bring me down, not tonight. They liked my music, they really liked it.'

'Of course they did, darling, and so did I. Marvellous and accessible, even to a layman like me.'

'Yes, I hope so. I was telling Sam Wright that I don't want to commune with myself and a few esoteric musicologists with a score in front of them. I want to reach my audience, and I think maybe I did.'

Nicola felt wildly proud of him and happy that everything had gone so well. Paul was on his way!

In bed, however, spurts of anguish flooded through her. As once a hard core of resistance had kept her from enjoying sex with Edward, now guilt over Julie was having the same effect with Paul.

Julie had been missing for more than a week, and not one crumb of information of her whereabouts had been transmitted from Europe, in spite of Edward's efforts.

Nicola couldn't stop thinking that while she and Paul were making love her daughter might be suffering from loneliness or hunger or abuse. She might be sick, she might be dead.

Paul, finely attuned to Nicola's responses, abruptly stopped caressing her and rolled over on his back.

'Forgive me, darling, it's not you, it's me. I simply can't stop thinking about Julie.'

'I know,' he said softly, kissing her hand as she touched his face. 'I wish there were something I could do to help but I can't think what. We just have to wait.'

Nicola dreamed that she was in Paris, walking up and down streets asking people if they'd seen her daughter.

'*Sale vache*' – dirty cow – one woman shouted at her, a woman who looked like Anne. Nicola suddenly saw Julie on a high hill in Montmartre. She called to her to stop, but Julie wouldn't. Nicola tried to run and found that her legs would hardly move. She saw her daughter's figure getting smaller and smaller, farther and farther away. Julie, the child of three, reached the summit of the hill and vanished. Nicola strained and strained to get up the hill but when she reached the top there was only blackness. She tumbled into the inky void shouting, 'Julie, Julie.'

Nicola awoke, sobbing, in Paul's arms. She remained tightly wrapped around him, but sleepless, until morning.

When she phoned Edward's office she was told that he had left for Paris.

Al was reading to Anne from the newspaper. ' ... the exciting première of "Sonnets", by composer-flautist Paul Kadin-Lurie ... colourful compositions, mostly tonal ... uncompromisingly romantic without being in the least reactionary ...'

Anne sat at her kitchen table drinking cup after cup of black coffee and chain-smoking. Her pleasure at the favourable review of Paul's music in the *Times* was soured by thoughts of Nicola, by the memory of Paul's public acknowledgment of his connection with her. How had he dared to credit Nicola with providing his inspiration when it had been Anne who had encouraged him from infancy, had got him the best teachers, worried over every phrase he played and every note he composed. Yes, his music was gorgeous, thanks to Anne and to nobody else.

'Are you listening, babe? Wright calls him a gifted composer, "his shifting mood alternating between contained intensity and effortless elegance ..." '

Anne was so hurt by the way Paul had lumped her together with Al when thanking his 'parents' that she couldn't even speak of it. And after she had hugged and kissed him backstage, letting bygones be bygones, although his apology had been inadequate to his crime.

What would Bernard Lassiter have written if he had attended the première? He had ignored her phone calls and formal letter of apology.

Anne had been irritated when Janet and Tom had come over to greet her, after they had been disloyal enough to sit in Recital Hall with Nicola. They had praised Paul and tactfully avoided mentioning Nicola. Anne had always felt they cultivated the famous sculptor hoping some of her success would rub off on them.

She had seen Nicola looking at her, expecting her to smile and kiss her and tell her everything was all right. Well, Nicola would never have that triumph as long as she lived.

'She looked terrible,' Anne said abruptly, breaking into Al's reading. 'I don't wish any harm to poor Julie, but it would serve Nicola right if she never saw her daughter again. She doesn't even deserve to have a daughter.'

'Sh, sh. What kind of talk is that? I'm surprised at you, babe, being so vindictive. You thought Nicola would hurt Paul's music, but as you saw, he was tremendous. So maybe she deserves a little credit –'

Anne jumped up, furious. 'If you're going to defend her you can get out right now!'

Al looked hurt and turned the newspaper pages glumly.

After Paul's speech at the party, Anne had been unable to remain. Unobtrusively she had slipped away without saying goodnight to her ungrateful son.

Damn that treacherous creature who had tinged Anne's sweet pride in her son with bitterness. Julie would pay her back though. Nicola would find out what it was like to see a child go wrong and not have the power to stop it.

'I've got to go to Paris, Paul. At least I'll be doing something. I can't just wait here listening to the clock tick minute after minute.'

'Even if you find her she'll run away from you. It's against you – against us – that she's doing this in the first place.'

'I know. But if I go she'll realise that I care.'

'Enough to leave me,' Paul finished tightly. 'That's what she wants. Are you going to give in to her? Is that a reasonable demand for her to make?'

With every moment Nicola's resolve weakened. She knew the minute she walked out of the door she'd be weeping. Would she have the strength to go through with it?

Paul saw her hesitation. 'If you give in to Julie it will confirm to her that you never believed in our love.'

'Of course I believe in it. I just want to know that she's safe.'

'Nicola, you don't understand Julie at all. If you go just to see that she's safe she'll know you did it for you, not for her. She'll be reinforced in thinking you just want to ease your own mind but don't give a damn about her.'

'But I do, terribly.'

'If you do, by her reasoning, you'll give me up. She's like a terrorist, don't you see? She wants what she wants when she wants it. She wants you home and living with her father, that's what she wants, and nothing else will do. God, it's so clear to me.'

What Paul was really saying, Nicola felt, was that *he* needed her. He was in competition with Julie.

'Edward's goons will find her and her little ploy will have failed, so maybe she won't try that again.'

'Don't call it a ploy! I saw her, Paul, you didn't. She's devastated. As my parents are. Do you think that's a ploy also?'

'Your parents have a religious justification, but I don't hate their punishment of you any less. Nicola, you have to decide which you want more – me, or the good opinion of the world. And if you choose the world, it makes you no better than my mother, your husband, or anyone who's been trying to break us up.'

'I've already chosen you, Paul, you know that. But Julie –'

Her words were muffled beneath his kiss. 'But nothing. If you love me you must stay.'

'I love you very much, but I – I can't,' Nicola murmured into his shoulder, beginning to weaken.

To their surprise, Fred Felix appeared at the door. 'Can we speak alone, Paul?' Fred Felix looked agitated.

Nicola resolutely reached for her suitcase. 'I'm going –'

'No, damn it, wait a moment! Fred, tell me what you have to tell me,' Paul demanded, anger and fear making him rude. 'I have no secrets from her.'

'Very well. Look at this score.'

Paul, trying to suppress his impatience, reached for it and began to scan it quickly. His eyes widened in disbelief. 'How did you get hold of this? It's *Sonnets*, at least an earlier version of it. I changed the cello and oboe here, and here, and altered some of the flute phrases.'

Paul turned back to the beginning. '*Fantasy in Blue Smoke*, by Ivor Lewes. What is this, some kind of joke?'

'No, I'm afraid not,' Felix said gloomily. 'I picked this up from Weetch and White, the publisher. You'll note the copyright is more than a month ago.'

'But this is my music. Nobody could have copyrighted it –'

'Ivor Lewes did. I know it's your music, and the ensemble knows it. The record reads differently.'

Felix leaned forward, his fine, lined face reflecting the pain he saw in the eyes of his protégé. 'John Weetch was sent a ticket to your première anonymously. Apparently the critics have heard the news as well. Weetch only called me because we know each other. I may be able to convince him not to sue. Ivor Lewes is in Paris and can't be reached. The black and white of it, Paul, is that *Sonnets* is considered a plagiarism.'

Nicola flew to Paul's side, her trip put off in the face of this incredible development that could wreck Paul's career.

11

Bernard Lassiter sat at his desk glancing from one musical score to the other. Kadin-Lurie, that snotty little fake, had overstepped his own arrogance. Not his mother, not even his grandmother would be able to help him now.

Putting a sheet of paper into his typewriter, Lassiter typed nimbly for some moments.

He was interrupted by a 'phone call from their music man in the Paris office. 'Bernard, you're in luck. I never thought I'd locate Ivor Lewes but he turned up at a party given by expatriates. Lewes was high on something, and I wormed the story out of him. Here goes.'

When Lassiter hung up he felt vindicated.

Paul Kadin-Lurie was going to learn what happened to musicians who had a false sense of omnipotence based on too-lavish praise given them by doting parents. Paul Kadin-Lurie was going to wish he'd been an orphan.

Ivor Lewes woke up feeling as if someone had removed his bones during the night. It was an effort even to turn his head. His mouth seemed made of absorbent cotton, his stomach full of needles.

Glancing at the blonde head beside him, he was hit by a tidal wave of guilt, remembering his crime. Someone had pumped him the previous evening, when he was higher than the moon and saying wild things he almost believed.

Wincing, he eased himself out of bed and rummaged in his jacket pocket.

When Julie awoke and sat up, she felt nauseous and dizzy. Her first sight was of Ivor sniffing cocaine. 'Do you have to blow that stuff first thing in the morning?'

'Quit moaning. I didn't ask you to follow me here. You can split any time.' She had become a stone around his neck, even if he was living mostly on her money now.

Julie's eyes welled. She blamed the deterioration of their relationship on that damn coke.

At first it had been so exciting, sneaking off to Paris by herself and hunting Ivor down in the hotel he had told her about. Although he hadn't been overjoyed to see her, once she had crept into his bed he wanted to keep her there.

Things were fine for a couple of weeks, and then a rival for her affections changed everything. Cocaine. The more he took the less he cared about sex. Once her body lost its charm her principal asset was her money.

Julie had thought she knew how to throw money away until she watched Ivor Lewes. He practically forced it on people, along with coke, until he acquired a following of flaky characters with twitching nostrils and both hands extended.

Julie groped on the nighttable for her bottle of Pernod.

'You're a fine one to talk,' Ivor said, 'you're blind with booze most of the time.'

'Because of you,' she shot back, topping up the liquid in her glass until it turned a milky yellow.

'Bullshit. You were an alchy when I met you.'

Julie gulped her drink, and a moment later raced to the bathroom where she was violently sick to her stomach. She had never felt so awful in her life. Awful every morning, whether she drank or not. Later in the day she usually improved, and then the Pernod picked her up.

When Ivor saw her looking so miserable he had a jab of pity. 'Let's go and get a croissant and some coffee, kid.'

'Yuk. I couldn't eat anything.'

'Keep me company, then, come on,' he said gaily. The coke was doing its job of masking the pain and the guilt.

At the cafe Ivor ate both croissants, noting that Julie was getting skinnier every day. The bones were showing above her chest, and even her bosom was disappearing. Strange, that he had ever thought her beautiful. Now he was just sorry for her – when he wasn't being sorry for himself.

'How much money do we have left, Jul?'

'About a thousand. That hotel is expensive. It would be cheaper to find an apartment.'

'Send for some more. Your rich dad will be glad to pay, just to find out you're alive.'

Julie put her head down on the table.

He patted her blonde curls. 'Come on, cheer up.'

'You say that now,' she mumbled. 'Wait until the coke wears off and you start climbing the walls.'

Ivor noticed a well-dressed, sharp-chinned American at the next table reading a paper and drinking *café au lait*. 'Hey, Duke. Glad to see you. I need to score.'

Duke shook his head. '*Rien*, baby. Sold out.'

Ivor felt his gut start to throb. 'That's impossible.'

'Sorry, babe. That's where it's at. I can lay some horse on you.'

'No!' Ivor began to sweat. Heroin would be the end of him.

Duke shrugged and put his cup down. '*A bientôt*, baby.'

'Hey, wait.' Ivor tried to get up but found it too much of an effort. Then he noticed that Duke had left his copy of the *Herald-Tribune*.

Picking it up, Ivor glanced at the front page, read the sports, and turned to the back page.

'Composer's Work a Plagiarism' hit him in the face.

'Paul Kadin-Lurie, 22, whose "Sonnets", a tone poem for seven instruments which had its première at Carnegie Recital Hall in New York City last week, has been accused of plagiarism by music publishers Weetch and White. They copyrighted an almost identical work two months ago titled "Fantasy in Blue Smoke" by Ivor Lewes. When reached in Paris, Lewes, an oboist and composition student at the Eastman School in Rochester, New York, expressed shock that Kadin-Lurie, whom he described as a talented flautist and composer, should have performed Lewes' work with very few changes. Lewes maintains that Kadin-Lurie asked to see his score last year with a view to premièring the work with the Felix Ensemble, associated with Yale University. Kadin-Lurie, after some days, returned the score with regrets. Lewes, at present negotiating for a Paris performance, believes that Kadin-Lurie may have reproduced the music "unconsciously" ...'

'Bernard Lassiter, music critic at the *New York Times*, excoriates "young men of no patience" who have been propelled by parental expectations into taking rash "shortcuts" such as "borrowing" the original work of another composer, making insultingly minor changes, and expecting to get away with it.'

'Paul Kadin-Lurie and Fred Felix have issued independent statements denying the charge of plagiarism ...'

The excruciating pain in his stomach doubled Ivor over. He lurched out of his seat and staggered away.

By the time Julie picked up her head Ivor was out of sight. Afraid any quick moves would cause her to begin retching, she sat erect and breathed deeply, waiting for the sick feeling to subside. Then she had a few gulps of coffee, and ordered a double Pernod.

Waiting for her drink, she started to move Ivor's paper out of her way. The name 'Paul Kadin-Lurie' jumped in front of her eyes.

Julie grabbed the paper, took a quick look and started back to the hotel without touching her drink.

Ivor was lying on the bed with his eyes closed. She shook him by the shoulders. 'You bastard, you've been telling me stories, never letting on you were a musician. Why did you do this to Paul?'

He groaned and lay limply without moving. 'Didn't do anything,' he muttered.

'You couldn't write a note if your life depended on it. Someone must have paid you to do what you did, and that's where you got the bread to come here.'

Getting no reply, she went angrily to the bathroom for water. On the basin she noticed an empty envelope. She dipped her finger into it and tasted. Heroin.

Julie flung a glass of water in Ivor's face. 'Pretending to be an actor, telling me rotten lies.'

'I am an actor,' Ivor sputtered. 'I've been acting for ages. Listen, you don't really want to hear this story.'

'Oh, yes I do, and you're going to tell it to me.'

Julie sat on the bed as he gave a rambling account, slurring his words, until his voice petered out into a whisper and he began to nod.

Julie jumped to her feet. 'Get out. Get your gear and split, right now, or I'll turn you in to the flics.' She fell on him with her fists, hitting him with all her might, venting her frustration on the only person nearby.

Ivor crawled out of her reach while, in a controlled frenzy, she packed his stuff into two suitcases. She flung them outside the door, threw some francs into the hall, and pushed Ivor out, slamming the door behind him.

Julie sat down on the bed, trying to keep her hands from trembling. Delirium tremens. She didn't care. About anything.

Julie poured Pernod into her glass, added water, and drank. By the time the bottle was empty she was feeling no pain. She passed out on the bed.

'Paul, I'm so glad you're home early.' Nicola kissed him. 'The 'phone has been ringing all afternoon. People wanting you to know that they believe in you.'

He took off his jacket, his face tight and unresponsive.

Since the vitriolic piece by Bernard Lassiter, Paul had retreated behind a stance of appearing not to care.

Nicola knew he felt deeply humiliated, and she ached for him.

At first he had reacted with indignation. 'I don't understand why a fellow I never heard of would make up such a story. He must be off his rocker.'

'Simply jealous, I would guess,' Nicola said. 'You've been studying under Felix, you've won prizes, had a private debut at which you performed some beautiful pieces, and quite a few important people were there to hear it.'

'Who probably think I stole that music as well. I don't know how anyone could get hold of my score. Only Felix and the ensemble had access to it.'

That part of the mystery was cleared up when someone remembered the fellow calling himself John who had sat in on one rehearsal for Joe Yarrow.

Joe, when questioned, looked blankly at the others. 'I never sent a substitute. In fact, that day was uncanny ...' A call to the *SoHo News* revealed that there was no reporter named Reilly.

When Paul realised that somebody had deliberately set up Joe's sickness in order to send a thief to steal his music, he grew pensive and withdrawn. Someone was behind it, someone who hated his guts and was out to get him. He could think of only one person with cause – Edward Harrington.

And now Paul felt he was going to fail. As if the original newspaper account weren't bad enough, Lassiter's attack had hurt him badly. Paul knew very well that the critic bore him a grudge for the unintentional snub. Unfortunately, people tended to believe that smoke was caused by fire.

'Darling, nobody who knows you or has heard your music believes it for a moment,' Nicola assured him. 'Who is Ivor Lewes? What has he achieved to indicate he could have written such exquisite music?'

'It doesn't matter. He copyrighted it. And short of a denial, which he won't make, there's nothing I can do.' Except find Harrington and break his arm. He had the motive, the means, and the cold vindictiveness to have engineered such a frameup. Ivor Lewes had fled to Paris – proof, for Paul, that Lewes was only reading from a script someone else had prepared.

Paul's pain hurt Nicola even more than her own over Julie, who still had not been found.

Although Paul didn't say so to Nicola, he now believed, as she did, that their love was doomed. He had counted on being successful, on obtaining lucrative commissions so that he could pay his own way at least. He had even dreamed of showering Nicola with money to buy their own studio.

Now he had to stop kidding himself. How much longer would she be able to hold out, scrimping pennies? All she had to do was jump into a taxi. In ten minutes she'd be back in luxury with a man who had it made. A man whose word nobody would question, who had not been cited in the papers as a pitiful fraud.

Even Al had been unable to lift Paul's depression. 'Listen, we'll take a full-page ad in the *Times*. Joe Yarrow is willing to go to court if necessary.'

'No. Leave it. Just leave it alone. I'll simply have to write something else.' Paul had looked at his father and Nicola with a new cynical expression. 'They say that suffering builds character, so let me at least capitalise on it in my work.'

Nicola, now watching Paul drink glass after glass of wine, felt powerless to help him. No matter what she said, he had a counter-argument. To her contention that everyone supported him, he retorted that nobody knew Nicola's unlisted number except Fred Felix, and it was he who was gathering support. Paul's enemies didn't know where to direct their venom.

'Darling, how about some dinner –'

'Not for me. I want to try something out.' He got up, holding the wine bottle, and went over to his flute.

Nicola felt hopeful. She ate a sandwich and kept out of Paul's way.

When the 'phone rang, she answered. There was a pause and then Anne's voice. 'Let me speak to Paul.'

'He's working now, Anne. It's the first time since – if he could call you back later.'

'Don't give me that crap. Just get him to the phone. This is important.'

Nicola acted purely on instinct in hanging up. Then she took the 'phone off the hook. She didn't care what Anne thought. The one thing Nicola would not do was distract Paul now. Inspiration was mysterious, elusive. If not carried to completion it might be lost forever.

She did some work herself, comforted by occasional bursts of music from the other side of the studio. Nicola didn't like the turn her work was taking but she couldn't control it. Her piece exuded pain, uncertainty, confusion. It wasn't any less powerful, perhaps, but it was certainly a departure.

A little after eleven Paul put aside his flute.

'Feeling better, love?' Nicola smiled at him.

'Much. Forgive me. I haven't been fun the last few days.'

200

Nicola stopped his words with her lips.

'You've been wonderful,' he murmured. 'Your faith has been about the only thing keeping me going. I'm so afraid you'll lose patience with me, with this life.'

'I love you and this life. Darling Paul, I believe in you utterly. I know you will be the composer you deserve to be, and that this injustice will be rectified in time.'

'Only this evening I thought I'd never be able to write another note, but now I feel stronger. Music is bound up in my nature, and if things go wrong, the inspiration doesn't dry up, it simply alters. I see my life in musical terms, and have to express my feelings that way, good or bad. Is it the same for you?'

'Exactly the same.' She pressed against him, loving him terribly, feeling close in their mutual understanding.

'Anything to eat around here? My stomach has that Henry Moore feeling again.'

They laughed, remembering their meeting in London at the Tate, when Paul had said those words to entice Nicola to have lunch with him.

'I'm glad the phone has stopped ringing, anyway –'

'Oh, God, I took it off the hook. Anne called.'

Paul dialed his mother, who was so relieved to hear his voice that she said nothing against Nicola.

'Paul, I'm sick over this business with Ivor Lewes. I wrote to the *Times* telling them what I think of Bernard Lassiter. Just because he missed a lunch is no excuse to write such a vicious article when he never even heard your music ...'

Paul was comforted by his mother's unquestioning loyalty.

'Ordinarily I would have seen to it that the music was copyrighted before rehearsals began. How the devil did that creep get hold of your score?'

When Paul told her, Anne could have kicked herself.

Later, Paul made love to Nicola, feeling better than he had in days. She had stopped talking of going to Paris, and he was going to write a quintet for flute that would leave no doubt in anyone's mind about who composed *Sonnets*.

Paul and Nicola worked long hours with the phone off the

hook. They felt closer than ever before.

Fred Felix wangled an interview with Sam Wright, the critic who had liked Paul's music. Producing scores and tapes of Paul's earlier works, Felix insisted that nobody else could have written the tone poem. He had signed statements from the members of the Felix Ensemble that Paul had altered the music constantly. They reported the circumstances of Yarrow's illness and the appearance of the unknown oboist who could have stolen the score. Wright agreed to a follow-up story.

One evening Anne appeared at the studio. 'Your line was busy. Off the hook, I suppose.'

Anne stalked past Nicola. 'Paul, I have to talk to you.'

Nicola went back to her work – or tried. Anne, when excited, had a voice that carried.

'I've got the goods on that Ivor Lewes. I went up to Rochester and spoke to his teachers at Eastman. The consensus is that he was a decent oboist but not worth a damn at composition. One boy hinted that Ivor Lewes had a problem with drugs, can you imagine? It seems the boy wasn't on good terms with his parents, who are divorced. The mother is married to a Hollywood bit actor and trying to pretend she's a sweet young thing, so she'd rather her son didn't exist. The father has money but thinks his son should make it on his own.'

'Does it matter?' Paul asked wearily. 'What's done is done. I'll continue to compose, and nobody will ever hear of Lewes again.'

'How right you are. He dropped out of school altogether. And do you know what he was doing? Playing in a trio on street corners,' Anne finished triumphantly. 'He could no more write music like yours than I can design furniture. Bernard Lassiter, that prejudiced little jackass, should know better. I'm writing an open letter to the *Times*.'

'I wish you wouldn't, Anne. I'd like to forget about it. I don't want to sink to Lassiter's level and get into a hassle that won't help. Whereas finishing my quintet will do more than anything else to disprove Lewes' claim.'

Anne's face lit up. 'You've already started on a quintet. That's wonderful.' She realised suddenly that he had been working when she arrived. 'I'm sorry for bursting in like this, but I couldn't reach you on the 'phone and I wanted to give you my news.'

'Thanks, Anne. I appreciate your concern but don't write to the *Times* or do anything more, please.'

Anne reluctantly agreed. 'Let me at least finish. Ivor Lewes had no money, but suddenly found the means to pay a publisher to print his music? I don't believe it for a minute. Nobody would publish the work of an unknown, especially before it has even been played, let alone reviewed, without some financial gain. So it means somebody paid. Some envious s.o.b., maybe a colleague of yours, bribed that kid. Paid him to escape to Paris ...'

'I know, Anne,' Paul said, 'I know, and I don't care. Can we drop it now, please.'

'Yes, of course.' Anne tried to be casual but she felt hurt that Paul didn't fully appreciate all the trouble she had gone to to try to salvage his reputation. Which was more than that selfish cow of a 'girlfriend' did for him. Anne couldn't bear to look at Nicola, working away on her scaffold as if nothing mattered in the world except her art. And what was it, anyway? A few pieces of metal stuck together.

But when Anne took a better look at it, she had to admire the power of the sculpture in spite of her feelings about Nicola. Anne's practiced eye immediately saw that Nicola's anguish – whether over Paul or Julie or both – had been transmuted into art. The piece had a nightmarish quality, as if the sculptor were haunted by unbearable memories.

Nicola, who had overheard the pertinent parts of Anne's narrative, was busy welding.

Anne observed that her own son was holding his flute, waiting for her to leave. She was irked by his impatience. 'I don't suppose I could get even a glass of water in this place.'

'Your sarcasm is inappropriate, considering that this is Nicola's studio and you aren't exactly being polite to your hostess.'

Anne tamped down her rising anger. 'It's Edward's studio, to be accurate. Anyway, I can see you don't want me here –'

'You know damn well you're welcome here when you can accept us as a couple,' he said tensely.

'Don't worry, I won't come again. It's only because I

couldn't get through on the 'phone. At least get an answering machine. It's so frustrating to dial and dial and get a busy signal.'

Paul, irritated, slipped the phone on the hook as he walked his mother to the door.

You see? It's ringing already.'

Paul picked up the receiver. 'Nicola,' he called. 'Important. Paris.'

Nicola scrambled down the ladder so quickly she banged her shin. 'Yes, yes, hello, Edward.'

'This is a terrible connection, but I've been trying to get through for hours. I've found Julie.'

Relief flooded through Nicola. 'Is she all right?'

'Well, yes, at least she will be. At the moment she's in the hospital –'

'Oh no! No!'

'She's getting over the effects of alcohol poisoning, but she'll be all right. Also, we're going to have to decide about an abortion.'

Nicola leaned weakly against the telephone table. 'I'll catch the next plane.'

Anne, smelling victory, hovered at the door.

Nicola hung up and turned to Paul, who had grown as pale as she. 'Julie's sick,' she whispered.

'I'm sorry,' Paul murmured. 'I'll come with you.'

She shook her head. 'Darling, you have your work, and of course I'm going to have to be involved with Edward. Julie is in a terrible way. She doesn't even recognise her father –' Nicola's voice broke.

'Paul, come home with me,' Anne spoke matter-of-factly. 'There is no place for you here now.'

Paul whirled. 'Keep out of this, Mother.'

Anne put her hand on the doorknob. 'Certainly I'll keep out of it. It has nothing to do with me. The two of you, in your selfish indulgence, have pushed that poor girl to the edge.'

'Goddamn it, Mother, if you say another word –'

'Please don't quarrel,' Nicola begged wearily, her hand on Paul's arm.

'We have nothing to quarrel about,' Anne agreed, speaking directly to Nicola for the first time. 'You're going to your daughter, as is your duty. Maybe she'll forgive you some day, not only for abandoning her but for seducing the man she was in love with herself.'

Nicola and Paul stared at Anne.

'Oh, yes, she was, it was obvious, the night of Paul's concert at my house. Everyone noticed it, even Al. If the two of you hadn't been so self-involved you would have seen it too!'

Anne left.

Nicola stood with her hands to her face, stunned.

'That's nonsense, darling.'

'No, no, it's not. Oh God, I remember the way Julie was talking to you, and you left her to search for me. She was so hostile to me that night, and I didn't know why.'

'Nicola, please, please let me come with you.'

'Don't you see that I can't? Julie's very ill with alcohol poisoning. She needs me.'

'I need you,' he murmured, his eyes wet with pain.

Nicola couldn't bear to look at him. She was bathed in guilt, drowning in it. 'It's not the same thing.'

Glancing at her watch, she ran to the closet. Her suitcase had been half-packed for weeks.

Paul stood watching her, clenching his fingers. 'Can't Julie return with Edward?'

Nicola shook her head. 'To him she's a pretty toy. He loves her in his way, but right now my baby needs her mother.' Tears sprang to her eyes.

Paul crushed Nicola to him. 'Let me come to Paris. I won't interfere. Let me just be there.'

'Oh, Paul, I wish you could, but it won't work. Julie must see that I'm alone. I must take care of her, get her well. Then, when she's stronger, maybe she'll understand how it is with us.'

Nicola moved out of his arms and snapped her suitcase shut. She put on her coat.

'Nicola,' he whispered. 'Edward may have exaggerated –'

'No. She – she's also pregnant.' Nicola burst into tears and flung herself into Paul's arms. She had never felt so awful in her life. The thought of leaving him caused her unbearable grief, which was compounded by worry over Julie.

'I've got to go now, please, Paul.' Nicola broke away once more and resolutely picked up the suitcase, wiping her eyes and swallowing her tears.

At the door she turned to look miserably at him.

He felt that she was already thousands of miles away. 'Please don't sacrifice our love to Julie,' he said, his voice low, unable to rise above the hurt in his throat.

'I don't want to, darling, but I'm afraid I've already sacrificed Julie to our love. If only it's not too late. No, let me go quickly. I'll call you as soon as – as I can.'

During the taxi ride Nicola sat with her hands over her face, thinking of Julie, pictures flashing into her mind of a beautiful, smiling little girl. Poisoned, and pregnant. It was agony even to think of it.

If only Paul could understand that just because Julie needed her more didn't mean that Nicola loved him less. But Paul was not a parent. How much maturity did she have the right to expect from someone who had been on this earth for only twenty-two years?

Paul sat in the studio for hours, not noticing that it was now dark. He felt as if he'd been dropped from the top of the World Trade Centre. his bones and blood and guts and heart shattered on the sidewalk.

Had it been only a dream, an illusion, lasting a few months? Had he fooled himself that Nicola loved him, that he could make her happy?

What if Julie was only an excuse? He had noted the way Nicola, without thinking twice, had reserved a seat on Concorde. Edward, of course, was paying.

Once Nicola was with her husband, surrounded by the comfort and respectability he could give her – and Paul could not – would she ever come back to him?

He moped around the studio for six days, unable to compose or do anything except brood and worry and miss Nicola terribly. Every once in a while he would rush to the 'phone from some far corner of the studio, sure that he had heard it ring. Several times it did, but the caller was not Nicola.

Finally, he forced himself to face what must be the truth.

Nicola was back with Edward, really back with him, in spite of everything she and Paul had meant to each other. No doubt it had tickled her sensuality to play house with Paul for a while, but at the first excuse she had opted for luxury.

Angrily Paul wiped away the wetness on his cheeks. A surge of pride went though him. He wasn't going to sit around here like a piece of her scrap metal waiting until she was ready to have dealings with him again.

PART III

WINTER – SPRING, 1979

1

At the first sight of her daughter, lying in a hospital bed, so thin that her face looked skeletal, Nicola had to exert all her control not to break down. She sat at Julie's bedside waiting for her to awaken. When she did, she looked at her mother but did not speak. Nicola saw from Julie's reflective expression that she recognised her. Putting her hand over Julie's, Nicola pressed it gently, tears glistening on her cheek.

Edward, hovering behind Nicola, expelled a sharp sigh.

There were no words, but Julie let her mother hold her hand until she fell asleep again.

In the corridor, Edward said, 'She's more than eight weeks pregnant. I've found a doctor who will perform the abortion –'

'We'll have to discuss it with her first.'

'What do you mean, discuss it? Surely there can be no question –'

'There is certainly a question, Edward. It would be Julie's baby. She has to make the decision.'

'You've flipped, you really have. All this fraternising with youth has caused you to lose whatever sense forty years of living ought to have given you. I just can't believe that you want your daughter to be an unmarried mother just because it's chic in some circles.'

Nicola did not let Edward's insults ruffle her. In his querulous tone she heard the first note of guilt. Julie had been in her father's charge when she had managed to get herself pregnant.

'We'll talk about it tomorrow, Edward, please. I'd like to go to my room at the hotel now. I'm rather tired. Julie will sleep for several hours, the nurse said. And it will take her some time to recover. There's no question of an abortion now.'

'She can't have that child. God only knows who the father is.'

'Our first thought must be for Julie, and what she wants.'

'She doesn't know what the hell she wants,' Edward snapped. 'You should have seen how she was living, and with whom. When I got a tip from my contact I rushed up to this sleazy hotel and found the concierge trying to break down the door. Outside was a character of the worst sort, so dopey on drugs he could hardly talk, claiming Julie had stolen his money and thrown him out. I actually had to give him a handout to get him off my back.'

For most of every day and evening, Nicola and Edward remained with their daughter. Julie refused to talk or look at Edward at all. Towards her mother she was watchful and rather triumphantly hostile. Nicola read her expression to mean, I've finally done something to make you take notice, to make you leave your lover and your art and come to take care of me, for a change.

During the four or five hours Nicola tried to sleep at the hotel, she thought of Paul with a mixture of emotions.

She wanted to call him but the situation was as yet unchanged. Julie was still so ill. Any day there would be an improvement, and then ...

'How long is this going to go on?' Edward asked, after a week. 'Julie's better. Isn't it time we got this business solved so we can go home? *I* can't talk to her about it.'

As soon as Nicola sat down in Julie's room, the girl turned her chair and looked at the window.

'Julie, I'm sorry. For everything.' Nicola did not know how to go on. She wanted to help Julie but she didn't even know how to communicate. Who had told Julie about birth and death, about love between a man and a woman, about pregnancy? Had she? Or the au pair?

'Darling, I'm sure you are aware of – of a matter we have to discuss very seriously because time is passing by, and the more we delay, the harder it will be.'

Julie felt a rage rising in her. Her parents didn't care about her, only about the inconvenience, the shame. She bolted out of her chair so quickly that Nicola jumped.

'Don't worry, I'm not going to have it. I don't want a whining, puking, shitting, horrible red-faced monster,' she screamed. 'I hate it! It makes me sick every morning. I don't want a big fat belly like some gross cow! I don't want it. I don't want anything!'

Julie tried to open the locked window, and failing, rammed her fist through the glass.

Nicola dialled the studio over and over. She asked the operator to try. But there was never any answer.

Finally she called Al's house, and was startled to hear Paul's voice.

'Paul, oh, Paul!'

'Nicola, for God's sake. What's going on . . .'

The rest of his words were lost in a noisy crackle.

'Paul, I'm afraid Julie is very bad, even worse than I thought. She wouldn't speak, then she tried to jump through a window and – and now she seems to have withdrawn into a trance.'

'I'm sorry,' he shouted into the phone, hearing the echo of his own voice. 'When are you taking her home?'

'Well, I'm not sure. The doctors here think she may be schizophrenic. I'm trying not to believe it. Oh, Paul, it's been a nightmare.'

Paul, hating himself for the bitterness he'd been feeling towards Nicola, shouted, 'Darling, please come back as soon as you can. We'll work it out –'

'I can't, Paul, not now. That's what I'm trying to tell you. We can't be together until Julie is better. It's just too much for me, and Edward blames me for everything.'

'To hell with Edward. I'll deal with him.'

'You can't. He's her father. Besides, there's some truth in his accusations . . .' Her voice faded.

'Hello! Hello!' Paul jiggled the 'phone button frantically. 'Don't hang up. Give me your number. I'll call you right back. Hello!'

'Paul, are you there? I can hardly hear you.'

'Yes, yes, I'm here. Please don't say we can't be together.'

'I'm trying to make you understand. This is more serious than I thought. It may take a long time. I can't be at the studio with you until my daughter ... ' Again her words faded.

'Nicola, I need you! I need you now! I'm not playing games –'

' – not a game for me either! You're supposed to be an adult, but she's still a child, and a very sick one.'

'She's manipulating you –'

'That's a monstrous thing to say!'

Nicola's anger was feeding his own, on top of his anxiety of the past week. 'You're giving in to Julie because it's too hard for you to be your own woman and do without luxury and respectability.'

'Oh, God, you refuse to understand! You're still so *young*, just as your mother warned me.'

'And you're just as stupidly conventional as my mother! You don't understand your daughter any more than Anne understands me!'

'I can't have this conversation now. Edward is waiting for me.'

'*I'm* waiting for you. Hello! Hello!' All he could hear was the echo of his own words, mocking him. She had hung up.

Nicola put her head against the phone and wept. Paul, for all his surface maturity, was his chronological age after all. It was madness to have entered into this affair. She could not go on with it, not now. Paul would have to wait. And she would have to wait. Julie had to come first.

Paul, after staying with his father for a couple of weeks, found a small two-room apartment in an old building on Sullivan Street. It had what he needed, even down to the street noises. They comforted him, and he found in the sounds of life corresponding notes for his quintet.

Paul advertised in the *Voice* for music students and succeeded in finding several.

He disciplined himself not to think of Nicola. When he couldn't help it, he remembered morosely that he had begged her to come back and she had hung up on him. And not called again. Al had tried to make excuses for her, but Paul could not be mollified. He was too angry, too hurt.

Nicola had taken the first opportunity to cut out. Her

spoiled little daughter was having a prolonged temper tantrum, refusing to speak, maybe even holding her breath until she turned blue, and Nicola was indulging her to the hilt. Meanwhile Edward paid the bills. Poverty wasn't Nicola's bag, and Paul had nothing to offer but that, and love. Well, she'd taken his love – great greedy doses of it, until she had enough.

Anne, as soon as she heard that her son had found his own place, invited herself for a visit.

'It's charming,' she declared, walking around the tiny apartment appraisingly. 'I'll make you some pillows for the couch.'

'Please don't fuss, Anne. I'm okay as it is.'

'I'm not fussing. I know you bought the furniture from the previous tenant and it's fine, only I thought with a little colour –'

Paul impatiently went to the window and turned his back.

Quickly Anne changed the subject. 'With so many students, do you have enough time for composition?'

'Plenty.' He had nothing but time. The last thing he wanted was to go out, see friends, be reminded.

'You must be short of cash.'

'No, thank you, I'm fine.'

'I understand that your precious Nicola hung up on you in Paris.'

Paul leaped to the sink and put water on the stove to boil.

'According to Janet, Julie is in a terrible way. Suicidal and hysterical. The Harringtons,' she said, dwelling on the name, 'had to put her in a private sanitarium in New York. Bars on the windows, the whole bit. Nicola, it seems, is there all day every day. Of course she's moved back home with her husband. A married couple closes ranks when tragedy strikes. Everyone blames them for neglecting Julie.'

Paul, his back to his mother, reached for a loaf of bread and cut four slices.

'So much for her grand passion for you. You're not to blame, of course. You don't have the experience to recognise –'

'Drop it, please Anne.'

She was pleased at his calm tone. 'Anyway, a mother always chooses her child. The pangs of childbirth are

215

nature's way of forging the closest bond in the world.'

Paul busied himself buttering toast, and then had to discard one slice because his knife ripped a piece out of it.

'I was speaking to Leila the other day. She knows Galway personally. If we could get him to première your quintet –'

'No. First of all, it's a long way from being finished. And second, I haven't changed my mind about doing things my own way.'

Anne, listening to her son's depressed voice, decided not to push further. Little by little she would regain his confidence and when his pride finally allowed it, she would resume her role in his musical life. Certainly she would see to it that the dreadful stain on his reputation was wiped away.

At least he wasn't defending Nicola any more.

'I was thinking, Paul, that if you wanted a few things from your room at home to put here –'

'No, thanks. I like the place uncluttered.' Paul took a deep breath and brought the toast and coffee to the table, keeping his head down and his eyes averted. He didn't want his mother to see his tears.

'Maybe you're right. It is a small place after all, but exactly right for one person.'

As soon as Nicola walked into the vastness of her studio she was hit with such an acute longing for Paul that she cried out his name.

Only a layer of dust, and a pile of mail, showed how long she had been away.

On the door Paul's keys hung. There was no other trace of him.

Prowling the empty studio and looking with shocked lack of recognition at her work in progress, Nicola admitted to herself that at the back of her mind had been the expectation that Paul would have come back and be waiting for her. In spite of their fight and the fact that she had hung up when her husband approached, she had been hopeful. Edward had assumed she was crying over Julie, and had comforted her. It had been dreadful. Nicola had hesitated to call Paul again and risk a replay of the anguish and frustration, heightened by a bad 'phone connection and the distance between them.

She blushed now to think of her misplaced vanity. Yes, Paul had said he needed her, couldn't do without her, and so on and so forth. But he was young and attractive, and a man. Why should he wait around for a middle-aged woman to sort out some severe problems with her daughter?

No, Nicola would have to let it be. Even though she had longed for Paul so terribly, and Julie was not yet in any condition to disapprove.

The fact was that Nicola's great romance had ended sooner than she wanted, but it would have to end some time. She wouldn't get in touch with Paul.

Up and down she paced for thirty minutes, unable to draw a fresh breath in the studio although she had opened all the windows.

In the end, she reached for the 'phone and dialled Al.

The woman Al lived with answered. 'Paul's not here. He got his own place. No, I don't know where. Al could tell you.'

Without giving her name, Nicola said that wouldn't be necessary and hung up. She was white and trembling. For Paul, it was definitely over. The reality struck her like a blow in the chest.

The studio reeked of Paul and their love. Every corner of the place had become invested with his aura. That was where he had kept his files, that chair was the one he had sat in when composing. There was the mirror he had installed for her so that she could see her work from a different perspective.

Nicola felt an unendurable aching depression. She couldn't live here. She couldn't even work here. Taking only the clothes she needed, she fled to Beekman Place.

The chief psychiatrist at Beckworth told the Harringtons that Julie was suffering from a complete breakdown and strongly recommended termination of the pregnancy.

While the abortion on her daughter was being performed, Nicola sat sadly in the waiting room, remembering the day she had learned she was pregnant with Julie.

It had been something of an accident. The doctor,

examining her diaphragm, found a pinpoint of a hole.

Before telling Edward, Nicola went to see Anne. 'I'm glad, I suppose, and yet scared. I hoped to have a baby eventually, but it seems so soon. We've only been married a few months, and my work has been going so well.'

Anne, who had the afternoon free because Al's mother was watching the boys, looked at Nicola thoughtfully. 'Motherhood is a fulltime job.'

'It can't be, for me. I'll have to hire someone. I must have time to sculpt. As it is, I don't know how I'm going to get near enough to my materials with a big belly.' Nicola smiled, picturing herself in an advanced state of pregnancy. 'Edward will be so pleased. He wants children before he gets too old.'

Anne made a face. 'For the first three or four years, fathers aren't terribly interested. Infants don't appeal to them, and I can understand why.'

'Anne,' Nicola asked, struck by her friend's reticence, 'if you wanted to go on with your music, couldn't you hire an au pair to take care of the boys?'

'No, Nika, it wouldn't work. I couldn't free my mind to concentrate, worrying if Paul fell and hurt himself in the playground or if Timmy had an upset stomach. Some mothers go off to work with a free conscience, but I just can't.'

Nicola sighed. 'Well, I can't give up my sculpture, no matter what. I'll just have to train myself not to worry. I'll get somebody really good, who will love the baby ...'

Or not go through with it. Nicola walked all the way home from the West Side, thinking about what to do. She could have an abortion without ever telling Edward a thing. Maybe that wouldn't be fair, but it was her life that would really change, not Edward's. She was still so young. Wouldn't it be more practical to wait until she was twenty-five or twenty-six, when she would be better established?

However, as she drew closer to Beekman Place she began to visualise an attractive golden-haired version of Anne's boys. A bright little boy or girl with an inquiring mind, whom she could teach all about art from infancy, who would watch her work and be inspired. Boys' and girls' names popped into her mind.

Nicola looked at their enormous duplex with new eyes.

How easy to install a nursery. There was space for a playroom, too, and an au pair. And Edward would be so happy.

Nicola poured herself a gin and tonic. She ought to have been overjoyed, like Janet Markham, pregnant for the second time. Janet had phoned Nicola absolutely overcome with happiness. Of course, Janet's set-up was different because Tom worked at home and shared in the raising of their daughter. Edward wasn't Tom, who had simple desires which mostly revolved around his family. Edward was engrossed in collecting and the managing of his estate, now that his parents were dead.

Did Nicola have a right to bring a baby into the world when she was already thinking of ways to have it cared for by someone else? And yet she didn't want to remain childless.

On an impulse, Nicola dialled her parents. 'Mama, I just wanted to say hello –'

'You must be a mind-reader. I was just about to call you. Papa had another attack. No, it's not serious, but he really has to stop working, except he won't hear of it. Says he would have nothing to live for –'

'He would, Mama. He's going to be a grandpa!'

Paul's loneliness was unbearable. The Felix Ensemble was back at Yale. Although Anne was trying to influence him to return to school and finish his master's, he was adamant in rejecting the academic life. Recognition was what he wanted. Popular acclaim, respect, and money. He was too much of a hedonist to live like Fred Felix, always shabbily dressed and dependent on some foundation for a grant.

Paul's only relaxation was to drink capuccino at the Cafe Figaro.

One evening he noticed a girl sitting near him. At her feet was a violin case. He looked her over carefully, the first woman he had had any interest in for weeks.

She was dark, pretty, and appeared sensitive. Paul felt a stirring that had long been quiescent. He went over to her table.

'Excuse me. I play the flute and compose. I'm writing a quintet and wonder if I could speak to you for a few moments about the violin part.'

She was studying at the Manhattan School of Music. Paul found her warm, intelligent, and forthcoming. He took her 'phone number.

For a few days he went out with her, trying desperately to forget himself in her company. But the streets, the restaurants, the cafes, the parks – everything reminded him of what he had lost.

The girl was a perfectly acceptable companion – for someone else. Her prettiness and sweetness were to no avail, simply because she was not Nicola.

Paul hurt in his soul. Being with someone else was worse than being alone.

2

Nicola's days took on the quality of a prison sentence. She awoke every morning exhausted from the battles she fought with herself when unconscious. Her first sensation was of an aching void because Paul was not beside her. Her second thought was for Julie.

Nicola had moved into the guest room the first night, making the clear nonverbal statement to Edward that she had no intention of resuming marital relations.

He had not commented. With Julie so sick any personal discussion would have been callously inappropriate.

Nicola walked the mile and a half to the Beckworth Nursing Home. Although Julie's psychiatrist, Dr Spivak, had advised Nicola not to force herself on her daughter, she wanted to be there when Julie needed her. Nicola had daily sessions with the doctor, who theorised about the silent girl's problems and resentments.

Julie had not spoken a word, after the last terrible things she had told her mother in the Paris hospital. The doctors were unable to agree on whether Julie was simply suffering from shock, was schizophrenic, or had decided consciously to withdraw from the world.

For a large part of the day, Julie sat in a chair and looked out at the East River. She did not react to her mother's presence. Nicola remained for hours, not speaking but trying to will her daughter to feel that she was loved. In the evening Edward came as well. However, he became disaffected at his daughter's continued silence and refusal to look at him. He began to make excuses for staying away.

Nicola didn't criticise Edward. She simply appeared every day, seven days a week. During the second week of Julie's stay at Beckworth, Nicola had vowed not to sculpt until Julie recovered. It was a severe penance, but she had not hesitated.

Julie had her meals in her room and ate only if the nurse fed her. Nicola ate hers there as well. She didn't read a book or listen to the radio, She sat without moving, simply being there with Julie, concentrating on getting through to her daughter. Julie, I love you. I'm sorry, I know it's my fault. I want you to recover, to be the bright, laughing girl you used to be once.

Julie was incontinent occasionally, and sometimes refused to let the nurse near her. Nicola was happy to take over, happy that Julie allowed her to do so.

Two months went by without any change.

Edward, cursing his bad luck, let himself into the apartment he had rented on East Fifty-seventh Street. He had just made the worst deal of his life – a mistake that could possibly cost him more than fifty thousand dollars. Stupidly he had sold a George Segal sculpture, completely forgetting that the Whitney was mounting a big show of Segal's work.

The fact was that Julie's illness had knocked every sensible thought out of Edward. Whenever he thought of his sweet little girl being mauled by that revolting drug addict in Paris he felt sick.

Edward blamed Nicola for everything. Julie had been fine until her mother started shacking up with that punk. And he himself had been in terrific form, his collection appreciating by more than a million each year, his virility never in question. With one rash, insane move, Nicola had destroyed her daughter and her husband.

At first Edward had been almost relieved at Julie's breakdown because it had caused Nicola to come back home. She had put herself in the guest room, certainly and there was her pride, and the preoccupation with Julie. But weeks had gone by without any change. Nicola, in what he thought of as excessive Catholic guilt, spent sixteen hours a day at Beckworth. When she returned to Beekman Place she was like a zombie. If she spoke at all, it was about Julie. She didn't eat with Edward, didn't drink with him, didn't communicate except in monosyllables. She would go to her room and shut the door and that was that.

Edward felt he had been patient and sensitive to Nicola's anguish but enough was enough. She was under his roof again and he expected some acknowledgment that he was still her husband.

When he saw that she was going to persist in her self-abnegation and punishment of him, he wanted to retaliate by having assignations with one girl after another in his rented apartment. But if Nicola even noticed that he wasn't sleeping at home she seemed totally unconcerned.

Edward was angry at Julie too, but underneath he was hurt. She had been his princess. He had petted her, made a fuss over her, and given her whatever she wanted. It infuriated him to be told by Dr Spivak that his time and interest would have been more valuable to his daughter than a too-big allowance.

Edward poured some scotch over ice. He disliked Dr Spivak, a dark, stocky man with intense eyes. A Paul Kadin-Lurie type, and a smartass to boot. Damn the man's impertinence and over-calm voice, reeking of superiority, when everyone knew that psychiatrists had the most maladjusted children.

When Edward was downing his third double scotch the 'phone rang. It was his date for tonight, telling him she would be unable to make it. Edward hung up, containing his impulse to wrench the machine out of the wall. Stupid, sassy little cunt, who did she think she was? She wasn't even a decent lay! He decided glumly to go home.

In his living-room he put on a Mahler symphony, but found it too gloomy. He tried a Bach cantata and found the voices irritating and absurd. Louis Armstrong was too hot, Jerry Mulligan too cool.

When Edward glanced at the walls he wasn't pleased with the paintings he saw. Tess Abrams was a bore. Her work was too slick, too arch. He would sell her off, and that Chagall, too. An inferior example of the painter's art.

Edward hated everything, most of all himself. From the day Nicola had walked out on him his life had gone awry. The cook was surprised to find him at home. Mr Harrington had said he was dining out, no?

Edward wasn't really hungry but he asked for French bread, pâté, and cornichons, drinking a full bottle of wine while he ate, his mind racing wildly from one extravagant idea to the next.

He came from a family that believed in winning, and he held up his end of the tradition with a vengeance. Edward's banker father had made his own, second fortune by combining perspicacity and guile. His speciality was refusing loans to small, promising businesses that needed a helping hand. He would keep his eye on such a firm, however, and if it failed to get the necessary funds he would buy it up for almost nothing under a subsidiary. He would advance the necessary money and turn the enterprise profitable.

Edward had learned well, always bearing in mind three simple principles. Never be sentimental in business dealings, always pay rock bottom prices and sell only when the item had appreciated tenfold. For thirty-odd years he had not failed, but now he was feeling like a loser, and even worse, behaving like one.

Nicola came home at ten-thirty. 'Come in here, Nika, and have a brandy with me,' he invited, trying to keep his tone casual.

She hesitated. 'I'm awfully tired, Edward.'

'At least tell me how Julie's doing. I just couldn't get away tonight.'

She sat down and accepted the cognac Edward handed

223

her. 'No change. We simply have to be patient. It took her eighteen years to become so disturbed, and we can't expect overnight miracles.'

While they spoke, Edward noted how distraught Nicola looked. Her hair, plainly pulled back and tied, had no lustre. She wore no makeup and was dressed in a simple shirt and blouse. She was playing the role of 'Concerned Mother'.

Edward became excited. Her guilt over Julie had apparently taken away her sexual appetite. He had an impulse to bring it back, only this time make sure it was directed only to him.

Edward moved to the arm of her chair and casually sat on it. 'We used to be such a happy family.'

Nicola, swirling the amber liquid in her snifter, didn't reply.

Looking down, he saw the swell of her breast beneath her shirt. He took the glass from her hands, as she looked up in surprise. Without speaking, he put his arms around her and kissed her chastely on the forehead. Nicola drew back.

'Don't you think, for Julie's sake, we might try again?'

Nicola cast him an apologetic look before moving away. 'I can't. I'm sorry, Edward. There's no reason not to be friends, but anything else is out of the question.'

Edward suddenly gleaned from her expression that she was still infatuated with that boy, and the realisation made him livid.

'Are you still thinking about that little prick?'

Nicola shut her eyes and winced, but couldn't stop the flush warming her cheeks.

'If you think you're going back to him, you can forget it. I'd sooner see you dead.'

Nicola rose and tried to leave but not quickly enough. Edward grabbed her, pinning her arms to her sides, while forcing her head back. He kissed her brutally and threw her on the couch.

'Edward, for God's sake.'

Blind with rage, he jumped on top of her with his full weight, while she gasped in pain. With one hand he mauled her breast, and put his other hand under her skirt, forcing her legs apart. He kept his mouth on hers, biting her lips, thrusting his tongue deeply into her mouth.

224

Nicola struggled violently. 'You're hurting me.'

'You've hurt me. I gave you everything for eighteen years and you walked out on me and your daughter, you evil bitch.'

He ripped off her shirt and bra in one motion and bit down on her breast, while she cried and struggled to escape.

'What did that little prick do to you that I can't do?' He tore off her skirt and pulled down her panties.

Nicola, fighting the sharp, stabbing pains, tried to push him away. He suddenly hit her in the face so hard that she felt as if her jaw would snap. She stopped struggling. Edward was drunk and irrationally jealous enough to murder her.

Julie. If Edward murdered her Julie would never come back from her own world.

Edward climbed on top of the unresistant Nicola in triumph. But when he looked at her face, eyes shut tightly against him, he suddenly wilted.

'Goddamn you!'

Nicola heard his cry and felt him roll off her. He flung himself against the corner of the couch, mumbling drunkenly, 'You bitch, you've finished me. I can hardly ever make it any more because of you.'

She sat up, her body bruised and tender. Every movement was painful. Gathering her shredded clothing together, she left.

Although she didn't really think Edward would attack her again, she locked her door.

For a long time she lay wide-eyed in her bed, pity vying with revulsion and sadness – to think that her half-lifetime with Edward could have come to this.

Julie watched the brightly painted wooden figures come out of the bag. The nurse was moving her lips but Julie couldn't really hear her. She was looking at a big boy, a big girl, a little boy, and a little girl.

Tentatively she touched the figures and moved them, while the nurse stood by.

After a while Julie put the big boy and the little boy back in the bag and lifted the little girl close to the big girl.

225

'Mommy,' she said. 'Mommy.'

The nurse pressed a button, and in a few moments Dr Spivak appeared and sat down next to Julie. He retrieved the little boy and moved it to the other figures. Julie flung it to the floor. She did the same when the doctor moved the father figure closer.

'No! Mommy. I want my mommy,' she yelled, and burst into tears.

Nicola found a note under her door from Edward. 'Forgive me. I had too much to drink.'

She would never be able to forgive him but she accepted a share in his frustration that had brought him to such a point of rage.

Nicola would have left Beekman Place without delay but finding her own studio took time – and more money than she had at the moment.

Nicola had a hot bath to ease her soreness and bruises and then, took a taxi to Beckworth.

Dr Spivak met her with the good news that her daughter's silence was finally broken.

Paul spent a few days at Yale, consulting with Fred Felix and greatly pleased that his teacher was excited about his quintet.

Back on campus, Paul ran into Kate Markham and asked about her family.

'Everyone's fine. Emmy's engaged, in fact, to an art student. My folks think she's a little young, but they like the fellow a lot. And speaking of art students, Mom told me some terrible news about Julie Harrington.'

Paul's temples began to throb.

'She's had a breakdown. Can't speak, and Nicola has given up sculpting and hardly leaves her daughter's side. Oh, but you probably know all this. I forgot. I mean, you and Nicola –'

Paul murmured goodbye and went quickly in the opposite direction. He felt a surge of tender love for Nicola, followed by a tightening in his chest and acute misery that he could not go to her, hold her in his arms, comfort her.

He had been wrong about Julie, his own needs causing him to underestimate her illness. If Nicola was not working she must be going through absolute hell.

Paul dialled long distance, his breath coming in uneven gasps.

'Mrs Harrington not here. Home late.'

He hung up without daring to leave a message. On an impulse he decided to write. She was back with Edward, and he hesitated to expose his feelings completely. He compromised with a short note containing a simple expression of sympathy and hope for Julie's recovery. Then he tacked on an ambiguous reference to work as being a necessary outlet for anguish, phrasing it so that Nicola would realise that his own anguish came from still loving her.

He thought of sending it to her studio, but if she wasn't working she might not get it. He put his new address and 'phone number on the bottom of the letter and sent it to Beekman Place special delivery.

Anne was feeling terrible, so bad, in fact, that she was trying to eat away her misery! Anne had 'phoned, written, and gone to see virtually everybody she knew in the music world with a view to getting Paul's quintet performed. And had come up against a blank wall.

First of all, nobody wanted even to look at the score. They offered all kinds of excuses: overwhelmed with new compositions; no time to include a new work in their repertoire before a worldwide concert tour; not looking for a quintet, although a cello sonata might be welcome.

Only her old friend, the impressario Max Furst, was honest enough to tell her the truth. 'Annie, I can't touch him. Do you know what money is like these days, and grants? Tighter than my grandma's girdle. And because of this plagiarism business – no, of course I don't believe it – nobody will stick his neck out, not for you, not even for Henrietta.'

Anne had thought the hardest thing would be to get Paul's score into her hands. Instead, he had handed it to her almost without thinking. But she had never anticipated such an unfavourable reception.

Thrashing about for someone to blame, Anne could only come up with Nicola. If that viper hadn't seduced her son, he wouldn't have quarrelled with his mother, and there would have been no scandal.

And for what? For a few months of fleshly indulgence which, like a good meal, was forgotten the moment it was finished. Because of a contemptible last-ditch effort of an aging woman to retain her youth, the career of the most promising composer in America was being ruined.

Well, Anne refused to accept defeat. She would hire the best public relations firm in New York to show proof of Paul's innocence, to present their case so as to have conductors, impresarios, and flautists crying into their coffee.

Paul's quintet would be heard if she had to bankrupt herself and her husband in the process!

Edward didn't go to his office or to Beckworth. He took a long walk through Central Park, trying to cheer himself up by enjoying the balmy spring day.

At the boat pond he observed little boys with their sailboats, wishing, not for the first time, that he had a son. Sons were a hell of a lot less trouble than daughters.

He came upon the Metropolitan Museum of Art but decided against going in. Instead, he stood on the steps watching the girls walk by. It had once been a favourite activity, one that relaxed him and cleared his mind of problems. Now it was only an aching reminder that his libido had gone haywire.

Edward developed a headache, and his stomach was upset. The events of the previous evening were only half-remembered. He had tried to make love to his wife and couldn't. And in his frustration he had slapped her. Well, it was the first time. Many men beat their wives regularly.

An attractive redhead smiled at him and asked for a light. Formerly he would have nibbled at the bait, taken her for a drink, and wound up in the sack for the price of a good dinner. Now he didn't dare risk humiliation.

Barely glancing at her, he lit her cigarette and then his

own. She looked disappointed as she walked away.

The more Edward thought about it, the more obsessed he became with the notion that he and Nicola had to resume their married life properly so that he would become a winner again.

He couldn't bring himself to go home, so decided to go to a movie house to see a revival of a Katherine Hepburn/Spencer Tracy comedy. Then he ate dinner at his club, had a couple of brandies, and tried to concentrate on the morning edition of the *Times*.

He began to take heart. Sooner or later he always got what he wanted, and Nicola was not going to be an exception.

When Edward finally came home, he was greeted at the door by the cook, telling him to 'phone Nicola at Beckworth.

'Edward, Julie is speaking! She's still very childish, but Dr Spivak now definitely sees hope and will be starting intensive psychotherapy. I'm going to spend the night. She's been calling for me.'

'Yes, that's a good idea. I'll come tomorrow first thing. Sleep well, my dear.'

Edward's spirits soared. The tide had turned. He had willed it to be so. Idly he scanned the mail on the hall table. A special delivery letter postmarked New Haven caught his eye. It was addressed to Nicola, and Edward didn't need to open it to know who had sent it.

He hefted it for a moment. Light. Not a long story. A feeler, most likely.

Edward tore the letter into shreds.

Julie had good days and bad days. She was lucid for minutes at a time, but only with her doctor. Towards Nicola she vacillated between playing like a child of three and silence.

Following Dr Spivak's advice, Nicola spoke to Julie only about the toys she played with, keeping her voice neutral, and not getting discouraged when there was no response.

After a while, Nicola brought some acrylic plastics to Julie's room and began to make little toys for her. She had taken to rising very early and going to her studio, cutting and melting her materials, shaping them when they cooled. She would take the pieces to Julie and encourage her to

229

watch while she glued them together.

Julie was usually uninterested in the bright bits of plastics, but Nicola persisted.

Three times a day Julie saw Dr Spivak. During those sessions Nicola would go for a walk or read. Often she thought with a pang of Paul, hurt that he had never contacted her, even to ask about Julie. Nicola did not dare call or write him – even if she had known where he was – and appear pathetic. She could find no words that would not immediately reveal that she loved him as much as she ever had.

She never got over the first chill that struck her every time she walked into the studio. Especially when she looked at her unfinished sculpture, *Moon View*. She retitled it *Absence* and refused to let Marshall have it in its present form.

She forced herself to converse politely with Edward but rebuffed all attempts at sociability. He was biding his time and did not force her.

Strangely, although Julie was often almost receptive to her mother, she shied away from her father as if she feared him.

Dr Spivak assured Edward that this was part of the illness, and that the past and present were confused. Edward was stonily uncooperative in talking about his own problems, especially as they related to his daughter. About his marriage he would say nothing.

Edward had contempt for shrinks. If Julie was improving it was simply time and good physical care, not to mention the belated devotion of her mother.

Nicola, although she had begun playing with acrylics because she thought the bright colours would please Julie, began to find a real interest and challenge in the medium. She made toy after toy with Julie in mind. Sometimes, while watching her daughter play, Nicola's eyes would well with tears. What joy there was in watching a child discover something new. She saw snatches of sweetness, of innocence in Julie. It was as if her daughter unconsciously was forcing her mother to experience the childhood she had missed.

One clear morning Julie rushed to the window shouting delightedly, 'Sun. Sun.'

Nicola was inspired to do something special for Julie. It

turned out not to be a toy but a real sculpture.

She made four triangles: blue, aqua, yellow and red and positioned them vertically and overlapping, set on a motorised platform. Each triangle was timed to revolve at a different speed so that the sun's angles would change the colours. For the room, Nicola had a special lamp installed to create the same effect.

Nicola set it on a table near the window. With the morning sun streaming into the room, the rotating sculpture gave off rainbow glints. On the bottom Nicola had lettered, 'Julie Looks At The Sun.'

Nicola would never forget Julie's delight in the piece. Lightly she put her finger on the slowly rotating mechanism and then traced her name.

Julie looked up at Nicola and smiled shyly – a smile that, to her mother, was nothing short of a miracle.

Julie sat with her elbows on the table for hours, watching the sculpture. She seemed very dreamy and abstracted. Every so often, though, when Nicola wasn't looking directly at her, she had the feeling that she was being observed.

As Nicola started home one night, something nagged at her. Julie had seemed unusually restless that day. The farther Nicola drew from Beckworth, the more anxious she became.

She jumped in a taxi and returned. The night nurse assured her that Julie was sleeping but Nicola insisted upon going to her daughter's room. A feeling of love and protectiveness pervaded her. She wanted to stay all night. With Dr Spivak not available, the nurse was dubious, but Nicola refused to budge. She made herself as comfortable as she could in the easy chair.

Listening to Julie's quiet breathing, Nicola eventually drifted into sleep.

Suddenly she was bolt awake.

'Mommy, mommy,' Julie was moaning.

Nicola rushed to the bed, where a small light burned. 'What is it, darling?'

Julie opened her eyes and stared at Nicola, but not as a child. Nicola hardly dared to breathe.

Tears filled Julie's eyes. 'I needed you. Why weren't you here? What did I do wrong?'

'Nothing. You did nothing wrong. Oh, darling, I'm so sorry. Forgive me. It was my fault, not yours. You were a wonderful, beautiful child. Everyone loved you, and I did too, always, only I'm afraid I didn't show you how much.'

'I needed you,' Julie wept, 'and you were never there.'

'I'm here now.' Nicola held a sobbing Julie tightly, rocking her, while her own tears fell unchecked onto her daughter's hair.

3

For days Paul didn't leave his apartment. He cancelled his students and would have taken the 'phone off the hook if he hadn't known that his mother, unable to reach him, would appear at his door.

He didn't want to see anyone or do anything. Idly he speculated on what would happen when his food ran out.

Nobody would perform his quintet, or even listen to it, thanks to his damaged reputation. Paul had been fighting with his mother, and even his father, deploring the steps they were taking to convince the music world that he was innocent. It was too humiliating. He didn't care if he never wrote another note. Couldn't anyway. He was finished.

Nicola had not acknowledged his letter. He had tried calling the studio but there was never any answer. In his desperate longing for her he had even called Beekman Place. Either he got the Korean cook, who told him that she was not at home, or a recorded message, in Edward's mellifluous voice. The last time Paul had called Nicola's home, he had dared to leave his name and number with the cook. Nothing.

How could he have been so wrong about her? Was it all a fake, her absorption in him and his music, her words of love?

For hours he sat looking out on Sullivan Street, watching the passing parade. He felt numb, disinterested. He didn't know how to make his life work again, and he was terribly ashamed of his earlier arrogance. Mr Know-it-all. He had screwed up.

Not bothering to shower or shave or change his clothes, Paul slept and ate at odd moments, hardly noticing if it was day or night.

One morning he got a 'phone call from Joe Yarrow. 'The word is out that Miles Fanchel is doing a new ballet and is looking for a composer.'

'Forget it, Joe,' Paul interrupted glumly. 'He's up and coming, and I've had it.'

'No, really, listen. The ballet is based on Mardi Gras in New Orleans. Jazz motifs. You would be the perfect person to write the score.'

Paul knew that Joe felt responsible for the business with Ivor Lewes, and he appreciated his friend's attempt to help, but –

'Just take down the address. You have nothing to lose by trying.'

Paul reached for a pencil, mostly to make Joe Yarrow feel better. Then he went to sleep.

He didn't know how many more days passed. When Anne or Al called he tried to sound normal to keep them from insisting on seeing him.

One night he awoke with a pain in his stomach. He couldn't remember when he had eaten last, but when he made it out of bed he saw there was nothing left.

Paul sat up until morning, feeling lightheaded, his thoughts drifting aimlessly.

When the bustle began in the street, he stood up, weak in the legs, and went into the bathroom. He couldn't remember the last time he had looked at himself in the mirror.

His hair was long and matted, and he had the beginnings of a full beard, threaded with a few grey hairs. Paul grinned sardonically at himself. So that's what people meant when they said that worry turned you grey.

He brushed his teeth, finding that the toothpaste made him terribly hungry. He wanted some warm bread from Zito's, smeared with butter, and a hunk of cheese, some freshly ground coffee.

Apparently he wasn't ready to give up yet.

Paul showered, washed his hair and beard, and trimmed both, looking in the mirror critically. He liked the beard. It made him look as old and jaded as he felt.

Over breakfast, visions of masked, costumed dancers on Bourbon Street danced in front of him. He heard rhythmic blasts of trumpet and trombone, a strummed guitar, a plucked banjo. The music was coming from somewhere inside him.

He was being idiotic, he told himself, as he dressed. Fanchel would have a composer by now. And even if he didn't, Paul had become a pariah.

But the music kept pouring into him, representing a good omen, a turning point. He made notations during the subway ride to Fanchel's studio.

'Janet, it's so wonderful of you to do this,' Nicola exclaimed, embracing her friend. 'Julie's with her doctor now. She's making great strides, although she's still very ambivalent towards me. But she's always liked you so much, and Dr Spivak thinks that weaving would be wonderful therapy for her. For some reason she refuses to paint.'

The two women talked in the private lounge. 'Julie is in group therapy as well, with young people who have similar problems.' Nicola smiled ruefully. 'I'm not the only parent who made a mess.'

'Don't be so hard on yourself. Another kind of child might have been fine. Julie is particularly sensitive and in a way strong-willed. I remember that she wasn't easy – not like Emily, but more like Kate.'

Janet was too tactful to mention Paul, and Nicola couldn't volunteer any information. The women met Julie in one of the therapy rooms, equipped with looms, materials for basket-weaving, jewellery-making, and painting.

Julie's face lit up with genuine pleasure, and she kissed Janet warmly. 'Nice of you to come and see me in the loony bin.'

'Only because you're my favourite loony.'

Julie laughed.

After a few moments Nicola withdrew to leave them alone and to have a word with Dr Spivak.

'Why, when Julie is expecting her father, does she hide away the sculpture I did for her?'

Dr Spivak pondered. 'Fear, probably. Little by little she's dealing with the hurts of her childhood, and one of them is feeling that her father loved you better because of your talent. It's one of her problems.'

Paul drank several beers in Minetta's, picked up a girl, and brought her back to his apartment with a bottle of gin. She was young, pretty, and happy to go to bed with him.

He drank enough to deaden his anguish, lower his inhibitions, and enable him to concentrate on her silky hair, smooth skin, shapely breasts and buttocks.

But afterwards he didn't feel satisfied or relaxed, only extremely sad.

Fanchel had said he would be in touch, but Paul despaired of getting the commission. His interview had been quick and inconclusive. Fanchel had been too busy to listen to any of Paul's suggestions on the spot, so he had had to leave his notations. His jottings for the ballet weren't, of course, copyrighted, and Paul amused himself grimly by imagining that Fanchel would give them to one of his gay composer friends to develop. It had already been two weeks.

Paul was drinking more than he should and finding himself strapped for money. The music lessons just about covered rent and food, and he flatly refused to accept any help at all from his parents. Anne took it personally, whereas Al tried in his jokey manner to call it a loan, but Paul was stubborn and proud. He was either going to make it on his own or not make it at all.

There were three girls he took out occasionally. Sometimes, in desperate loneliness, he saw all three the same day. The girls were pleasant, companionable, and giving. Two of them were in love with him, but although he tried very hard he couldn't feel anything but the most impersonal biological attraction. Unfortunately, he had begun to dread being alone at night with a telephone that never rang.

One night it did ring, after eleven. Paul's heart beat very quickly.

'Paul, I was getting worried,' Anne said. 'You haven't

called or been to see me in so long.'

'I'll call you tomorrow.'

'Is everything all right?'

'Yeah, terrific.'

'Oh. Okay. I just wondered.'

'I've got a girl with me,' Paul broke in brutally, knowing he was being mean because it was his mother on the 'phone and not Nicola.

'Oh. I'm sorry. I'll try to get you in the daytime. Maybe we could have lunch?'

'Sure. I'll call you tomorrow.'

Paul hung up feeling rotten, and tried to change his mood by draining himself sexually.

He was awakened, exhausted, very early by the 'phone.

'Miles Fanchel. I like your music.'

'Janet's awfully understanding,' Julie told her mother one afternoon as they walked in the garden at Beckworth.

'She's always been fond of you, Julie, and she's so pleased with the remarkable progress you've made with the weaving.'

Julie looked sideways at Nicola. 'That's not why she comes all the way into Manhattan twice a week. She does it for you.'

Nicola curbed her tendency to contradict Julie glibly. 'That's only part of the reason. Mostly it's for you. You know how kind she is.'

'Yes, I remember. I used to envy Kate and Emily.'

Nicola swallowed the hurt. 'I don't blame you. I would rather have had Janet for a mother than me.' Suddenly feeling tired, Nicola sank down on a bench. 'I regret not giving you what you needed.'

'I'd like to visit grandma and grandpa in Florida,' Julie said unexpectedly. 'I used to love to go to Brooklyn when I was a kid. Grandma made such wonderful things to eat, and she fussed over me.'

'I know.' Nicola looked at Julie, pain in her eyes. 'She fussed over me too and I guess I took it for granted. I never realised how awful it is for a child to do without it.'

Julie looked intently at her mother. 'If you had realised, would it have made any difference?'

Of course. Every difference. But Julie's arresting gaze disturbed Nicola.

'Probably not a lot,' Nicola finally admitted, meeting her daughter's eyes sadly. 'I would have tried harder and no doubt done a little better but – but being an artist means being selfish. Visions were always going through my head. I had a compulsion to work, which made me put aside everything and everyone as extraneous – even people I loved.'

'I never felt loved, by you or Dad.'

'Well, you were, very much.'

'I always felt that the only way you and Dad would accept me was if I turned out to be a great painter.'

'That was never true. We want you to be what you want to be. Haven't we always told you so?'

'Maybe, but I didn't feel you meant it. Art is so important to both of you.'

'Julie, you're important, and what you want to do.'

'Do you think I have any talent as a painter?'

Nicola hesitated. 'Well, that depends on what your goal is. Your flowers are lovely. No doubt you could earn a living selling your work to people who love watercolours. But if you want recognition, you have to do something nobody has ever done before. And just hope your timing is right. Many talented representational painters languished when abstract art was the rage.'

Nicola paused for a few moments, then said slowly, 'You seem to have felt pushed into art. Maybe you ought to explore other fields and see if anything really excites you. Discovering what's right for you is a talent in itself.'

Nicola smiled at Julie, who looked at her reflectively for a long moment.

'Thanks, Mom.'

The Markham house and garden were overflowing with people of every age and description. Although Nicola knew that Janet and Tom were particularly sociable, she hadn't expected anything like this.

'Nicola, so glad you could make it,' Tom called out, coming over to hug her.

'Me too. Happy twenty-second, Tom. What fun. I'm never going to miss another of your anniversary parties.'

He laughed and handed her a glass of punch. 'Be careful. It tastes innocent but it's lethal as hell. Jan, come and see who we've enticed out to the boondocks.'

'Nika, how wonderful.'

'Now I see why hardly any of your friends ever get divorced. They come here once a year to have their faith in marriage renewed. I have never seen two happier people. How do you do it, you two?'

'The secret is sex,' Tom whispered, drawing an embarrassed smile from his wife. 'Janet just gets more irresistible every year.'

'Oh, stop, Tom,' she chided. 'I have to talk to Nicola for a moment.' Janet drew her into a corner. 'Anne Lurie is here. I invited her, of course, as I do both of you every year, but I never dreamed she'd come. I can't remember the last time.'

'It's all right,' Nicola said woodenly. 'I don't mind seeing Anne. She's the one who's upset over me.'

Janet looked quickly at Nicola. 'Edward isn't with you?'

Nicola shook her head. 'We live under the same roof, that's all.' She decided to answer Janet's unasked question. 'I'm not in touch with Paul. Julie actually had a crush on him, and I was so stupid I never even noticed.'

Janet squeezed Nicola's arm. 'How is Julie doing?'

'Fine. She's in Florida visiting my parents. It was the first place she wanted to go after she got out of Beckworth. She's still in therapy, however, and her group has helped her so much. We're now able to talk, really communicate, for the first time.'

'Wonderful.'

'Julie has woven a lovely little rug for you and Tom. She'll never forget how much you helped her.'

'It was my pleasure.'

Nicola drank her punch, nibbled the delicious fried chicken and salad, and wandered around the garden.

Emily came to say a few words. 'I'm sorry Julie couldn't be here but I'm definitely expecting her at my engagement party in a few weeks. I didn't want to share my folks' limelight today. I must introduce you to Brian, if I can find him anywhere ...'

238

Emily looked radiantly happy. A few weeks ago Nicola couldn't have been able to stand the contrast between this girl and her daughter.

'It's Nicola, isn't it?' A tall young woman with curly brown hair stopped her. 'Kate Markham. I suppose I've changed, but you look exactly the same.'

Nicola's heart pounded. Kate was a friend of Paul's. Someone she had actually been jealous of, and with good reason. Kate was lovely, and so intelligent. Did Nicola dare to mention Paul? Did Kate know about them?

Nicola never found out because Kate was called away to deal with a country music band that had just arrived.

Nicola tried to enjoy herself but she felt Paul's absence so keenly she almost wept when she thought of him. She knew she was being foolish, but she couldn't help it. The punch and the music and the laughing, happy people all around her reminded her of what she had had, and lost.

Whenever she caught a glimpse of herself in the mirror she was startled to see how ravished she looked. She had aged years, in spite of Kate's kind words. Nicola no longer wore her hair loose or cared what clothes she put on, as long as they were nondescript and nonseductive.

The music went on and on, and there was square-dancing. After a while Nicola drifted away. At a certain point it began to seem monotonous.

Stepping into the cool shade of the living room, Nicola found herself face to face with Anne.

She stopped, startled and uncomfortable.

The women stared at each other sadly.

'Hello, Anne.'

'Hello.' Nicola looked so thin and pale that Anne found it difficult to hate her enemy with her former intensity. Nicola had suffered, that was plain. The joyous light had gone out of her eyes.

'I understand Julie is much better. I'm glad.'

'Thanks. She's come out more whole than she ever was.'

'You were lucky to get another chance.'

'Yes, I was.' Nicola looked at former friend with unhappy eyes. 'Artists are selfish people. Their work comes first, and it makes them rotten parents.'

'Yes, I know. I had my own mother as the shining

239

example of the breed.'

Anne nervously reached for a handful of peanuts. 'That so-called music out there sets my teeth on edge.'

Nicola smiled faintly. 'I remember. I can't listen to it indefinitely either, but everyone is having such fun.'

Anne shrugged, indicating she couldn't for a moment imagine why. 'Emily looks beautiful and so happy. She's landed a job teaching.'

Nicola could hardly control her breathing, and she was aware of a terrible clash of emotions. Anne was making conciliatory overtures. Nicola would have given anything to be friends again – almost. She missed Anne. The trouble was that she still loved Paul. Making up would be dishonest.

With a start Nicola realised that Anne had stopped speaking and was looking probingly at her. 'Paul's life was almost ruined because of you. I have to say it, Nicola. That business with the plagiarism would never have happened if I'd been making the arrangements. It is only a measure of his strength and talent that he was able to come out of it better than ever.'

Nicola bit hard on the inside of her lip to keep her face expressionless. At all costs she must not let Anne see what she was feeling.

'My son has grown up in the last few months. He's paid for his mistake dearly but not fatally. He was given a commission to write the music for a new Miles Fanchel ballet.'

'I'm glad,' Nicola said, in as flat a tone as she could muster, while a ripple of elation went through her. How happy Paul must be.

'The thing that gets me is that it was all for nothing, as I knew it would be. You're back with Edward, where you belong, and you're damn lucky he took you back.'

'Oh, God!' The cry broke from Nicola's lips involuntarily. 'I'm not back with him. It's only because of Julie –'

'Stop! I don't want to hear it.' Anne's eyes flashed a warning of her anger. 'If you haven't learned your lesson yet, there's not a shred of hope for you! Fortunately Paul has broken free of your influence and found himself a lovely young girl, a musician, and he's terribly happy with her.'

Anne turned and walked into the garden.

SUMMER, 1979

4

Julie came back from Florida, tanned and ten pounds heavier. Nicola thought she looked wonderful. She had made friends in her therapy group and went out a lot. Edward didn't approve. 'I'm not sure they are the right sort of friends for you.'

'They're a lot better than the junkies and porno kings I used to hang out with.' Julie grinned at her mother.

Edward was not amused. 'What is this, a conspiracy?'

'No. Mom understands that I'm to be trusted now. And it's not as if I had any virtue to lose.'

'Do you hear the way she talks to me?' Edward said, when Julie had left. 'Her little caper has cost me thousands of dollars.'

'Yes, that seems to be your attitude, and Julie senses it. Try to understand that we were both at fault. We didn't mean to be bad parents but we were. The only thing we can do is learn from our mistakes.'

'We?' he echoed bitterly. 'As long as you sleep in the guest room there is no we. You and your daughter seem to think I have unlimited funds. When, for instance, was the last time you sold a sculpture? Marshall tells me you have an unfinished piece at your studio he could sell for a hundred thousand.'

'Yes, but until Julie was really well, I haven't been able to work properly.'

Edward walked out of the room. He was fed up with the women in his family treating him as if he were a leper when he could snap his fingers and a dozen beautiful girls would gladly fling themselves into his arms.

Nicola admitted to herself that Edward had a point. She had been messing with acrylic toys for months, unwilling or unable to start on anything big. Julie was well. It was time she got her own life together. Wishing for Paul was a useless exercise.

Nicola went to the studio, steeling herself for the wave of depression that interfered with her breathing.

Looking with a fresh eye at *Absence*, she saw at once all the rough places that needed fixing, and how to give the piece the unity it now lacked. She buckled down to work until it was finished.

When her payment came, Nicola handed Edward her personal cheque for twenty thousand. 'For my room and board.'

Edward glanced at the cheque and shifted his gaze to her. She was looking very attractive although still sad around the eyes.

'Look, Nicola, I don't really want to take the money – not like this. You make me feel like an ogre.'

'Not at all. I'd rather be self-supporting. In fact, I have been looking for *my* own studio.'

'I wish you wouldn't. We've been through a lot together, with this business with Julie. I think we should make another try at being a family again.'

Nicola slowly shook her head, the memory of the way he had assaulted her making her shrink from him with contempt and revulsion. 'We can't fool Julie by pretending everything is all right. One of the things she so resented in us both was what she felt was our dishonesty.'

'Well, I don't accept that you and I aren't going to get together,' Edward said, his mouth tightening stubbornly.

Nicola was suddenly aware of how much he had aged in the last few months.

He hadn't really intended to take the money, but he put it in his pocket. The less she had, the harder it would be for her to leave him.

Dr Spivak assured Nicola that her daughter would not return to her former habits. The drinking and promiscuity had been symptoms of a deep disturbance that had been successfully treated. Yet Nicola found she simply could not get to sleep until Julie came home.

One night when Julie was still not in at twelve forty-five she was so agitated that she phoned Dr Spivak.

'Have you any reason to think she's not all right?'

'Well, no, only it's so late. Oh, I think I hear her now.' Nicola rushed out of her room, startling her daughter.

'What's the matter, Mom?'

'I was worried because it's so late.'

'I should have 'phoned, I guess, but I was having such a wonderful time.' Julie smiled dazzlingly, looking so beautiful and happy that Nicola had a momentary panic. 'You haven't been drinking, have you?'

'No, of course not. Oh Mom, I'm in love.' Julie hugged her mother, something she had not done since the first night they had spoken at Beckworth.

Stunned, Nicola followed her daughter to her room.

'Someone in the group?'

'Yes. Luke Simmonds. I always liked him, of course, but the last few times we've been out together there was something really special between us. And tonight – well, I went back to his place. I mean, his parents' place, but they weren't home. Don't worry, it's not at all the same as the past. That was hostility, but this was so super. And we took precautions.'

Nicola was assailed by warring feelings. Joy for her daughter, apprehension, and gratification that Julie wanted to confide in her.

The two women sat on the bed like college roommates, Julie speaking in spurts, her enthusiasm communicated to Nicola.

'Mom, I'm happy, really happy! Luke is going to medical school in the fall. And I'd like to go too. I want to be a doctor.'

'Let me catch my breath,' Nicola begged, overwhelmed.

'It's not because of Luke. I mean, one reason we love each other is that we both think and feel the same about wanting to help people. To do something important. You know I can't be a painter.'

'That doesn't mean there is no other artistic aspect.'

'I don't want the arts. I want medicine.' Julie's voice rose.

'Okay, okay. Actually, I think that's wonderful,' Nicola said, as Julie's words sank in. 'If that's what you want and you're willing to work hard you'll succeed.'

'Will you help me to convince Dad?'

'Well, yes, but do you think he'll need convincing?'

'Yes. He doesn't understand me at all, and he doesn't try.'

'Julie, I think he's hurt by your evasiveness. Your illness hit him hard.'

'I know.' Julie slipped her dress over her head.

Nicola was startled to see how her daughter's body had matured to womanliness in the last few months.

'Mom, stop worrying. I'm fine. I really have a sense of myself for the first time. I want to be with Luke as much as possible, live with him, and study medicine. His folks have a lot of money, and he has trust funds and things. He loves me too, really, and we want to get our own place.' Julie hesitated. 'At least in November, as soon as he's eighteen and gets control of some of his money. He's a few months younger than me but it doesn't matter at all.' Julie stopped when she discerned her mother's expression.

'Mom, I'm sorry I was so horrible about Paul.'

Nicola felt the colour rushing to her cheeks. 'I don't blame you. I was insensitive to your feelings, inexcusably so.'

'My feelings were really confused. I didn't care about Paul the way I do about Luke. Do you remember which one he is? The redhaired fellow with the green eyes. I think he's gorgeous. And we're like two halves of the same wooden nickel. I mean he has similar family problems, only the other way around. It's his father Luke felt he couldn't live up to …'

Julie couldn't seem to stop talking. In spite of the hour, Nicola sat up drinking in every word. Julie was a different person.

'All the cliches about falling in love are true,' Julie said in wonder, stretching luxuriously. 'I hardly have any appetite, think about Luke constantly. Every song reminds me of him. And I keep writing Mrs Julie Simmonds on pieces of paper, although I know we're a long way from that. Did you ever do such a thing?'

Nicola smiled, enjoying Julie's enjoyment. 'Maybe.'

'Mom, are you ever going to move back into the bedroom?'

'No, I'm afraid not,' Nicola replied sadly.

'Did you used to love Dad?'

'Yes, I suppose I did.'

'Like Luke and me?'

'Not exactly.'

The first time Nicola had seen Edward he was sitting at a table in the Limelight Cafe in the Village, where she worked as a waitress. Attractive, in his thirties, well-dressed and obviously well-heeled, Edward flirted with her whenever he got the chance. If he had been female, his pearly-toothed smile could have won him a Miss Rheingold contest. Nicola privately thought of him as Mr Rheingold.

After six months of attending classes at the Art Students League, Nicola had begun to get discouraged. New York was the art mecca, where hundreds of young artists were struggling and competing for recognition. Poverty was getting her down. The four years away from home had made it impossible to live with her parents again, much as she loved them. They were mystified by her work, and as an unmarried daughter she could not have come and gone with freedom.

A typical day for Nicola was to rise at seven and work in the studio for a couple of hours until it was time to leave for her art classes. Then, she went home and sculpted until she went to the Limelight.

Nicola was abstracted by thoughts of sculpture as she took orders and served food from six until closing.

'What can I call you except Miss?' Mr Rheingold asked her one evening. 'At least, I assume you're not Mrs.'

'Nicola,' she said tersely, setting down his espresso.

'That's a beautiful name, and you do it justice. Tell me what you do – I mean really. I can see you're not just a waitress.'

'I'm too busy to talk,' Nicola moved away. She had become inured to the men who tried to pick her up. The best way to discourage them was to be polite but distant. They usually took the hint.

Mr Rheingold didn't. Soon after her snub he asked her to have dinner with him.

She declined without even looking at him and asked again for his order.

During the following weeks he did not ask her out again, but confined himself to a few pleasant words and the toothpaste smile.

Nicola wasn't interested in him or even curious. Since the disappointment with Gareth Howe she had not left herself open to fresh hurts. Her art meant everything to her, and no man would ever again get in her way.

Nicola's spirits soared when she received a call from the O'Casey Gallery, which operated from a derelict storefront near First Avenue. Jeannie and Burt O'Casey were mounting a group exhibit and wanted five of Nicola's welded mobiles and collages. She had shown them her slides so long ago she'd almost forgotten about them.

Although the O'Caseys seemed like nice kids, Nicola had a traitorous feeling of going over to the enemy. The artist, as always, would be getting screwed. The O'Caseys took fifty percent of every sale. Nicola's soul revolted at making such a deal, but fifty was better than nothing. Better than shoving her work into a corner of the studio to gather dust.

Her reservations vanished in the excitement of the opening – and she learned that she was the gallery's second choice because at the last minute someone else had backed out of the show. It didn't matter that the opening wasn't very big or black tie and that nobody famous was there. What mattered was that it was the first time her work was on show at a New York gallery.

The Luries attended and insisted on buying a small collage. When Nicola saw the red dot appear on it, evidence of her first professional sale, she almost wept.

The tiny paragraphs the opening received in the art press picked out Nicola as being worth watching in future.

During the next week her other four pieces were sold.

One day as Nicola tore out of her art class she literally bumped into Mr Rheingold on the street.

'Nicola Di Candia, you are going to have lunch with me, and I will reveal to you the fate of your mobile, *Beech Tree*.'

Nicola, stunned into open-mouthed silence, let the man lead her across the street into the Russian Tea Room.

'I'm not dressed for this place –'

'That doesn't matter when you're with me.' He helped her off with her coat and checked it.

Feeling rather out of place, Nicola followed the *maître d'hôtel* into the restaurant full of white tablecloths, flowers, and a clientele bejewelled and smelling of expensive perfume. She was out of her element completely in her patched jeans and a baggy old sweater, her hair tumbling into her eyes.

The *maître d'hôtel* called her companion Mr Harrington, so it was clear he ate here often. Edward ordered Nicola a Black Russian and told the waiter they would have *shashlyk*, rice, salad, and a bottle of château something-or-other.

'What about *Beech Tree*?' she asked shyly.

'It's hanging in my study.'

'Oh.' She was embarrassed. 'How did you find out about me?'

'By accident. I saw a review of the show and went to the O'Casey Gallery, where I was very much taken with your mobile. I realised that their Nicola was my Nicola.'

The way he said that sent a peculiar shiver down her back.

Smiling, he handed her a card. 'As a matter of fact, I'm a collector.'

She was not impressed but thought cynically that he had money to burn, so it didn't hurt him to throw some of it away on the sculpture of an unknown. Especially when he was hoping to get the sculptor herself.

'I've been back to the gallery and note that everything was sold. I wonder that you work as a waitress when you not only dislike the job but the side benefits.'

Meaning, she supposed, the possibility of being taken out by men like him.

'I don't know what you mean.'

'I mean that if you can command such good prices for your work – and I figure the gallery took half – you should have got one fifty for *Beech Tree* alone.'

Nicola put down her fork. 'Are you telling me you paid three hundred?'

'Yes, ma'am. I bought it from Burt himself. I'm not a fool, Nicola, I've been collecting for almost ten years. It's not unknown for a gallery to cheat artists. I investigated further and discovered to whom all your pieces were sold, and for how much.'

He read from a piece of paper. 'In all, you should have received five hundred dollars. I'll eat my skewer if you got anything like that.'

Nicola sat slumped in her seat. 'I got two fifty.'

'That's what I thought. Now, little girl, let me tell you something about dealers. Unless they come personally reecommended, they can be crooked as blazes. In this case, it's easy to see what happened. They told you one price, and maybe even intended to stick to it. But the good reviews sent collectors like me to the gallery, and they upped the prices and never bothered to inform you.'

Nicola felt ill, thinking that the work she had sweated to produce brought someone such an enormous profit.

'I'll get your money back for you.'

'No thank you. You have no reason to do anything for me.'

'I disagree.' He smiled. 'I think you have great potential, and find your dedication to your work utterly admirable.'

Nicola blushed. He seemed so sincere, and was nice, really, but as a collector he counted as one of the enemy. 'It's people like you who are in cahoots with galleries, making private deals –'

'You remind me of the hills of Rome, the villas of Florence, and, when you erupt, the volcano of Mount Etna.'

'I'm sorry.' Nicola laughed at the picture he painted.

'I'd like to help you make that success you're heading for first by getting back your money.'

'Thanks but I'm going to let it drop. It's hard to explain but – but I can't dirty my work by quibbling over money.'

Edward Harrington leaned over the table, his eyes suddenly shrewd, his expression almost crafty. 'Money is currency. Money makes the world go round. It buys all the good things of life, it buys time, it buys you lunch.'

Nicola jumped up. 'I'll reimburse you when I get my pay cheque!'

He didn't try to prevent her from leaving.

At the door, Nicola, feeling like an imbecile, rummaged in her purse for a quarter to buy back her coat.

Yet, after days of stewing over the way she had been cheated she changed her mind after all. Damn them, it was her money and she wanted it. On an impulse she went to the gallery.

Jeannie was there alone. She listened to Nicola's claims without expression. 'I don't know what you're talking about. We sold your stuff for what we said.'

While Nicola argued, claiming she would bring Harrington around, and he could prove her case, Burt came into the gallery.

'Okay, kid,' he said quietly, and Nicola whirled, her eyes blazing. 'Okay, so we did a little deal.'

'But why? Why? It's as much stealing as if you robbed a bank. I trusted you.'

He shrugged and reached into his pocket. 'Here's fifty on account. That's all I've got. Come back a week from Friday and you'll get the rest. Promise. Okay?'

'Okay.' The naked larceny of these people she had liked depressed her, and she just wanted to get away.

When she returned on the appointed day, the O'Casey gallery was cleaned out, a padlock on the door.

'Them? They split last week,' the shopkeeper next door told her. 'California, I think. They owe you money?' He laughed. 'They owe everyone money. Forget it. They're gone.'

Nicola had thought it only fair to tell Edward Harrington her story. Instead of taunting her with I-told-you-sos, he was sympathetic and offered to lend her money if she needed it.

Of course she declined.

A few weeks later he called her over to his table and counted out two hundred dollars. 'I traced your friends to San Francisco. I have my contacts. Anyway, those two were doing business the same old way.'

Her respect for Edward Harrington went up several notches, and she began to have an occasional drink with him or dinner. She still thought his interest was not essentially platonic but he never made passes at her.

Two months later Edward told her that the Marshall Faber Gallery, newly established on Tenth Street, wanted to give her a one-woman show.

'How can that be? I mean I'm nobody.'

'Faber likes your work and he's willing to take a chance. A new gallery often makes its reputation by discovering new talent. And you're it.'

Nicola was delirious with joy. Edward bought the biggest mobile on opening night, the reviews were excellent, and six months later Nicola agreed to marry him.

'Did you love him, Mom?'

'I thought I did, at the time. Maybe not the way I loved Gareth Howe.' She told Julie the story.

'Maybe it wasn't fair to have married your father.'

'You still love Paul, don't you? You gave Paul up because of me, didn't you?'

'He was much too young,' Nicola whispered.

'That's old-fashioned, if you really loved each other.'

'We – we looked ridiculous, and you were disgusted at the idea.'

Julie made a gesture of apology. 'I only said that because I was so jealous of you always. God, I never realised how hard you struggled. I mean, to me, you were always so successful, so perfect. Anyway, I don't care if you go back with Paul. I'm over my jealousy of you. Oh, Mom, I'm so happy I can forgive you and Dad and the whole world!'

'Forgive Dad for what?' Nicola asked, after a moment's thought.

'Oh, nothing. Luke wants to meet you. Really, not just as part of the group. He's really impressed with your work. His mother's a social worker. She was awfully nice to me. Can we invite Luke over to dinner? I'll help you cook.'

Nicola lay awake for the rest of the night, shedding tears of joy for Julie, and tears of sadness for herself.

Anne invited Paul to have lunch out with her. 'You're working so hard, between the ballet and your students, I don't think you ever take time to get a proper meal.'

'Stop fussing.'

Anne looked critically at her son. 'I'm not sure about the beard. It hides so much of your face.'

250

Paul laughed. 'I'm sure about it. Stop picking on me, will you.'

Anne stopped. She had developed a new respect for her son and didn't mind his independence too much, although it had hurt her initially. He had become more mature, and his realistic self-confidence would help him in his music.

'Is it going well, Paul?'

'There are good and bad days. Miles is a genius but he can be very irritable, and there are constant squabbles with the cast. But I feel so damn lucky to get the chance to compose for his ballet.'

'It will be a success, I know it will. And then flautists will be falling over each other to play the quintet.'

Paul looked at his watch. 'Thanks for lunch. I've got a student at half past.'

'Paul, I'm having a soirée next Saturday, if you'd like to come.'

'Thanks, Mom, but I can't make it. I have a date.'

Her ears pricked up. 'Well, bring her. Somebody nice?'

Paul sighed. 'Yes, nice. They're all nice but they're not right for me. Don't push, please.'

'Who's pushing? I always said you had plenty of time. I don't believe in early commitments. Oh, I went to the Markham's anniversary party. Quite a mob of people. Emily is engaged. The boy seems very ordinary, but so is she. The Markhams have always been simple people. Kate is the only one in the family with any ambition. Oh, Nicola Harrington was there. Troubles with Julie have taken away her looks. She told me she and Edward are very happy now. She's lucky he took her back.'

Paul stood up abruptly. 'I've got to run.' He pecked his mother on the cheek and darted out of the restaurant, his cheeks flaming.

Hardly aware of what he was doing, he rushed to a 'phone and dialled the number of Nicola's studio.

'Hello. Hello? Who is it?'

The familiar husky voice sliced into him like a rusty knife. He hung up without speaking and leaned his head against the cold glass, hating her.

And loving her as much as he ever had.

5

'All this is too quick for me,' Edward declared, looking at his wife and daughter reproachfully. 'In the same breath Julie tells me she's in love with some boy and wants to be a doctor. Who is this kid?'

'Luke Simmonds,' Julie said impatiently. 'His father's chairman of Simmonds and Strang, brokers, with a seat on the Stock Exchange.'

'That sounds all right,' Edward said reluctantly, 'but a boy from your therapy group, disturbed –'

'I'm disturbed. We're all disturbed. Dad, Luke and I have a chance to go to Africa for a month under the auspices of a medical team doing research there. After Luke and I finish medical school we want to work in Africa –'

'What is this? You go from one extreme to the other. First you indulge yourself in – in a way that makes the jet set look puritanical, and then you want to put your health and life at risk for no reason.'

'There is a reason,' Julie cried, growing excited. 'There are many diseases in Africa and hardly any trained doctors.'

'Hold on there one minute. Although it's a bit of a shock, I'm not displeased that you're interested in medicine. I'll be happy to send you to medical school, if you can get accepted. It's hard to get into them, especially a particular one –'

'I'll get in. I'll study day and night for the entrance exam. I'll impress them at the interview with just how much I want to be a doctor.'

Nicola had a surge of pride in her daughter.

'Please, Dad, I need money for the trip to Africa. And I intend to work all during medical school to help pay my expenses –'

'It's not the money, Julie, it's the idea of exposing yourself to danger.'

'There are dangers of a different sort right here. I have to go to Africa and see what it's like.'

'You have some highly romantic notions, young lady, but the reality is far different. You've always lived in luxury.'

'I never needed it. I wouldn't have cared if we were dirt poor but were a real family, like the Markhams. I loved going there, even though by your standards they live like slobs.'

'Edward,' Nicola broke in, 'you may find it distasteful to deal with disease in Africa, but if that's what Julie wants to do –'

'That's what she wants now. She may want something different a few months from now,' Edward said morosely, 'when she gets turned off the boyfriend or she remembers how comfortable it was living here.'

'Edward, why don't we take it one step at a time.' Nicola was trying to be reasonable, as she saw father and daughter heading for an angry fight. 'Why not let Julie go to Africa. We can discuss the rest later –'

'Thanks, Mom,' Julie said, her chest heaving.

'All right,' Edward agreed sullenly. What he really was afraid of was that when Julie left so would Nicola.

'Why can't you go to Barnard or Columbia, and see this boy of yours on weekends? I'll pay for the transportation.'

'I don't want to do that but I will come down to New York often.'

Edward nervously lit a cigarette. 'I don't understand this, I really don't. For years you said you wanted to be a painter, and just because you meet a boy who's interested in medicine you're going to throw away all your training and all your advantages. Medical school is a long haul. And the art field has endless possibilities, even if you're not a painter. I'd help you start your own collection. I want to pass on my work of a lifetime. You're my only daughter.'

'I'm sorry, Dad, but I don't want it. Give it to a museum. I don't want to be a collector any more than you wanted to be a banker.'

'Well, I think you're trying to work out some mental problem by scorning the help I can give you, all the contacts

I've made over the years in the art world.'

'I HATE THE ART WORLD,' Julie cried, growing excited. 'I hate it. It's phony, phony, phony. A playground for rich, selfish, gross people mostly interested in the big money.'

'That's enough,' Edward said hotly. 'You've inherited your mother's contempt for money, but both of you, I notice, are happy to come to me when you need it.'

'I don't have contempt for money,' Julie shouted, 'only for the way you use it. Money should be used to do some good in the world.'

'All I need is a do-gooder in the family,' Edward groaned.

'Edward, don't sneer at her idealism. I hope Julie never becomes cynical.'

'You're too late, Mom. I learned it from my dear old dad, wheeling and dealing with people's lives. You sneer at doing good because all you've ever done is bad!'

'Julie,' Nicola said, 'maybe you ought to stop.'

'No, I won't stop. He thinks money can buy anything and anyone, and he goes after weak, pathetic characters and offers them impossible temptations and ruins their lives!' Julie was red in the face and out of control.

Edward, looking at her reflectively, suddenly grew quiet.

'Julie,' Nicola said gently, 'I can see you're upset, but you're saying wild things.'

'They're not wild at all. I have proof. What he did to Ivor Lewes, for instance.'

Nicola snapped her head up. 'What? What are you talking about?'

'Dear old dad knows, Ivor told me all about it. Dad arranged the stealing of Paul's music and all the rest. Ivor wasn't supposed to know Dad was behind it but he found out from the doorman when he was trying to locate the detective, a man named Fry. I didn't know a thing until after I followed Ivor to Paris. It was on his conscience. He sold his name for five thousand dollars, which he spent in one month on dope. That creep outside my hotel room was Ivor. When I found out about that dirty deal to hurt Paul I just wanted to die. I was so ashamed of having a father who would do a thing like that!'

254

'Coming from a girl in an alcoholic coma and knocked up to boot, that's almost comical!'

Edward stood in the centre of the room glaring at his defiant daughter and his horrified wife.

'You think it was so terrible what I did to Paul? Well I don't. I'd do it again. As long as we're having a family psychodrama, let me tell you that when your mother went to live with that shit she broke my heart. I begged her to give him up, for your sake, too. I begged him. You should have heard him, arrogant little bastard, talking back, implying he could offer a woman more than I could, taunting me about my age. I warned him but he just laughed in my face!'

'Everyone fights with his own weapons. He had youth and talent. I had only my love for my wife and daughter –'

'And money,' Nicola said, in a cold, hard voice, 'and sleazy detectives, and the morals of a gutter rat.'

Edward swallowed, his pallor deepening. He turned to Julie. 'Are you satisfied now?'

'Satisfied isn't the right word. I'm glad all of this is out in the open, finally. People can't make a real choice in their lives unless they have all the facts. Anyway, I'm going now to meet Luke. What a breath of fresh air that will be!'

'You can whistle for money for that trip to Africa,' Edward shouted after her.

'I'll give you the money,' Nicola said, staring at Edward with hatred.

'At least you're fighting like real people, instead of all that pretence that used to make me sick!' Julie's face softened. 'I used to think I hated you both but that was because you'd hurt me so much. I know you didn't mean to, but it worked out that way. One of the things I've learned is that I love you because you're my parents, even if I don't admire everything you do. I guess everyone makes mistakes.'

After Julie left Nicola and Edward were silent, sharing a last parental moment.

She spoke first. 'I can't stay here a moment longer.'

'Don't be hasty. Try to understand. They say all's fair in love and war –'

'Not in my book,' Nicola retorted, rising.

'What should I have done? Let you go, just like that, after nineteen years?'

'Yes, if that's what I wanted. I'm going in any case!'

'Nicola, don't.'

'I must. That you could even hatch such a despicable plot shows me I never really knew you. If you were going to harm anyone it should have been me, and not Paul.'

'Why didn't Paul raise a stink? Why did he take it lying down? You're a babe in the woods, Nicola. The name of the game is winning. And a person either has what it takes or he hasn't. And if he hasn't he deserves to lose.'

Nicola looked at Edward sadly. 'Oh, great! How about murder? Is that acceptable in this winning of yours?'

'Goddamn it, we're talking about wife-stealing. In some cultures murder is justified.'

'Yes, where a woman is considered a part of the furniture. You can't differentiate between me and something you paid a high price for. You want value for money –'

'You're goddamn right I do. Who wouldn't? I damn well did pay a high price for you. I promoted your talent, and now when you're at the top of your profession you're cutting out because you suddenly don't like my methods. But you didn't question them when they were pushing you up the goddamn ladder.'

Nicola stared at him. 'I don't know what you mean. You helped me, yes. You bought my early pieces. Of course the deal with Silversmith was despicable. If I had known about it then –'

Edward lost his temper. 'You goddamn bitch, to look at me like that, as if I'm beneath contempt, after you've profited from my efforts!'

He advanced upon her. 'I'm not going to hit you. I just want you to wise up. If it weren't for me you'd be doing paper cutouts in a kindergarten. You'd be nowhere.'

'That's not true,' Nicola whispered. 'The O'Caseys chose my stuff for their show –'

'The hell they did! *I* chose it. *I* found out who you were and what you were doing. I assured them that all your stuff would be sold. As a matter of fact, except for what the Luries bought, I bought the rest myself and paid a higher price than they agreed with you. I knew they wouldn't be able to resist ripping you off. Then I stepped in, the hero, and got your money back, right? Wrong. I never saw the O'Caseys again. I reimbursed you out of my own pocket.'

'Why?' she asked, stunned.

'Because I wanted you. It was the only way I could attract your notice. I was intrigued. Most girls in your position would spread their legs just for a beer. You were different. I found it an enjoyable challenge. Besides, I really believed then that you had a certain amount of talent. But having it and getting it noticed were two different things.'

Nicola was almost speechless. 'And when Marshall Faber offered me a show in his gallery –'

'There is no Marshall Faber Gallery, you naïve infant. It's my gallery. You should have guessed the truth years ago. Marshall was under curator at MOMA, gutless and spineless. He's licked my boots for years just to have his name over the door. I bought the whole goddamn shebang for you.'

'Oh, God.' Nicola crumpled into a chair, her face on her arm.

Edward came closer. 'And that's reality. You artists have your brains in your fingertips. Art is a business, like banking, like manufacturing. You have to grab your opportunity ...'

Nicola could hardly hear him. Her brain was twirling in her skull. For years she had suppressed her anxiety about her talent, reasoning that the proof was in her success. But now?

She got shakily to her feet.

'Don't look at me with such hatred. Think rather that I loved you enough to put myself out for you, always, getting you commissions, sweet-talking critics, fraternising and socialising so that my reputation for picking talent would rub off on you. I put my reputation on the line for you, as a matter of fact. I cherished you. I loved you body and soul. And you denied me, pretending all your sexuality was going into your art, frustrating me so much I had to resort to other women. I suppose that revolting boy of yours told you that. And to go and live with him publicly, making a laughingstock of me –'

Nicola started to run from the room.

'If you leave me you'll be just another middle-aged dabbler who's lost her touch. Where is your art? You haven't sculpted one piece in a year. From this day forward, Marshall is through with you.'

Nicola faced him, her lips trembling with rage and self-loathing. 'Are you planning to do to me what you did to Paul?'

'I don't have to do a thing. It's what I won't do that will finish you. Your talent is a dime a dozen. Name or not, you'll see how far you get without me.'

6

Nicola bought a studio on West Broadway in SoHo for a greatly reduced price by putting fifty thousand down in cash. It nearly cleaned her out. Although the loft wasn't half as large or grand as the one on Eleventh Street, it had the forty-foot ceilings she needed and the potential of being quite livable.

Nicola invited Julie and Luke to lunch in a restaurant, and eased out of her depression when she saw how happy the two were.

Luke was arrestingly funny-looking, with a freckled face and wide mouth. He was very, very sensitive to Julie, Nicola noticed, treating her with respect and kindness and a shy appreciation of her beauty.

'Mom, I've sort of made up with Dad and he's given me the money to go to Africa after all. I'm sorry if I was the cause of your breakup.'

'You weren't. It would have come anyway, and in this case, sooner is better.'

Julie hesitated, looking probingly at her mother. 'We're leaving next week, but when we come back, before we go up to Ithaca, I could stay with you that last weekend if you'd like.'

Nicola smiled. 'I'd love it, but don't expect Eleventh Street. My new studio is a mess. And so am I.'

Nicola encouraged Luke to talk about himself.

'You know, my father pestered me for years to be a doctor, like just about everyone in his family. He couldn't make it because his eyes were too bad. I always resisted. I didn't want a Park Avenue practice. But after Beckworth and seeing medicine in a new light, I decided it's what I really want after all.'

'I like Luke a lot,' Nicola told her daughter when he excused himself for a moment.

'I can see he likes you too, Mom. I just wish everyone were as happy as we are.'

Nicola hoped that Julie could retain her enthusiasm for a long time. Of course, disappointment of some sort was bound to come. Perhaps Julie now would be able to handle it without falling to pieces. Her daughter's new strength gave Nicola relief from her own anxiety.

'Julie, do you suppose I could borrow the sculpture I made for you?'

'Of course, if I can have it back. It really did help me to look at the sun.'

When they parted, Nicola gave her daughter her phone number and post office box. 'I need to be by myself to work out some things. Except you, I don't want anyone – and I mean anyone – to know where I am.'

'Okay.' Julie suspected her mother was thinking of her father. 'Do you think you and Paul might get together?'

Nicola looked pained and shook her head. 'He's found someone else. Anyway, it couldn't have worked for long.'

Nicola withdrew from all social contacts. She worked like a maniac to clean up the studio and furnished it with bits and pieces found in thrift shops. She had left everything on Eleventh Street except some tools and things she had bought with her own money.

Nicola went to her lawyer to arrange for a divorce as soon as possible. She was asking for nothing but her freedom. The constant question in her mind was how much of her

259

success was based on talent and how much on Edward's influence. Yes, of course she had something, she had to have. However, she knew very well that certain artists had been popular during their lifetimes because of their patrons or their winning personalities, only to have their work judged as unimportant by critics of succeeding generations.

Had a single commission ever come her way except by Edward's intervention? Everything had been handled through Marshall, and Nicola had no way of knowing, no way of proving anything to herself.

The only proof would be what she did from now on.

She spent a chunk of her remaining money on materials. Then she shut herself up in the loft and worked sixteen hours a day or more until she was ready to drop from exhaustion. It was as if six months of inspiration, blocked by her concern over Julie, were suddenly bursting forth.

Nicola hardly knew the time of day because she had rigged up lighting so that she could work whenever she wished. She ate only when discomfort in her stomach reminded her that it required fuel. She sculpted as she had never done before, even during her most productive periods.

She was fighting for her creative life. At the same time that she felt apprehensive and angry with herself for having been so stupid all those years, she existed in a fever of excitement at what she was producing.

After working with grey metals, Nicola was fascinated by the coloured acrylics and loved the effects she could achieve by combining them.

When her 'phone rang one morning she was startled.

'We're back, Mom. What's the matter? You sound funny.'

'Has a month passed already?'

'Of course. Didn't you get my cards?'

Nicola hadn't even been to the post office.

'There's also a pile of mail at home. I'll bring it over, okay?'

'Yes.' Nicola hung up, willing herself to step from the plane of her own imagination to the real world. Julie was coming for the weekend as she had promised.

*

Edward was relieved to meet Luke Simmonds and find him a reasonable young man in spite of being so unattractive. Well, Julie had enough beauty for both of them.

He had never seen his daughter look more radiant, like a young goddess. That painful, coltlike awkwardness had gone, along with the skinny, fragile quality.

Julie was bursting with health and enthusiasm and strength. They had loved Africa and were sticking to their plan to work there after medical school.

'Dad, there's nothing to worry about. We took pills to avoid malaria and we got all the shots we needed.'

'We can make a real contribution to world health and even political peace, Sir. We felt like magicians watching people's faces light up when they saw the miracle medicine can provide!'

Edward decided he liked this polite and respectful young man. Besides, he came from a damn good family. Plenty of money there on both sides, and distinguished surgeons, too. Luke was not even eighteen. He would surely change his mind over the next four years and follow his uncles into a lucrative private practice in New York or Boston.

Edward was feeling good again. The reality that Nicola had gone, that she would never come back to him, had given him the impetus to try to form an alliance with someone else. He had been running through women like a millionaire's profligate son through the family fortune.

He had got back his confidence and his virility. He didn't feel he had lost Nicola. Rather, they had simply outgrown each other. Theirs had been a nineteen-year marriage, period. Nicola was undeniably neurotic and Edward now thought himself lucky to be rid of her. He saw that once she had proved herself disloyal he had stopped loving her and it was only stubbornness and hurt pride that had caused him to try to get her back.

Things were looking up for Edward in every respect. The career of Marc Rubetsky, the painter he had discovered, had taken off like a rocket, and Edward was making a fortune on his early work. Several new talents had come to him of their own accord, one of them a beautiful woman, Nora Rambleaux, recently divorced from a French businessman. She was doing wonderful sculptures that combined architecture with video images. She thought Edward was absolutely marvellous. At the same time, she was modest and not sexually aggressive. Just what the doctor ordered. Edward persuaded her to move into the empty studio on Eleventh Street.

When the divorce papers arrived, Edward couldn't believe that Nicola wasn't asking for a penny. She could have made a big court case out of it, and probably proved that he had been womanising for years. Of course she had left him, not once but twice. He could have dragged her name and Paul's through the papers, though he had no appetite for that kind of publicity. Nicola had never been a businesswoman. Edward, not sure whether to respect her for her integrity or feel contempt for her stupidity, signed the papers gratefully.

Nicola enjoyed the two days with Julie and Luke. She turned her mind off her work and listened with fascination to their experiences in Africa.

'You can't imagine how wonderful it was, Mom. In spite of their superstitions, the people out in the bush are so quick to learn, so friendly and warm. By the time we're back there working they'll have their own doctors. Our role will be to teach them to apply the latest medical techniques.'

Julie was like the young Nicola, only stronger for her ordeal and more sophisticated. Nicola was glad that she was living at a time when women were encouraged to have careers instead of having to fight the world, as well as their own doubts.

Going through her pile of mail, Nicola opened letter after letter from the major galleries. Learning that the Marshall Faber Gallery had closed, no fewer than ten others were offering to represent her.

Nicola decided against telling Julie what she had learned from Edward. She simply said she was changing her medium and asked Julie not to mention her acrylics to her father.

Julie was enthusiastic about the new works, which pleased her mother. She felt closer to Julie than ever.

'Oh, Janet Markham called. I told her I was sworn to

secrecy about your address and 'phone number. I think she's a little hurt.'

'I'll call her,' Nicola promised.

'I've interrupted your work, haven't I. You would rather not have seen me at this time.' Julie's happy face clouded over.

Nicola looked directly at her daughter. 'It's true that you interrupted me but not that I would rather not be with you. When you were so ill I couldn't work at all. Seeing you well and happy will help me to work better. I've learned, far too late, the importance of a person one loves. You come first, Julie.'

Julie put her arms around her mother and they hugged.

When her daughter had gone, Nicola didn't give herself time to dwell on the emptiness of the studio. She went right back to work, not stopping until, after another month, she had amassed fifteen maquettes.

She had slides made, put them in a box, and sent them out to one of the galleries that had expressed enthusiasm for handling Nicola Di Candia.

The name she had decided to use was Frances Gray.

FALL, 1979

7

'Anne, I feel honoured you could fit me into your busy life, and when everything is going well, too.' Al Lurie was having an elaborate meal in a Chinese restaurant with his wife.

'Oh, don't be silly.' Anne was feeling good, bubbling over with talk about Paul. 'Al, have you seen him lately?'

'Sure. We have lunch or dinner every week or so. He's doing fine.' Al's expression, however, was wary.

She immediately caught it. 'You sound doubtful, but I'm sure. I've heard some of the music for the ballet, and it's wonderful. I'm so thrilled that it's going to be performed at Lincoln Centre. We hadn't hoped for that, but Miles seems to have all the contacts. I only hope Paul can keep out of the gay world.'

Al smiled. 'He can take care of himself. He's learned a lot in a few months. This ballet is going to be his big break, and then watch him take off.'

'Yes. If only he would find himself a nice girl. He's wearing himself out, going with one after another.'

'I thought you wanted him to play the field.'

'That was before *her*. If he can't find a replacement he might still be vulnerable.'

Anne leaned forward, a mischievous smile lighting up her face. 'I did something maybe not so nice, but necessary. I told Nicola when I ran into her at the Markham's that Paul had a new girlfriend. Later I mentioned to Paul that Nicola was back and happy with Edward.'

'Jesus, babe, that's playing with dynamite.'

'Never mind. Sometimes a person has to step in to save someone from making a big mistake.'

Al shook his head. 'You can't play God, especially not with Paul, and when he finds out you lied to him –'

'He won't find out. Why should he?'

Al took Anne's hand. 'Because, sweetie, Nicola has split with Edward for good.'

Nicola felt a chill of terror when her slides came back from the Castelli Gallery with a polite rejection. Immediately she sent them to Marlborough. And when they came back from there, to Sidney Janis, and then to Fischbach.

All of them had wanted Nicola Di Candia. Not one was willing to handle Frances Gray. Not one appeared to see anything in the work. Regardless of the medium, any knowledgeable dealer should have been able to recognise Di Candia work when he saw it – unless she had failed utterly. Unless her stuff was really lousy. Had Edward been correct that her work was only mediocre and it had been his influence that made her name? Or was it simply that blue-chip galleries would take on only blue-chip names, regardless of quality?

Each rejection had made her feel as if another link to the world had been broken, isolating her with her misery.

She was in limbo. She could not continue to produce maquettes that might have no merit, and she didn't have money to buy more materials. She needed a commission.

For days Nicola sat in the studio and brooded. It was already October. Soon Julie would be coming down to New York with Luke.

Nicola dreaded having to be cheerful or spoil Julie's good time. The only thing keeping her from total despondency was the cheerful letters and 'phone calls from her daughter. Julie was working in a local hospital and had applied for premed but would have to wait until the following September to go if she were accepted.

Increasingly, Nicola thought and dreamed about Paul. Every time she imagined him with another woman she felt as if her body were being unfleshed by gall into a useless collection of bones. She wasn't eating or sleeping properly. At odd moments a terrible panic would seize her, causing her to break into a cold sweat and tremble. Her entire artistic life had been a lie and a fake. And her affair with Paul had been a make-believe travesty, embarrassing in retrospect.

She finally 'phoned Janet.

'Nicola, thank heavens! Tom and I have been so concerned.'

'I'm all right,' Nicola said woodenly, 'but I'm going through a crisis. I really need time to work it out.' Very briefly she sketched the points of Edward's revelations.

'I can imagine what you're feeling, Nika, but surely you can find a new gallery without Edward's help?'

'I'm trying, Janet. My love to you and Tom.'

Nicola put down the phone with trembling fingers. Panic had overcome her and made her mouth so dry she couldn't speak.

'Nicola sounded so down, Tom. Being out of contact with everyone is terrible.'

'Yes it is,' Tom agreed thoughtfully. 'What I can't

understand is that she's having to look for a dealer at all. Galleries should be falling over each other to handle her. It doesn't make sense.'

'I wish I could find out where she is,' Janet mused. 'Julie has been asked not to tell, but I think we ought to do something.'

'Try telling Paul.'

'How would that help? I mean, so much time has gone by.'

'I think he'll find her if he wants to.' Tom put his arms around Janet. 'True love always finds a way.'

The day Nicola had to pay her next monthly maintenance on the loft, she saw that the balance in her cheque book was only a thousand dollars. When she wrote a cheque for three seventy-five there would hardly be anything left.

Nicola began one of the interior dialogues she had been having with herself lately.

You do have talent and you'll make it. Don't give in. It's only been a couple of months, you big sissy. You stuck it out when you were young and all the odds were against you.

Yes, but I *was* young, that's the point. And I had faith. I was too ignorant to realise how easy it is to fail.

If you don't have the courage to find out the truth about your art, just send your slides to Luigi Bianchi under your real name. Presto, you'll have a gallery, money, fame. Everyone will talk about the exciting new Di Candia acrylics.

I can't do that. Because not knowing where I stand is worse than having my work turned down.

Okay, hot shot, what *are* you going to do?

Pull myself together, climb out of the pits, and survive.

Nicola put on her jeans and an old shirt and jacket. Tying a scarf around her head, she went out into the windy street to look for work in the very places she had sometimes posted notices for day help.

She found a job assembling a complicated neon sculpture. Sticking to the name Frances Gray, Nicola worked hard, spoke little, and was relieved that nobody recognised her.

At the post office her slides were waiting for her.

Edward Harringon was having a drink with Luigi Bianchi in his office at the gallery uptown.

'You're looking good.' Bianchi smirked and hit Edward's arm playfully with his fist. 'Bachelorhood agrees with you, eh?'

Edward grinned his old toothpaste grin. 'Can't complain. The best thing about woman's lib is all that available pussy.'

Bianchi roared. 'You can say that again. You look like you're getting plenty. Makes you look fifteen years younger. I wish I had your energy and time. Speaking of which, you want to show me something, right?'

'Right.' Edward smiled pleasantly. 'I've found an astonishing sculptor, Nora Rambleaux, turning out wonders like you wouldn't believe.'

Edward began to arrange the slides in the projector.

A young girl in large glasses came into Bianchi's office with the mail.

'Uh, I thought you might be interested in these. I found them intriguing.'

Both men smiled at the girl's earnest tone.

'Show them here, Jill. What name?'

'Frances Gray.'

'Okay, Jillie, I'll have a peek.'

'What a funny little mouse,' Edward said after she left.

'Yeah.' Bianchi was holding one slide after another up to the light. 'She's a smart kid, though. And you'll never guess whose daughter. Svenson's.'

Edward whistled softly. Svenson was a big collector, a Swedish-born millionaire.

'These are very interesting, the kid is right,' Bianchi mused. 'I haven't seen acrylics handled quite this way. This guy's no amateur. Wonder where he's been hiding. No, it's Frances female. What do you think?'

Edward held one up, and then another. He shrugged. 'Pretty mediocre.' He glanced cursorily at the rest. 'Some skill, but no pizzazz. Not like what I have here. Rambleaux has me more excited over sculpture than I've been in years.

In my opinion she's going to turn out to be another Nicola
Di Candia.'

After exhausting the uptown galleries Nicola sent her slides
to a gallery in SoHo. She felt like an ageing courtesan reduced
to walking the streets. It wasn't that she didn't have respect
for these newer showcases, which were more receptive to
unknown and avant-garde artists. But she had been a star,
and it was difficult to start again from the bottom.

Back came the slides from one, two, three, four SoHo
galleries.

Nicola got up one very cold morning realising that she
would not be able to pay the December rent. Her day work
barely kept her in food and postage.

Bundling up some of her designer original dresses and
suits, Nicola took a Madison Avenue bus uptown to a
second-hand shop she had heard about.

She was humiliated to find the door of the shop locked.
She had to wait like a criminal while the suspicious lady
buzzed her in.

Looking disdainfully at Nicola's jeans and sheepskin
jacket, the saleslady offered her insultingly low prices. 'It's
the best I can do. These are out of fashion. Someone may
have paid a fortune for them,' she said, her sarcastic tone
indicating that Nicola had stolen them or had them handed
down, 'but I can't sell them for much. Take it or leave it.'

Nicola took it, her face flushing with mortification and an
upsurge of the fearful panic. When she took the money she
was trembling and perspiring. The woman looked at her
with contempt as if she were a drug addict desperate for a
fix.

Nicola couldn't wait to get out of there. A cold blast of
damp air hit her in the face and cooled her burning cheeks.
Never again. She would get a job, anything.

She decided to save the fifty cents and walk home. That
turned out to be a mistake. It got colder by the moment, and
Nicola felt weak from having eaten very little. She got more
and more exhausted but stubbornly refused to spend the
money for the fare once she had started walking.

She stopped at the post office, sensing her slides were

there. They were. They had been returned by every well-known gallery in SoHo.

By the time she reached her studio she was flushed and achy. Not hungry, she undressed and crawled into bed. Fitfully she slept, but awakened in the middle of the night with a killing headache and a burning sensation all over her body. When she tried to get up she fell weakly to the floor.

'Dad,' Paul said to his father over a pre-dinner drink, 'Did you know that Nicola left Edward and moved into her own place?'

'Yeah. That is I heard they split up but not where she was living –'

'Why in hell didn't you tell me!'

Al looked reflectively at his son's agitated face. 'I only found out last week –'

'Anne had assured me they were happy together.'

Al, uncomfortable, glanced away.

'That wasn't true, was it? She purposely said that, to throw me off.'

Al sighed. 'Your mother is a wonderful woman in many ways but she's wrathful, like a biblical character. And I can't stand to see her unhappy. It hurts me, kid, it really does me damage.'

Paul looked soberly at his father. 'Even though she's always treated you badly.'

Al made a face and moved his hand from side to side. 'No, not always. In her way, she cares. Besides, I can't help myself. The rabbi said till death do you part, and that's the way I feel. She's my Annie, for better or worse.'

'I'm the same as you,' Paul said fiercely, leaning over the table and fixing his father with his compelling eyes. 'Nicola is my woman. Now tell me where she is.'

'I don't know, Paulie, honestly. I only heard accidentally from that old windbag, your mother's friend Max Furst, who I ran into on Sixth Avenue. He bent my ear for fifteen minutes, gossiping about this one and that one. Said he'd seen an item about the Harrington divorce in the paper.'

'I have to find her. Janet Markham called to tell me but she doesn't have her 'phone number or address, just that it's

269

in SoHo. The Marshall Faber Gallery has folded. I've even tried to reach Julie in Ithaca.'

Paul gulped his drink and ran his fingers through his hair. 'I haven't been able to write a note since I heard. Al, she needs me, I can sense it. Goddamn it, where is she?'

Julie was sweeping the floor of the hospital ward. The ward was dark, the quiet broken by an occasional moan from one of the patients.

She glanced at the big clock over the night nurse's desk. Luke would be phoning her before picking her up when she came off duty.

He was the most wonderful person in the world and she was awfully lucky to have met him. In spite of his long hours of study, he insisted on setting the alarm to get up and take a bus to the hospital.

A weary groan came from a bed on the aisle. Julie, looking up from her sweeping, saw a pair of glittering eyes in the face of an old lady.

'Hello,' Julie whispered. 'Having trouble sleeping? Can I ask the nurse to get you something?'

'Could you possibly just sit for a minute?'

Julie sat down and took the woman's hand. She appeared to be very old.

'Ninety-seven,' she told Julie proudly. 'Never sick. Four children, nine grandchildren, fifteen great-grandchildren.'

'That's wonderful.' Julie smiled at her.

'You must be a fine girl,' the woman murmured, 'to work in a hospital. You could be an actress, a girl like you.'

Julie squeezed her hand. 'I don't want that. It makes me feel happy to help people the way I was helped when I was very sick. I'm going to be a doctor.'

The old lady nodded. 'What's your name?'

'Julie.'

'Well, Dr Julie, thanks for sitting with me. It takes away the loneliness of the night.' Her grip grew slack as she dozed.

Gently Julie detached her hand and resumed her work. Just as she reached the end of the ward the 'phone rang. It was answered by the night nurse.

'Julie, for you.'

'Hello. Luke?'

'Julie, this is Paul Kadin-Lurie.'

'Oh. Oh, hi, Paul.'

'Have you spoken to your mother recently?'

'Not in about a week.'

'Julie, please, please let me have her 'phone number. Nobody's heard from her, not even Janet Markham.'

'I'll call her right now, but I can't give you her number unless she says it's okay. I'm sorry but I promised.'

After a moment of silence Julie heard him mutter, 'Oh, Christ,' under his breath. 'Okay, but tell her I must speak to her. Please call me back collect.'

Julie dialled her mother as soon as Paul hung up. She let the phone ring fifteen times but nobody answered. Maybe her mother was out, maybe with a man. Julie decided to try again first thing in the morning.

Nicola lost track of time. She had no idea how long she remained in bed without eating. She was aware that her head felt as if it were being split with an axe into kindling wood, her back ached, and her legs were burning. When she looked at herself she saw that she had a splotchy rash on her chest and belly. She sank back gratefully into a half-doze.

She didn't care. She had nothing to get up for.

Nicola Di Candia. A myth created by Edward Harrington III. He had brought her art to life and now that she was not with him it had died a natural death.

She would die a natural death.

A bell rang and rang and rang ...

'Nika, get up, we have to put up the meal,' her mother was calling. 'I purposely set the alarm.'

Nicola didn't want to help her mother in the kitchen. She wanted to go out in the backyard with her brother and her father, who were doing all sorts of exciting things with blowtorches.

'What's the matter with you? What are you dreaming about? I told you to beat the batter. You're moving it around like you're half asleep. How're you ever going to learn to be a good cook if you don't pay attention?'

'I don't want to be a good cook. I want to weld fenders like Vincent.'

'I told you a million times, a girl doesn't weld fenders.'

'Why not?'

'Because ... Don't ask me stupid questions. Come and help me stuff the zucchini.'

Nicola awoke drenched in perspiration.

'Girls aren't doctors, they're nurses,' she suddenly heard her mother say. She tried to argue but fell asleep.

When Nicola awoke in the morning she felt cool and clear-headed for the first time in days. She was still weak, though. Shakily she got out of bed and turned on the radio. Friday, November twenty-third. It couldn't be. She had no memory of the last nine days.

Nicola didn't recognise the apparition she saw in the mirror. Pale, gaunt, horrible. When she dressed, her clothes hung like a tent draped over a clothes rack.

She went slowly to the kitchen and made coffee, eggs, and toast.

Between her wallet and her cheque book she had a grand total of sixty-seven dollars and forty-eight cents. For two months she hadn't paid her 'phone bill or Con Edison. And the maintenance on her loft was way overdue.

Get a job.

Doing what? I can't even type.

You can make frames. Weld fenders. Get a job in a garage. No excuses, now. You can be a salesgirl. A waitress. It's better than losing the loft.

Is it? What do I need all this space for? I can't work any more. I've found out for a fact what I suspected all these years. That's it!

When the prince was dressed as a pauper nobody believed he was the prince. Life is like that. You're expecting a miracle.

Nicola, dressed and made up, looked only marginally better than before.

She stood at the doorway, uncertain of what to do. Go out and look for work? Stay in and wait to be evicted?

When her eye fell on the maquettes, her vision became distorted. Suddenly panic closed in. Here we are, your ugly creations, they seemed to be shouting at her, the monsters that nobody wants.

Nicola rushed blindly through the door. As soon as she was halfway down the stairs her telephone began to ring but she didn't go back.

8

Paul sat hunched over his desk, spread with his music papers. He tried to work but couldn't. He simply had to find Nicola.

Agitation caused his thoughts to wander fitfully. If he hadn't been so foolishly proud he would have called even though she had never responded to his letter.

When the 'phone rang he jumped.

'It's Julie. I've tried my mother but there's no answer.'

'I must have her address. I feel there's something wrong.'

'I can't. Mom made me promise.'

'But nobody else knows where she is. Marshall Faber closed his gallery. Does she have another dealer?'

Surprised, Julie said, 'I really don't know anything about it.'

'Julie, I'll take the blame. Just give me her address.'

'I'll keep trying to call her. I should reach her by tonight.'

Paul put down the 'phone, not relishing the irony that the girl who had gone out of her way to cause her mother pain was now so scrupulous about following her instructions. Or was Julie still trying to keep him and Nicola apart? It struck him that Nicola might have another man. That could be why she had left Edward, and why Julie was so hesitant in helping him reach her.

He couldn't bear to sit still. Putting on his jacket, he rushed out.

Nicola stood on the corner of Houston and Sullivan, wondering what she was doing there. Had she decided to try to find work? Her head felt very light, and there was a buzzing in her ears. Maybe she wasn't really here at all, and this was only another dream.

Flip a coin. Heads you look for work in the Village, tails you try SoHo.

Nicola's fingers, without gloves, were numb. How did one flip a coin anyway?

Throw it in the air and catch it on the back of your left hand with your right palm.

She tried but missed. Fascinated, she watched the quarter roll into a pile of debris in the gutter.

'Nicola!'

There was Paul coming towards her, disguised in a beard.

He stopped in front of her. They stared at one another.

'I'm only dreaming,' she whispered. 'I've been doing that lately.'

When he put his hands on her shoulders, she could feel his warm breath on her forehead. 'I'm very real.'

She looked at him in wonder. 'Paul?'

'Nicola!' He drew her to him, enfolding her in his arms, holding her close, but gently. She seemed so cold, so frail.

'Paul, Paul,' she repeated against his rapidly beating heart.

'We need a brandy.' He took her icy hand and led her into a bar.

Like an obedient child, Nicola sipped her drink, glancing at him to confirm that this was really happening.

Paul, looking at her, was close to tears. She was deathly pale, her skin almost transparent. She seemed to have retreated into herself. 'How are you feeling?'

'Warmer.' She managed a wan smile. 'I think I've had the flu, and I'm still weak.'

'Would you like me to take you home?'

'No!' She had a sickening memory of those mocking sculptures.

Paul was uneasy. What was at home? A lover? He ordered another round.

The brandy made Nicola feel better. She had been standing on the street and met Paul, remarkable as that was. They were now having a drink, like two old friends. Except she must not spill out her troubles. As it was he was regarding her with pity.

'I – I was happy to hear that you're writing music for a new ballet.'

'Thanks. I was lucky to get it.' Paul talked on, hoping to put her at ease. She was behaving like a person who has been isolated from human companionship for a long time.

Nicola watched him as he spoke, her visual impression vying with her concentration. Paul Kadin-Lurie, the young man she had adored, was no longer quite so young. There were lines in his forehead that hadn't been there eleven months ago. Life had caught up with Anne's golden boy and added a little tarnish.

Nicola dropped her gaze so that he wouldn't see the tears hovering in the corners of her eyes. If he looked so much older to her, how ancient she must seem to him. She felt miserably self-conscious, and at the same time deperson-alised. He was strong, self-contained, sure of himself. And she was – what? Who?

How she had longed to see Paul. Now that she was seeing him, she wanted only to get away.

He had grown silent and was looking at her with pained concern. 'Nicola, please speak to me. I am still your – your friend.'

She returned his glance and sighed. How could she tell him her whole life had been a fraud? Paul had admired her work, but he was not an expert. How much had been his interest in her? How much influenced by her fame?

She felt strange with him, alienated. He was on his way up, and she was already smarting from the rocks at the bottom. She was glad they were no longer together. He would have felt responsible, obligated to carry her on his back. Every moment with him now was a confirmation of the rightness of her decision, and what madness it had all been.

Paul smiled sadly. 'It's been such a long time. There's so much to say that it's difficult to know where to begin. You haven't begun yet.'

The smile cut her in two. He was more attractive than

275

ever. He would continue to be attractive, while she shrivelled and wrinkled and faded into eccentric middle age – if she lived that long.

'I understand you've moved into your own loft.'

'Yes.'

'I'm happy that Julie is recovered and interested in becoming a doctor.'

'Yes.'

Paul refused to give up. He leaned forward tensely. 'Why did you never answer my letter? Or my 'phone call?'

'You – you wrote me a letter?' Her skin began to tingle. 'And you called? And left your name?'

'Of course. Many months ago, when I first heard how sick Julie was.'

'I never got the letter or the message. I suppose that was Edward's doing.' Nicola swallowed with difficulty.

'God, what you must have thought of me, believing I wasn't even concerned enough to get in touch. Nicola, I was, and am, very, very sorry about what happened. I was totally wrong about Julie. I behaved childishly and selfishly. Forgive me for having made the situation even worse for you than it needed to be.'

'Of course,' she murmured, finding it hard to look at him. With every word he said she was being drawn to him, frighteningly so.

'I'd heard that you had stopped sculpting to take care of Julie. I know what that must have cost you, and – and I shouldn't have stopped trying to contact you, but I was afraid to impose, if you didn't want to be in touch. I mean, Anne told me that you and Edward were – together.'

Nicola smiled sardonically. 'She said that, did she? Good old Annie. Consistent, anyway. A killer, Al once called her.'

'It wasn't true? You were living at Beekman Place ...'

'In the guest room, on the advice of Julie's doctor. Anyway,' Nicola said in a flat, sad voice, 'Julie's all right, Edward's all right, and I'm all right. I must go home now.'

Paul felt as if he had been slapped. Maybe her coolness was a desperate attempt to deal with her vulnerability, but he couldn't help taking it personally.

Nicola, in fact, was determined not to show how much she still loved him. She stood up.

276

'I'll take you home in a taxi. It's snowing, and – and I wouldn't put an invalid out on a day like this,' he murmured very low.

Nicola felt she was going to cry, and she grabbed her coat and ran out of the bar. She had to get away.

He ran after her and caught her arm. 'Can't we be friends?'

'Someday, maybe.' *When you're married and I'm too ludicrously old for anything but.*

They stood on the street, a snowy wind blowing into their faces. Paul was desperate. When he saw a taxi he hailed it and grabbed Nicola, catching her by surprise.

'What's your address?'

She hesitated and then gave it to him.

He sat back in the cab, looking at her reproachfully. 'You're being silly, hiding out as if a gang of criminals were after you. I'm just going to deliver you to your door, not beat it down.'

Nicola was silent. The panic began to hit her when she remembered those sculptural abortions waiting for her.

'I was surprised to learn that Faber closed his gallery. Have you found another dealer?'

His question accelerated her panic. 'I can't talk about it.'

He divined then that her crisis had to do with her work.

Before Nicola could leap out of the taxi Paul had paid and was at her side. He pulled out his card. 'Promise you'll call if there's anything I can do. The offer of friendship is for all time.'

Nicola's eyes filled and she quickly averted her head. With feigned casualness she took the card and put it in her pocket.

He swallowed hard and looked at the snow swirling on the sidewalk. How could he leave her here, like this?

'Thanks for the drinks and the ride. Goodbye, Paul.'

She turned her back and inserted her key in the door. When she opened it and glanced behind her, he was still standing there looking stiff and cold and miserable.

'Go home, Paul. Your life is working. Don't look for trouble.'

'I've only felt half alive since you left,' he said in a low voice. 'It hurts that you won't even be friends.'

'I can't.' She refused to acknowledge what was happening to her flesh along the backbone.

'Please let's not say goodbye like this, Nicola.'

She saw a way of making him realise how low she had fallen.

'Okay, come up for a minute,' she said, almost mockingly.

He had a surge of hope as he followed her.

She entered the studio first and turned to face him, so as to catch his reaction the moment he saw her work.

His eyes widened in surprise and delight. Slowly he walked around the studio, where the sculptures were arranged in a semicircle. He looked at each in turn, touching gingerly with his fingertips.

For a long while he stood in front of *Julie Looks at the Sun*, slowly revolving under its special light.

Nicola glided silently beside him. His eyes were brimming.

'This is the best thing you've ever done. It touches me so much.'

Nicola burst into tears.

They were in each other's arms, holding each other, kissing each other's wet cheeks and eyes.

But when Paul tried to find her lips, Nicola wrenched away from him. This time she must be strong, cruel even. She could not start it all over again. He had a girl. This was pity, or maybe nostalgia.

'Please excuse me,' she gasped out. 'The brandy hit me on an empty stomach, and your reaction to my work –' She moved to a file cabinet. 'Every gallery uptown, downtown, and all around the town has rejected my slides.'

Paul, upset at the way she had pulled away from him, tuned in to her words. 'I don't believe it. It's impossible.'

Nicola flung papers at him. 'There they are, the rejection letters.'

He looked at them. 'But these say Frances Gray –'

'So what? A sculpture is a sculpture is a sculpture. What's in a name? If they were any good, the name wouldn't matter.'

'Oh, Nicola!' Paul was completely stunned.

'Nicola Di Candia was invented by Edward. Without that name nobody's interested.' She told him how Edward had schemed, lied, connived, and meddled in her career from the moment of their first meeting.

Through her resentment, Paul heard the hurt, and the fear. A great tenderness for Nicola filled him. And anger against Edward. He wanted to murder him, take her in his arms and kiss away all her pain. But she didn't want him.

'Regardless of what Edward has done, you are very talented. Have faith in yourself. At least half of the letters told you to try them again –'

'If my work were as good as it's supposed to be, one of those galleries would have wanted to represent me.'

'Try newer ones. Keep trying. You mustn't give up.'

She looked at him, a challenge in her voice. 'Do you think I'm wrong to use a pseudonym?'

'No. Not if you feel you really must know for sure.'

Nicola was afraid she would cry again. She saw that she would never stop loving Paul. 'Please go now.'

He forced himself to stand up. 'May I call you?'

'No.'

At the door he looked sadly at her but she kept her back turned.

They left it like that.

As sad as she felt, the interlude with Paul had restored Nicola's will to survive. She decided to look for some sort of temporary job.

The next morning, when Nicola was out shopping, she overheard an argument as she passed Vito's Body Shop.

'You promised my car days ago and you still haven't done a damn thing on it.' The well-dressed man pounded impatiently on the hood of his sleek red Jaguar.

'So I promised,' the grizzled old man shouted hotly. 'Did I know my son was going to get the flu on me? I'm all alone here.'

Nicola was reminded of similar confrontations between her father and his customers. He could only estimate the time it would take to make repairs, and if he ran into a snag ...

'If it's not ready tonight I'm taking it elsewhere.' The car owner walked away.

On an impulse, Nicola approached the old man. 'Do you need help? My dad used to own a body shop in Bay Ridge.'

Nicola spoke quickly, flushing at the look of incredulity on Vito's face.

'You want to fix cars? Gowan, lady!' He said something to her in neighbourhood Italian.

Shyly Nicola answered him.

He grunted. 'Okay, so you're a *gombara*. You don't look like you could even lift a hammer!'

Nicola had already moved away and was examining the Jaguar's dents and jagged edges, beginning to rust.

'Lady, don't waste my time. Sure I need help, but –'

'Give me an hour. If you don't like what I've done I'll walk away.'

Her quiet confidence puzzled him. 'I must be crazy, but okay. One hour. Hey, don't practice on that. Over there's a Chevvy ...'

In the tiny room behind the workshop Nicola found an old pair of pants and a jacket. They were miles too big but she rolled the sleeves and cuffs and got to work.

Vito stood back a little, hands on his hips, watching her, until his 'phone rang.

When she looked up from her torch, half an hour later, he was shaking his head unbelievingly. 'I don't know where you hide them muscles but I ain't complaining. If you can get the Jag ready for tonight you got yourself a job until my boy gets well. Eh, the whole world's topsy-turvy.'

As Nicola worked she felt she had stepped back a million years. Once again she was her father's assistant facing the challenge of repairing a car to make it 'as good as new.' There was a particular physical thrill to welding that she had been missing working with acrylics. Behind the blowtorch she felt powerful and in control. About the usefulness of this kind of work she had no doubts at all.

She saw, as she attacked the dents, that her despair had been masking a great deal of anger at the art world.

By mid-afternoon Nicola had the fenders smooth and ready for painting. Vito was busy with another customer so she went to the supply of spray paints and found one to match.

When her boss saw the finished job his mouth flew open.

At six the owner of the Jaguar appeared. Nicola, back in her street clothes and about to leave, was gratified to see his face crease into a satisfied smile. He was astonished to learn that Nicola had been the waver of the magic wand. 'Score one for the distaff side,' he said, smiling at her.

She declined his invitation to have a drink and simply went home.

Her feet and arms were sore but she felt better than she had in weeks.

In the studio the 'phone was ringing.

'Oh, Mom, I've been trying to reach you. Is everything all right?'

Julie's worried voice astounded Nicola. 'Yes. I had the 'flu and was sleeping a lot, but I'm recovered now. How are things with you –'

'Terrific. Mom, Paul called me.'

'Paul?'

'Kadin-Lurie. He was desperate for your 'phone number. Janet Markham had called him, worried at not having heard from you. Mom, why are you being so secretive?'

Nicola, her head whirling, didn't reply.

'Well, can I give Paul your number?'

'No, it won't be necessary.'

Julie hung up, puzzled and slightly uneasy. She was going to have to tell Paul her mother did not want to speak to him. It was awkward. Then she recalled that it was because of her that they had broken up. In the course of her recovery, Julie had realised that she would never be a decent human being let alone a doctor, unless she accepted responsibility.

She dialled Paul's number. 'I just reached my mother. She's fine.'

'Thanks for letting me know.'

He sounded deeply depressed. Julie's face grew warm. 'I'm afraid Mom's still not giving out her 'phone number.'

'I see.'

Julie took a deep breath. 'I'm sorry for all the trouble I caused between you and my mother. I had a few problems I needed to work out.'

'I understand. I owe you an apology too, Julie. I didn't take your illness seriously. I thought you were faking. My mistake. I'm glad things are going well for you now.'

281

'Thanks. I'm glad they're going well for you, too.' She paused. 'And I'm sorry it's too late for you and Mom –'

'Why too late?'

'Well, your new friend –'

'What new friend?' He sounded agitated.

'Look, I'm sorry. It's none of my business –'

'Julie, please tell me what you're talking about.'

'Well, I once asked Mom if you and she, well, you know, would get together again and she said you had somebody new.'

There was a long silence.

'Hello? Paul?'

'Thanks, Julie.' He hung up.

9

The next morning a white box was delivered to Nicola. It contained a bunch of anemones, her favourite flowers, incredibly out of season. There was a note:

My darling Nicola,

There is no other woman, no matter what you may have been told – no doubt by my incredibly meddling mother.

The two things that matter most to me are music and you. Music is always with me. The absence of you has made me restless and miserable for eleven months five days, thirteen hours, twelve minutes, and forty-five seconds.

Love alters not with brief hours and weeks but bears it out even to the edge of doom.

Still yours,
Paul

Nicola read the letter once and put it aside. It didn't matter, really. He was on his way up as a composer, and she had come full circle.

She was glad to lose herself in her work at the body shop. The noise and the exertion were stupefying, keeping her from thinking or feeling at all.

The nights were bad, however. She would fall into bed achingly tired, but her dreams were disturbing. The nightmares bothered her less than the erotic dreams with Paul, from which she always woke short of fulfilment. Although she hadn't intended to memorise his note, words and phrases kept flitting into her consciousness.

One morning on her way to work Nicola grabbed her slides and dropped them off at a new gallery.

When Anne opened the door she was astonished to see Paul. 'What a nice surprise.'

'No, not nice, not nice at all.'

His mother was dressed for the evening, and he could hear musicians tuning up inside.

'You have guests, so what I have to say I can say here. You told Nicola that I had a girlfriend, just as you told me she and Edward were happy together. Both lies. How dare you manipulate people's lives so callously?'

'I meant only to protect you –'

'I don't care what you meant. Only what you *did*. I've been miserable for a year. Damn it, do I interfere in your life? Do I tell you to go back to Al, who's a great guy you don't even deserve? Do I ask you why you seem unable to love any man?'

'I love you, Paul.'

'Like hell you do! You don't care how unhappy I am.'

'I – I didn't realise. You were going out with so many girls.'

'Thanks to you, I thought it was hopeless. I was trying to forget Nicola. But it didn't work. Now she's hurt and ill and in despair. Edward has done terrible things to her. She needed me.'

'We'll talk about it tomorrow, I promise.'

'You can stuff tomorrow! If I lose Nicola I'll never forgive you. I've always loved you, respected you, admired you, but what you have done to keep us apart is contemptible!'

Paul rushed down the hall, tears streaming from his eyes.

Anne stood frozen. She hadn't seen him cry since he was a child.

On Saturday there was a lineup of cars, and Nicola didn't have time to stop except for half a hero and a coke in the little office at lunchtime.

The prospect of an empty weekend increased her aching loneliness. She kept eyeing the 'phone and thinking of Paul.

Walt, the owner of the Jaguar she had repaired, dropped in to talk, as he had several times since the first day.

He was terribly curious about her but she had not felt much like enlightening him. All he knew was that her name was Nicola Harrington.

'Don't spoil your appetite, Nicola. I'm taking you to dinner tonight. If you like, we can talk about cars.' He smiled at her pleasantly.

Nicola returned his smile tentatively. He was an attractive, well spoken man about her age. Why shouldn't she accept? She felt restless. Maybe all she needed was companionship, and later, another body next to hers.

They ate in a Spanish restaurant in the Village. Not even a pitcher of Sangria and two double brandies were able to lift Nicola out of her depression.

Walt, recently separated from his wife of twenty years, was an architect living in a loft. Although he was intelligent, kind, and of Nicola's generation she felt unconnected and unresponsive. He lacked the raw nerve endings, the intuitive grasp of her essence Paul had shown from the first moment they had spoken at his concert.

In the taxi she silently cried for Paul ... Paul ... Paul, until her throat ached.

When she emerged Paul was standing in front of her door, catching his breath.

'I was at home working when I had the weirdest feeling. I had to come and see if you were all right.'

Nicola flung herself into his arms, kissing his lips wildly. He held her tightly, feeling her tears against his cheek.

'Paul, I'm so afraid. I don't want to drag you down with me. I'm working at an auto body shop!'

'Christ, you don't have to do that. I have enough money

for both of us. Let's go in. It's freezing out here.'

'I've already caused you too much unhappiness. Did you know Edward was behind the Ivor Lewes business?' Haltingly, guiltily, she told him.

Inside the loft, he took off their coats and held her hands.

'It wasn't too high a price to pay to have you,' Paul said huskily, his eyes scorching her. 'I'm all right now. If you love me.'

'You know I do. You heard me calling you.'

'We are meant to be together. And we will be. Our love has survived our enemies' hatred.'

'Paul, Paul,' she whispered, her fingers digging into his back.

They kissed until they had no breath.

'Nicola, I want you so much I'm not going to be able to stop.'

'I don't want you to stop.'

'You're not too tired, from working –'

'I've been on my feet, not on my back.'

Their shared laughter dispelled the tension, but a moment later amusement changed to desire.

Nicola touched him with trembling hands, making him moan and pull her down on the couch.

She was brimming over with love, remembering his wonderful hands and lips, the insistent hardness of his body, the silky feel of his hair, the smell of his skin.

He kissed her face and lips, her neck, her breasts, and the satiny wetness between her legs. Nicola crested and ebbed, each climax making her hungry for another.

She pulled him on top of her.

'Darling, I can't hold it –'

'Nor I,' she breathed in his ear.

Their bodies exploded into love-fed spasms that rocked them off the couch onto the floor.

Moments later they climaxed again.

He felt as if an electrical charge had started in his centre and radiated to his extremities.

Her nerve endings tingled and she was sure she would disintegrate into quivering bits and pieces.

She believed she was dying.

He knew he was only beginning to live again.

285

They stayed in bed all day Sunday.

'I'm supposed to work tomorrow,' she murmured, examining his beard with great concentration.

'Tell them you've quit. Something's come up,' he teased, poking her with it and making her smile.

'What about your music? Don't you have to meet Miles Fanchel tomorrow, with some more written?'

'It's being written every moment I'm with you.' He traced notes on her belly with his fingers. 'I missed this part,' he said, kissing it, 'and this, and this, and this. But there's less of you than there used to be. About fifteen pounds less.'

'Less is more. Haven't you heard?'

'Not if it's less of you. Do you like my beard?'

'Mm. Very much,' She kissed it. 'It adds ballast to your face.'

'Oh, thanks a heap. Casting slurs on my chin.'

'It's an adorable chin, as I remember. But the beard lends dignity, authority.'

'Then let me use it.' He rolled on top of her and kissed her, smoothing her face with his hands, studying her.

She averted her eyes. 'I look awful, I know. Haggard, and with many more wrinkles.'

'No, my sweet, you've been looking unloved, but not now or ever again.'

'How is it you didn't meet some wonderful girl in all this time?'

'I met many wonderful young girls. I tried like the devil to feel something for them, especially torturing myself imagining you with Edward. But I couldn't. It seemed obscene to be doing, without love, what we did together.'

Nicola felt a surge of passion.

'Aha, that turns you on, I see.' He smiled wickedly. 'And so it should, to know that you have absolute power over me. Nicola, my sweet one, I don't ever want another woman as long as I live.'

'You will, and then I won't be able to bear it. I mustn't love you as much as I do.'

'You certainly must. Kiss me.'

Eventually they got up to eat. Paul poured wine into their glasses.

'To our happiness.'

'To our happiness,' she echoed, but he saw that she was smiling only with her mouth.

'Do you know what you're going to do tomorrow?'

She frowned and shook her head.

'Go out and get the materials for a full-scale sculpture of *Julie Looks at the Sun*. I can see it under a real sun, the star of the next Biennale.'

'But I can't, without a commission. Do you know what something like that would cost? The motor, the engineering involved?'

'You can. My ballet music is going to be recorded. I'll be rolling in money, sprinkling it over your head like confetti.'

He managed to infuse her with his enthusiasm. She began to visualise the piece, and her depression floated away.

When she smiled with the whole of her face, he hugged her joyfully. 'Julie's Mother Looks at the Sun. And that's the way it's always going to be.'

10

'I just can't believe that Paul's given up his apartment and moved back with Nicola.'

Al patted Anne's hand. 'He's crazy about her, babe. Stop fighting it.'

'I can't help it. I hate the idea of them. He went out with one beautiful girl after another, and intelligent too. What is it with him?'

Anne poured herself another glass of wine, while Al nursed his beer. 'Oh, Al, I'm so unhappy. I only wanted the best for Paul, and now he's so angry he won't have anything to do with me.'

'When you accept his choice he'll forgive you.'

'It's ironic that Paul, who got so much of my time and devotion, should have turned out like this. Timmy I practically ignored, and he's turned out fine –'

'Excuse me, sweetie. Do you know what Timmy once told me? He said he was glad he wasn't musical. That way you wouldn't have expectations and he wouldn't worry about disappointing you.'

Anne looked at Al miserably. 'I feel such an emptiness in my life. All the running around I do to concerts and benefits. The hundreds of people I know and entertain – when they all go home I'm alone.'

'That was your choice, babe. Doesn't have to be that way.'

Anne laughed nervously. 'I couldn't start all over again, even if I met a man I was remotely interested in.'

'How about starting all over again with me?' Al asked and then took her in his arms so that she could not answer. 'Annie, Annie, Annie. I wish you'd stop making life tough for yourself. I'll help you by loving you so much you won't have time to worry about who's loving anyone else.'

Al stroked his wife's hair gently. 'It won't be all bad, you'll see, even if I'm not the ideal man for you. You wanted a Paul for yourself. Maybe that's why you can't stand to see him with Nicola.'

Anne jumped away from him. 'That's ridiculous.'

'Is it? Paul is everything you wanted him to be – educated, charming, talented, sophisticated. You look at him sometimes like you could eat him up. He's your ideal, and I'm a *schlemiel*. I can't help it, without being a phony. I am what I am, and you are what you are. It's no good wishing you were someone else.'

Al watched Anne take another drink of wine. She had drunk almost the whole bottle on an empty stomach.

'But I do wish I were someone else,' she burst out bitterly ...

When Anne first met Nicola she was as ignorant as dirt, with the most appalling manners. Yet in a matter of weeks Nicola was dressing and speaking like a girl born to the purple. In addition to her beautiful hair and eyes and slim, perfect figure she was also graceful. Very quickly she became more popular with Anne's friends than Anne was herself.

288

'Lennie Baron told me, Nika, he thinks you're cute and would like to ask you out, only he's too shy.'

'Good. That he's too shy, I mean.'

'You don't like him?'

'He's okay but not my type.'

'He could be my type, not that he knows I'm alive – as a girl I mean.' Anne sighed. 'Gentlemen prefer blondes.'

Nicola laughed. 'I'm not interested in boys who go only for looks.'

'Me neither. Especially as I haven't any looks to go for.'

'You do too. Stop tearing yourself down, Annie. You have an interesting face and beautiful eyes.'

'So does a cow. Oh, never mind how I look. The boy who marries me will just have to lump it and love me for my talent. He'll have to be a boy with musical sensibilities, a Mozart or a Beethoven, who will compose a cello sonata just for me,' Anne said dreamily.

'Mm. Serious, but with a mysterious smile. Someone with depth and feeling who really cares about art.'

Anne looked curiously at Nicola. 'Have you ever actually had a date?'

'No. Nobody is right, somehow.'

'Yeah, I know what you mean.'

'But you seem to spend a lot of time with Al Lurie. He has a terrific crush on you, I can see it in his eyes.'

'Oh, God, I don't take him seriously. He's strictly for practice, not for real. Not in a million years.'

'Nicola was who I wanted to be,' Anne told Al drunkenly. 'She was born lucky. Beauty, intelligence, talent, charm. And loving parents who didn't torture her the way my mother tortured me. Her father didn't let his wife push him around. You know, I believe my father died just to get out of Henrietta's way. Nicola's always had what she wanted, including marrying rich. She can even dare to throw over a wonderful man like Edward because she can attract a man half her age –'

'Sh, sweetie, wait a minute –'

'Don't shush me,' Anne cried. 'Do you think I don't know I look old enough to be her mother? Do you know something, I purposely wear matronly clothes and comb my hair in a bun! I know I can't compete with her and I don't want to appear to try, and come out pathetic. But don't think it doesn't hurt me. It always has. I wanted to be beautiful and beloved by men!' Anne hid her face in her hands.

'*In vino veritas*,' Al said softly. 'Bet you didn't think I knew such million dollar words, huh. Annie, for what it's worth, to me you have always been beautiful and beloved.'

'You must be blind,' she said bitterly. 'I was always clumsy and overweight. I used to feel like an overgrown elephant.'

'What a thing to say. It's totally wrong. You know something, I loved you the first time I saw you, changing classes in the hall. I couldn't stop looking at you. You were walking with Nicola, and I saw those wonderful eyes you have, and the proud way you held your head, and I heard you speaking in your classy way. You know what I thought? Now there goes a gorgeous babe.'

'*Me*? Oh, come on, Al,' Anne said incredulously. 'You thought I was gorgeous next to Nicola? Don't insult my intelligence.'

'Don't insult mine,' Al countered. 'I won't say I don't like to look at Nicola. Sure I do. Sure, she's beautiful, but in an exotic way, like a Picasso painting, always a little out of reach. Terrific in a museum. But in my own living room, I'd rather have a Renoir any time.'

Anne looked at Al as if she had never seen him before.

'That's right, sweetie. Different strokes for different folks. That I'm not good enough for you is another story.'

'Not true,' Anne said morosely. 'You're a fine person.'

Al smiled ruefully. For the first time in years Anne noticed what sensitive eyes he had.

'I'm sorry I've hurt you, Al. You deserved better.'

'People deserve what they get, and I wanted you, so shut up. What I started to say before was that you had Edward figured all wrong.' Al told her what Edward had done in the matter of Nicola's career, as well as his infidelities. He had heard everything from Paul.

'I would never have guessed such things in a million years. He was always so pleasant, so delightful –'

'So hypocritical. I'll tell you, he's the worst. He's the one who tried to ruin Paul!'

When Al had finished, Anne stared into space for a long time. 'I don't know anything any more.'

'That's the beginning of knowledge,' Al said, patting her hand.

'Damn it, Edward has to rectify the wrong. He has to clear Paul's name.'

'No way, babe, forget it. He'll never make such an admission. There's no proof, and even if there was, Paul wouldn't have it. He's doin' fine.'

'But to let Edward get away with it, no. I can't, I won't.'

'You will, sweetie. Respect your son a little more. What he's really angry at is the way you disregard his feelings. First, he loves Nicola. Second, he doesn't want to do anything about Edward. That's it. Finished. Okay? You admire a strong man, huh, someone who puts his foot down. Well, I'm putting mine down. I really mean it. Butt out. Instead of worrying about everyone else, come to grips with yourself for once in your life.' He had never spoken so harshly to her.

'What do you mean?' Anne asked, subdued.

'You know what I mean,' he said in a softer tone. 'You spent your life envying Nicola and never admitting to yourself why you didn't become a professional cellist.'

'You know why. First there was Paul, and then Timmy.'

Al was silent.

'I couldn't have an abortion. You know all about that. And I wanted to be a decent mother to the boys.'

As she spoke and drank the rest of the wine in the bottle, Anne's voice began to quaver. 'They were both accidents –'

'Paul was no accident. You didn't want to take any precautions. I offered to get some condoms and you said nothing could happen, it was the wrong time of the month.'

'I never said that.'

'You did, sweetie. Think harder. Yetta had big plans for you. Juilliard. A concert tour with her accompanying you. She expected you to practise six hours a day, every day, and I remember you were so miserable.'

'She hated me!' Anne burst out. 'She was hoping I'd fall on my face so she'd be justified in hating me! She used to smile with satisfaction when I flubbed a note. And I was so scared, Al. I knew if I failed I'd be nothing. She'd spit on

291

me. Oh, I couldn't face it, I just couldn't face it.' Anne put her head down on her arms.

'Maybe without realising it I did want to be a wife and a mother so she wouldn't blame me for failing. She'd have some compassion, and love her grandchild, and maybe even me, a little.' Anne broke down in sobs.

It was the first time Al had ever seen her cry.

'My whole life has been a cop-out,' she wept. 'I didn't give up my career for Paul after all. I did it for selfish reasons, and I've been punishing him for nothing.'

'We do most things for selfish reasons but that doesn't mean we don't help others too. You were a wonderful mother to Paulie, and he loves you.'

'Love, love,' she cried bitterly. 'What is it anyway, that we wreck our lives and other people's just to get some.'

'Who knows. I only know we need it. You couldn't get love at home so you came to me.'

'It's true,' she sobbed. 'You're the only one who ever really loved me, and look at the way I've treated you.'

'Sh, sh, it's all right, Annie. Everything will be all right, you'll see.'

'Oh, Al, hold me, please.'

11

When Paul put his flute away he was surprised to see that the table was set for dinner and a bottle of champagne was cooling in the ice bucket.

He came up behind Nicola, who was making a salad, and put his arms around her. 'Darling, you spoil me terribly.'

'No more than you spoil me.'

'What are we celebrating? It's not your birthday or mine.'

'I have a surprise for you.'

'Every moment with you is that,' he whispered, caressing her neck with his fingers.

292

'Have you noticed my slides hanging around?'

'Nicola! You've found a dealer.'

'I think so. Barbara Maralek. She wants my fifteen maquettes for an all-woman show she's mounting.'

Paul was elated. This was the one area in which he was helpless to make Nicola happy, the one thing he'd been hoping for.

'The letter came today. I haven't spoken to her yet.' Nicola showed it to him, her smile radiant.

'You sly thing, making it sound so cut and dried. "I'm really excited about your work," it says. While I open the champagne, call up the lady, for heaven's sake!'

Nicola liked Barbara Maralek. She was thin, young, intense, and direct.

'I thought I'd come to see you,' Nicola said, 'and then we'd go to my studio.' She glanced curiously around the gallery and approved of what she saw. After her first euphoria, she had wondered if this was just another feminist gallery that would exhibit anything produced by women, regardless of quality. What she observed reassured her about Barbara's artistic taste.

'Will I be the only sculptor in the show?'

'Yes. Most of my experience is with painters.'

From her conversation, Nicola gathered that Barbara had been around. 'You're no novice at dealing.'

'No. I've worked for Marlborough and a couple of others but I'm tired of the whole scene, of new talent – especially female – not getting viewed, and the established ones acting like rock stars.'

Nicola flushed, and saw that Barbara was looking at her reflectively. 'Your slides show you're no novice either. Who was your last dealer? How did you happen to come to my gallery?'

Nicola didn't answer the first question. 'I happened to be passing by.'

'Oh, come on,' Barbara implored, with a sceptical smile. 'Stuff of your quality doesn't come out of the blue. I'll have to have some credentials. Nothing personal, but I can't afford to show work that might belong to someone else, to

293

put it bluntly. The critics are already antagonistic to an all-woman show. They'd love to get something on me.'

Nicola made a quick decision. 'Okay, I'll level with you. My name is Nicola Di Candia –'

'Oh, wow. I knew there had to be a catch.'

'No catch.' She told Barbara the story.

'I should find it incredible but I know from the inside that things are like that. It's the main reason I wanted out. In fact, I have an idea that will shake some of the smugness out of them!'

'In case Paul gave you the wrong idea,' Anne said to Nicola, over a drink, 'I didn't suggest this meeting to tell you that all is forgiven.'

'No. Paul simply said you and he had come to an understanding, and that you wanted to see me. You're looking well, Anne, much happier than you have for a long time. I'm glad.'

Nicola could afford the compliment, Anne reflected enviously, when she herself looked so radiant. Tragedy hadn't ravaged her permanently. No sooner was Julie all set and Paul back than she magically became young and beautiful once again.

'What I wanted to say,' Anne continued coldly, 'was that I'm sorry I was dishonest with you and Paul – for reasons I don't want to go into. Not that the two of you made it easy for me either. But what's done is done. I can't bear to be at odds with my son, so I'm willing to call a truce. Of course, you and I can never be as we were.'

'I'm sorry, Anne,' Nicola said sadly. 'I wish it could be otherwise.'

'Friendship needs trust. I no longer trust you. Matter of fact I've become suspicious of the whole world. Who would have dreamed that Edward would turn out to be such a bastard. He fooled me for years. Did you ever suspect?'

'I had inklings but I dismissed them. My real life was my work, and the rest was almost shadowy.'

'I'll never understand why, when you came out of the shadows, you had to pounce on my son, of all the men in the world. I won't ever be happy about it either.'

'No, I guess not. It's not a thing easily explained. I like the way I am with Paul, and he lets me be myself.'

Anne, working on her second martini, smiled cynically. 'Funny. Al has always let me be myself and I was contemptuous of him for it. I wanted to be someone else.'

'Who?'

'You, of course.'

Nicola frowned and shook her head in disbelief.

'Yes, I did. It seemed to me you had everything.'

'Nobody has everything,' Nicola whispered, pained. 'You give up something to get something. The devil must have his due. Sometimes the choice is agonising. Julie, for my art. And now your friendship, for Paul.'

Barbara Maralek had learned her craft from experts. She borrowed money from an all-woman bank as well as prominent feminists, to mount her show and buy the best publicity she could. The result was a stunning black-tie opening studded with beautiful people happily drinking champagne and milling about the way they did at the better known galleries.

Barbara had sent invitations to all the leading uptown and downtown dealers, as well as the prominent art critics. She picked a day on which nothing else was happening in order to get the largest attendance possible. Also invited were unknown artists, budding writers for little-known publications – people who ordinarily did not get the chance to rub elbows with the art crowd.

The paintings of nine women and of one sculptor were on exhibit.

From the start of the evening to the close, the biggest crowd hovered around four triangles revolving under a special lamp. The piece was untitled and not for sale. More than a dozen people expressed an interest in the sculpture by the unknown Frances Gray and tried to pump Barbara about the artist's background. She was evasive, and explained that Gray's works were meant only as maquettes. The sculptor wanted to obtain a commission for a full-scale work.

The show was very favourably reviewed in the *Times* and

the art press. Without exception, each writer picked the sculptures of Frances Gray as the most interesting work at the show, and the triangle piece was reproduced in colour in two of the magazines.

Frances Gray was called 'an astonishing talent,' and 'proof that promising female artists are being neglected by the blue chip galleries'.

Only one critic, Stan Ferrin, commented that the 'extraordinary maturity of technique is surprising in an unknown and seems somewhat derivative of Nicola Di Candia'.

Half a dozen institutions contacted Barbara Maralek with offers to commission large-scale works, and all were puzzled and disappointed to be put off.

Two weeks after the final reviews were in, Barbara Maralek gave an exclusive story to a journalist friend of hers on the *Times*.

When Luigi Bianchi read the paper every morning, he skipped the news section and the editorials, usually signalling gloom and doom, and turned first to the art page.

On that particular morning, he would have done better to start with the obituaries.

'An extraordinary deception has been perpetrated on the art world. SoHo gallery owner Barbara Maralek revealed yesterday that 'Frances Gray', who was part of a recent all-female show at Maralek Gallery, is really well known sculptor Nicola Di Candia. For reasons Maralek declined to mention, Di Candia had sent slides of her new acrylic works to all the prominent dealers under her pseudonym and had them rejected by every one.'

As he read, Bianchi turned choleric. His breakfast uneaten, he rushed to the telephone and called the writer of the article.

'This is Bianchi, you prick. After all I've done for you, you could at least have given me a call before printing that. Yes, I know I turned down Di Candia's slides, but let me tell you who was looking over my shoulder and describing them as "mediocre"!'

SPRING, 1980

12

'To you, Nicola,' Tom Markham said, raising his glass at the celebratory dinner at the Four Seasons, 'for having the guts to put your talent on the line, and for exposing the art business for the phony baloney we always knew it was.'

'Hear, hear,' Janet echoed.

Paul raised his glass, smiling at Nicola, who was faintly embarrassed by it all.

'Thank you. It wasn't guts I had, only fear that I'd been fooling myself all these years.'

'Oh, Nika, how could you have doubted your talent?' Janet said. 'You had only to ask anybody.'

Nicola smiled wryly. 'Anybody or everybody seemed to be dazzled by the name. I needed objectivity. Anyway, Tom, it was never my purpose to expose anyone. That was Barbara's idea. I'm afraid my actions were entirely selfish.'

'Your relentless seeking for the truth knocks me out, no matter how you deny it,' Tom said. 'I wonder if Calder, trying the same sort of thing, would have met the same fate.'

'What's interesting,' Paul chimed in, 'is to see how the dealers are trying to squirm out of it, claiming they never saw the slides, that it was their assistants who rejected them.'

'All except Luigi Bianchi,' Tom noted. 'What a letter he wrote to the *Times*. The man was enraged. He certainly didn't do Edward's reputation any good. It's a wise collector that knows his own wife's work. Are you going to stay with Maralek, Nicola?'

'Yes, I think Barbara's a terrific dealer, on her way to success.'

'Watch out when she makes it,' Tom cautioned. 'I hate to

'appear cynical but many big dealers started off small and idealistic.'

'We're celebrating another piece of news,' Nicola said, beaming at Paul. 'Jean-Pierre Rampal has agreed to give Paul's flute quintet a world première in Paris in September.'

Paul accepted the Markhams' congratulations and then said, 'Good news comes in threes, doesn't it. Nicola's *Julie* sculpture has been commissioned for a new outdoor plaza in São Paolo.'

'Wonderful,' Janet said. 'I could listen to endless good news about you both, but my head is about to float off from the wine. Can we maybe eat a toast or two?'

During dinner, Paul said to Tom, 'To feed your cynicism, I think that Barbara Maralek is one sharp little operator. She put off confirming any commissions for Frances Gray, waiting for the story to break. Of course a Di Candia can command ten times the price anyone would pay for an unknown, and paying they are.' Paul smiled at Nicola and squeezed her hand.

'Nicola,' Janet said to her when both were in the ladies room, 'I was so sure you were going to say that you and Paul are getting married.'

'Did you? Well, don't expect it.'

'Why not? Paul seems so crazy about you.'

'I am about him, too. That's why I wouldn't marry him or allow him to make a commitment he'll want out of a few years from now.'

Nicola waved aside Janet's objections. 'Paul doesn't yet have a full sense of himself as a man. Wait until the ballet is a success, and the quintet, and all the music to come.'

'But he's also concerned about your career, and so supportive –'.

'I know. That's just it. At the same time that I drink it up like a person dying of thirst in the desert, I think he deserves better than being second to me. All you have to do is walk into the studio. Paul's music is neatly on pieces of paper tucked out of sight, whereas my sculpture is growing like some science fiction monster, crowding out everything else. The point is, though, that when he reaches his peak I'll be on the way down.'

'Of course you won't. Look at Nevelson.'

'Look at us. Did you notice how people were staring in the restaurant? When Paul is only thirty I'll be nearly fifty. I don't give us five years, if that long, and I wonder if I ought to wait around and watch his love turn to indifference, then obligation, finally resentment.'

'Nonsense. If people stare at the two of you, they're only admiring what an attractive couple you make. You look younger and he looks older. Nobody would guess there was such a difference, unless you insist on pointing it out. Trust Paul enough not to spoil what you have right now, Nika, by worrying about what may happen in the future – or more likely, will never happen at all.'

It was good advice, and Nicola tried to follow it, but as the weeks drew on she became increasingly anxious about her relationship with Paul.

At first, after their reunion, she had been so deliriously happy with him she had hardly stopped to think of anything but her immediate, palpable joy, so exquisite after her year-long agony. Even her parents had been won over, to the point that they confined themselves to saying prayers for their daughter.

Nicola had never loved Paul more. She delighted in every moment they spent together. It was only his encouragement, during her period of doubt and stress, that had kept her sculpting before the breakthrough.

Her problems began when Paul asked her to go to rehearsal. She became increasingly uneasy by the attention he commanded from the dancers and the girls in the orchestra.

Especially a violist, Serena Parvey, young, lovely, all flowing hair and sensitivity, both in her playing and her behaviour. Nicola began to rail against the fate that had caused her to be born twenty years too soon.

The way Serena Parvey kidded with Paul was, for Nicola, a preview of what the future would hold. Although Paul's attitude towards Serena was one of gallant male appreciation without even a hint of personal flirtation, it was obvious to Nicola that she would someday lose Paul to a girl like Serena.

Don't go to rehearsals, you fool, she told herself sternly. But when her work was finished, when four assistants came to her studio to dismantle and pack her sculpture for

299

shipment to São Paolo, a vast emptiness descended on her. Her worry about Paul accelerated.

One lovely spring Sunday, they walked up to Washington Square Park and watched the roller skaters and Frisbee throwers.

A big ball bounced over to them. Paul, smiling at the little girl who owned it, bounced it back to her.

Nicola felt a chilly draught through her chest, and she grew very quiet.

'What is fermenting in that beautiful brain?' Paul asked, kissing her cheek.

'Nothing,' she murmured.

'Hey, baby, speak to me,' he demanded gaily.

'Paul, do you like children?'

He smiled at her in astonishment. 'What a question. I like some children, some cats, some dogs, some unicorns, and even some ladies – especially you.'

'I'm serious. You're going to want children some day, and I won't be able to give them to you.'

'In that case, I'll kidnap a likely brat on the street. Or take fatherless boys to baseball games.'

'Please don't make a joke of something not as – as trivial as you think.'

He looked quickly at her. 'Sorry. I didn't realise you were so touchy on the subject. Frankly, I've never given it a second thought.'

'Please do.'

'Okay.' Holding her by the hand, he sat them on a bench and was silent for ten minutes.

'Okay. I've thought about it. Although on one level – a highly romantic one – I can imagine a gorgeous little Nicola, realistically, I'd probably be jealous of a child. Besides, it might turn out to be a bratty little Paul. I don't think my ego requires a replica of me. I plan to reach immortality through composing. Creative, rather than procreative, is how I see myself. To be good at the job of fathering a man needs time and patience. I don't have either one.'

'What if I wanted to have your child? I mean now, before it's too late? I might not be able to, of course, but it's still biologically possible.'

'If that's what you want, it's okay with me. I'd do anything to keep you happy.'

'I don't want a child,' Nicola said perversely, 'for all the reasons you mention. Plus I'm too old, and it wouldn't be fair. But I think you will want one someday, even if you don't realise it yet.'

Paul began to laugh. 'I may want to live on the moon someday. So what? Forgive me, Nika, but you really are being difficult. I guess it's because you're between sculptures while I, selfish beast that I am, have been working like a madman and not giving you the time you deserve. Tell you what. A week or two after we open – well, a month, anyway – let's take a vacation in South America. We'll get to São Paolo in time for the unveiling of your sculpture. Okay?'

'Okay,' she sighed.

'Right. Now let's have an end to this silliness. Unless it's only an excuse, an oblique way of expressing your dissatisfaction with me.'

'Of course I'm not dissatisfied. It's just that I can't see any future for us.'

He drew her to him and held her close. 'I can't see any future for me without you. Nicola, you are my other self, and you must never leave me again. Let's get married, please, darling.'

Nicola closed her eyes and surrendered to his arms. 'Thank you for that. But no.'

'Why not? Don't you love me enough?'

'I do. That's why it's no. Ask me again in ten years.'

13

The last couple of weeks before the ballet was to open, Paul was constantly tense and harassed. Miles Fanchel, under pressure, became trigger-tempered.

'Please come to every rehearsal,' Paul begged Nicola. 'I need someone there who's outside the madness.'

Nicola went to the theatre to please Paul, but she was tortured by terrible spurts of jealousy over Serena Parvey. It didn't matter that Paul never flirted with the violist. Objectively Nicola could see that they were perfect for one another.

She was struck by the way the female dancers and musicians regarded Paul as if he were a god. Surely they were in love with him, every one.

Don't be dumb. Of course they look at him, he's conducting the music. They look at Miles too, even though he's gay.

Nicola tried to control her obsession but it began to dominate her, causing her to grasp at Paul tenaciously, fearful she would lose him at any moment. He absorbed all her attention, devotion, and insatiable love.

Watch out, he'll get tired of you that much more quickly.

It was a miracle, she thought, that so far he revelled in her fierce passion. Never had they made love so often or with such intensity.

Nicola had received a new commission but she couldn't make a decent start because of her preoccupation with Paul.

Arriving early at a rehearsal, Nicola overheard an exchange between Paul and Serena.

'Paul, I don't know how I'm going to survive until opening night, with Miles picking on me constantly. This is one time I'd love to be a fag hag.'

Paul laughed and boffed her shoulder. 'You're too beautiful, too feminine to play that role. Too womanly.

Maggie is more that type ...'

Nicola tiptoed back the way she had come. The words 'too beautiful, too feminine, too womanly' reverberated through her.

She had never been jealous of Edward but now that feeling made her think that she was going to crack up.

I must leave him before it's too late.

I can't leave him because I love him more than anything in the world.

No, not more than her art.

On the morning of Paul's opening he went to the theatre after having exacted a promise from Nicola that she would come early for the last rehearsal.

While lingering over her coffee and looking at the maquette for her sculpture, she suddenly felt the surging power of inspiration. She could visualise the full-scale work, a series of complex swirling loops meant to suggest infinity. Paul and her own worries were banished, overwhelmed by the mysterious force within her. She drilled into huge tubes of plastic and smoothed the edges with sandpaper. Then she heated what she had cut, removing it with gloves from the oven, intending to shape it quickly before it cooled.

When the doorbell began to ring insistently she was so startled that she pulled off her glove and burned her hand.

Her visitor was a very attractive dark girl who smiled pleasantly at her. 'Hello, my name is Marcia Jensen. I was told by Fred Felix that Paul Kadin-Lurie lives here. Is he at home by any chance?'

'No, at rehearsal.' Nicola heard the echo of her flat voice in the hallway.

'Oh. I thought I might catch him before he left.'

'I can give you his number at the theatre –'

'No, thanks, I won't disturb him at rehearsal. I'm on my way to Germany. If you wouldn't mind telling him good luck for me ...'

Nicola shut the door feeling dizzy and dry in the mouth. Marcia Jensen, French horn player, from the music department at Yale. Paul had never even mentioned her name, and yet she had created the impression that they were close friends. Had Paul had an affair with her?

For an hour Nicola brooded while her plastic tubes turned

cold and the burn on her hand began to show an angry red mark.

When she looked at the clock she went to have her shower. She dressed and applied makeup, looking critically at herself in the mirror. Two images superimposed themselves on either side of her. One, the beautiful Serena with the flowing fair hair, the other, the beautiful Marcia. In her own face Nicola saw faint lines in the forehead and around the eyes. No grey hairs yet, but for how long?

The 'phone must have been ringing for five minutes before Nicola was aware of any sound.

'Are you still at home? I expected you at rehearsal an hour ago. What's wrong?'

'Nothing. I'm sorry, Paul. I guess I lost track of the time.'

'You must be working.'

'Well, I've been thinking about it.'

'Darling, can I be awfully selfish, just this once? It's mayhem at the theatre. The primary dancer is having a fit, and Miles is joining her. I'm about ready to walk out of here!'

'Last minute nerves. The ballet will be a tremendous success. It's wonderfully conceived, and your music is divine. I mean that literally.'

While Nicola soothed him, a panic began to rise. 'Paul, Marcia Jensen stopped by to wish you luck.'

'Who?'

'From Yale. Marcia Jensen. Tall, dark, velvety, violet eyes. Plays the French horn.'

'Oh. Oh, yes. Nice of her to stop by. Darling, are you dressed yet?'

'Yes,' Nicola murmured. She knew what she must do.

'I hope you're wearing that little beige nothing of a dress that makes you look so gorgeous and every other lady like a fugitive from a thrift shop. We'll only put in an appearance at the party, which may be more like a wake. I'm thinking of the way I'm going to adore your flesh tonight, to show you how very much I love you and to make up for what I've been putting you through the last few days ...'

Nicola put her hand over the mouthpiece to keep him from hearing the way she was breathing.

After he hung up she began to fling clothes into an

overnight bag. Nicola didn't know where she was going. She didn't know anything except that the only way to break with Paul was to do it brutally. If she didn't appear this evening he would never forgive her, no matter whether he attributed it to her capriciousness or selfishness. He would be devastated and look for comfort nearby – to Serena Parvey.

Edward took a last look around the duplex and gave final instructions to his Korean cook. 'Mr Beaumont will be having lots of dinner parties for all the dealers and collectors in town.'

'When you come back, Mr Harrington, you change telephone?'

No, he wouldn't. He would retain his new unlisted number.

Nora Rambleaux was waiting in the Rolls. When Edward kissed her he had a recurrence of the feeling that had been with him for some weeks. Did she really love him or was she merely tolerating him because he was in a position to make a famous sculptor out of her?

Whatever the truth was, she certainly excited him. He wished they were already in Paris ensconced in René Beaumont's exquisite house near the Tuileries. Swapping apartments with René had been a stroke of genius on his part.

Nora had lived for years in Paris and felt at home there. That was fine with Edward. For six months he would concentrate on her career. And it would be a relief to be away from New York, from the jeers of certain nasty individuals who had enjoyed his public mortification. Worst of all had been the vicious anonymous calls in the middle of the night. Talentless painters and hard-core lesbians, he suspected.

Only a perverse bitch like Nicola could have thought of such a plan to humiliate him. *Of course* if he'd taken a careful look at the goddamn slides he would have recognised her work! It simply hadn't occurred to him that she could be so sneaky and in cahoots with Maralek who saw a way to give established galleries the finger.

Nora was a far better artist than Nicola, as well as more

305

practical. She recognised the importance of dealers and collectors in influencing public taste. In fact, Bianchi had been on the point of accepting Nora when the *Times* story had rocked the art world. Of course, not everyone was against Edward. Several dealers and collectors had privately expressed their support, noting that an ex-wife could be a formidable enemy.

Edward took satisfaction in believing that Nicola would never get the kinds of commission from Maralek that Marshall, through him, had got her. She had looked awful the last time he saw her. Ageing fast. Her young lover would leave her soon enough!

Just as Nicola was dashing out of the studio the phone rang. Was it Paul again? She couldn't bear to speak to him. She'd break down.

But what if it was Julie? She hadn't talked to her daughter in about a week. It would be better to answer.

Nicola lifted the receiver without speaking.

'Hello, Nicola?'

'Oh, hello, Janet.'

'I'm glad I've caught you.'

'You sound strange, Janet. Is something wrong?'

'Yes. I have something terrible to tell you, and sorry to have to do it today. But I wanted you to know why I won't be at the ballet tonight. Tom died this morning.'

'Oh, no! Janet, no!'

'It was a heart attack. He wasn't feeling very well, and after breakfast went to lie down. An hour later, when I tried to awaken him ...'

'Oh, God, it's so unbelievable, he was so young,' Nicola babbled, hardly aware of what she was saying.

'Tom had a checkup only recently. The doctor said he was fine.'

'Janet, dearest, I'll come right out to be with you –'

'No, thanks, Nika, it's not necessary. Paul needs you tonight. And Emily is with me. Kate is flying down later. We'll mourn quietly together, the three of us.'

'God, what you must be feeling. I could jump in the car and be with you in half an hour.'

306

'I appreciate it, but I'm all right, really. Sad, of course, and I guess still in shock. It will hit me later on.'

How Janet could speak so calmly mystified Nicola. She would have been in hysterics. She was half-hysterical as it was, over Paul, and now Tom ...

When Nicola put down the 'phone she didn't know what to do. It occurred to her that she couldn't possibly leave town because of Tom's funeral. And Janet would need every friend she could muster in the next few days, no matter how composed she seemed now.

Nicola shoved her overnight bag in the closet. Her brain was reeling, the decision about Paul complicated by the shock over Tom.

She left the studio with no clear idea of where she was going.

Paul hung up the phone, feeling better for having had Nicola's reassurances.

'No, no, no,' Miles was shouting. 'You're out of sync, start again. Where the hell have you been, Paul? Nobody takes a pee unless I say it's okay.'

They started from the top, Paul conducting, the musicians playing, the dancers dancing, all trying vainly to please.

Paul kept glancing at the empty seats, anxiety threatening to overwhelm him as time passed and Nicola did not appear.

He had never thought of himself as superstitious but now, when he was on the point of dissolving into nervous exhaustion, he had the idea that as soon as Nicola arrived everything would be all right. What could be taking her so long?

When there was a two-minute break, Paul dialled the studio but got no answer. Then he returned his parents' 'phone call.

'Rehearsals are always impossible, Paul,' Anne told him. 'In fact, the worse it goes, the better the performance is likely to be.'

'Hey, Paul, hang loose,' Al chimed in. 'Like Annie says, the more crap that comes out now, the less there'll be when it counts. I once played a gig with a drunken bass player and a piano player with ulcers. At rehearsal they were fighting over some dame. She'd left one that morning to go and live with the other one. I thought those guys were going to murder each other, only they'd miss and there I was in the middle. But came the performance, they played like angels. I don't know who killed who 'cause I cut out of there quick.'

'Thanks for calling, you two. I'll do my best tonight.'

'You bet, Paul. And your mother and I will be sitting right up there in the first row, so don't make any wild moves with that baton.'

Nicola still had not arrived, and Paul's anxiety took a giant leap. Now that he thought of it, she had sounded unlike herself. Subdued, a little remote, even when she had been trying to cheer him up. Why? Surely nothing to do with that girl who had wanted to say hello. Paul hardly knew her.

He went back to rehearsal, feeling tense and horribly worried. He was afraid he would lose Nicola if the ballet fell on its face. Nicola Di Candia was up among the stars again, as he had known she would be, stronger than ever. And here he was, still struggling, pestering her, interrupting her work, imploring her to hold his hand, as if he were an infant. He burned to show her his love and maturity, as soon as his opening was past.

It was almost four o'clock. During a moment when Miles was fighting with one of the dancers, Paul rushed to the phone, feeling the blood pounding in his ears and certain that something was wrong.

He let the phone ring twenty times.

14

Nicola, walking aimlessly north, found herself in Washington Square Park just outside New York University.

She sank onto a bench, for the first time noticing what a beautiful day it was. Tender leaves had blossomed overnight, and the air was fragrant and soft. It was the kind of day that ordinarily would have made her supremely happy just to be alive. The kind of day that drove everyone outdoors to breathe deeply and long for romance.

Nicola's sadness was heightened by the spectacle of a pigeon lady. Eccentrically dressed in a creased long brown skirt, plum-coloured, short sleeved chiffon blouse, and red bedroom slippers, she kept pushing her frizzy bleached hair out of her eyes with one hand and tossing the pigeons crumbs from a paper bag with the other.

Nicola turned her head, hoping to lose her aching depression amid the vibrant buzzing on all sides of her. Bike riders zigzagged precariously around pedestrians, playing children, and romping dogs, revelling in their skill at avoiding last-minute collisions. Competing roller skaters in colourful clothes danced forward and backward to music coming from big radios or earphones clamped to their heads.

Everywhere Nicola saw couples – young student, middle-aged, interracial, homosexual, beer-swilling, and pot-smoking. She couldn't take her eyes off a woman of about fifty strolling hand in hand with a man at least ten years younger, the two looking lovingly at one another.

A convertible stopped at the corner for a red light, It, too, contained couples. The young girls in back were flirting animatedly with the two boys up front.

Nicola had a vivid recollection of the day not very long ago when she and Paul had invited the Markhams for Sunday brunch and were preparing to go for a drive in their new Porsche ...

'The women had better sit in back –' Paul started to say.

'Oh, really? Brandy and cigars for you guys, knitting for us?' Janet interrupted gaily.

'Don't fuss, my love,' Tom said, kissing his wife on the nose. 'The back of this buggy has no leg room. It's okay for lapdogs, infants, dwarfs – and, of course, lovely petite ladies like you. But I'm six two, most of it legs!'

'Tom's right,' Nicola said, laughing. 'We're the obvious candidates. We'll just curl up happily and look out the window.'

'Just as long as you don't blow kisses to strange men,' Tom joked.

It had been such a fun day, the four of them so relaxed, so unaware of what was to come. Nicola and Paul. Janet and Tom. And now Tom was no more.

Nicola began to cry. Wonderful, cheerful, sweet Tom had squeezed every moment of pleasure from his life and given so much to everyone who knew him. Tom and Janet had been so happy together. Life was more unfair than it had a right to be.

'Are you all right over there?'

Nicola picked up her head and saw the pigeon lady looking at her with concern.

'I guess so.' Nicola blew her nose, embarrassed. 'A – a very good friend died suddenly, a dear, dear man.'

The woman clucked sympathetically. 'Your man?'

'Well, no, not mine –'

'Then you should thank God,' the woman said fervently, flinging a handful of crumbs to the pigeons.

Nicola, wiping her eyes, remembered Janet's final words on the 'phone earlier. 'We had so much, Tom and I. The thing is, when he was alive I gave him all the devotion and love I was capable of. I can't think of anything I should have done, could have done. That will make it easier to bear.'

Nicola, glancing at her watch, jumped up, waved at the pigeon lady, and ran into the street to hail a taxi.

She was being ridiculous. The world was perverse and unpredictable. She had no right to destroy her happiness and Paul's prematurely. Nobody could say how long love would last, or anything else.

As the taxi approached Lincoln Centre, Nicola took out her mirror and lipstick to repair her face. She couldn't let Paul see her like this. Now was not the time to tell him about Tom.

Shoving six dollars at the driver, she raced up the steps to the New York State Theatre.

The strains of Paul's wonderful, joyous music filled her ears, and she halted behind the last row in the orchestra to listen and catch her breath.

Miles Fanchel was leaping around on the stage, admonishing the dancers. 'That's it for now. Take ten, and we're going to get it right or so help me ...'

Paul lowered his baton wearily and turned to look at the empty seats.

Nicola ran forward waving.

The smile of sheer relief on Paul's pale, strained face made her weak with the realisation of what she had almost done to them both.

He crushed her to him. 'Where have you been? I almost called the police!'

'A good thing you didn't. They'd have arrested me for indecent exposure, in this little nothing of a dress you like so much.'

'Not so much that I won't rip it off you, later.'

Nicola hugged him tightly. The only love that was real and worth anything was the love she and Paul felt for each other right now. And she would show her love as fully as she could and never have a single regret.

HEYWOOD BOOKS

TODAY'S PAPERBACKS
– AT YESTERDAY'S PRICES!

Heywood Books is a new list of paperback books which
will be published every month at unbelievably low prices.
It will range from up-to-date contemporary women's
novels to exciting romantic thrillers and the best in
historical romance, from classic crime to nerve-tingling
horror and big adventure thrillers, presenting a superb list
of highly readable and top value popular fiction.

Look for this month's new titles:

DOWN TO A SUNLESS SEA	*David Graham*	£1.75
LADY IN WAITING	*Rosemary Sutcliff*	£1.75
THE ROOT OF HIS EVIL	*James M. Cain*	£1.50
CRISS-CROSS	*Alan Scholefield*	£1.50
LOVENOTES	*Justine Valenti*	£1.75
THE WOODSMEN	*Michael Falconer Anderson*	£1.50

LADY IN WAITING
The powerful love story of Walter Ralegh and
his beloved

Rosemary Sutcliff

Handsome and gifted, Walter Ralegh glittered brightest
in a court of brilliant men ruled by one of the greatest
monarchs of all time, Elizabeth I. Ralegh held position
and power, and was loved by the Queen, but his dream
was to conquer new lands for his Queen, and to find El
Dorado.
Bess Throckmorton was one of the Queen's Maids of
Honour. Shy and retiring, her dream was to capture the
heart of the proud and restless Ralegh, in whose life it
seemed she would always come second.
Set against the dramatic backdrop of their times, theirs
was a passionate and enduring love.

'A sensitive, delightful novel that no woman could fail to
enjoy'
The Daily Telegraph

CRISS-CROSS

What would *you* do if someone was trying
to snatch *your* child?

Lee Jordan

Divorced from her American husband, Walter, after a
disastrous marriage, Jane had been awarded custody of
their four-year-old daughter, Susie. Determined to take
her safely back to her own family in England, Jane was
keeping her daughter close to her. Walter had succeeded
in kidnapping her once and she swore he would never get
near her again . . .

But now someone is on their trail. Alone and with
no-one to turn to, Jane has no choice but to attempt a
desperate getaway with Susie. Holed up in a remote
seaside village, they appear to be safe. But, all too soon,
Jane is caught up in a new web of intrigue and before
long not only Susie's life, but her own as well, is in
mortal danger . . .

THE ROOT OF HIS EVIL
Marriage to a millionaire . . .
Any woman's dream – but not Carrie's

James M. Cain

Author of *The Postman Always Rings Twice*

All his life, Grant Harris had been known as the heir to
a great railway fortune. But for waitress Carrie Seldon,
an orphan making her own determined way in the world,
he was just Grant, attractive, rather mysterious, infuriating – and the man who marries her on impulse.
When she subsequently discovers that their secret marriage has caused a public scandal, she is at first horrified,
but decides to stand by her man. The wealthy Harris
family discover that Grant's unsuitable new wife cannot
just be pushed out of his life, for now they have Carrie
herself to reckon with . . .

HEYWOOD BOOKS

FICTION
One Little Room	*Jan Webster*	£1.50
The Winnowing Winds	*Ann Marlowe*	£1.50
The Root of His Evil	*James M. Cain*	£1.50
Criss-Cross	*Alan Scholefield*	£1.50
Lovenotes	*Justine Valenti*	£1.75

SAGA
Daneclere	*Pamela Hill*	£1.75
Making Friends	*Cornelia Hale*	£1.75
Muckle Annie	*Jan Webster*	£1.75
The Windmill Years	*Vicky Martin*	£1.75

HISTORICAL ROMANCE
The Caretaker Wife	*Barbara Whitehead*	£1.50
Quicksilver Lady	*Barbara Whitehead*	£1.50
Lady in Waiting	*Rosemary Sutcliff*	£1.75

THRILLER
KG 200	*J. D. Gilman & John Clive*	£1.75
Hammerstrike	*Walter Winward*	£1.75
Down to a Sunless Sea	*David Graham*	£1.75

HORROR
The Unholy	*Michael Falconer Anderson*	£1.50
God of a Thousand Faces	*Michael Falconer Anderson*	£1.50
The Woodsmen	*Michael Falconer Anderson*	£1.50

NAME ....

ADDRESS ....

....

Write to Heywood Books Cash Sales, PO Box 11, Falmouth, Cornwall TR10 9EN.
Please indicate order and enclose remittance to the value of the cover price plus:
UK: Please allow 60p for the first book, 25p for the second book and 15p for each
additional book ordered, to a maximum charge of £1.90.

B.F.P.O. & EIRE: Please allow 60p for the first book, 25p for the second book,
15p per copy for the next 7 books and thereafter 9p per book.

OVERSEAS: Please allow £1.25 for the first book, 75p for the second book and
28p per copy for each additional book.

Whilst every effort is made to keep prices low it is sometimes necessary to
increase cover prices and also postage and packing rates at short notice.
Heywood Books reserve the right to show new retail prices on covers which may
differ from those previously advertised in the text or elsewhere.